THE PIRATE'S SECRET

LYNDEE WALKER

BRUCE ROBERT COFFIN

SEVERN RIVER

PUBLISHING

Severn River Publishing
www.SevernRiverBooks.com

ISBN: 978-1-64875-613-9 (Paperback)

ALSO BY THE AUTHORS

The Turner and Mosley Files

The General's Gold

The Cardinal's Curse

The Pirate's Secret

The Pharaoh's Tomb

BY LYNDEE WALKER

The Faith McClellan Series

The Nichelle Clarke Series

Never miss a new release!

To find out more about the authors and their books, visit

severnriverbooks.com

For all the teachers who tirelessly encourage students to reach for their dreams: you rock, and we thank you. And to our readers, who help us keep the flame of imagination burning brightly.

"Life is either a daring adventure or nothing at all." — Helen Keller

PROLOGUE

London, 1664

The pungent odor of burnt fish oil hung heavy in the air from the wall-mounted torches illuminating the castle hallway, the light emanating from them dancing along the rough stone walls. Errol's lips disappeared into a tight line as he stood outside the monarch's chamber, shaking his head in disapproval.

"The king will not be disturbed," the aging manservant said, staring flatly at a taller, stronger guard intent on waking His Majesty.

Burgess raised his hand above Errol's head and reached toward the heavy wooden door, intent on rapping his knuckles against it. Errol grabbed onto the guard's arm and tugged it away, releasing it only after a conveyed look of warning from the formidable younger man.

Proper protocol meant everything to King Charles II, who had been restored to power in London three years earlier, following a nine-year exile and the execution of his father, King Charles I. On that point the monarch could not have been clearer to all who served him.

"Tell me what it is you want," Errol said. "In the morning I shall pass the information along to His Majesty."

Burgess leaned in close until his face was mere inches from Errol's, gritting his teeth as he spoke. "This is an urgent matter, Errol. One which needs to remain strictly confidential."

"And I am the king's most trusted adviser," Errol said.

"You are nothing more than a glorified butler," Burgess said. "I will speak of this only to the king, and it must be now."

Errol crossed his arms in defiance and stood his ground in front of the door.

"Then you leave me no alternative," Burgess said as he withdrew his sword from its scabbard. "Step aside, old man."

"Guards!" Errol shouted.

The sound of rapidly approaching footfalls echoed throughout the hallway.

"Guards," Errol shouted again. "Help!"

Burgess stepped toward Errol and shoved him aside with an elbow. Before either man could engage further, the door to the private chambers swung open to reveal the king himself standing before them in a fine silk dressing gown.

King Charles had the rumpled and disoriented appearance of one who had only just awakened from a deep slumber. A handful of castle guards rushed toward the two men until the king raised his hand signaling for everyone to stop. "Enough," he bellowed.

Charles pointed at Burgess. "Return that sword to your scabbard."

"My lord." Burgess bowed his head slightly as he complied.

"What is the meaning of this?" Charles demanded.

"My apologies for the disturbance, sire, but I must speak with you in private," Burgess said. "It is a matter of the greatest urgency."

"I should say." Charles regarded the other men. "You may return to your posts."

"Very good, Your Majesty," the closest guard said.

Charles turned his attention to Errol. "That will be all for now."

Errol nodded. "As you wish, sire."

After everyone else had departed, Charles beckoned Burgess into the lavish chamber and closed the door.

The fireplace had gone cold, reduced to nothing but embers and ash.

The bedchamber smelled of tallow candles and spruce. Burgess stood at attention in front of the mantel, awaiting permission to speak.

Charles gestured to the empty bed. "You are most fortunate that I was not entertaining anyone this night, Burgess."

"My only good fortune, sire."

The king hid a smile from one of his most trusted guards as he poured himself a splash of brandy from a crystal decanter. He strode to the opposite side of the chamber and plopped down in the center of the divan before taking a sip. "Now, what was of such great importance to warrant disturbing my sleep at this hour?"

Burgess met his gaze. "Thieves have accosted the tower tonight."

Charles lowered the glass. Unblinking, he awaited the rest of Burgess's story.

Burgess flexed his fingers closed and then open. He wasn't one for fidgeting, but upsetting the king wasn't something to take lightly. There were torture devices in the white dungeon he'd rather withstand.

"We have the finest guards under God's creation, and I have faith in your command." Charles tipped his head to one side. "Are you at a loss for how to deal with the intruders, then?"

"No, of course not." Burgess pulled in a deep breath. Best to just get it out there. "I fear your faith might be misplaced this night. The crown jewels, Your Majesty. They are missing."

1

"Carter Mosley glided along beneath the ocean waves mere yards from the thirty-foot black-and-white orca. The majestic member of the dolphin family dwarfed even the tall, muscular shipwreck hunter. Mosley, an experienced deep-water diver, was keenly aware of how dangerous the animal often referred to as a "killer whale" could be. A single swipe of the creature's tail might leave him paralyzed...or worse." The honey-voiced baritone narrator looked up from the page.

Flynn Harding, the director, pointed to Carter and mouthed, "You're on."

Carter leaned toward the microphone windscreen and began to read from the script.

"During one of the most harrowing dives I had ever undertaken, I remained hypervigilant as—"

A harried and disheveled gray-haired man rushed onto the set, Carter's speech faltering as he looked at Harding and pointed to the gatecrasher.

"Cut, cut," Harding said. "Where is our security?"

"I'm terribly sorry, Mr. Harding," a uniformed security guard said, catching the man's arm. "I don't know how he managed to get in here."

"I'm late for my call time," the man mumbled, Harding talking over him as he glared at the guard.

"Isn't that why we pay you?" Harding asked. "Is there any chance we could at least act like professionals, people?"

Avery Turner did her best to suppress laughter as she stood at the wings of the soundstage next to Josh, Carter's agent, who was videoing the nine-foot-tall version of Carter swimming across the wall-sized digital screen playing in the background. Avery watched the guard lead the older man away with mild interest—he looked more lost than dangerous.

"Just get him off my set." Harding waved one hand at the guard. "No one else go anywhere. Reset—we'll go again."

The bespectacled narrator looked annoyed, reaching for his cigarettes.

Harding got up from his chair and approached Carter. "Everything okay, Carter baby? You seem a bit off."

"No, I'm good," Carter said, suppressing an eye roll at Harding's extreme overuse of the word *baby*. It was like his own little version of pig latin—he just squished it onto the end of everyone's name. Well. Everyone he thought was important. And every time he said it, it came out faster—almost more like one word than two at this point.

"Actually, you aren't," Harding said, squinting his disapproval before he flashed a grin. "Sorry, Carterbaby. No offense meant." One-word mark officially crossed. Carter stared at the camera behind Harding.

"None taken. I think," Carter said. "What do you mean I'm not good?"

"Well, you're talking too fast. You seem a little amped up."

"Okay, I'll slow it down."

"It's more than that. See, Carterbaby, you've got to modulate your voice more. We're trying to build suspense here, okay? I need feeling in those words."

Five feet away, Avery swallowed a laugh, thankful she wasn't deemed important enough to have her name changed to Averybaby. This guy was like a caricature of Hollywood brown-nosing bravado.

"You're not really gonna try and tell me how to tell a story, are you?" Carter snapped, throwing his arms up. "I record narration for a living, you know."

The narrator scoffed, earning a dirty look from Carter.

Harding raised both hands in mock surrender. "Relax, Carterbaby! Telling a story to television viewers is different than regaling a bunch of drunks in a bar or adding voiceovers to video snippets online. You need those pregnant pauses. Modulate your voice a little. Lower tones add an ominous touch. Your entire demeanor is just too excited, from your hand gestures, which thankfully we can't see on screen, to your pitch."

"What the hell is the matter with my pitch?"

"It's a bit too high," Harding said, his tone conciliatory. "What we're going for here is drama, not just information. I know this is exciting for you, but our viewers are more couch potato than adrenaline junkie—this is terrifying stuff to the average person. We want to feel what you felt."

"I felt excited," Carter said. "Seeing a perfectly preserved wooden ship for the first time in a hundred years? Doing something few people have ever done? Why isn't that exciting?"

"You could have *died*, Carter." Harding looked around until he spotted Avery. "*She* could have died. I want that. Give the audience that."

"Now I have to kill Avery with my voice?"

"Might as well," the narrator said. "You're killing me with it."

"Do we have to use this guy?" Carter looked to Josh for support.

The narrator removed his reading glasses and tossed them atop the podium. "I can't keep doing these stops and starts, Flynn. It completely throws off my rhythm."

"I got something that will throw off your rhythm." Carter half stood, glaring at the narrator.

Josh rushed to center stage. "Hey, guys, what do you say we take a break and regroup after lunch? What do you think, Flynn? Seems like everyone might be suffering from low blood sugar here."

Harding folded his arms over his chest, gaze bouncing from the narrator to Carter and back again before landing on Josh. "Okay, everyone, one hour, then we go again," he agreed. He turned and clapped Carter on the shoulder. "You got this, Carter. See you back here in sixty."

Avery raised a brow as she approached. "Tall and muscular shipwreck hunter, huh? You write that line yourself?"

Grinning, Carter sat back in his skintight black tee and ran his hands through his wavy hair. "Hey, I don't even have script approval. Though the description is uncanny, isn't it? It's almost like they know me."

Avery rolled her eyes. "You want to grab a bite to eat, He-Man?"

Avery, Carter, and Josh stepped outside into glorious seventy-five-degree early summer sunshine. The prevailing westerlies drifted through the studio lot carrying just a hint of the salt air of Santa Monica Bay. They donned their sunglasses and headed down the sidewalk to a waiting caravan of food trucks. The smell of cooked meats and spices made Avery's stomach grumble.

"My God," Avery said. "There're celebrities everywhere I look. Is that Gal Gadot?"

Carter spun completely around as his eyes followed the actress. Gadot busted him with a quick backward glance and a sly grin.

"Serves you right," Avery said.

"What?" Carter said, wide-eyed, trying to project his innocence. "I was just trying to confirm who it was. For you. Right, Josh?"

"By all means," Josh said.

"Josh doesn't count," Avery said.

"Why not?" Carter said.

"Because he gets ten percent of everything you do, Carter. He'll agree with anything you say."

"That's harsh, Avery," Josh said. "Entirely true, but harsh. Very harsh."

"I still don't understand why we need a director anyway," Carter said. "Millions of people like my self-direction just fine."

"The point of this is to add to that total, Carter." Josh wiggled his eyebrows and Carter scowled.

"Say 'baby' and I'll fire you," he growled.

Avery laughed in the middle of ordering her gyro, Josh joining in.

"Harding is a professional, man," Josh said. "This is what he does. Trust him."

"Whatever." Carter waved one hand and ordered his birria tacos. "I don't like that narrator guy either. He's a total di—"

"Carter," Avery warned. "I've almost broken Harrison of street lingo. Don't tell me I have to worry about you now."

"I was going to say dip. He's a total dip."

"Hmm," Avery said, narrowing her eyes in disbelief. "What do you think, Josh? Is Carter telling the truth now?"

Josh shook his head. "Nope. He's lying for sure."

"How can you say that?" Carter said, feigning injury.

"Because I don't get ten percent of a fib. And regardless of what you may think of that guy, he is the best voice since Don LaFontaine."

Carter's phone began buzzing in his pocket.

"You gonna get that?" Josh asked.

"Nope," Carter said as he silenced the call. "Whatever it is, it will keep until after lunch."

2

Following lunch, Avery grabbed a table in a semi-secluded area of the soundstage, intent on getting some work done. If Carter punched the narrator, she figured there would be video, and she couldn't listen to any more of Flynn Harding's Splenda-laced direction. The guy was as fake as a chocolate coin, and Avery could get along with many different kinds of people, but that wasn't one of them.

She was engrossed in writing a speech about real-world applications of technology when the crew took a taping break and Harding sidled up beside her.

"So, what's it like to dive with the great Carter Mosley?" Harding asked.

"It's great," Avery said.

"Bit of a risk taker, isn't he?"

"I can tell you I've never felt unsafe diving with him. Not once. Carter is very methodical about safety."

"He's certainly done some amazing things," Harding said. "I understand that the two of you have formed a company together. Treasure something, isn't it?"

Unsure where the conversation was headed, Avery smiled politely. "TreasureTech Designs."

"Fascinating." Harding leaned so close Avery knew he'd had the gyro for lunch, too. "Tell me more about that."

She sat back in her chair and flashed a weak smile. "We've created applications that help locate, decode, and digitize hand-drawn maps using millions of files, centuries of records, and global-positioning systems. Another one of our apps is used by professional deep-sea divers to maximize and pinpoint the necessary safety protocol measures by utilizing their own biometric data."

Harding nodded. "Incredible, Avery baby."

Oh Lord. She tried to keep from flinching visibly. Carter didn't need this guy being more difficult because he was annoyed with Avery.

"I'm sorry," Avery said. "I guess I kind of turned that into an elevator pitch. I don't imagine you're interested in purchasing anything."

Harding laughed, inching forward. "You never know. Tell me about your target clientele."

Harding was standing closer than Avery was comfortable with, but she couldn't back away any farther without getting up. Her eyes going to her computer screen, she realized for the first time that her speech was still open. She couldn't tell if Harding was a creep, simply a close talker, or if he was trying to get a look at her work. Avery closed the laptop and pushed her chair back slightly before answering his question.

"Our clients are mostly government institutions, police, branches of the military, and the like. We do have a few non-government organizations, though."

"Do you and Carter personally do dives for any of those outfits or is it strictly programing that you provide?"

Avery wasn't sure she was completely comfortable with the strange vibe Harding was giving off.

"Are you a diver by chance, Mr. Harding?" she asked, shifting gears on him.

"Please, call me Flynn. And no, I'm not a diver, but I have the greatest respect for those of you who are. I did go on a vacation dive once, right after taking a resort class, but it didn't end well."

"What happened?"

"I came face-to-face with an eel. Think I may have walked on water all the way back to the resort."

"Oh." Avery laughed, then pinched her lips together. "Sorry."

Harding pointed at her laptop. "So, what are you working on? Another cool TreasureTech app?"

Avery maintained her phony smile, but something about this entire encounter had her skin crawling right up her arms—away from the director. "Just catching up on some email," she lied.

Harding's smile—more of a smirk, really—didn't even try to look genuine. Avery couldn't help wondering if he had picked up on the falsehood.

"Well, it is nice to have you on set, Avery baby. You sure you don't want a part in this documentary? I could probably pull a few strings. Who knows, you might be more of a natural than Carter."

"I appreciate the offer, but I think I'll just stay in my lane. And Carter is plenty natural. He just likes to do things his own way."

He cast one more glance at her laptop, and Avery laid her hand on it. Harding pointed behind him.

"I've got to get back. If you change your mind, be sure and let me know."

"I will."

Avery watched as Harding strolled back to the set. There was something off about the man. Too slick? Too Hollywood? She'd been there for forty-eight hours, so she didn't know. Was everyone here like him? Or was Harding a special flavor of creepy?

It was late by the time filming wrapped for the day, but Carter felt like he was finally beginning to get a feel for what the director wanted. At the recommendation of one of the film crew members, Avery made a reservation at a popular LA Mexican eatery, then hired a car to drive them across town to meet Harrison, Avery's right hand, for a late supper.

"Harry, these pics are fabulous," Avery said, flicking through photos of his day on his phone.

"Thanks," Harrison said, taking the phone from her and scrolling through more pictures. "I've always wanted to visit this city. Grauman's Chinese Theater was so cool. Here's some pictures I took on the walk of fame. Check this one out." He showed Avery and then passed his phone across the table to Carter.

"Barbara Stanwyck?" Carter furrowed his brow. "Wasn't she on *I Dream of Jeannie*?"

"That was Barbara Eden." Harrison snatched his phone back with a withering look.

"Heathen. I had a crush on Barbara Stanwyck since she played Victoria Barkley in *The Big Valley*."

Carter blinked. "I know that was all English, but I have no idea what any of it meant."

Avery laughed. Harrison shook his head and put his phone on the table.

"So, how goes the filming?" Harrison said. "Are you gonna be the next big Hollywood star?"

"Hardly," Carter said. "Besides, it's only a docufilm."

"He's doing a great job," Avery said.

"The director thinks we'll be able to wrap up my part in this by end of day tomorrow," Carter said.

"That's too bad," Avery said. "The weather has been so great I was thinking about leasing the beach house for another week."

"We still can, can't we?" Carter said. "I'd love a real vacation."

"When exactly aren't you on vacation?" Harrison said.

"You're one to talk, Harry," Avery said, waving a hand at his "I love LA" shirt and Muscle Beach ball cap.

"How is everything?" the waiter asked, stopping at the end of the table with a smile.

"These are fantastic." Harrison pointed to the remnants on his plate.

"Ah, you like the chile rellenos. I will bring you another order if you like, señor."

"You just became my favorite person," Harrison said.

The waiter laughed. "I've heard that ten times just today. It's easy when the kitchen does good work. Can I bring anyone else something?"

"Another round of margaritas, please," Avery said.

"Very good, señorita."

"I like this place." Harrison rubbed his stomach.

They were halfway through the second round of margaritas when Carter's phone chimed a voicemail reminder.

"Missed call?" Avery said.

"No, it's the one I blew off at lunch." Carter shook his head. "Who even leaves voicemails anymore? Doesn't everyone text?"

"I still leave voice messages," Harrison said.

"I rest my case," Carter said as he pressed the rectangle at the center of the screen and placed the phone to his ear, his smile fading as the message played.

Tension coiled every muscle as he replayed the message. Only a dozen words, but they made Carter's blood run cold. He lowered the phone to the table and stared at it.

"Jeez, you look like someone just pulled your Instagram page down," Harrison said.

"What is it?" Avery asked.

As Carter searched for words, Harrison leaned over and looked at the call screen.

"Who's Jeff?"

"Jeff Shelton. He's my oldest friend."

"Jeff, your old diving partner?" Avery asked.

Carter nodded. "Yeah. We haven't spoken in four years."

"What did he say?" Avery said.

Carter motioned for them to lean in before he activated the phone's speaker and replayed the message.

"Hey, buddy, just calling from London to wish you a happy birthday. Hope this year is the absolute best. Love you, brother."

"Your birthday isn't until October," Avery said.

"How good a friend could he be if he doesn't know that?" Harrison asked.

"Jeff and I were best mates growing up. My ride-or-die buddy back in the day. Trouble always seemed to find us even when we weren't looking for it."

"And especially when you were, I'll bet," Harrison said.

"Well, at least he thought about you, even if he mixed up the date," Avery said. "I think that's sweet."

"He didn't mix up the date, Avery," Carter said. "Jeff and I worked out a code, kind of like our underwater signals. Like, if we were at a club and one of us complained about the DJ not playing enough Madonna, that meant 'I'm about to throw a punch.' The word *equestrian* used in a sentence meant 'Let's get out of here,' like in case we got trapped by someone at a party or were on a bad date."

"So this is a coded message?" Harrison said.

Carter nodded.

"Then what does happy birthday mean?" Avery said.

"Five-alarm emergency," Carter said. He looked to Harrison for confirmation. "Dudes don't remember their friends' birthdays."

"It's true," Harrison said. "Hell, I barely remember my family's. Yours and your mom's are the only two I do remember, Ave."

"So, Jeff's in trouble," Avery said.

"Again." Carter ran a hand through his hair.

"How bad do you think it is?" Avery said.

"Life or death," Carter said. "He would never tell me he loved me unless he was scared."

"Is London a code too?" Harrison said.

"No. He'd have to tell me where he was if he expected me to help." Carter flashed a tired grin at Avery. "What are the chances you could run interference with Flynn and Josh tomorrow?"

"Of course," Avery said. "You're really going to London?"

"Got to," Carter said as he picked up his phone to search for flights.

Avery pulled it out of his hand. "You're really worried about him." Her forehead furrowed into concerned lines.

"Jeff is a lot of things, Avery. Overly dramatic isn't one of them. His life could be in danger, and I'll never forgive myself if I don't try to help."

Avery returned his phone, then removed hers from her pocket.

"What are you doing?" Carter said.

"Texting Marco," Avery said. "We're a team. If you're going to London, then so am I. This is what private jets are for."

Harrison signaled the waiter for the check.

Carter couldn't help but worry about putting Avery in danger. Jeff had never been known for hanging out in the safest places.

"I can't ask you to get involved in this," Carter said. "Jeff has been known to cross paths with the kind of people who use weapons to settle scores."

"Too late," Avery said. "Marco will be waiting for us at the airport by the time we pack our stuff."

"We got your back, kid," Harrison said as he stood and clapped Carter on the shoulder. "That's what family does. And you're family."

"Thank you, both." Carter let out a deep sigh and picked up his phone again.

"You're worried about telling Flynn?" Avery said.

"Not at all," Carter said. "But Josh—he's going to lose his mind."

3

It took them less than an hour to pack up their belongings and vacate the beachfront property. Avery couldn't believe how quickly they had moved from extending the lease for an additional week to moving out. Ninety minutes later, Avery's Gulfstream lifted off from the Bob Hope Airport in Burbank with Marco at the controls.

They refueled in Charlotte, North Carolina, and Marco got them back in the air in record time.

The transatlantic flight was uneventful. Harrison snoozed, likely the result of his extra margaritas, while Avery caught up on work and kept an eye on Carter, who was still wired. He managed almost zero shut-eye and probably clocked ten thousand steps pacing around the cabin.

Avery had never seen Carter truly worried, and given that she'd seen him face down death more than once, she found it unsettling. MaryAnn, the Keys museum director turned TreasureTech chief information officer, had been a godsend when it came to research largely thanks to her contacts, spread literally all over the world. But right then, Avery was interested in MaryAnn's long history with Carter—she sent an email requesting a detailed report on Jeff. If they were about to walk into trouble, she didn't want to do it blind.

They landed at Heathrow late in the afternoon. A receptionist directed them to a car standing by to transport them to a private lounge while customs formalities were handled.

"This might be the swankiest lounge I've ever been in," Harrison said as he enjoyed a plate of mashed potatoes and Lincolnshire sausage. "What do you think, Ave?"

"It is pretty nice. It's funny, some days I barely notice luxury surroundings. Others I feel like I'm just waiting for someone to come and kick us out." She knew it was the price of overnight success.

Avery had spent her early and mid twenties as a rising star in computer programming. She'd been working for Mark Hawkins at Hawkins Technologies when she developed a cutting-edge app that catered to a high-end market and had altered the possible applications of mapping and location software forever. The result was a bidding war to purchase not only the app but Mark's entire company. Per the terms of Avery's original contract with Hawkins, she'd received half of the price paid by a German company for the app, which was enough to make her a billionaire literally overnight.

She watched as Carter continued to pace the lounge.

"I've never seen you like this," Avery said. "Sit, Carter. Have a drink."

"I'll get it," Harrison said as he rose and headed toward the bar. "What do you want? Grape Nehi?"

"Ha-ha," Carter said, waving him off. "I'm good, Harry."

"I don't get it," Harrison said as he returned to the table. "In all the time I've known you, I haven't heard a word about this guy, and last night it sounded like you didn't even like him anymore. I figured you'd had a falling out."

"It's complicated," Carter said. "Jeff was once a big part of my life. Our families were intertwined. We were both raised by single moms—often each other's."

"But *you* cut ties with him, didn't you?" Avery said.

Carter nodded. "Because of stuff like this. But the more I think about it, the more worried I am. After all this time, Jeff wouldn't have reached out to me like he did if he wasn't really scared. And Jeff doesn't get scared."

"I might say the same thing about you," Avery said, concern flooding the words. "Until today."

"This doesn't make sense," Carter said. "Jeff has always been so far out there. The number of times I saw him"—Carter ran one hand through his hair—"like, literally walk past death with a big stupid grin on his face. If he's afraid of something, I'm not sure I want to know what it is."

"Yet you dropped everything and ran halfway around the world," Harrison said. "You're a good friend, kid."

"I hope I'm not too late." Carter resumed pacing and Avery used the opportunity to check and see if MaryAnn had responded yet. There was nothing in her inbox.

The customs official was exceedingly kind and genial. He introduced himself as Officer Bobbin, then proceeded to check their passports.

"Business or pleasure?" Bobbin asked.

"A little of both, I imagine," Avery said.

"I've heard of you two," Bobbin said, directing his comment to Avery and Carter. "You're world-famous treasure hunters."

Avery laughed. "Carter's the world-famous one. I'm just a treasure hunter. And a computer geek."

Bobbin regarded Harrison. "And what is your story, Mr. Harrison?"

"I'm just a lowly retired New York homicide detective," Harrison said as he presented his passport.

Bobbin's expression grew serious. "I assume you're all familiar with British gun laws."

Avery exchanged a quick glance with Harrison.

"I know they're stricter than American laws," Harrison said. "But I can't say I've ever had occasion to read them."

"There are war zones with stricter gun laws than your country," Bobbin said with a chuckle. "This is the point where I'm required to ask you if you have any firearms to declare."

Avery and Carter shook their heads. Harrison raised his pant leg, revealing an ankle-holstered .38.

"Oh, Harry," Avery groaned.

"What? I never thought it would be an issue."

Bobbin held out his hand. "It's customary for visitors to apply for a permit to carry six weeks in advance."

Harrison unloaded the weapon and handed it to Bobbin.

"Our decision to fly here was a spur-of-the-moment thing, I'm afraid," Avery said.

Bobbin's eyebrows jumped to his hairline. "Hunting treasure here, by any chance?"

"Nothing so exciting, I'm afraid." Avery smiled. "Just seeing an old friend. I don't suppose there might be a way to expedite a permit for Harry?"

"I could help you process the paperwork," Bobbin said. "There is an exception for law enforcement, as he has met all the training requirements."

"And you can put in a good word for me?" Harrison grinned.

"I can," Bobbin said as he picked up the phone. "I'm calling a friend at the Met right now."

"Great," Harrison said.

"What I can't guarantee is that they will choose to expedite it," Bobbin said as he dialed. "At a minimum it would be twenty-four to forty-eight hours before the approval and permit come through. In the meantime, I'll secure your weapon in a locker."

"When can I get it back?"

"When you bring me the permit or when you leave the UK."

After leaving a message for his friend at the Met, Bobbin directed Harrison to a website where he could fill out the required forms.

"Remember, the sooner you file, the quicker it might come through."

"Thanks for all your help," Avery said.

"You are most welcome," Bobbin said. "Enjoy your stay in the UK, Miss Turner."

They shouldered their overnight bags and ambled to a black town car where their driver was waiting to transport them to their hotel.

"Where to?" the driver asked.

"The Rosewood Hotel," Avery said.

"Very good."

"Sounds swanky," Carter said.

"It is," Avery said. "I booked us in Lincoln's Suite."

"Abraham?" Harrison said.

"Um, not in London." Avery laughed. "Try Lincoln's Inn Fields."

"What's he famous for?" Harrison said.

"It's not he," the driver said. "The fields are a place where they used to execute thieves back in the seventeenth century. Gangs of vagrants called the Mumpers and the Rufflers."

"What great words," Carter said with the first smile Avery had seen him flash in hours. "Why don't we use fun words like this anymore. I bet Harry would have made a great Mumper."

"Ha-ha," Harrison said. "Very funny."

Avery checked her email three times on the short ride. Still nothing from MaryAnn. She reminded herself that it was still early back home.

Following check-in, they went directly to the suite to drop their bags. Double doors opened to a tastefully decorated living area, off of which they found three large, well-appointed bedrooms.

"Jeez, my place in New York would have fit in here three times over," Harrison said.

"I love that our lift goes only to this room," Carter said. "It's like our very own penthouse."

"Lift?" Harrison said. "Don't you mean elevator? Look at him, Ave. One hour in London and Carter's already turning British."

"Anybody hungry?" Avery said.

"I'm famished," Harrison said. "Although I have no idea what time it is now. Are we having breakfast or dinner?"

"Dinner. I reserved a table for six thirty in the mirror dining room downstairs."

"That's ten minutes from now," Carter said, checking his watch.

"We'd better get a move on, then," Harrison said.

They ate until they were stuffed, returning to the suite around nine thirty.

"I may not eat again until we're back on American soil," Harrison said, rubbing his belly. "But I don't regret a bite of that."

"Me neither," Carter said. "You think the best thing was the Scottish beef or the homemade ice cream?"

"I'm thinking it may well have been the Harviestoun Lager." Harrison chuckled. "Unless Avery can convince me that her salad was special."

"I liked the ice cream better. You two are just gluttons for punishment." Avery pulled antacids from her suitcase and passed the bottle to the guys. "We need to figure out what we're doing in the morning."

Harrison wrinkled his nose, and Carter laid a hand on his stomach when it made a gurgling noise, gobbling the antacid tablets. "Can't we talk about this tomorrow?" Harrison asked.

"No, she's right," Carter said. "The first step is to find out where Jeff is and go see him." He pulled out his phone.

"It's a little late," Avery said.

"I came to England to help him out of whatever jam he's gotten himself into," Carter said, swallowing hard when his stomach gurgled again. "He can take a call after ten."

Carter found the number on the voicemail message and called. "Voicemail." He sighed. "Hey, man, good to hear from you. Thanks for the birthday wishes. We should catch up soon." He ended the call and put his phone down, both hands running through his hair and making it stick up in a way that would've looked funny on anyone else.

Avery crossed the room. "You good?" she asked softly, because she could tell he wasn't but didn't know what else to say. She'd never seen Carter worry about much of anything really, and they'd been through some crazy things together.

"I don't want to be too late," he said finally, meeting her eyes with a pained look. "He saved my life more than once when we were kids, and I owe him."

"We're not too late," Avery said firmly. "He's asleep. We'll call him tomorrow. If you want to help him, the best thing you can do is rest." She steered him toward his room.

When Carter's door closed, Avery turned to Harrison. "This isn't like him."

"No," Harry agreed. "He says it's not like his old buddy either, which is what's throwing him, I think. It's disconcerting when people we know behave in a way we're not used to—sometimes it helped your mother and me solve murders. Here it's making our Mr. Devil May Care worry. But you're right. His friend will likely get his message in the morning and call back."

Avery bit her lip. "Aren't you going to call your old captain about pulling some strings for the firearm permit?" she asked.

"I called Roger during dinner, when I skipped to the loo," Harrison said.

"Look at you, multitasker," Avery said. "And who's 'turning British' now?"

"So maybe he was right about the fun words." Harrison patted her shoulder. "It'll be okay, Avery. This kid can't be in so much trouble."

She told him goodnight wishing she felt as sure of that as Harry sounded.

Avery retired to her own room and logged into the hotel Wi-Fi with her laptop. She pulled up her email account and found a response from Mary-Ann. She had known Carter a long time and was dating his brother, Brady, so surely she'd have some insight.

Oh boy. There's a long history there that Carter didn't ever even talk to me about, but I did some checking and I think I know why Jeff took off for London. He has two minor theft convictions in Florida and three active warrants, one of them for robbery. I have a request in for the police report, but that charge could get him prison time with two priors. I asked Brady, too. He confirmed that Jeff and Carter were like brothers, and Jeff was good at finding all kinds of trouble—including sleeping with one of Carter's girlfriends. Brady said Carter took it really hard, so he can't understand why Carter would fly halfway around the world to help Jeff.

Avery thought about Carter's face when he said he owed Jeff. Carter was a lot of things that exasperated her from time to time, but he was loyal and honorable above all.

MaryAnn's closing line was underlined and highlighted by exclamation points.

Be safe!!!

I'll do my best, Avery thought as she closed the laptop and placed it on the nightstand. She'd reply, probably with more questions, after they found Jeff.

Her eyelids drooped. She hadn't slept much on the flight over and was paying for the jet lag. She fell back onto the plush oversized canopy bed fully clothed and plunged instantly into a deep sleep.

4

London, 1664

Burgess and several other guards ran through the streets in the faint light of dawn, hounds baying as they tracked the scent of the intruders. His men had located an abandoned royal guard's uniform in the White Tower dungeon. The thief responsible for stealing the crown jewels had been a fool to think he could lose His Majesty's dogs by simply crossing the Thames. The animals were bred to hunt. Barring death, Burgess knew they would track the person responsible to the very ends of London. He was confident that the treasure would be returned to its rightful place in the fortress before nightfall.

Burgess and the others herded the anxious animals into a wooden boat and transported them across the Thames to the opposite bank where they resumed tracking. Their handlers shouted words of encouragement while struggling to control the dogs' progress against the leashes.

Noses to the ground, the hounds turned abruptly in unison down an alleyway. They scampered along the road until reaching a dead end. As the dogs jumped and clawed at the stone walls of a livery yard in Whitechapel, Burgess realized that they must have lost the scent.

"There's no door on this side," Andrew DeGuille, Burgess's right-hand man, said, stating the obvious.

"Damn," Burgess said with a stomp of his foot. "In what part of the dungeon did you discover the cloaks?"

"Not far from the scavenger's daughter, sir."

Burgess knew the dark corner that held the scavenger's daughter well. It was a truly terrifying place. And the uniform being left there mattered here, but the baying of the dogs muddled his thoughts. "Can't you quiet those blasted beasts?" he snapped. "I can't hear myself think."

"What would you have me do with them?" one of the dog handlers asked.

"Have them search the stables."

Burgess followed their progress back down the alley.

"Shall we accompany them, sir?" Andrew asked.

"No, come along, Andrew, and leave them to it. If I am right, there will not be a single trace of the thief at the stables."

"Then why did you send them there?"

"Because we're going somewhere else."

"And where would that be?"

"Back to the tower—and then under it."

Burgess was certain he knew what had happened. The thief, or thieves, had escaped into the tunnels that ran beneath the tower's dungeon. And toting the heavy bounty of jewels, he'd wager they hadn't gone far enough for him to need the dogs.

Scavenger's daughter was the nickname given to a new torture device located inside one of the chambers. It was innovative technology given over to extracting information from enemies and traitors to the crown, but a ghastly business requiring a disposal tunnel located between it and the rack. The tunnel was born of necessity—for ridding the tower of blood and other unpleasant bits, which were periodically flushed out with buckets of water.

Burgess knew that only a limited number of people in the king's employ knew of the tunnels' existence, drastically narrowing the list of suspects capable of having committed the crime. He wondered, though, why the dogs had led them across half the city. Had the thief planted a scent trail to throw off the animals?

Back inside the dungeon, Burgess removed the heavy steel grate covering a drainage hole in the stone floor, then leaned it up against the wall. Using a torch, he peered down inside the tunnel. The stench of rotted flesh wafting up on stale air was nearly overpowering. Grimacing, he had to acknowledge that this was a brilliant way for a thief to escape. Few would think that anyone had gone down there, and no one—himself included— would want to follow. He knew the tunnel ran downhill and ended at another grate positioned out near the riverbed. But if a person could bear the god-awful smell, the tunnel would make a suitable place to hide. His thought was the thief might have planned to double back after the search was called off.

Burgess took one last deep breath before dropping down inside the tunnel. His boots splashed into the foul-smelling water that ran along a trough cut into the bottom of the tunnel. With the torch burning in one hand, he moved forward and drew his sword with the other. If the thieves were hiding down here, Burgess would send them to meet their maker.

5

Carter was wide awake before sunup. Lying on the satin duvet cover staring at the ceiling, he was too preoccupied to notice or appreciate his lavish surroundings. All he could think about was Jeff. The more he replayed the coded message, the more worried he became. For the last half hour, he'd been lying in bed calling Jeff's cell phone every ten minutes. Each time, the call went directly to voicemail. Was the phone off because he was still sleeping? But then why hadn't Jeff called him back last night? Maybe because… Carter didn't dare finish the thought. He wouldn't—no, couldn't —let his mind go there.

His memory played a loop of Jeff, free-falling way too far, Carter screaming uselessly into the wind for Jeff to pull his chute already while Jeff grinned and cackled, BASE jumping, deep-sea diving, fending off an unusually aggressive tiger shark that had Carter by one leg with nothing but a diving knife. Sharks, rays, eels, broken bones, irate thugs—they had gotten up to a lot of fun and more than a little trouble together, and these days the betrayal stung way more than the loss of a girl Carter knew he wouldn't still be with anyway. He was cold-sweat terrified of what had Jeff scared, and gut-wrenchingly uncertain about Avery being anywhere near Jeff or whatever mess he was in, Carter's mind chasing that possibility down a thousand trails until he found the most unsettling one: What if Jeff had been forced to make the call? Was someone using Jeff to bait Carter into coming to London? If he'd been baited, so had Avery, and that would be his fault.

Carter tried the number again. Again, straight to voicemail.

Speaking of voicemail, his own was overflowing, and Josh had moved on to blowing up Carter's phone with texts laced with so much profanity, Carter learned a few new words scrolling through them. The gist, of course, was predictable: The director and producer, not to mention the network executives, were furious. The lawyers would be out for blood. Not even the king himself should have been able to summon Carter to London, and if he didn't want to lose everything he'd worked for, he'd better get himself straight back to California. Carter was confident that his relationship with Josh, if not entirely over, was on life support. But he couldn't focus on that now. Not while his childhood friend was in serious trouble.

He dropped the phone onto the bed and resumed his ceiling gazing. His brain wasn't about to let him sleep.

Thank God for Avery and Harrison, he thought. Who else would have dropped everything to fly to another country at a moment's notice to help someone they didn't know? Someone they had never met. Which made Carter wonder: Did he even know Jeff anymore? He hadn't seen or talked to him in years. Once upon a time, Carter thought he'd known Jeff better than anyone in the world—until his friend turned out to be a cheat and a thief, which had made Carter wonder then if Jeff had changed or if he'd just never noticed those particular personality traits. Surely he wouldn't purposely put Carter in harm's way, no matter how much water roared under that bridge. If someone had forced him to make that call, then why a cryptic message, using a code they'd invented a decade earlier and trusting that Carter would remember it? Nah. He'd have been more straightforward if this was just about getting Carter to London.

Carter let his thoughts wander the memory halls of his teenage years. It had been clear for a while that Jeff was headed down an entirely different path from the one Carter wanted for himself. A reckless path. Carter hadn't wanted to see it for probably entirely too long, but Jeff had a propensity for acquiring things that did not belong to him. It started with pickpocketing and went from there. He had liked to haunt the posh beaches of the most exclusive stretches of the Florida coast, not to ogle models and heiresses, but because they were a pickpocket's haven, populated by people with zero street savvy—everything was there for the taking. And it hadn't even been about the money, really. Like everything with Jeff, it was about the high. Getting away with it was the ultimate rush. The fear of being caught, the relief when he wasn't. Carter half thought it was the thrill of the escape, and not particularly the girl, that had led Jeff to mess around with Chelsea in the first place.

It wasn't like Carter didn't understand chasing adrenaline. Their bond over that was one of the things that had made his friendship with Jeff so strong and deep. Carter had even made a very nice, if accidental, career for himself out of it. His Instagram adventure video diary—scaling mountains or sheer cliffs because they were there, though there wasn't a cable or harness in sight, jumping out of perfectly good airplanes, swimming with sea life that could kill him with a single bite or flick of the tail—had caught the eye of a reality show star and hugely popular fashion influencer. That brought him legions of followers who kept coming back because they liked the way he looked and that he was brave and witty, which eventually parlayed into the TV special...that he had run out on to help Jeff.

But there was a dramatic difference between chasing a natural high and stealing from rich people. Carter had warned Jeff long before they parted ways that he would eventually find himself in hot water he couldn't talk his way out of. Jeff had always laughed and said, "If I can't talk my way out of it, you sure can, C. I believe in you."

Jeff believed in him. And so here he was.

Carter picked up the phone again and touched Jeff's number. He waited for the voicemail to kick on again, but the phone rang. And Jeff answered.

"Hello, my old friend," Jeff said, his voice cracking. "You came for me, didn't you?"

He sounded off, Carter thought. Tearful.

"Of course I did," Carter said. "Where are you and what have you gotten yourself into?"

"I can't tell you anything over the phone. These people, they're—" He stopped, and Carter heard a couple of deep breaths followed by a door closing.

"They're what?" Carter prompted.

"Can you meet me in half an hour?"

"Where?"

"South Bank. The Black Penny Café."

Before Carter could respond, the phone beeped the three-tone call-end sound in his ear. Jeff was gone.

Carter got up and dressed quickly. He toyed with the idea of waking Avery, but after a moment's thought he knocked lightly on the door to Harrison's room.

A sleepy-looking Harrison opened the door. "This better be good," he said.

"I just spoke to Jeff," Carter said. "He wants me to meet him in half an hour. Will you come with me?"

"That depends."

"On what?" Carter blinked. He figured Harry wouldn't hesitate.

"This place where you're supposed to meet, will there be coffee?" Harrison smiled.

"It is a café."

"And Avery?" Harrison asked, his eyes shifting toward her closed bedroom door. "Have you told her what we're up to?"

Carter shook his head. "I'd rather keep her out of danger. Jeff sounded... not like himself. I have no idea what we're getting into."

Harrison nodded. "Sound thinking, young man. Give me five minutes."

The early hour meant the London streets were empty in a way that bordered on eerie, a chilly, damp wind kicking up the only noise. Carter and Harrison hopped into a waiting taxi at the queue in front of the hotel and made the trip to the café in less than five minutes.

The Black Penny was exactly what Carter had envisioned. Located directly across the Thames from Covenant Garden in South Bank, the small bistro, with indoor and outdoor seating, was shoehorned between two boutiques in the heart of London's shopping district. The café hadn't opened for business yet, but Carter could see the staff inside preparing for the day. Carter and Harrison commandeered one of four deserted outdoor tables standing atop a brick patio under a large awning. Harrison sat with his back to the establishment, facing the street.

"What exactly did Jeff say?" Harrison asked, raising his voice over the wind whistling between the buildings.

"Not much," Carter said. "He sounded scared. Said he couldn't talk on the phone, that it had to be in person. He said something about 'these people,' like someone's after him."

"Did he mention anything about the people?"

"He started to. I think he wanted to but decided against it."

"You do know Ave is gonna be pissed when she finds out we came here without her, right?" Harrison said.

"Yeah, I know. You think I should have woken her?"

"Hell no, my young Jedi. It's better if we find out what's going on first."

"Then you'll smooth it over with her?"

"I never said that." Harrison chuckled, but the smile withered like a flower in a vase as he tipped his head forward, clearing his throat. "Heads up. Three o'clock. Is that Jeff?"

Carter's head swiveled to the left until he caught sight of Jeff's face peering around the corner from a nearby alley and winced. "Oh, man. He looks pretty worse for wear, but yeah, that's him."

Carter raised a hand in greeting. After looking both ways, Jeff scurried toward their table.

6

Jeff looked downright antsy. *Like a long-tailed cat on a porch full of rockers.* The memory of Jeff's mother saying that exact phrase popped into Carter's head as vividly as if she had just spoken the words. Jeff's clothes were filthy and wrinkled, like he had slept in them. More than once.

"I can't believe you actually came for me." Jeff blinked against tears in his eyes as he sat down at the table beside Harrison.

"Hey, dude, I made a promise," Carter said.

Harrison exchanged a silent nod with Jeff.

Up close, it was clear that someone had worked Jeff over. His lip was split and swollen and one of his eyes was an angry potpourri of black and purple.

"Now, what the heck is going on?" Carter asked.

Before Jeff could utter a single word, three dark-haired men approached them from the south at a dead run.

"We've got company," Harrison said, rising to his feet and assuming a defensive posture. Carter and Jeff followed suit, jumping up and sending their chairs clattering to the ground.

"You were followed," Jeff said, the fear registering clearly on his face.

"Give it up, Shelton," the tallest man growled, swinging a meaty fist into Jeff's jaw as the trio of assailants pounced.

Amid a flurry of punches and elbow strikes, the tables were upended, clanging to the patio and drawing the attention of the people inside the café.

Fighting a man approximately his own size, Carter gave as good as he got—which was saying something. It was clear that their attackers, whoever they were, were well trained in hand-to-hand combat. Carter managed the occasional glimpse of Jeff, who despite his sleep-deprived and beaten-down appearance, was giving his assailant the fight of his life. Adrenaline was indeed a powerful thing, though Carter would take a shark over a thug any day of the week.

Harrison fought his way out of a hole and knocked out his attacker, then slid over to give Carter a hand. Carter used the distraction to put his man in a chokehold from behind.

"Help Jeff, Harry," Carter said as his assailant struggled to get free. Harrison sprinted toward the alley, which ran alongside a dry cleaners, where Jeff was clearly losing his fight. "Just bloody hand it over," Jeff's attacker squawked.

"I don't have it," Jeff grunted. "And it's not yours, anyway."

The man caught in Carter's grip wriggled around like a hooked fish, and Carter pulled his forearm in tighter, hoping to take some of the fight out of him.

"What do you want?" Carter demanded.

The only response came in the form of a vicious elbow strike to his ribs. The pain was intense, but Carter managed to hold on, squeezing even tighter. Fighting was like any other endurance activity Carter had ever mastered, whether it was rock climbing or wrestling: the trick was to power through the pain.

"Knife," Harrison yelled.

Carter glanced over and saw Jeff and Harrison jump back as their attacker swung his blade in a wide arc. It looked to Carter like the man knew exactly what he was doing. After slashing at Jeff to put him off balance, the man readjusted his grip on the knife, then lunged, jabbing at Jeff's torso. Carter heard the man shout something else at Jeff but couldn't make out the words over the grunts and growls coming from the guy he was trying to hold on to.

For the distraction, Carter was rewarded with an elbow strike to his side, followed by one from the opposite side directly to his jaw when his grip loosened. That blow stunned Carter long enough for his attacker to produce a knife of his own, and just that fast, the dynamics of the brawl flipped. Tracking both hands and leaning back on the edge of an over-turned iron table, Carter kicked with both feet and shoved his attacker backward. The man tripped over his own feet and began to tumble, the knife clattering to the cobblestones. He scrambled after the weapon, but Carter was quicker and pounced on his attacker's wrist before he could retrieve it.

Carter risked a glance back at Jeff in time to see his old friend turn away from the fight, intent on escaping down the alley—and leaving Harrison and Carter to deal with his mess. Typical.

Jeff managed all of three steps before Harrison's assailant touched his ear, then disengaged and stumbled backward into the middle of the road. A bright burst of crimson bloomed on the back of Jeff's grungy shirt a split second before his legs straightened and he pitched face-first to the ground.

7

Carter snatched the knife up off the pavement as his own assailant scampered off, then Carter hurried toward Jeff's motionless body. The man Harrison and Jeff had been fighting with had already disappeared down another alley. Carter heard the angry shouting of the bistro owner behind him like the guy was across the river: muted, dull. The man was yelling something about phoning the police. *Good*, Carter thought. The only thing that mattered was helping Jeff. He knelt at his old friend's side and checked for a pulse, but couldn't find one, noticing that the blood pool on the ground underneath Jeff wasn't getting larger, because his heart had stopped. Hoping against hope, Carter rolled Jeff onto his back and saw that it really was too late. Jeff's eyes were wide open and fixed. The wound left behind where the bullet had exited his body was large and ragged. Jeff never stood a chance.

"Get down, Carter," Harrison shouted. "The shooter might still be up there."

Carter turned and saw Harrison hunkered down behind one of the upended bistro tables. He was scanning the rooftops on the opposite side of the road.

"You see him, Harry?" Carter said as he, too, scanned the rooftops.

"No, but he was up there. On the roof of the bank. It's the only place he could have taken that shot."

The sound of approaching sirens grew louder, and Carter recognized the telltale hi-low tone associated with British police vehicles from old movies.

"Give it up, Shelton," the tall one had snarled. Whatever their attackers had been after was likely on Jeff's person. Or at the very least those guys thought it was. He quickly went through Jeff's pockets.

Harrison ran over, squatting and pulling Jeff's eyelids closed. "What are you doing?" he hissed at Carter.

"Looking for something that will tell us what Jeff had gotten himself into. They thought he had something they wanted."

"You can't be messing around with the body, Carter. This is a crime scene."

"Just give me a minute," Carter said.

"You don't have a minute," Harrison said as two police vehicles slid to a stop directly in front of the bistro. "Hurry up."

"Stop right there," one of the responding officers yelled.

Carter and Harrison raised their hands and waited for the inevitable.

Carter couldn't tear his eyes off the lifeless shape of his friend beneath the white sheet laid over his body by the medics. Standing beside him was a young blonde uniformed officer who'd been one of the first on the scene and was now assigned to keep an eye on him, he supposed. Carter was only half listening to the words spoken between Harrison and Inspector McGregor, the police detective who had arrived at the behest of the first-responding uniformed officers.

There had been a lot of shouting and confusion as the first officers converged on the scene. It wasn't until Harrison identified himself as a retired NYC detective, and the bistro owner backed up their account of the other men being the knife-wielding aggressors, that the police began treating them as the victims they were.

"I'm sorry about your friend," the policewoman said.

"Thanks," Carter said absently. Given the circumstances, it was the only reply he could think of.

McGregor approached and sat down beside Carter on a stone retaining wall across the street from where Jeff's body lay.

"Mr. Mosley, tell me again how you and Mr. Harrison happened to be here with the victim this morning?"

"I told the other officers already," Carter said, nodding toward the woman. "Jeff asked me to meet him here."

"And Mr. Shelton called you?"

"No, I called him. Jeff had left a coded message telling me that he was in trouble and that he was here in London."

"A coded message?"

"It's a long story. But I knew he was in trouble."

"And when was this?"

"Day before yesterday I think," Carter said. "We just got here last night. Flew in from LA."

"LA?"

"Los Angeles, California."

"And Jeff Shelton was a close friend?" McGregor asked, jotting notes.

"A long time ago."

McGregor raised a brow.

"I hadn't talked to him in some time," Carter said. "We had a—falling out."

"May I ask what it was about?"

"Just stupid friend stuff," Carter lied, not wanting to share more with the inspector than he needed to.

McGregor nodded his understanding, but Carter read the doubt in his eyes.

"One of the witnesses said they saw you doing something over near the body. You didn't remove anything from the scene of the crime, did you?"

"No," Carter lied again, far less convincingly this time. "I was checking to see if I might be able to perform CPR on him. But when I rolled him on to his back I saw the hole in his chest, and I knew."

"The reason I ask is because we haven't found any identification or cell phone on his person. And you did say you called him, right?"

"I called him this morning and he had his phone then."

"And the wallet?"

"I didn't see him with one."

Carter was distracted by the arrival of the morgue transport and the two attendants who went to work removing Jeff's body.

"Where will they take him?" Carter said as he watched them lower the stretcher into position next to Jeff's body and realized he was going to have to call Jeff's mother and tell her that her son was dead.

"The city morgue, as is routine," McGregor said. "They will perform an autopsy on the body to confirm the cause of death."

Carter didn't bother to say that the gaping hole in his friend's chest was a pretty safe bet. The cops had their procedure, and this guy didn't make the rules.

"And how will his family go about getting his remains released to return him to the States?"

"We can go over all of that later," McGregor said as he stood up from the wall. "I'll make sure to keep you and Mr. Harrison in the loop as we work to identify your attackers."

"What about the shooter?" Carter said. "We just got a lecture yesterday from customs about British gun laws. There can't be but so many people here who have a rifle that can do that kind of damage."

"I'll be in contact, Mr. Mosley."

Before Carter could mount a proper protest, he heard rapidly approaching footfalls and one of the officers yelped, "Ma'am, this is a crime scene. I'm sorry—"

Carter turned to see Avery standing just behind the yellow crime scene tape with her hand over her mouth. He watched her gaze travel from the bloody spot on the road where Jeff's body had been only moments before, to Harrison. Finally, she looked directly at him. The relief on her face at seeing him and Harrison alive was unmistakable. Almost as clear as her irritation at having been left behind.

8

Avery ducked inside the bistro and ordered coffee and scones for all of them while Carter and Harrison finished speaking with Inspector McGregor. She exited and grabbed one of the empty patio tables as soon as the police crime scene tape was taken down. Sipping her coffee, she watched as McGregor and a blonde policewoman both handed business cards to Carter before departing. Avery couldn't help but notice that Harrison only received a card from the inspector.

Carter and Harrison joined Avery at the table. Avery slid a hand over Carter's. "Are you really okay?"

Carter nodded. "There were three of them. Harry and I held them off as long as we could."

"But a sniper got to Jeff before we could speak to him," Harrison said.

"I'm so sorry about your friend, Carter," Avery said.

"Thanks." Carter winced as the hot coffee stung his busted lower lip.

"You're bleeding." Avery leaned closer, dabbing at his wounds with a napkin.

"My guy got a lucky punch in," Carter said.

"It was more than that," Harrison said. "They had knives, too, Ave. These guys, whoever they were, were serious. We're lucky we weren't stabbed to death."

Holding up one finger, Avery turned to the next table, where a middle-aged couple sat whispering and pointing at them. "Do you mind?"

"Indeed I do, miss," the man said. "Who wants to listen to such talk over pastries on a lovely morning?"

"You are perfectly free to move." Harrison half stood. "You might not want to sit at that table, anyhow. I'd pick another if I were you."

"Why not?" the man demanded.

"I mean...the last guy who sat there is on his way to the morgue." Harrison shrugged. "If you're okay with that, go ahead and stay there."

Eyes wide, the couple immediately sprang from the chairs and left.

"That was a little cruel, Harry," Carter said.

"But effective, no?" Harrison winked.

"Very."

Carter turned to Avery. "Are you mad that we didn't wake you?"

"Sure am," Avery said. "But we'll discuss that later."

"Told you," Harrison grumbled.

Carter shook his head. "So much for your Young Jedi schtick," he muttered.

"That was before you made her mad," Harrison retorted.

Avery tapped on the edge of the table to call for order. "So, if you didn't get a chance to speak with Jeff, then we still don't know what he was into that got him killed," Avery said.

"I don't know about that." Harrison fixed Carter with a scowl. "Mr. Crime Scene Wrecker there might have some clues."

"What?" Avery asked.

"Carter took stuff from Jeff's pockets before the police arrived." Harrison stared at Carter. "And don't pretend you didn't. I saw you pocket some stuff when you thought you were being slick."

"Did you, Carter?" Avery asked.

Carter nodded again. "I found his cell and wallet."

"Jeez, Carter, you took his phone?" Avery said. "Won't the police be looking for that?"

"Of course they will," Harrison said. "They're not stupid. And they've probably got eyes on us right now."

Avery studied the people milling around. Aside from the crime scene team examining the buildings near the alley, all but two of the uniformed police had departed. Nobody appeared to be paying them any mind.

"What are the evidence techs down there looking for, Harry?" Avery asked.

"Bullet fragments or damage to the buildings. They're hoping the shooter messed up and fired more than one round. They won't find anything. Whoever did this was a pro."

"How do you know?" Carter said.

"Because this was a hit, plain and simple. The three goons we fought with were nothing but a distraction. Whoever was behind this planned to kill Jeff all along."

"But why?" Avery said.

"No idea," Harrison said. "But it sure sounded like they wanted something he claimed he didn't have."

"Jeff said they followed us," Carter said. "Could that be true?"

"Way more likely they'd been tracking him than you," Harrison said.

Carter sighed and picked at his scone. "I'm sorry I dragged you guys into this. I didn't manage to help Jeff at all. I just got us in trouble and we don't even know what kind. Jeff's dead, and those guys saw us. I think the smartest thing we could do at this point is head home."

Harrison brushed the crumbs from his scone off his shirt onto the ground. "Um, in case you weren't paying attention, we aren't going anywhere, Slick. McGregor ordered us to stick around while they investigate."

"Then I guess we'd better get started," Avery said as she wadded up her napkin and tossed it into her empty coffee cup.

"On what?" Carter asked.

"Finding out who Jeff crossed paths with that wanted him dead."

"I'm not sure that's such a good idea, Ave," Harrison said as Carter shook his head.

"Harry, the police said we weren't free to leave. They didn't say anything about conducting our own investigation, did they?"

"Well, no, they didn't actually say those words but—"

"You know better than I do that an American thief is not going to be a high priority for the police here." Avery stood and slid her chair under the table as Carter and Harrison exchanged an uneasy glance. "Carter's right, the killers saw you two. And as you said, Harry, we're stuck here for a few days. I'm not interested in spending them at the hotel waiting for a sniper to find a clear shot, and Mom always said the best defense is a good offense. So we'll find them before they find us."

9

"I can't ask either of you to do that," Carter said. "I've already put you in enough danger just by coming here."

"Nonsense." Avery waved one hand. "Are you forgetting how I dragged you into chasing after the General's Gold after Mark was murdered? How many times did we almost die that week?"

"That was different," Carter said.

"Because it was me and not you?" Avery asked as she exchanged a look with Harrison and motioned for him to stand up.

"Yes," both men said in unison.

"Spare me." Avery shook her head.

Harrison stood and placed one hand on Carter's shoulder while gathering up their trash with the other. "Looks like you've been overruled, sport."

As they walked along in front of the shops on their way back to the hotel, Carter continued to try to talk them out of staying. "Look, Avery, someone just shot Jeff in plain sight in a city where guns are hard to come by."

"True story," Harrison said as he pretended to reach for his own gun.

"I have no interest in having your death on my conscience," Carter continued.

"Hey," Harrison said. "What about my death? You dragged me into a brawl this morning without batting an eye."

"Oh please, Harry," Avery said. "That's the most fun you've had in months, and don't try to say otherwise. You always were up for a good fight."

"Guilty as charged." Harrison laughed.

Avery stopped walking and turned to face Carter. "Look, I'm a grown woman, Carter. This isn't my first rodeo. We've been up against bad guys before. I know you want to find out what happened to Jeff and why. You wouldn't have run halfway around the world to find him if you didn't."

"That was before people were getting shot." Carter held up Jeff's cell phone. "Maybe we should just let the police handle it. Take them the evidence and go."

"The police will be focused on finding the shooter," Harrison said. "You heard that guy yesterday—they don't like guns here. That will be their priority. But Avery has a point here—just sitting around waiting for them to come knock on the door isn't the smart play. We might be able to help McGregor's investigation along by finding out who we're dealing with."

"And what they were after," Avery added.

"Assuming we don't end up like Jeff," Carter argued. "And no one is knocking on our door without getting past hotel security—we're in the penthouse and there's a private elevator."

"I like our chances of finding something helpful without getting killed." Harrison touched one finger to his chin. "It's going to take more than a little digging, even if we assume our mercenaries are well-connected, for them to find out who we are. We're in a foreign country. They're not."

"Two-thirds of them aren't internet famous, though," Carter said, his shoulders already drooping because he knew he'd lost the fight.

As they reached the door to the Rosewood Hotel, Avery stopped again and faced Carter.

"I know that no matter what happened between you and Jeff all those years ago, this has rattled you."

Carter opened his mouth to protest but Avery stopped him.

"I know you, Carter Mosley. I've been messaging MaryAnn and she told me that Brady said you three were inseparable as kids. Jeff was like the third Mosley brother."

Carter gave a weak smile at the memory. "It's true. He was."

"We can't go home anyway. So, let's just look through his stuff and see if we can pick up a trail. Okay?"

"Harry?" Carter cocked one eyebrow at the retired detective, but the big man stood resolute, arms folded in front of his chest.

"Okay," Carter said. "You win. Just do me one favor. Both of you."

"What's that?" Avery said.

"Don't get killed."

Avery grinned and snatched Jeff's phone from Carter's hand. "Got you covered."

Back in their suite, Harry checked the entire space for hidden cameras, bugs, or any sign that someone else had been there.

"Harry, is that really necessary?" Avery asked.

"You want to take that chance again? Perhaps you've forgotten Antarctica."

"I haven't forgotten," Carter said. "Need any help looking?"

"I think we're in the clear here," Harrison said as he returned a lamp to one of the end tables.

Carter laid the wallet on the table and Avery added Jeff's cell phone.

The wallet was a plain brown leather bifold. Avery attached Jeff's Android smartphone to her computer. It took all of two minutes on her laptop to bypass his password.

"I'm in," she said.

"Just like that?" Harrison said. "Remind me to change all my passwords when we get home."

"The text messages have all been erased." Avery ignored him, her eyes on her computer screen. "But the call logs are still up. I can see the incoming calls from you, Carter."

"Were those the last ones?" Carter said.

"No. There was one more. Looks like a local number and it came in just before you and Harry went to meet him at the bistro. Give me a sec and I'll check it in a reverse directory."

"Odds are they're just going to tell you it's a mobile number," Harrison said.

"Yup, it is. But now we have the carrier, and I'm sending the information to MaryAnn to see if she can sweet talk someone out of the name on the owner's account."

"She does seem to know everybody," Harrison agreed.

While Avery checked through the phone, Carter held up his own and excused himself to call Jeff's mother.

Avery watched him disappear into his room. "What a terrible thing to have to do."

"It's never easy news to deliver," Harrison said. "No matter how many times you have to do it."

"Carter!" The water shut off in the background and Carter could practically see Miss Loretta, probably a little more gray these days, wiping her hands on a sunny yellow dish towel. "This is a nice surprise. I just watched your last video on my computer this morning."

"How'd I do?" he asked, trying to keep his voice light. How in the world was he supposed to tell her that her only son was dead?

"You're too skinny. You need to come let me make you dinner," she said. "But the dive was something. My favorite was the one at the south pole, though. My goodness, I was stressed out watching that." She laughed.

"I'm glad you like them."

"I wish you boys hadn't fallen out," she said softly. "But I am so proud of you. Your momma would be, too."

Carter swallowed hard. "Thank you, ma'am. I sure hope so."

"My Jeffrey just hasn't figured out how to be happy with what he's got. I tell him, he's young, he's healthy, he's smart." She clicked her tongue. "He'll grow up someday."

Oh, man. Carter winced.

"I'm in England, Miss Loretta," he said slowly. "I came to see Jeff because he called me day before yesterday and said he was in trouble."

"What kind of trouble?" Her words came slowly.

"I'm so sorry." Carter's voice cracked on the last word. "I came straight here, and I tried. But he…" Carter tried to force the word *died* out and it just wouldn't go. He blinked hard and took a deep breath. "He was shot this morning. He didn't make it."

As long as he lived, Carter would never forget the scream that ripped from her throat. He stayed quiet for what felt like hours while she sobbed. "I'm so sorry," he said again when she got a little quieter. "I didn't want the London police to be the ones to tell you."

Loretta Shelton sniffled. "I appreciate you, Carter. You were always a good boy at heart. I wish my Jeffrey had taken more after you. Too much of his daddy in him." She stopped there, but Carter was a little shocked she'd said that much—in their whole lives, Jeff and Carter had never heard three words about Jeff's father.

"I wish I could have saved him." He didn't know what else to say.

"How do I… What now? He's in England…" She sounded so sad, a woman he'd rarely seen without a smile even when she was bone-tired from working two jobs.

"I'll take care of getting him home, Miss Loretta," he said.

"No, that's going to be expensive—" she began and Carter cut her off.

"I insist," he said. "It's the least I can do."

"Carter," she said softly. "I know what Jeffrey did. With Chelsea."

"It's the least I can do for you, ma'am," Carter said.

She started crying again. "Did they get the shooter?" she asked.

"Not yet," Carter said. "But one way or another, I'll make sure they do. I promise." He had zero ideas for how he could make good on that, but he'd give it his all.

"You're a good kid, Carter Mosley." She sniffled.

"I'm so sorry, Miss Loretta. I'll see you soon." He ended the call and went back to the living area, where Harrison was removing everything from Jeff's wallet.

"He had a UK driver's license," Carter said, clearing his throat and plucking it off the table. "Looks like it was issued only months after our last contact."

"When was that?" Harrison said.

"Four years ago."

"Let me see that," Harrison said, taking the ID. "It looks real enough but I'm not familiar with the British government's counterfeit measures. If it is a fake, it's a good one. It would fool me."

The wallet itself contained six hundred pounds in large notes and a five-dollar American bill.

"Certainly not enough money for someone to kill him," Harrison said.

"No but that's still a lot of money for Jeff to carry around," Carter said. "I'm guessing he just fenced something."

"Maybe whatever it was is what those guys were after," Avery said.

"Just how good a thief was your buddy, Carter?" Harrison asked.

"Pretty good," Carter said. "It was about the rush for Jeff. So the more he got away with, the more he wanted—his skill pushed him to try bigger scores, which was one of the reasons we lost touch. It started innocently enough—he got a metal detector one Christmas that he used to find lost things on the beach when we were kids. At first, he was excited about just finding things, sometimes even returning them if he could find the owners. Then one day someone gave him a reward for finding a wedding ring, and all of a sudden everything he returned, he wanted a reward. It was like a race where the finish line jumps back ten steps every time you reach it. He moved on to pickpocketing, then small-item theft, and finally bigger stuff. I tried to pretend it wasn't a problem for way longer than I should have. Kept hoping he'd get bored and want a new kind of thrill. The legal kind."

"I knew quite a few burglars and robbers with the same addiction," Harrison said. "They want the high as much as the loot."

"Anyway, that's part of why I cut off all contact with him."

"I'd say it was safe to assume that the person or persons we're up against were probably the last ones that Jeff stole from, and they want whatever it is back," Avery said.

Carter held up the cash he'd found in Jeff's wallet. "Well, if these six hundred pounds are any indication, I'd say he fenced whatever it was."

"But that's not near enough money to kill someone over," Avery said. "There's something else, clearly."

Harrison picked up the wallet and kneaded the worn leather.

"What are you doing?" Avery said.

"Looking to see if he stashed anything inside."

"Like what?" Carter asked.

"Like this," Harrison said as he folded back the nylon lining and turned the wallet upside down over the table. A brass key clattered across the tabletop toward the edge. Carter grabbed it out of the air before it hit the floor. The key was long with a decorative round head and a hole in the middle to allow it to be attached to a ring.

Before anyone could speak, the phone on the high glass sofa table bleated.

The whole room froze momentarily before Avery shook her head like she was trying to clear it and crossed the thick carpet to pick it up. "Hello?"

"Good morning, Miss Turner. I'm terribly sorry to disturb you, but there's a gentleman at the desk here who is insistent that he must speak with you."

"In private," Avery heard a deep, muffled voice say in the background.

No way.

Carter crossed the room and put one hand on her shoulder, mouthing, "Everything okay?"

Avery waved her hand at him. "I'm afraid I'm not taking meetings today," she said. "Please tell him if he'd like to leave a card, I'll get back with him at my earliest convenience."

Harrison's eyebrows shot up.

"Very good, miss," the concierge said, hanging up.

"What was that?" Harrison asked.

"He said there's a man at the desk who wants to speak to me," Avery said.

"Surely they didn't find us that fast." Carter turned to Harrison.

"Doubtful. But now I'm curious," Harrison said. "Sport, you feel like some recon in the lobby? Avery said to have the guy leave a card."

"And I'm supposed to sit here alone?" Avery shook her head. "No thanks. If y'all are going downstairs, I am too."

"Fine. But we're being casual," Harrison said. "Surreptitious."

"That word-of-the-day calendar coming in handy for you?" Carter quipped.

"I know a few words I didn't get from the calendar." Harry glared.

"No time for that, guys," Avery said, tucking Jeff's phone and wallet into the room's safe and turning for the door.

She put her hand on the knob just as a knock came from the other side.

10

Avery jerked her hand back like the door handle had turned into a snake. She turned to Harry, who looked around for something that could be a weapon and hustled over to stand by the bar cart, putting his hand on a heavy cut-crystal decanter full of scotch that cost more per bottle than his rent in Brooklyn had been. He nodded for Avery to check the hallway.

She peered through the peephole. A tall, clean-cut guy who was very easy on the eyes stared back like he could see her through the door. He was wearing a suit and shiny wingtips. She waved Carter over to check him out since she hadn't seen the thugs who'd attacked them that morning.

Carter shook his head, whispering, "He wasn't one of them."

"Miss Turner, I know you're in there." A voice that rivaled Harry's for depth and authority rang through the thick wood door like it was a flimsy screen. "Mr. Mosley, Mr. Harrison—there's only one elevator and I was just in it. Open the door."

"How did you get up here?" Avery called, proud of the fact that her voice didn't shake. "I told the desk no meetings."

"You want to talk with me," the man said. "I promise. I'll explain if you'll open the door."

"How about you explain and then she'll think about it?" Harrison called.

"Mr. Harrison, you can trust me."

"Didn't Ted Bundy tell women that?" Carter asked.

Avery's eye was smashed to the peephole, watching their uninvited visitor's every move.

"Miss Turner, I need your help finding a missing jewel," the man said, his voice lower. "Moreover, I believe helping me might help Mr. Mosley find some closure."

"What?" Harrison muttered, scratching his head.

"Take off your jacket and spin around," Avery said.

"I'm not carrying a weapon." He did as she asked, raising his arms high for good measure.

Avery stepped back and opened the door, allowing him in. Harrison's grip on the decanter tightened.

Once the door was closed, the new guy turned to Harry. "You swept for bugs?"

Harry's brow furrowed. "I did. But how—? Did McGregor send you?"

The man faced Avery and put out his hand, flashing a small but charming smile. "I'm Rowan. MI5. And at the risk of sounding very dramatic and therefore not British at all, Miss Turner, Mr. Mosley, Mr. Harrison...the Crown needs your help."

Avery gaped at the new guy. "MI5." She stammered when she could talk. "Like James Bond? Do you have a double oh number?"

"Top secret, that." He smiled again as she shook his hand. "It's a pleasure to meet you."

"What do you mean, you need our help?" Carter folded his arms across his chest when Rowan extended a hand to him. "You're the...like the CIA, right? Why in the name of anything holy would you need us to help you find so much as a restroom?"

Rowan tipped his head to one side. "Is it possible that you're really that modest, Mr. Mosley? Do you not understand that you and Miss Turner and the gadgets she's invented seem to have a real gift for locating things considered lost forever?"

Carter's shoulders relaxed. "Well. When you put it that way."

Avery gestured to the silk-upholstered settee, and Rowan sat down. She took a blue armchair across from him and waved Carter into the matching chair. Harrison ignored her invitation to sit.

"Why couldn't you just say that?" Harrison asked, his hand not leaving the decanter.

"To a random desk clerk or in front of the hallway security camera?" Rowan raised his eyebrows and Harry nodded grudgingly.

"So what is it you need our help finding?" Avery asked as Harry let go of the decanter and put his hand out wordlessly for Rowan's badge, which he examined and then handed back.

"A ring that we believe Mr. Shelton might have stolen," Rowan said, tucking it back into a pocket inside his suit coat. "And that could be the key to cracking a secret of historical significance that stretches back centuries."

"What kind of ring?"

"A five-carat round ruby set in heavy gold," Rowan said.

"And where do you think Jeff stole it from?" Carter asked. Avery could read on his face that he was thinking about the fistfight and the hole in Jeff's chest.

"That's part of why we need your expertise, Mr. Mosley," Rowan said. "We haven't the faintest idea. If our intel is accurate, Mr. Shelton was the first person to see the ring in several centuries."

Avery chewed the inside of her cheek. "A long-lost ruby ring." She glanced at Carter and Harrison. "If you don't know where it was, how do you know Jeff stole it?"

Rowan frowned as he considered that. "It wasn't his, was it? So he must have stolen it from someone."

"You said several centuries," Avery said. "How many?"

"Nearly five, as far as I know."

Harrison whistled, and Avery tapped one finger on the sofa table. The money they'd found in Jeff's wallet would barely insure shipping on a five-hundred-year-old five-carat stone. What was Carter's buddy into?

"What kind of secret?" Avery asked.

"If I knew that, Ms. Turner, I wouldn't be here," Rowan said. "The information I have is that Mr. Shelton grazed the tip of an iceberg when he came into possession of this ring, however that happened. I'm told several historical documents hint that it was priceless, and part of something larger. However, I have read your file. I trust you all will know more in a matter of days than our historians have managed in decades."

"That's it? A huge ruby ring and a secret?" Avery raised one eyebrow, her face dripping skepticism.

"Honestly, I think my superiors sent me here hoping Mr. Shelton confided the stone's location in Mr. Moseley," Rowan said earnestly, his arms relaxed along the contours of the settee.

Avery's skeptical look melted, her shoulders relaxing.

"He didn't have a chance to tell me anything," Carter said, holding Rowan's gaze.

"Pity. But I have faith in your abilities, and in Ms. Turner's brilliance." He smiled at Avery and she felt her cheeks warm. "What I know is that the ring has some historical value, likely because of where it came from or because it belonged to a duke or a bishop or something, maybe. I'm afraid my file is thin, but my orders were very clear: get your assistance in solving this puzzle."

"So what do we get for helping you?" Harrison asked.

Rowan blinked. "I'm sorry?"

"You're asking Carter and Avery to take some personal risk looking for a long-lost bauble, but if it's so hush-hush, chances that they get anything for their time, or for possibly putting their lives at risk, even, given what happened to Jeff just this morning, are slim I'd wager. So what are you going to do for us?"

"What could you possibly have in mind?"

"I want to know who killed Jeff," Carter said without hesitation, Miss Loretta's anguish echoing in his head. Maybe this guy, and finding a lost ring, were the key to making good on the promise he'd just made her.

"Me too," Avery added.

"I'm sure the local inspectors—" Rowan began and Harrison shook his head.

"I'd feel better about getting answers faster if MI5 was on this case," Harrison said. "Your murder rate is lower here. The local cops are less experienced than I was working in New York."

"I'd wager even Scotland Yard has nothing on your experience in this arena, Mr. Harrison." Rowan gave a nod and a smile.

"But I don't have connections or channels to work here," Harry said. "You have more than Inspector McGregor, I'm sure."

"That is true."

"We'll find your ring and decode your secret," Avery said confidently. "You find our murderer. Deal?"

Rowan put his hand out and shook all three of theirs in turn. "Your cooperation is much appreciated," he said. "I'll be in touch."

He let himself out and a few seconds later they heard the faint *bing* of the elevator.

"James Bond in our hotel room," Carter said, nodding. "Pretty lit."

"Or an invitation to get yourself shot," Harrison said.

"You said yourself McGregor told us not to leave, Harry," Avery said. "I'd bet chasing a jewel at the request of the government is less dangerous than chasing a murderer, at least a little."

"And we did get British intelligence looking into Jeff's death," Harry conceded. "That makes me feel more like there will be an answer at some point."

"Anyone else way more curious about this thing in light of what the double oh cool guy said?" Carter held up the funny key they'd found inside the lining of Jeff's wallet.

Avery and Harrison both raised their hands.

"We need to find what it goes to," Avery said.

Carter flipped it around in the light. "It's rather fancy. A safe? A trunk maybe?"

"Let me see it a sec," Harrison said.

Carter passed it to him.

"Any thoughts, Harry?" Avery said.

"It looks a lot like a key my grandmother used to have when I was a kid." He handed Avery the key and wiggled his eyebrows. "It was her safety deposit box key."

Avery and Carter exchanged glances.

"I'll bet this is what they were after," Avery said, her voice shooting up an octave midway through the words. "That's brilliant, Harry."

"Assuming we can find the box, you might have just gotten yourself a pretty cheap expert murder investigation," Harrison said.

"Any idea how the heck we do that?" Carter asked.

"I would bet it's not far," Harrison said. "Jeff was on foot. He had to have been staying somewhere close by or he wouldn't have asked you to meet at South Bank."

Avery pulled up her laptop GPS and searched for banks in the area. "According to Google Maps there are five banks in a six-block radius from here, including one right near the café."

"It could be a coincidence, but I believe that is the building the shooter fired from," Harrison said.

"What if that was why Jeff wanted to meet us there?" Carter mused. "Maybe he planned to take us to the bank as soon as it opened?"

"We should start with that bank and work our way out," Harrison said.

"That's a great plan, guys," Avery said, typing in a search bar. "But what makes you think they're just going to let us waltz in there and check out someone else's safety deposit box? They're supposed to be secure for a reason."

"Maybe that James Bond dude could help," Carter said.

"His name is Rowan," Avery said. "But I got the impression he was asking us to go do this on our own, not offering to assist."

"You think he can really help the cops find out who killed Jeff?"

"I think if the secret police can't catch the killer, then probably nobody can," Avery said. "But that doesn't help us with the safety deposit box."

Harrison picked up Jeff's license from the table and studied it.

"When the box holder dies, there are rules and procedures about next of kin and wills," Avery read from her screen. "And we don't have either."

"Maybe we don't need to," Harrison said, staring at Carter with a furrowed brow. "How good are your acting skills?"

"What are you talking about?" Carter asked.

Harrison turned the license around so Avery could see it. "Jeff could have been the third Mosley brother for real. At least back when this picture was taken. If he says he's Jeff, who's going to look too hard?"

"No kidding," Avery said as she looked back and forth between Carter and the image on Jeff's license.

"Tell me you are in fact kidding." Carter's eyes popped so wide Avery could see white all around the brown. "In addition to almost being killed this morning, I had to lie to the police today already."

"Don't forget stealing evidence from a crime scene," Harrison added.

"Thanks, Harry," Carter said. "That's helpful."

"Don't mention it."

"I don't want to go to British jail for bank fraud. Or to hell for pretending to be my dead friend to get at his valuables."

"As jails go, I bet the British ones are the most polite," Harrison said. "If that helps."

"Not really," Carter said.

"No one is going to jail," Avery said. "Carter, the picture is small enough. I think if you put some wax in your hair to make it stick out like Jeff's and present this license to the bank along with the key, nobody would think twice. And you can't go to hell for trying to help the police."

"Says who?"

"It's a rule." Avery winked. "I'm pretty sure."

Carter looked at Harrison. "Is this stupid?"

"I really think it's worth a shot," Harrison said. "But the only opinion that matters is yours. What do you say, sport?"

Carter sucked in a deep breath and stared at Jeff's photo.

"It may be the only way we find out what this is all about," Avery said.

"Fine," Carter said. "I'll go."

Avery smiled. "We'll start with the bank across the street from the café. You and I can go inside and check the safety deposit box while Harry checks the roof to see if he can find anything the gunman might have left behind."

"I thought that was Rowan's job," Harrison protested. "And how exactly am I supposed to get onto the roof?"

Avery shrugged. "The gunman made it up there. There has to be a way. And just because Rowan is looking into Jeff's death doesn't mean you can't look too. What else are you going to do, come inside and watch Carter commit fraud?" She put one hand on Carter's arm when he yelped a protest to her choice of words.

"Interfering with a police investigation is also a crime," Harrison grumbled in a way that told Avery he was going to do it anyway.

"No worries, Harry," Carter said. "If you get caught, we'll go to polite British prison together."

"Great," Harry said. "Old Bailey here we come."

11

London, 1664

The odor intensified as Burgess continued down the length of the tunnel, working to both ignore his surroundings and control his gag reflex. One hundred meters from where he had entered, the small bits of human remains were still visible beneath the water trickling along the floor, the remnants a stark reminder of just how cruel the men who worked the dungeons were. Burgess realized how fortunate he was to maintain a loftier position within the Crown's hierarchy, far removed from the distasteful world that existed in the bowels of the tower.

A chilled breeze wafted past the skin of his exposed neck, causing him to flinch. He was tough as they came, but like anyone who believed in the existence of heaven and hell, Burgess couldn't discount the possibility that the lost souls of the departed still haunted the tunnel, for if hell and Earth had an intersection, it was here.

He picked up his pace as he sloshed along through the ankle-deep foul water, moving the torch from side to side in search of any sign that someone had recently been down here. He found nothing but gore, filth, and things he would rather not contemplate too deeply.

As he continued on, the water began to clear. Traces of the nightmare he had been wading through mercifully began to dissipate along with the accompanying odor. The fresher air told him he was nearing an exit. As he rounded the final bend in the tunnel, he stopped. To his right, there was another opening in the wall. It began several feet above the tunnel floor and continued up to chest height. It was so small that any man his size would be forced to crawl once inside.

"What in blazes?" he mumbled aloud, spooked for a moment by the sound of his own voice.

He examined what looked to be freshly chiseled markings in the stone as if someone had recently created a new tunnel through the wall of the first. He ran his fingers across the rough hatch marks left behind by the chisel. Most troubling was the fact that the marks appeared to have been made toward the tunnel, not away. Which meant someone had tunneled their way into this one, not the other way around.

He held the torch just inside the darkened opening hoping to see something more, but the light would not penetrate the inky blackness beyond. If there were thieves lying in wait, he might easily be ambushed and left to die down here in the putrid darkness.

Burgess spun around and hurried back toward the dungeon. He began shouting for help and weapons long before anyone would hear him.

12

"I'm very sorry, Mr. Shelton, but we don't seem to have a record of you having a safety deposit box here," the auburn-haired bank officer said. Carter had handed Jeff's ID to a teller when they first arrived, and he directed them to the woman they were with now. The teller hadn't shown even the slightest hesitancy about believing Carter was Jeff, and the redhead hadn't asked for ID.

Carter stared wordlessly at the officer. How exactly would he explain not knowing where his own deposit box was?

I'm sorry, ma'am, but I get a little absent-minded from time to time, he thought but did not say. *Especially after my friend gets gunned down in a foreign country.* He wondered absently if Harrison was faring any better in his search of the roof.

Had Jeff used one of his aliases to open an account, or were they simply at the wrong bank? Did his old friend have his usual collection of bogus IDs? Carter took a deep breath. If Jeff had used another identity, this one was clearly blown. Carter wondered if this was his punishment for posing as a dead man to gain access to his valuables. He turned to Avery, his eyes wide with panic.

"It has been a while since he's been to London," Avery said as she patted

Carter's arm and presented the teller with her most disarming smile. "Come on, hon. We must have the wrong bank."

"I'm so sorry to have troubled you," Carter said.

"Not at all," the woman said. "I hope you find it."

As they turned away from the redhead, Carter's eyes were immediately drawn to a man walking into the bank lobby. The same man he had put in a headlock only hours before—and he couldn't risk being recognized. He pulled away from Avery and turned back to the bank officer.

"How would I go about opening a business account for processing UK transactions for—" He paused and looked over at Avery for help again.

Avery jumped in and took over. "The reason we ask is because Jeff and I own a technology company in the US, but we've been considering branching out internationally. The UK just seems like the logical place to start."

Carter nodded along with everything Avery said while his eyes scanned the lobby to see where his attacker had ended up. The man was now standing in a teller line. The very teller they had spoken to upon entering the bank. As Avery and the redhead continued to converse, Carter watched the man step up to the window and engage the teller. The teller's expression shifted from friendly to puzzled and she looked around the lobby until she spotted Carter and Avery. Carter felt his heart rate increase as the teller signaled for the man to wait. He watched in horror as she left her station and made a beeline toward them.

"We really shouldn't bother this nice lady any further," Carter said as he took Avery by the hand. "Thank you so much for putting up with us."

Avery's eyes widened as the teller stepped up to the bank officer and whispered something in her ear.

Carter and Avery had taken exactly two steps toward the door when the bank officer called out from behind. "Excuse me, sir. May I see your identification again?"

Carter froze. The man at the counter had spotted them. The recognition on his face was immediate and the menacing look impossible to miss as he moved in their direction, his lips moving as if he were speaking with someone. Caught between the bank officer and a hired goon didn't leave Carter and Avery with many options.

"Come on, Avery," Carter said as he pulled her toward the door. "We gotta go, now."

As they passed through the bank's front entry doors, Carter risked a glance backward. The goon was now surrounded by the bank officer, the teller, and a uniformed security guard.

"What the heck was Jeff into, Carter?" Avery asked as he hurried outside and around the corner.

"I wish I knew," Carter said. "And how did that guy know to go to a bank? This bank?"

"We've got to warn Harry and get out of here," Avery said.

They fled down an alley and around to the rear of the building, where Harrison's motionless body sat slumped against a stone wall.

13

"Harry!" Avery yelled as she rushed over to Harrison and knelt by his side.

"Is he breathing?" Carter asked as he squatted and checked for a pulse.

"Yes, thank God," Avery said.

"I've got a good strong pulse here too." Carter released Harrison's wrist.

It took several moments before they were able to rouse him. Harrison seemed a little loopy as he came around.

"What happened, Harry?" Avery said.

"Dunno. I remember climbing down the fire escape from the roof. As soon as I hit the ground, something stung the back of my neck. That's the last thing I can remember."

Avery gently pushed Harrison's head forward and pulled his collar out of the way.

"Right there," Carter said, pointing at the tiny red mark on Harrison's neck.

"Harry, are you allergic to bee stings?" Avery said.

"I don't think so. Never had a problem before."

"It's not a bee sting, Avery," Carter said. "That's an injection site."

"You're kidding me," Harrison said.

"No," Carter said. "I'm not. One of the goons we fought with was in the bank. He probably spotted you on his way inside."

"I must be slipping," Harrison said. "I didn't see anyone around."

"Are you missing anything?" Avery asked.

Harrison quickly patted his pockets. "Damn. My phone is gone."

"What about your wallet?" Carter asked.

"I was a cop too long to carry my wallet in my pocket when I'm skulking around in back alleys in a strange city. It's back in the hotel room."

"Funny, I never thought of London as a strange city," Avery said.

"It's getting stranger by the minute," Harrison said.

"Well, if that guy we saw inside the bank has your phone, then he has all your information too," Carter said.

"Not to worry," Avery said as she and Carter helped Harrison to his feet. "Even a master hacker is going to have trouble cracking all the security I put on your phone, Harry. We have a couple of days at least, if they know what they're doing."

"Can you walk?" Carter said.

"I think so," Harrison said.

"Good, then we need to get out of here before—" Before Avery could finish her thought the man from inside the bank rounded the corner.

Carter grabbed Harrison by the arm. "Let's go."

Harrison wasn't yet capable of running. He stumbled, his limbs seeming like they'd forgotten how to move in tandem.

If they couldn't run, they would stand and fight. Avery and Carter positioned themselves between the goon and Harrison without a word, both assuming a fighting stance. Avery liked their odds—maybe the guy would just take off.

The goon snarled, then charged at them. He didn't appear to have a weapon, but Avery could tell immediately that this guy was well trained in martial arts. He gave as good as he got, blocking both her and Carter easily and moving to attack even though they had a two-on-one advantage.

The goon landed a solid punch to Carter's solar plexus, stunning him. Avery's attention veered to doubled-over Carter just long enough for the goon to grab her from behind.

He probably thinks he's won this round, Avery thought as she flung the crown of her head into his chin, catching the satisfying clack and squeal of his teeth meeting each other before she flipped him over her shoulder onto the cobblestones where he landed hard, a cell phone clattering out of his pocket. Harry's phone.

Carter recovered enough to dive and grab the phone as Avery moved to tackle the goon, intent on making sure he stayed down. He was too fast—rolling out of Avery's path, he sprang to his feet like a cat and sprinted down the alley.

Avery jumped back to her feet like she hadn't just skidded across three yards of cobblestone and took off behind him, making it three steps before Harrison grabbed her elbow.

"Let him go," Harrison said.

"Why do we want to do that?" Avery asked.

"Man, that guy can fight," Carter said, winded and rubbing his chest.

"We got my phone back, Ave," Harrison said. "They had a sharpshooter this morning. Let's not press our luck."

"Harry's right," Carter said. "We need to regroup and get Harry back to the hotel. There's still two more of those guys out here somewhere."

"But what about checking the other banks?" Avery said as she hooked her elbow through Harrison's to steady him. "We still need to locate that safety deposit box before they do."

"We will," Carter said, taking Harrison's other arm.

"Man, I wish I had my gun right about now," Harrison said.

14

After safely stowing Harrison at the hotel, Avery and Carter resumed their search for Jeff's safety deposit box. After two more awkward exchanges with bank officers who couldn't find a record of Jeff, they hit pay dirt at the fourth bank on their list.

"Irony: he used a bank here in swanky Covenant Garden, farthest from where we met this morning, but closest to our hotel," Carter muttered when the teller turned away to look for keys.

Avery found Abigail, the young brunette at the teller station, pleasant and helpful. She didn't even raise an eyebrow at their assertion that Carter was Jeff and that he and Avery were siblings—maybe because it left an opening for Abigail to flirt with Carter.

"Very good, Mr. Shelton, I'll just go and get the key," Abigail had said in a voice that was somehow cutesy and breathy at the same time before she stepped away.

"Could you be any more shameless?" Avery asked.

"What?" Carter said, making a failed attempt at projecting innocence.

"I do declare, I just love your accent, Abigail," Avery mimicked Carter's Southern charm.

"Can I help it if I've got swagger?"

"Someone needs to invent a shot for what you have."

They knew instantly something was wrong when Abigail returned empty-handed, the bank manager in tow.

"This can't be good," Avery said.

"What do you think the problem is?" Carter said.

"Not a clue." Avery shrugged.

"If I can have your attention for a moment," the manager said, addressing the teller pool. "I need to know which one of you checked out the key to the safety deposit vault last. It is supposed to be returned to the bin when you're done."

Carter snorted behind his hand. "Those two security guards at the door don't mean much if they can't keep track of a key," he whispered.

"Let's not panic just yet," Avery said.

Half the staff dispersed, crisscrossing the lobby with small, tight but quick steps, their shoes clicking rapidly on the tile and their arms straight at their sides, fists balled and lips tucked between teeth.

After several minutes of the almost comically tense yet dignified search that Carter pointed out was worthy of a Benny Hill skit, a goateed teller located the key—still stuck in the lock to the open vault door.

Carter ran one hand down his face. "I bet Jeff picked this place thinking it was safer because of the neighborhood."

"Maybe they don't have as much to worry about in this part of the city?"

"Bank robbers in London can't have cars?" Carter grinned.

"Touché," Avery said.

Abigail hurried back over with a wide smile. "If you'll just follow me, Mr. Shelton."

"Is it okay if my sister accompanies me?"

"That is entirely your choice."

They followed Abigail into the vault and Carter handed her the key. She unlocked the door and removed a metal box from inside, placing it on a table at the center of the room.

"I'll be in the next room," the teller said. "Let me know when you've finished, and I'll come in and resecure the box for you."

"Thanks so much," Carter said as he watched her leave.

"You're most welcome, Mr. Shelton." She smiled and batted her lashes.

Avery stared wordlessly at Carter.

"What?" He chuckled.

"Don't," Avery said. "Just, don't. Can we do what we came here for?"

Carter opened the box. Inside was a capped thumb drive and an envelope with his name scrawled across the front.

No ring.

He swallowed hard as he reached for the envelope while Avery poked her fingers into the corners of the box to make sure they weren't missing a giant ruby.

She laid one hand on Carter's arm when she saw his eyes fill, as he looked at his name written in Jeff's handwriting. She plucked the thumb drive from the box, then tucked it inside the small handbag slung diagonally across her torso. After a moment Carter picked up the envelope and slid it into his pocket.

"Aren't you going to see what's inside?" Avery said.

"Later," Carter said, calling for Abigail.

After securing the safety deposit box, the teller led them back to the lobby. "Is there anything else I can do for you, Mr. Shelton?"

She was not talking about banking.

"Um, no I think that about does it," Carter said.

Avery jabbed her elbow into his ribs, fixing him with an aren't-you-forgetting-something look. Carter stared back blankly, his eyes still a little shinier than normal.

"Weren't you planning to get an update on your account balance, *Jeff*?" Avery asked.

"Oh, right. I totally forgot. I'm expecting a money transfer to come through and I'd like to check my balance. Is that something you could help us with?"

"I most certainly can. Give me just a moment."

They returned to her teller station and waited while she logged back into the computer. "Do you have your account number, Mr. Shelton?"

Carter slapped himself on the head. "I'm sorry, I can barely remember my own name before my third cup of coffee."

Avery bit her lip to keep from snickering and Carter tapped her foot with his, shooting her the tiniest sideways smile.

"That's okay. I can search by your name. Just take a moment." Abigail looked up at him through her lashes. "I don't suppose you'd like to go for coffee, would you, Mr. Shelton? I'm due a break."

"I'm afraid my day is booked. But I'd like that a lot. Rain check?"

"I'll hold you to it." Abigail looked up and grinned so widely Avery half expected canary feathers to poke out of her mouth. "Here we are. It looks like your transfer came through yesterday."

"For the full amount?" Avery asked.

"Eight hundred thousand pounds," Abigail murmured as she spun the screen around to face them. "Is that what you were expecting?"

"Um, that is exactly what I was expecting," Carter said. "Thank you so very much, Abigail."

"Abby," she said. "And I'm going to hold you to that coffee."

"Looking forward to it." Carter winked, and Avery looked away before the teller melted into the marble-tiled floor.

Avery was sure they were walking too slowly, trying to play it too cool, as they left the bank, and as such would get themselves caught. But hardly anyone even glanced at them as they stepped out into the sunshine. Neither said a word until they were almost a block away.

"Nearly a million pounds?" Avery said. "That's more than a million dollars. No wonder people are after us."

Carter shook his head. "Could he have fenced this ring Rowan wants us to find for that much, you think?"

"Very possibly," Avery said. "Can you think of any other place he'd get that much money?"

"Nowhere good. Let's get back to the hotel," Carter said. "I need to read this letter."

"And I want to check on Harry," Avery said.

———

They found Harrison unharmed right where they'd left him. He was feeling better and whistled when they told him the amount.

"A cool mil," Harrison said. "Not exactly chump change."

"And a long way from his pickpocketing days," Carter said.

"I wonder why they killed him, though?" Harrison mused. "I don't know what use he'd be to anyone dead."

"Couldn't that be a dozen things, though?" Avery asked, pulling the flash drive out of her bag. "Maybe those goons were hired by whoever he stole the ring from and when they didn't get it back, they took him out. Maybe he convinced them he didn't have it, so they killed him. Maybe they had threatened him with death and were making good on a promise when he didn't give them what they wanted. Without knowing what led up to the brawl this morning, we have no way to know why they shot him."

Harrison nodded. "It's too bad we don't have a bank confirmation code. It would be helpful if we wanted to know where the transfer came from."

Avery pulled out her cell and unlocked the screen. "You mean this confirmation code?"

"How did you manage that?" Carter said, his jaw loosening.

"Easy," Avery said. "When Abigail turned the screen around, I snapped a pic."

Carter made a face. "I meant how did you do it without anyone seeing?"

"Magic." Avery winked.

"Who's Abigail?" Harrison said.

"Carter's latest conquest," Avery said. "Except she thinks his name is Jeff and that he recently came into quite a lot of cash."

"Whatever," Carter said. "I'm never going to see her again. So, can we do anything with that number?"

"I have a friend who should be able to tell us which bank it was sent from at a minimum," Avery said. "Maybe even the account number."

"Too bad we still won't know why they sent it," Harrison said.

"I may be able to help with that," Carter said as he removed the unopened envelope from his pocket.

15

Avery watched Carter's expression change as he read Jeff's letter, his brow furrowing so quickly she was almost afraid to ask.

Harrison, true to form, blurted it right out: "Oh Jesus, what now?"

After a moment, Carter looked up from the letter. "Jeff knew those guys were coming to kill him. I think he just wasn't sure when."

"Did he take something of theirs?" Avery said.

"He says he didn't even know who they were. Only that they were going to kill him."

"Does he say why?" Harrison said.

"The letter says he was diving a few weeks ago and found an old ring. A large ruby set in thick twenty-four-karat gold. Definitely a handmade, one-of-a-kind piece. He took the ring to have an appraisal done. The jeweler confirmed that the ruby was real with several insignificant flaws. Probably worth at least a million dollars."

"Come on," Harrison said. "Who just happens to find a million-dollar ring in the ocean?"

"That certainly would explain where the money came from," Avery said, ignoring the comment. "Did he sell it to the jeweler?"

"No. He sold it to a private collector using a fence as a middleman. And he wants me to make sure the money goes to his mother."

"Well, that's admirable," Harrison said. "But does he say if he told those guys that he no longer had the ring? He looked a little worse for wear before they even came up this morning."

"Didn't seem to matter to them." Carter waved the pages. "He had no idea why they wanted it so badly or how they learned that he had it. He said they just kept coming. They beat the hell out of him and trashed his place looking for information on where he had found the ring."

"Did he tell them?" Avery said.

"He gave them phony coordinates."

"That might explain why they were so pissed when we met them." Harrison nodded thoughtfully.

"Did he happen to include the actual coordinates in the letter?" Avery asked.

"He did. It's a place called Cromer Shoals Chalk Bed."

"Sounds made up," Harrison said. "You sure that's a real place?"

"It is," Carter said. "More commonly known as Britain's Great Barrier Reef. Jeff and I used to talk about diving it together."

Avery removed the thumb drive from her bag. "Guess it's time to see what else he left you."

"There's a lot of pictures of the ring here," Avery said as she scrolled through the photos on the thumb drive.

"That doesn't really help us," Carter said. "He fenced it."

"Anything else?" Harrison asked.

"These maps of the dive site should help pretty directly," Avery said. "Looks like Jeff marked several locations where he dove around the reef."

Carter stood looking over her shoulder at the maps. "Doesn't tell us which site he recovered the ring at, though."

"Of course not," Harrison grumbled. "That would be too easy."

"Any other documents?" Carter asked as he crossed the room and opened his own laptop.

"How about Jeff's bank account number, online access information, and the contact information for the fence he used?" Avery waved one hand at the file she'd just opened on her screen.

"The bank information will come in handy at some point," Carter said. "But I'm not reaching out to any of Jeff's criminal contacts. His fence won't tell us who he sold the ring to anyway—that's the entire point of the middleman."

"If they're friends though..." Harrison began.

"Thieves don't have friends, Harry. Jeff should've learned that years ago."

"What makes you think the fence isn't a legitimate pawnbroker?" Avery said.

Carter looked over his computer screen at Harrison. "Harry, you ever meet a legitimate pawnbroker?"

"They're kind of like the Easter Bunny, Ave," Harrison said.

"Meaning they don't exist," Avery said.

"Not that I've ever seen."

"Pawnbrokers aside, at least we know where the deposit came from without wasting time running it down," Avery said.

"What are you doing?" Harrison asked as Carter started typing.

"Looking into chartering a boat for our dive."

"Sure," Harrison said. "Because diving for treasure a bunch of heavies are after worked out so well for us last time."

"No, that's actually a really good idea," Avery said. "It's not treasure we're after, it's intel. Seeing where Jeff found the ring, examining the dive site, talking to the locals—that could help us figure out where it came from, which might give MaryAnn a clue about who would want it and have the kind of money it took to buy it. She knows collectors and historians everywhere."

"Tell you what, Harry," Carter said. "I'll give you a couple of different places to call and you can set it up. That way, you won't be able to blame me if something goes awry."

"I'll gladly set it up," Harrison said. "Though I think I'll leave blaming you on the table for now."

Avery composed a short email to MaryAnn with as much information as she had pertaining to the diving area, plus three photos of the ring and a comment about Rowan's mention of a lost secret. It bothered her that Rowan said he didn't know much about it, yet someone with power wanted it badly enough to send a special agent to their hotel to enlist their help. Whatever the reason, there was clearly more to the story, and Avery wanted to know what they were getting into.

If there's a way to find out what this is and who might want it, I think it might hold a clue. The guy said it was linked to a secret they want us to uncover. Their people are stonewalled. And whatever history on the reef you can come up with might help us with the dive, she typed before signing off.

After sending the message, Avery looked up at Carter. "How computer savvy was Jeff?"

"Not sure. Why?"

"Because it's possible he deleted things from this memory stick."

"Because?" Harrison said.

"In case it fell into the wrong hands."

"And you can recover that stuff?" Harrison said.

"Maybe," Avery said. "Let's see what I can do."

Avery searched through the backdoor coding of the memory stick until she located one deleted folder. It took her several minutes before she was able to restore its entire contents.

"Any luck?" Carter asked.

"Yup," Avery said, scrolling through the first document. "This one is an article from a website." She opened the next file. "And this is photos of pages from a really old book. But it's all about a pirate from four hundred years ago called Captain Ace Mullins."

"Cool name," Harrison said. "Always better to have your village pillaged by a guy named Ace."

"That tracks, though I'm not sure it matters to us," Carter said. "Jeff was always into pirate lore. He watched every movie about pirates ever made. Even managed to read a few books about them. So that might not have anything to do with this, Avery. Could just be that Jeff was too cheap to buy a new memory stick, so he wrote over an old one."

"I'm saving it anyway," Avery said. "Never hurts to know how Jeff's brain worked when you're following his trail."

"That's just the problem," Carter said. "His brain wasn't working, or he never would have gotten into this mess. The minute he had that thing appraised and found out what it was worth, he should've taken it to a museum or something."

"You wouldn't have tried to sell it?"

"I wouldn't even know where to find someone who could sell it," Carter said. "But Jeff always did. He always knew how to find trouble. And while I think he started stealing for the thrill, at some point it became about money, I think. Greed will get people every time, my mom always said—it's like a monster you can't get away from once it has its hooks in you."

"Not you, though," Avery said.

"Money is nice, don't get me wrong, but I was just as happy without it. I'm just less worried about bills now and I have a better view from my porch than a shed and a set of train tracks." Carter shrugged. "I started posting my stunts because I wanted to remember them—living, having done what I wanted—that was enough for me. All this other stuff was almost an accident. Jeff was different. He chased it because somewhere along the way instead of stealing from those rich people on the beaches, he decided he wanted to be one of them. It consumed him. Pushed him to make dumb choices. Seems like it might've cost him his life."

"My mom always said in a homicide case if there's a money trail to follow, you should do it," Avery said. "Let's go see what's in Cromer Shoals —maybe we'll learn something about more than just the ring. You never know."

Avery copied Jeff's files and saved them in two separate places, then put the memory stick and the letter in a small, nearly invisible compartment in her bag.

"I understand that, but what I'm asking is, how much is it if we want to forego the captain?" Harrison said into the phone. "We know how to pilot a boat you know."

He paused to listen.

"How could the insurance company stop you from running your business as you see fit?" he asked.

"Harry," Avery whisper-shouted to get his attention. "Triple it, if you have to."

"How about if we agree to pay three times your normal rate, plus the insurance? Done."

Harrison finished the call and hung up.

"Are we good?" Carter asked.

"We'll have a serviceable vessel at the Blakeney Docks as soon as we arrive," Harrison said. "For as long as we want it."

"How far is Blakeney?" Carter asked.

"About 180 kilometers," Avery said.

"What's that in American?" Harrison asked.

"About a three-hour drive, Harry." Avery rolled her eyes.

"Then I guess we'd better get packed," Carter said.

"I'll order up a car," Harrison said.

"And driver?" Avery said as she headed to her room.

"No way," Harrison said. "If I don't trust a boat captain, I sure as he— um, heck—don't trust a driver."

"Wise man," Avery said. "Just book a car, Harry. We'll have Carter drive like last time."

"Great," Harrison said. "I have always dreamed of riding on the wrong side of the road with Carter behind the wheel."

"I can hear you, you know," Carter said as he popped his head out of his room.

"Just get packed, Boy Wonder," Harrison said. "Christ, it's not even noon and I'm exhausted."

Thirty minutes later the front desk clerk phoned to inform them that their car had arrived.

"Car's out front," Harrison said. "Everybody ready?"

"I am," Carter said.

Lugging all their belongings, they exited the suite and locked the door. As they turned toward the elevator, the doors opened and the three goons from earlier stepped out into the hallway.

"If only the car had gotten here five minutes ago," Harrison said.

16

London, 1664

Burgess returned to the tunnel with four additional yeomen, each equipped with a torch and various weapons. He had grown accustomed to the foul odor permeating the air, but to the new arrivals the scent was nearly overpowering. One of his guards vomited into the wastewater flowing at their feet.

"Apologies, sir," the guard said when he had finished. "It's just—this smell."

"Worry not," Burgess said as he laid a hand upon the guard's shoulder. "Take solace in the knowledge that the treasonous thieves had to endure this foulness too."

The guard smiled weakly before falling in line with the others.

They continued forward in relative silence. The only sounds were the sloshing of wastewater and the popping of their torches.

They reached the newly formed tunnel and gathered at its entrance. Burgess knew the opening wasn't there two years ago, the last time he'd ventured inside this unholy place. There were literally miles of tunnels, a labyrinth carved into the bedrock beneath the city over decades, used for a multitude of purposes but largely for storing everything from food to corpses in the winter months when the ground was too frozen for proper burial.

Burgess also knew the tunnels were used by criminals to skulk from one place to the next, as criminals were wont to do. A filthy treasonous lot who somehow always managed to twist innovation to their purpose.

As he studied the freshly chiseled entrance, Burgess knew that the tunnel had to have been created with the plot to steal the crown jewels in mind. Why else excavate so close to the tower dungeons? What he couldn't make sense of was how the thieves managed to get into the tower past his men in the first place. Surely they didn't slip through the entire fortress from dungeon to turret without detection—that was the odd piece of this puzzle.

Once inside, the escape route made perfect sense. Slipping beneath a floor grate into the tunnels in the dead of night where no one—or almost no one—would dare follow, not even the inhuman savages who worked the dungeons. Especially not them, perhaps, for they knew what was down here. There was no security needed in the tunnels; who would try to break into a dungeon?

Burgess came from an extensive line of security officers, and like those before him, duty was everything to him. He would get the jewels back or die trying. The king's authority must not be questioned by the public, especially so soon after having been restored to power.

One by one, the men followed Burgess into the dark cramped tunnel, their torches lighting the way. After a few dozen steps, the tunnel floor began to rise on an incline. Burgess squinted into the blackness until he caught sight of another light in the distance. It was the dim light of dawn, he realized.

"This way," he shouted as he hunched over and scurried up the rise. "Hurry!"

17

Carter watched as Avery slid her duffel bag behind her hip and assumed a defensive stance. He almost felt sorry for these men—especially the two who didn't have to contend with her this morning. Though he was known for being foolishly brave, even Carter wouldn't take on Avery in hand-to-hand combat. He'd seen her put Harrison on his butt repeatedly when sparring, and Carter knew he'd be hard-pressed to best the wily old barrel-chested detective in a fair fight.

"Carter, which one did you fight with this morning?" Avery said.

"The one on the right," Carter said.

"The smaller one," Harrison chimed in.

"He's not exactly a pushover, Harry," Carter said.

"And how did that go?" Avery said.

"I held my own," Carter said with confidence. "I mean he needed a knife to try and—"

"Okay, he's yours," Avery said as she stepped toward the largest of the three. "Harry, you take the other one."

"Gladly."

Carter's goon swung wildly, telegraphing his first punch like his name was Alexander Graham Bell. Carter easily dodged before connecting with a knee strike to the man's midsection. As they traded blows, he glanced over in time to see Avery spin and deliver a perfect roundhouse kick to her assailant's stomach. Carter grinned before taking a hard shot to the side of the face for his lack of attention.

Recovering, Carter sent his man reeling with a right hook before catching a glimpse of Harrison using his assailant's body like it was a heavy bag. After several minutes of trading blows it occurred to Carter that the goons weren't as vicious as they'd been in the street earlier. Were they holding back? Harry had said he thought they were hired mercenaries whose only job had been to distract them long enough for the sniper to put Jeff down for the last time. Were they buying time again?

"I thought you said these guys were good?" Avery asked as she delivered a knee strike to her goon.

"They were," Harrison said.

"Something about this feels off," Carter said.

"Like what?" Avery asked.

Before Carter could answer, the man he was fighting dropped him with several well-placed body blows followed by a leg trap. Carter landed hard, the floor knocking the wind out of him. He turned his head to see that Harrison was also flat on his back and Avery was suddenly struggling to keep up with her man. As Carter struggled to regain his feet, he noticed Avery's goon reach into his pocket.

"Avery, knife," Carter yelled just before his man delivered a devastating punch to his jaw.

Avery dropped low, landing on her bag before sweeping the goon's legs out from under him, sending him crashing to the floor, his knife bouncing across the hallway. The man scrambled to his feet and ran for the stairwell, setting off the emergency alarm as he hit the crash bar on the door. Wide-eyed, the other two exchanged a glance before they followed him.

"Well, that was fun." Avery straightened her sweater, pausing to catch her breath. "Everybody okay?"

"I was just getting warmed up," Harrison said, brushing himself off. "How about you, Ace Ventura?"

"Oh, I'm just ducky, thanks for asking," Carter said as he rolled onto his back and lowered his head to the floor. "Just ducky."

"Why aren't we going after them, Ave?" Harrison said as Avery helped Carter to his feet.

"Because something feels weird about all of this."

"Something besides getting our asses kicked twice in the same day by the same people?" Carter said.

"Hey, speak for yourself," Harrison said. "I scared my guy away."

"Yeah, Harry, he looked petrified when he saw you sprawled out on your back like a beached—"

"Watch it." Harrison shot Carter a warning glare.

"Let me know when you two are finished," Avery said.

"I'm done," Carter said.

"Yes, you are," Harrison said.

"You guys also got the feeling they weren't giving it their all, right?" Avery said.

"Not until the very end anyway," Harrison agreed.

"My guy grabbed for my pocket a couple of times while we were fighting," Carter said.

"Copping a feel?" Harrison chuckled.

"Maybe they know we found Jeff's safety deposit box," Avery mused.

"But then why did they leave before they got what they came for?" Harrison asked.

"Anyone else notice how they all seemed to step up their game at the same instant?" Carter asked. "Almost like someone was giving them orders?"

"I'll bet my American Express Black Card that they were after your wallets," Avery said.

"Why?" Harrison asked.

"Our IDs." Carter pointed at Avery.

"Exactly," Avery said. "These guys aren't common thugs. I mean, who comes looking for trouble in a place this nice?"

"So, what's the plan?" Harrison asked as he retrieved his bags. "Assuming we don't want to hang around here waiting for them to come back."

"I say we jet before they throw us out," Carter said as he ran a hand across a dented piece of drywall. "Look at the damage to these walls."

"I'll take care of that when we check out." Avery waved one hand. "As for our uninvited guests, I think our best bet may be to disappear out to the coast. We need time to figure out who they work for and what exactly they're after."

"What about fingerprints?" Carter said. "None of them were wearing gloves."

"That's a good idea." Avery stepped into the elevator. "My guy grabbed a hold of this shoe."

"It just so happens I have my nifty-difty fingerprint kit and scanner," Harrison said.

By the time they reached the lobby, Harrison had lifted a full print from Avery's shoe and a partial from Carter's leather computer bag. Walking outside, they moved into the shade of a large tree, giving Harrison a chance to capture the prints with his scanner.

"Tell me again where you got that thing?" Carter said.

"No can do," Harrison said.

"Why not?"

"Because then I'd have to kill you," Harrison said with a wink. "I'll forward these to McGregor once we're safely out of the city."

"Don't look now," Avery said. "But the doorman is giving us the hairy eyeball."

"Maybe he's how those goons made it into our elevator," Carter said.

"You mean those goons?" Harrison said with a nod toward the crowded sidewalk where the three assailants were hustling back toward the Thames.

Avery watched them go, trying to work out why they had just up and left when the fight started to turn in their favor. It didn't make any sense.

But she was pretty sure they'd get another chance to find out. Whatever they were getting into with this ring the British government was after and Carter's dead friend, Avery knew they hadn't seen the last of those guys.

"Let's go, gentlemen," she said. "The ocean beckons."

18

Over the next several hours, Avery would've sworn on any sacred document that their rental car came equipped with a wormhole to a land where time was meaningless. The drive to the county of Norfolk was long, green, and never going to end. They made the most of it, enjoying the scenic country-side, bantering about the unending similarity of the rolling green hills, and checking some things off the to-do list.

Avery texted Rowan to tell him that they'd been attacked at the hotel by the same guys who'd accosted Jeff that morning, because he could probably get security footage that would show them how the goons got upstairs, and also that they were on the trail of the ring, headed to the coast, before she asked for an update on his investigation of Jeff's murder. When he didn't reply immediately, she began her own research into pirate Captain Ace Mullins and his exploits, figuring anything Jeff was recently infatuated with might be a clue. Harrison availed himself of the encryption software Avery had previously installed on his phone to forward the fingerprints to Inspector McGregor. Carter kept the car on the road, and one eye trained on the rearview mirror to make sure they weren't followed.

As they closed in on the coastal village, Avery's phone buzzed.

"Check out how the whole town looks like it's glowing gold," Carter said, waving an arm. "What a gorgeous sunset." The low, golden rays washed every ancient stone building in the little town with a patina that made it look like a mythical lost city.

"Wow," Harrison said as Avery studied her phone. "I've never seen anything like that."

"It's Rowan," Avery said, ignoring them. "He says he'll get the security footage from the hotel. He's annoyed that the goons didn't arrive while he was still there."

"Maybe they waited him out because they know who he is," Harrison mused.

"What kind of hired muscle can spot the secret police?" Carter asked.

"The kind who has a sniper capable of making that shot at your friend in the glaring sun with the wind we saw this morning."

Avery pondered that and then typed something into her phone. "Doesn't hurt to warn him," she said. "He says they don't have any solid leads on Jeff's murder yet but he's waiting for return messages from a couple of paid informants he thinks might know something."

"Maybe this will go somewhere after all." Harrison grinned as Carter drove across a small bridge that was likely older than New York City and into the most adorable little town any of them had ever seen.

"I feel like I'm in one of those Christmas movies where the big city executive girl moves home to the delightful little town over her high-powered lawyer fiancé's protests, and he was right to protest because she falls in love with a goat herder and stays on a goat farm happily ever sugarcoated after." Carter looked around.

"You looking to be someone's goat herder?" Harrison asked.

"Not really." Carter glanced at Avery, then clambered out of the rental.

With a population of less than eight hundred, Blakeney Parish could've been lifted right out of an antique painting—or one of the British mystery shows Harry liked to watch on TV. Once a thriving commercial seaport, Blakeney had evolved into a summertime tourist destination as large corporations consolidated shipping into bigger harbors. The River Glaven, lined on one side with small fishing boats, resembled a side street with parallel parked cars as it cut through the village center from Blakeney Bay.

Avery had booked them separate rooms at the Blakeney Hotel. Nestled on the bank of the River Glaven, it was an immaculate, sprawling, three-story affair, with a façade of stone and brick, and a terra-cotta tiled roof.

"I hope the boat I rented isn't one of those," Harrison said, pointing toward the water where a bevy of crafts lay canted to one side upon the exposed sandy river bottom.

"Glaven is a tidal inlet, Harry," Avery said. "It must be low tide."

"I knew that," Harrison said.

"If the boat you rented was listed as a diving boat, it should be docked on the ocean," Carter said.

"Good thing," Harrison said. "That's not much of a river at low tide."

"Um, Harry." Avery blinked when he turned to face her. "You can't go inside looking like that."

"Like what?"

"Wow, man," Carter said, rounding the car and stopping next to Avery. "She's right. You'll scare people with that shiner. Looks like you lost a fight."

"Well, I didn't. I scared that guy off, remember?"

"Come here, Harry." Avery set one of her bags on the hood of the rental and unzipped it, producing a tube. "I can hide it."

"Never thought I'd see the day," Carter said. "The big bad New York homicide detective wearing makeup."

Avery put her hands on her hips. "What are you laughing at, Captain Camera Ready? That bruise on your cheek doesn't look any better. Get over here."

"Yeah, Carter," Harrison said. "If you ask nice, she might throw in some eyeliner."

Avery shook her head and pulled Harrison's down so she could reach to make his face presentable. Finished covering everyone's bruises, Avery stepped back to inspect her work.

"What do you think?" Carter asked.

"It's better than nothing," Avery said. "But makeup doesn't hide swelling. People who don't know you probably won't realize you look like you went ten rounds with Rocky, though."

"Gee, thanks," Harrison said. Why are you the only one without bruises?"

"Sorry." Avery patted his arm. "Just lucky I guess."

They lugged their bags inside and checked in at the front desk.

"Ah, yes, Ms. Turner," the concierge said as Avery displayed her identification. "We're so glad you chose to stay with us. Are you here on holiday?"

Avery exchanged a glance with Carter before answering.

"Something like that," Harrison said.

"We're hoping to relax and take in some of the local sights," Avery said.

"Maybe do a bit of diving, too," Carter said.

"I don't suppose you can recommend a place for us to grab some dinner?" Avery asked. "We've had a long day, and I could kill for a drink and some fresh seafood."

"I second that motion," Harrison said.

The desk clerk recommended a pub within walking distance of the hotel called The Moorings. After stashing their belongings in their rooms, Avery, Carter, and Harrison walked over and found the quayside restaurant was set at the center of a row of shops near the end of a street. The building was a traditional structure of brick with white painted mortar and bay windows bookending the front doors. On the sidewalk outside the entrance, they found an easel-style chalkboard listing the day's specials.

A petite blonde waitress led them to a window booth overlooking the River Glaven.

"Welcome to The Moorings," the waitress said, her British accent crisp and melodic. "My name is Andie and I'll be taking care of you. May I start you off with some drinks?"

"Yes please," Avery said a little too forcefully.

Andie laughed. "Been that kind of a day, has it?"

"You have no idea," Harrison said.

"What's your poison, then?" Andie asked.

Avery ordered a glass of the house white, while Harrison and Carter opted for the local India Pale Ale.

As they continued to peruse the menu, Andie returned with their drinks.

"Can I interest anyone in an appetizer?"

"I don't know about anyone else, but I'll have an order of your spiced crab cakes with squash and apple chutney," Avery said.

"Anyone else?" Andie asked.

"That actually sounds really good," Carter said.

"Better make it three," Harrison said.

"Very good," Andie said. "Would you like more time to think about your dinner choices?"

"Please," Avery said.

After the waitress departed, Avery raised a glass. "What should we drink to?"

"How about getting out of South Bank in one piece, more or less?" Harrison asked.

Carter was solemn, staring into the foam topping his beer.

"How about we drink to Jeff?" Avery asked, nudging his foot with hers under the table.

Harrison nodded, shooting her a smile that radiated pride.

"To Jeff." Carter's voice caught as he raised his glass.

"To Jeff," Harrison and Avery chorused.

Glasses back on their coasters, Avery changed the subject. "So, what's the plan for tomorrow?"

"I'd like to check out the boat and the rental shop tonight if we can," Carter said. "There's still some work to do before we can plan a reef dive. We'll need to supplement our equipment, rent tanks, and get a look at the area by boat."

A big man sitting alone at a nearby table while nursing a pint craned his head around. "Couldn't help but hear you talking about diving the reef? Americans, right?"

"Guilty as charged," Harrison said, raising his glass to the man. "I'm Harry. This is Avery and Carter."

The man returned the gesture. "I'm Jeb. Jeb Wells."

Wells had snow-white hair with a matching beard and mustache and the ruddy complexion of a man who had spent his life on the ocean. Add in a yellow rain slicker and he'd have been a doppelgänger for the Gorton's fisherman.

"You know anything about scuba diving, Mr. Wells?" Carter asked.

"It's just Jeb, and I know a thing or two about fishing," Wells said as he turned his chair around toward them. "Been working on the water all my life."

"What can you tell us about the reef?" Avery said.

"I can tell you it's tricky. The currents are strong here. The temperature shifts create a vacuum of sorts in some areas."

"Does that extend below the surface?" Carter said.

"Aye, it's worse underwater. One of the reasons reef diving never really caught on around here. We've had folks go missing. Sometimes the bodies floated up weeks later, if at all."

"Well, that bodes well," Harrison said as he fixed Avery and Carter with a disapproving stare.

Wells chuckled. "What's bad for tourism is good for fisherman, if they know how to work it right."

"You fish?" Avery asked. "Like for a living?"

Wells nodded. "I was raised by a fisherman, who was raised by one before him. Those same currents carry huge schools of halibut into the cove every summer. The fishermen feed their families all winter, and us good ones fill up our bank accounts too."

"You must know a lot about the town's history," Harrison said. "With so many generations of your family here."

"Aye, Blakeney is said to have been founded originally by pirates."

"Seriously?" Avery sipped her wine.

"I wouldn't joke about such a thing, miss. They picked this spot to run their ships in and out unmolested by the constabulary. The spice trade, oriental cloths, and silks for all of England went right through this port."

"We drove by the river coming into town," Carter said. "Glaven doesn't look deep enough for large sailing ships."

"It isn't now," Wells said. "But centuries ago, before it filled in with silt, the quay was plenty deep enough. The pirates basically came here and squatted, snatching most of the land straight from under a ne'er-do-well duke, who liked booze and gambling a bit too much to put up a fight."

Avery studied Carter's face. She could see by his constant nodding that Carter was entranced by the old fisherman. Listening to Wells talk, Avery was thinking about Ace Mullins and Jeff's fascination with pirate lore. She wondered if it had been what brought Jeff to Blakeney in the first place.

Avery removed the phone from her bag and began typing out a message under the table to MaryAnn, asking her to research the town and its history. Much to Avery's surprise, MaryAnn responded instantly.

I'm on it, she texted back. *How's Carter?*

Avery took another look at him as the old man droned on, typing, *He seems okay at the moment.*

Her phone buzzed. *Brady said to tell you that Jeff's death hit Carter hard no matter what he tells you. Carter tends to get tunnel vision and a little too reckless when he's emotional. Keep an eye on him, Avery. Make sure he makes good choices.*

Will do, Avery responded. But as she watched Carter chat with Jeb Wells, she wondered if the ship of good choices had already left port.

Avery returned the phone to her bag and rejoined the conversation just as Wells mentioned another American who had recently visited.

"Don't suppose you'd know him, would you?" Wells asked. "Jeff something. Escapes me at the moment."

Carter said nothing.

"America's a pretty big place," Harrison said. "Believe it or not, we don't all know one another."

"I suppose that's a fact," Wells said with a chuckle. "I only mention it because this fella frequented the pub for a while this spring. He was pretty interested in diving the reef and hearing about pirates and lost treasure."

"Interesting," Carter said.

"I thought so," Wells said. "We had a couple of pints here one night and he mentioned a friend of his who was a treasure hunter, too."

Avery couldn't tell whether Jeb was baiting them or not. It all seemed too much of a coincidence that they were seated next to him and that he'd just happen to butt into their conversation, but stranger things had probably happened. Probably.

"So did this Jeff guy ever find anything?" Avery asked.

"Don't know," Wells said with a shrug. "One day he just up and right vanished. I figure he must have run out of money. The scuttlebutt is that one of the local inn owners was trying to track him down for an unpaid bill."

"Leave these nice Americans alone and drink your pint, Jeb," Andie admonished as she returned with a heaping tray of food.

"He's not bothering us," Carter said.

"Thank you, young man," Wells said before turning back toward his own table.

"Jeb can't help himself. He's always had an unhealthy interest in Americans. The best day of his life was when he signed up for Netflix and he could watch your TV shows to his heart's content."

They ordered another round of beverages—Avery got Jeb another, too —then dug ravenously into their meals. As she watched Carter and Harrison fill their bellies, Avery's eyes shifted to Jeb. He seemed honest enough and the waitress did know him—maybe his mention of Jeff was just a coincidence. But they should be mindful of who they spoke to and what they shared: experience had taught Avery that talk of treasure tended to bring out the pirate in everyone.

19

After dinner they walked back to the hotel and retired to their respective rooms, exhausted. Between the meal, the libations, the jet lag, and the two donnybrooks, Carter wasn't sure how much more energy his body would allow him to expend, but he couldn't sit still, much less lie down. He paced. His brain wouldn't allow him any quiet. All he could think about was what he had gotten Avery and Harrison into, and what surprises might still await them.

They hadn't even been in England thirty-six hours and already they'd been attacked three times and visited by the secret police. Carter needed to know what happened to his old friend. He wasn't sure he owed Jeff a thing, really, but he did owe Jeff's mother some answers, so answers he would find.

He couldn't help but worry that the police, particularly Inspector McGregor, wouldn't pull out all the stops to try to catch the killer of an American with a sordid past. But if they did their part and found this ring the secret agent guy wanted, it might get them somewhere. That Rowan guy seemed like he knew his way around an investigation, and since he wanted their help, he had reason to care about Jeff.

Then there were the thugs—they kept popping up such that Carter had checked his whole suite after dinner, half expecting one of them to charge out of the closet or shower. But he couldn't shake the feeling they had taken off at the London hotel because they were following orders, likely through headsets. Which meant...what? Organized crime? If so, then who was behind it—and were they really after the ring Jeff had found, or did they want something else? Like the mysterious secret Rowan mentioned. Which wasn't mentioned in the letter Jeff left, either because he didn't really think he'd die or because he was keeping secrets from Carter like always.

Secrets. Carter wondered if there were any more for Avery to find on that flash drive as he checked the time—it was late. Would Avery already be asleep or was she doing the same thing he was doing?

Only one way to find out.

Light leaked out into the hall from under the door to Avery's room. Carter knocked gently. After several moments the door swung open, Avery smiling at him in her pajamas.

"Can't sleep, huh?" she asked.

"Nope. My brain won't shut down."

"Mine either." She waved him into the room.

After locking the door, Avery returned to an armchair by a leaded glass window where her laptop sat open.

"Am I interrupting anything?" Carter asked as he perched on the edge of the sofa.

"I wouldn't have invited you in if you were. I was just researching the science behind the tidal patterns since Jeb was talking about the currents. If my hunch is right, this might even turn into something that we can market as part of our TreasureTech offerings. One more feature we could add to the DiveNav."

"Cool," Carter said.

"I found a ton of stuff on that pirate guy, too. Ace Mullins." Avery clicked something. "Listen to this journal from one of his crewmen: 'What better home for we than a town what glows golden in the waning light of day. 'Tis truly a light at the end of the rainbow.' Doesn't that sound like what we saw when we got here?"

"Sure does," Carter said. "You think there's a connection between this pirate Jeff was reading about and the ring Rowan asked us to find? Or the secret he claimed to know so little about?"

"Sure seems like it's at least worth looking into since Jeff's letter said he found the ring here," Avery said.

Carter nodded. "About what Jeb told us at dinner. Maybe I should dive alone."

"Um, I don't think so, Mr. Mosley. I didn't save you from marauding seals in the freezing waters of Antarctica just to be benched on a shallow dive in relatively warm water off the coast of England."

Carter opened his mouth to protest but Avery raised her hand to stop him.

"Especially when there might be ancient jewels lurking under there as a bonus." She raised one eyebrow. "I know you're thinking the same thing I am: If your friend Jeff really did find that ring here, and this place was a pirate hideout, and there really are extraordinarily strong currents in this area often, then there might be more jewels. But maybe not in exactly the same area. Right?"

Carter nodded. "I mean, pirate treasure would be a heck of a secret for the ring to lead to. And we'd be the people I'd call to look for that. But what do you know about staying safe in dangerous underwater currents?"

"I know that diving is always safer with a partner." Avery smiled. "My diving instructor taught me that."

Carter had taught her to dive. And he did tell her that. He sighed. "I'm not going to talk you out of this, am I?"

"Not a chance," Avery said, folding her arms across her chest.

"I know when I'm beaten. I would like to take a look at the images of the ring again, though."

"The memory card is right there in my bag."

Carter opened her bag and looked inside. "Where exactly? There's a lot of stuff in here."

"In the inside pocket, right where I left it."

Carter plunged his hand into the pocket and rifled around. There was nothing inside but a tube of lip balm. He shook his head.

"What do you mean it isn't there?" Avery said as she sprang up from the chair. "That bag hasn't been out of my sight."

"Did you have it with you at dinner?"

"I think so. No wait, I—I left it here."

Carter watched as Avery dumped the bag's entire contents on the bed.

"It's gone," she said after turning the bag inside out.

"Didn't you make a copy?" Carter said.

The worried expression melted from her face, replaced by a grin. "Not a physical copy, but I backed everything up to the cloud."

Avery returned to her laptop and quickly accessed the pictures she had stored on the cloud drive. "Here we go. Every picture that was on that card, safe and sound."

They spent the next ten minutes examining the photos from every angle, looking for anything that might be a clue. As they searched through the images, Carter's overtired brain kept replaying all the places they had been where someone might have had an opportunity to swipe the memory stick. Avery's bag had been with them in the hotel hallway just outside the elevator when the three goons paid them a visit. Could one of them have snatched it during the fight? That might make their hasty retreat just after they started winning the fight make a lot more sense.

"Earth to Carter Mosley," Avery said. "Are you still looking at these?"

"I'm sorry. My mind is all over the place. Just trying to figure where someone might have grabbed the flash drive. I'm wondering if one of our punch-throwing buddies might have nicked it back in London."

"Don't worry," Avery said as she continued to scroll through the photos. "I'll recheck all the luggage and cell phones for trackers."

"If there was one thing Jeff had a knack for, it was collecting enemies," Carter said. "But I know we weren't followed. I kept an eye peeled during the drive up here."

Avery pointed at the screen. "What is that?"

"I don't know." Carter leaned closer to the screen as Avery zoomed in on the ring, both sets of eyes focused on a mark on the underside of the band so faint that it might have been a smudge or even a shadow. "Can you rotate it?"

Avery did. "It looks like a squiggle."

"Is 'squiggle' considered professional treasure hunter vernacular?" Carter asked.

"It is now." Avery smiled.

"Wait, see? There." Carter pointed at the faint lines. "Looks like your squiggle is underscored with a square and the letter *W*."

Avery switched screens and opened a search bar. She typed in every word she could think of that might be associated with the symbol. The first few pages of results turned up nothing.

Carter watched her hunch over the computer, knowing how knotted his shoulders would be after a few minutes of that much tension. As her keys clicked, his eyes started to feel heavy.

"I'm going to call it a night," he said. "I'm falling asleep standing up."

"I'm not far behind you," Avery said as she walked him to the door. "Good night, Carter."

"Night, Avery."

Avery locked the door behind him, then returned to her computer to continue her research. She added information specific to the ring's description to her search and tried again.

The algorithms just hooked onto the word *ring*, returning nothing but jewelry advertisements. Avery waded through what felt like thousands of ads, everything from large companies to obvious clickbait scams, looking for a ruby with historical importance attached to it. She went back and added the word *lost* to her search and began again.

Finally, on the eighteenth page of results, she found an interesting article about a ruby ring called the Heart of the Night. It had been gifted by a Spanish nobleman to his English mistress as a symbol of his fiery and undying love for her. Avery felt the first twinges of excitement ripple through her as she clicked through the accompanying images. Interestingly there were no photographs of the actual ring, but there were several oil portraits of the woman, a British spinster who never married, wearing the ring in question. Based solely on the color the artists had used to render the ring, the band was gold, and the mounted solitaire stone was a golf-ball-sized ruby. While it wasn't exactly like the photos of the ring Jeff had discovered, it was close enough for an artist's rendering.

Avery kept reading. Ten minutes later she sat back and let out a heavy sigh. According to the author, the ring had been buried with the woman in 1723.

But.

If there was one thing that hadn't changed in the past three hundred years, it was the unscrupulous nature of some people. What if the ring hadn't been buried with her? Or what if grave robbers had unearthed it after it was? The odds of something so unique and valuable remaining deep in the ground undisturbed for all these years seemed low.

Avery's eyelids drooped. She saved the link to the article and sent it, along with the rest of Jeff's photos of the ring he'd found and a close-up screenshot of the markings she and Carter had noticed, to MaryAnn by email. If anyone could confirm whether Jeff's find was the Heart of the Night, MaryAnn could.

Avery shut down her laptop and crawled onto the soft mattress. As she pulled the heavy quilt up around her and closed her eyes, Avery wondered how many other people might be searching for the ring. Somehow, being asked to find it by an MI5 agent had given her both purpose and a sense of authority in her mission, but she'd learned enough about treasure hunting to know that if Jeff had found it and the British government wanted it, so did plenty of other people. Which begged the question: How many enemies could Jeff have made in the few years he'd been in the UK before being gunned down on the streets of London?

20

Avery awoke with the sun streaming on her face. Panicked, she checked the time: 9:20. How could that be? She had set an alarm for 8:30. Grabbing her phone, she opened the alarm app and flopped her hand down on the quilt when she realized her mistake. Exhausted, she'd set the alarm for 8:30 p.m.

She showered and dressed in record time, then hurried downstairs to the restaurant, where Carter and Harrison were waiting.

"There she is," Harrison said. "I told you she wouldn't go off treasure hunting without us."

"Not until I'd had a proper breakfast anyway," Avery said as she slid out a chair and joined them.

"We ordered you the same thing we got," Harrison said.

As if on cue, their server brought everyone plates laden with baked beans, sausages, and eggs. Avery asked for coffee. Lots of coffee.

"While you were sleeping, Harry and I had a nice chat with the gentleman that checked us in yesterday," Carter said.

"His name is Carleton," Harry said.

"Guess what Carleton told us?" Carter said.

"That Ace Mullins haunts the men's loo?" Avery asked, scooping up a forkful of beans.

"Wouldn't that be convenient?" Harrison chuckled. "But ghosts didn't come up, I'm afraid."

"Carleton told us that the last American to stay here left the room in shambles and skipped out on his bill," Carter said.

Avery froze mid-chew. "Does that sound like Jeff?"

"It does not," Carter said. "Jeff had a lot of unscrupulous tendencies, but he wouldn't have burned a bridge like that. Especially if there was even the remote possibility that he might return to dive the reef again. We know he had money. We found plenty of cash in his wallet."

"You think someone else tossed his room?" Avery asked, biting into a sausage.

"I do," Carter said. "And I think he bailed when he knew someone was onto him."

"Meaning?" Avery said.

"Meaning, assuming we're right, whoever was after Jeff knows he was here," Harrison said as he topped off his mug. "Ergo, they didn't need to follow us to Blakeney."

"Did you actually just use the word *ergo*?" Carter said.

"Harry's becoming quite the wordsmith," Avery said with a laugh, taking a last bite before she pushed the plate away and gulped coffee.

Carter checked his watch. "We'd better get going, Captain Wordsmith. Daylight is wasting, as my granny would've said."

The drive to the marina took less than ten minutes. Carter went to check on the boat situation while Avery and Harrison unloaded the gear.

The temperature turned chilly as the sun disappeared behind a bank of clouds, but for the moment at least, there was no precipitation.

Carter approached, carrying their rented tanks.

"How'd you make out?" Avery said.

"Good. The rental guy said based on the tidal report we should be okay. We'll have to be careful, but it is doable."

"Yeah, well, if the bad guys show up again, the currents will be the least of our problems," Harrison said.

"That's why we have you, Harry," Avery said.

"Riiight. 'Cause there's nothing scarier than a disarmed ex-detective."

Their rented boat—a converted fishing vessel called *The Tempest*—still bore disgusting remnants of its former duty, both visual and olfactive.

"Did you bother looking at options before renting this thing, Harry?" Carter groaned. "Everything smells like fish."

"Sue me," Harrison said. "I've never chartered a boat before."

"It isn't that bad," Avery said as she began to check her diving gear.

"Oh, no?" Carter said, pointing to something that looked like dried entrails.

"So, there's a bit of leftover fish guts here...and there." Harrison pointed. "Just don't sit in them and we're fine."

"That's called the gunwale," Carter said.

"Gen-el, shmenal," Harrison said. "It adds character to the boat."

"Nasty, smelly character." Carter wrinkled his nose.

"We'll be underwater most of the time anyway, Carter," Avery said.

"I won't," Harrison said. "But I'm not complaining."

Despite its disgusting accessories, *The Tempest* fired right up and ran smoothly. Following the dive map coordinates they'd found in Jeff's safety deposit box, Carter had them in the area in less than thirty minutes.

Avery kept an eye peeled for following boats, but there wasn't another vessel in sight.

"Why is it I have a bad feeling about being the only boat out here?" Harrison said.

"You always have a bad feeling about being on the water, Harry," Carter said. "Besides, it's a Sunday. Even fishermen take an occasional day off."

"Pirates don't," Harrison grumbled.

"I don't think that's on our list of modern-day worries," Carter said as he pulled back on the throttle and shifted into neutral. "Here we are."

Avery peered over the gunwale, careful to avoid the fish bits, as Harrison lowered the anchor. The water was clear enough to allow glimpses of the reef below.

"You know, Harry, this reef is more than twenty miles long," Carter said.

"Must be how you found it so easy."

"Even cooler than that, it might be over a hundred million years old,"

Avery said. "Isn't it wild to think we're looking at something that may have been here since dinosaurs roamed the shore?"

"We see Harry every day, Avery," Carter said with a chuckle.

"Laugh all you want," Harrison said. "Some of those carnivores swam in the ocean, too, junior."

After one last safety check of their equipment, Avery and Carter back-flipped over the side and into the chilly water of the North Sea. No matter how many times she'd done it, Avery still marveled at the way all surface noise simply disappeared as the seawater closed over her head. She looked to Carter, who gave her the okay, then started her descent.

The ocean was beginning to feel like a second home to Avery, the wet suit a second skin. A city girl who'd grown up riding the subway and barely gotten her feet wet on rare beach trips, Avery now couldn't imagine life without underwater exploration. She glanced over at the man responsible and wondered what her life would have been like if Carter hadn't come to talk to her as she hid behind plants at a museum fundraiser nearly two years before.

Like the hull of a monstrous ship, the reef loomed large as they drew nearer. The sky, though overcast, was bright enough to illuminate the coral ridge. Clusters of pink sea fan coral and strawberry anemones swayed with the movement of the ocean water. Even though they were on a mission of sorts, Avery excitedly pointed out the coral and the brightly colored sea creatures residing within the reef. She pulled out her underwater camera and snapped several pictures of a sea slug cluster, their bright lavender-and-pink antennae plumes making them some of the most beautiful marine life anywhere. Carter signaled to get her attention, pointing out a blue lobster scuttling along the bottom. Avery attempted to focus the camera on the crustacean, but it was too fast and all she captured was a blurry shadow.

Carter pointed to his watch. They needed to get on with the search, the reason they came here in the first place. Avery nodded, then stowed the camera and followed him along the reef. The current was stronger here and they let it pull them along like an underwater stream, conserving their strength and air supply.

Carter pointed to his left and Avery noticed what appeared to be a shadow near the reef's edge. They swam nearer until it became clear that the shadow was a cave, though the mouth wasn't exceptionally large. Carter signaled that he wanted to look inside and pulled a guideline from his belt, handing one end to Avery. She tied him off to a chalk reef protrusion near the cave's entrance and watched as he shined his light around inside the opening, looking for inhabitants. He signaled an all clear, then headed inside. She watched the guideline to make sure that it didn't become snagged as Carter swam out of sight.

Avery quickly grew bored and swam a few feet away, looking for more colorful sea life—the bright creatures were especially striking against the pale background of the ancient reef. About fifteen yards from the cave, she felt an odd tug on her leg—no—on both legs. She kicked her fins as hard as she could, trying to pull away from whatever it was, but the tug grew stronger and she lost ground. Twisting, she looked back, trying to see if she was stuck on something—or had been grabbed by an animal—but there was nothing there. Yet the sensation of icy, invisible fingers dragging her toward the ocean floor raced up her thighs and over her hips. She kicked harder, pulling with her hands as she fought to swim upward, but it was no use. She was alone, and one of the currents the area was famous for was pulling her under. Avery did her best to fight off the panic stirring in the pit of her stomach as she looked around for something to grab hold of, but even the reef was now out of reach.

The water temperature seemed to change by the second. She'd read something, she thought, but the panic made it hard to recall her own name right then. Temperature fluctuation, location...thermally unstable water columns! The phrase popped into her head like a light bulb flicking on. And the article she'd read said they caused strong undertows.

She would only exhaust herself by fighting. Avery was an experienced diver with plenty of air, so she needed to think like one. Relaxing, she allowed the current to pull her. They hadn't been that far from the bottom, there was only so much farther down she could go. A sudden flurry of silt and rocks grazed her leg, and she thought she'd reached the bottom. Seconds later, a ragged edge of what she would've said was the ocean floor five minutes before passed in front of her mask.

Damn. She was being pulled into a chasm that might be hundreds of feet deep, for all she knew. Avery scrambled to locate her handheld light, barely managing to turn it on before she was fully immersed in the long narrow space. A few feet into the fissure, the current seemed to abate. Keeping her breathing steady, Avery looked around. She had never seen anything like this up close. It was like swimming inside an underwater fault line.

Using her light to illuminate the crevasse, Avery kicked her legs and rotated her body, looking for lurking eels. Or any other swimming nightmares. Satisfied that she was alone, she swam horizontally for a bit before attempting to move back up. She wanted to locate a spot where the current wasn't pressing down, giving her the best chance of escape. Several meters in, her light glared off something ivory near the bottom of the fissure. The object stood out in sharp relief against dull gray walls. Avery dove down for a closer look.

Was that a chunk of the reef that had broken off? No. It looked too... round?

Just a foot or so away, Avery realized what she was looking at, her eyes widening in terror.

A skull. A human skull. And moving her light, she could see that much of the accompanying skeleton was still intact.

Horror bubbled up Avery's throat, her mouth opening around her regulator reflexively. Briny saltwater trickled in before she clamped her lips back down, shaking her head. No matter how much she wanted to, underwater, there was no way to scream.

21

London, 1664

Burgess wriggled out of the mouth of the tunnel like a snake, his torso barely squeezing through. He found himself on a bed of peat beneath an overgrown stand of Fortingall yews. He stood and brushed himself off, waiting as his fellow guards exited one by one. They were far outside the city's edge, meaning the thieves could have fled in any direction.

He wandered away from the trees toward a patch of exposed topsoil. There, he knelt and examined the mud where three different sets of boot prints remained. Each set was a distinct size, headed in the opposite direction from the others. Burgess ordered the men to split up and follow the tracks into the woods.

It wasn't long before the tracks vanished as the dirt was replaced by the heavy moss floor of the forest. The guards turned and gathered back at the starting point.

"Without horses, this is a fool's errand," one said. "I suggest we head back to the tower."

"Is that what you'd suggest?" Burgess said, his eyes narrowing.

"I meant no offense, sir. It's just that we don't even know if these prints belong to the thieves."

"Who else would they belong to?" Burgess thundered.

"Anyone could have been walking out here. The mouth of the tunnel is well hidden. It would be impossible to find unless the person knew what they were looking for."

Burgess stared the insolent guard down.

To his credit, the man met his gaze unblinking.

Burgess nodded. "Then by all means let's head back. Above ground this time."

As the men moved toward the city, Burgess hung back, grabbing the arm of his most trusted subordinate.

"What is it, my lord?" the guard said.

"I want you to keep an eye on him and report back any findings directly to me. I want to know where he goes and who he meets with."

"You think he may have been involved in the theft?"

"I think someone inside the tower must have been complicit. Finding the traitor may be our only chance at locating the crown jewels. Can I count on your discretion?"

"Leave it to me, sir."

22

Carter was careful to make sure his tether didn't get stuck on anything as he moved. The interior of the cave was pitch dark and the last thing he could afford was to have the line tangle—or sever—leaving him disoriented and trapped.

Slowly and methodically, he shined his light over each section of the cave wall before moving deeper inside. Bits of shell and chunks of broken reef that had drifted inside the cavern over time now lay piled along the bottom of one cave wall like some avant-garde baseboard molding. Carter checked the other walls and found them devoid of debris. Shining his light into the depths, he could see that there were larger objects farther in than he would've thought. Objects significantly larger than he had found while exploring other caves. He wasn't sure what to make of this. On one hand, they could've come from someone working inside to enlarge the tunnel—on the other, the currents beneath the surface could've simply been strong enough at times to move things around more than usual. Carter rechecked his safety line, then continued.

Approximately twenty meters in, the cave began to narrow, and Carter spotted what looked like a sliver of light up ahead. Curious, he started toward it, then paused to think that through. Exploring the cave alone meant he didn't have the luxury of his usual forgiveness-is-better-than-permission attitude. Every choice he made could affect his ability to get out of the cave alive, so he had to think more like Avery—logic, likelihoods, and caution. With the light from the other direction and his dive light, he could see better here, and nothing looked obviously dangerous. But the opening shrank with virtually every inch forward now—close to the light, the cave passage looked dangerously narrow, and the prospect of getting himself stuck down here for all eternity wasn't high on his bucket list. Inching forward, Carter checked for any protrusions that might hang him up, but the walls were all worn smooth. Interesting, because that meant the water did move inside the cave, and it moved often and fast. With only a few meters left to reach the light and whatever might lay beyond it, he decided to chance it.

He drew his knife from the sheath on his dive belt on the off chance that the light was caused by something other than the sun. Reaching the source, he discovered an opening in the cave ceiling. Just a slice, really, but the sun was bright and nearly directly overhead. Just below the opening, the cave vaulted upward, creating a pocket of air about a foot high and three feet wide below the ceiling. Carter kicked hard and propelled himself into the pocket, conserving his tanks by breathing fresh air while his head was above water. He examined the stone around the slit and could see that it, too, had been worn smooth. So the water did get up there, it just wasn't today.

Restarting his tanks and diving back under, he backed out of the narrow tunnel until the walls were wide enough to twist his body around. He retraced his path along the safety line, reeling it back in as he went, until finally he popped back out of the cave beside the reef.

He looked around for Avery, excited to share his find with her, but she was nowhere to be found. Carter swam one way along the reef from the cave entrance and then the other, but he didn't panic. Avery was a strong diver, and she could take care of herself.

He'd been inside the cave for a while, and Avery had a habit of letting her curiosity get the better of her. But he knew she wouldn't abandon him. He untied the safety line that she had secured to the reef, then turned to see if he could locate her nearby. He swam in the same direction that they had been traveling before he stopped to explore the cave. Gliding along with the current, Carter kept his head on a swivel as he searched for Avery, but it was just him and the rainbow slugs and the reef. Not so much as a bubble trail to follow.

Where was she?

___

Avery swam as far as she could until she found the far end of the crevasse. She turned and swam back toward the water above, hoping she had guessed correctly, and the current would be weaker here. The pull was still present, but much less so, and she managed to power through it until she was out of the hole.

Looking around, she spotted Carter's blue-striped wetsuit a few meters back toward the reef. She tried to get his attention, but he was looking the other way. She kicked her legs, pushing hard against the current toward him. As she neared him her diving computer vibrated, signaling that they had seven minutes remaining before it was time to head for the surface.

Carter turned and spotted her, smiling around his regulator. Avery could see the relief in his eyes as he pointed to the cave. She nodded and pointed to the crevasse behind her, willing to bet the cave wasn't harboring a dead person—but they were out of time for any more poking around. Avery flashed the thumbs-up. Carter nodded, and they began their ascent through a school of brightly colored fish.

At fifteen feet they performed the standard safety stop. Avery looked to the surface, making several turns in the water as she checked for *The Tempest*. The hull of their boat was the only one in sight, thank goodness. She turned back to Carter, who was watching seconds tick by on his dive watch. Avery wanted to talk to him—and Harry, too, since there were human remains in the underwater vacuum crack she'd accidentally found. At last, Carter gave her the thumbs-up.

As she broke the surface, Avery peeled off her mask and regulator and blurted, "There's a skeleton down there." Simultaneously, Carter said, "That cave has weird tidal wear on the walls and a hole in the ceiling." They continued shouting over one another as Harrison looked on from the deck of the boat.

"You gotta see that cave, Avery," Carter said. "It could have easily been a pirate hiding place for treasure."

"I got sucked into a crack in the ocean floor and before I could find a way out I found a body, or what was left of one, anyway," Avery said.

Realizing at the same time that each had important news to share, they stopped talking and blinked at each other. Harrison's shouting from the deck of the boat broke the standoff.

"You found what, Avery?"

They swam to the boat, and Carter gestured for Avery to climb the ladder first.

"What do you mean you got sucked into the floor?" Harrison demanded, alarmed, as he helped Avery onto the deck.

"But see, I'm fine, Harry." She shrugged out of her vest and set the tanks on the floor of the boat.

Harrison helped Carter up, then grabbed two bottled waters from the cooler. "Here."

"Thanks, Harry," they said in unison, opening them.

"You're welcome. Now tell me about this body." He stared at Avery.

"It was most of a skeleton," Avery said. "We definitely need to track down the local police."

Their attention shifted to the sound of a rapidly approaching black-and-white vessel.

"I think they're called the constabulary here, Ave," Harrison said. "And it looks like they're coming to us."

23

"Morning," the pilot of the police boat said after he'd pulled alongside *The Tempest*. "I heard from the dive shop that you had rented a boat and some dive gear; thought I'd nip out and check on you."

"How'd you know it was us?" Harrison said.

The constable pointed. "The diver down flag sort of gave it away."

"I guess it would," Harrison said.

The constable was an older man sporting a gray mustache, salt-and-pepper hair protruding from beneath his ball cap.

"Thank you for taking the time. You saved us the trouble of contacting you," Avery said.

"How's that, Miss—?"

"Turner. Avery Turner. You've already met Harrison, and this is Carter Mosley."

"Pleased to meet you," the constable said with a nod. "Name's Constable Paine. Now what was it you needed to see me about?"

"We found a body down there," Avery said.

Paine's eyes widened.

It took the better part of an hour for the dive unit, coroner, and forensics team to arrive at the site. As additional vessels dropped anchor all around them, Avery marveled at how much their remote diving site had changed since morning, and eavesdropped on Harrison's chat with Constable Paine.

"You guys have any unsolved missing persons cases?" Harrison asked.

"None that I can recall," Paine said, tipping the bill of his cap back and scratching his head.

"Could be it was before your time," Carter said.

"Doubt that, lad. I've been on the job thirty years next April."

Paine turned to Avery. "Tell me again what you saw?"

"It was more skeleton than body, truly. I found it in a crevasse not far from the port side of the reef."

"A crevasse that she got pulled into by the current," Harrison grumbled.

"The current gets a mite tricky this time of the year," Paine said. "It's why we don't have any tourists diving out here. Besides you folks."

Avery heard the condescension dripping from his words and fought the urge to snap back, but before she could, the coroner sidled up beside Paine. "Did you notice anything usual about the remains, Miss Turner? Any signs of foul play?" she asked.

Avery exchanged a glance with Harrison. He gave her a barely perceptible shake of the head. She knew he didn't want her getting involved more than they already were.

"I did," Avery said, ignoring Harrison. "There was a hole in the skull on the top right side." She pointed out the spot on her own head."

"Like a bullet hole?" Paine asked.

"No, not like that. It was bigger than that. And part of the cheekbone was missing beneath the eye socket on the opposite side."

"Body dump?" one of the police divers mused.

"The killer would have to be incredibly lucky to drop the body in the water and have it just happen to land in a ravine," Paine said. "More likely they knew the depression was there and carried it down to its final resting place." Paine turned to the coroner. "Wouldn't you say, Annie?"

"Aren't we getting ahead of ourselves?" Annie asked. "We don't even know the cause of death yet."

Avery looked around until she found Carter. He was seated on the stern watching the activity all around them, an unusually pensive set to his lips.

"What's up?" Avery asked as she sat down beside him.

"Just thinking."

"What about?"

"Jeff. Until the other day I hadn't spoken to him in a long time."

"I can't imagine how tough that must be," Avery said.

"It isn't that. I just don't believe in coincidence. First Jeff gets murdered by three thugs and a sniper. And now while we're looking around the last place Jeff dove, we just happen across a body."

"I'll give you that it's bizarre," Avery said. "And I don't know a lot about human decomposition. But I'm fairly sure that the body I found has been down there longer than a few weeks, Carter. Those bones were clean."

Carter shrugged. "That ring looked old. And that cave would've been a good hiding place for treasure, too." He tapped one finger on his knee, mulling the facts alongside his suspicions.

"Not everyone stashes gems in underwater caves." Avery winked, trying to lighten the mood. Carter kept his eyes on the water.

"Miss Turner," Paine interrupted, waving her over. "Would you mind speaking with our divers?"

Avery sat below deck at the battered dining table, sipping hot coffee and answering questions from Constable Paine. She couldn't help but feel like she had been shoved out of the investigation.

After debriefing her for information, the dive unit dove without her or Carter, telling them it was too dangerous for them to go back down. The leader of the unit was firm about it, saying that his team trained at the reef and knew how to deal with the underwater currents. While part of her wanted to be down there leading them to the remains, there was also a part that was grateful to be topside, away from the horror lying at the bottom of the North Sea.

"You say you saw no clothing at all?" Paine said.

Avery shook her head and lowered the cup. "No. All I saw was part of the torso and head of the skeleton. The rest was either missing or buried beneath the silt. But I was a little preoccupied at the time."

"How so?"

"Because the current had sucked her into a hole under the freaking ocean." Harrison crossed his arms, his exasperation clear.

Paine frowned at Harrison's intrusion. "I'd rather she answered the questions herself, Mr. Harrison."

"It's okay, Harry," Avery said. "Yes, I was a little freaked out at the time. I do remember that there appeared to be significant wear to the bones."

———————

It took over an hour for the divers to return, hauling several evidence bags containing the recovered remains. Avery watched as they turned everything over to the coroner.

"Any signs of equipment or clothing that might indicate the person was diving the reef?" Paine asked the lead police diver.

"Nothing that we could find."

"Maybe they were skinny diving," one of the other divers joked.

"I think that is highly unlikely," Paine said.

Avery watched as the forensic technician and the coroner inspected several of the larger bones. The coroner removed her glasses and waved Paine over. Avery followed.

"These bones show significant wear," she said.

Avery glanced at Harrison, who raised both eyebrows.

"How significant?" Paine asked.

"I think these remains have been there a while. They appear fairly old."

"How old is fairly old?" Paine asked, impatience creeping into his tone.

"I won't be able to give you an estimate without further examination, but if I had to pick a word to describe what I'm seeing, it would be ancient."

Pirates? Treasure? Murder? Avery couldn't help wondering what Jeff had discovered.

24

After being dismissed by the constable, Carter fired up *The Tempest* and turned the boat back to port. He had overheard the coroner's comment about the age of the bones, and he prayed she was right. His initial thoughts had been much darker: He was afraid that Jeff might have killed someone over whatever he'd found down there. Still, the fact that the body might have been the victim of a murder, regardless of how long ago that had occurred, left Carter feeling uneasy about the entire venture.

Jeff had obviously stumbled into something big. Something way beyond anything he could have foreseen. Wherever the ring he had found had come from, people were still killing each other over something to do with it. Whether it was an attempt to get the bulk of the treasure first or to keep its discovery buried didn't much matter—neither motive boded well for their safety. Carter had blindly, perhaps even foolishly, raced to England to try to save his old friend, but at what cost?

This wasn't the first time Carter had found himself in the crosshairs while hunting legendary treasure, so he couldn't fault Jeff there. But Carter wasn't motivated by greed, and he had Avery—a capable partner valuable not just in diving but in all the other adventures the two of them had gotten up to together. Jeff had a tendency to let greed drive him, and... Carter sighed. He couldn't easily dismiss the possibility that Jeff had double-crossed someone.

Jeff wasn't a terrible person, he just often had bad luck and, perhaps more often, bad judgment. Was Carter being unfair? Had Jeff merely found something he wasn't supposed to? But then, who both knew about that and cared enough to send three armed thugs and a sniper after him? Considering that, another question occurred to Carter: Had the thugs' mission been to take something, like Carter and Harrison assumed, or had they hit Carter's meeting with Jeff because they wanted to keep Jeff quiet?

The hum of the engine and the whoosh of the boat cutting through the waves were soothing. Avery and Harrison seemed content to leave Carter to his own thoughts—they were all exhausted to the point of near brain death from the whirlwind of the past couple of days.

They made it back to the harbor a little after five o'clock. Carter returned the boat and the tanks while Avery and Harrison loaded their gear into the rental. Following a short ride to the hotel, they headed inside, speaking for the first time in a while.

"How about we get cleaned up, then meet in the bar for a drink?" Avery asked.

"I'll second that motion," Harrison said. "How about you, Captain?"

"I'm in," Carter said as he exchanged a wave with Carleton, the registration desk attendant.

"Sounds like all in favor to me," Harrison said.

"Let's meet back here in thirty minutes?" Avery asked.

———

Deciding to take advantage of the temperate summer weather to see a little more of the town and the shore, they strolled from the hotel to the nearby beach between drinks and dinner.

"I told Constable Paine where we're staying, in case he needs anything," Avery said.

"Maybe we should have told the front desk where we were going, then?" Harrison asked.

"I'm not going to report my every move to the police," Carter snapped.

"Hey, easy there, Commodore," Harrison said as he stopped walking. "No one said anything about that."

"Carter?" Avery said.

"Sorry." Carter pulled in a deep, slow breath. "Guess I'm a little stressed out."

"Understandable," Harrison said. "Completely understandable."

Avery put her arm around Carter. "You know Harry and I are with you on this one hundred percent, right?"

"One hundred and ten," Harrison said.

"That's mostly why I'm stressed," Carter said. "I'm worried that I've dragged you both into something dangerous."

"Um, excuse me," Avery said. "Wasn't it me who dragged you into helping me find the person responsible for Mark's death?"

"Yeah but—"

"And let's not forget how you dragged him down to Antarctica," Harrison said. "And South America, and Norway, and..."

"We all remember, thanks." Avery pursed her lips, and her hands went to her hips. "Not sure anyone needed that much help. Anyway, Carter, you get the point. Harry and I wouldn't be here if we didn't want to be. We are partners, right?"

"All for one and one for all," Harrison said as he pantomimed raising a sword.

Carter smiled. "I guess we are, then."

"Okay, enough with this sentimental sh—"

"Harry," Avery said, giving him a warning look.

"What?" Harrison asked, trying hard to convey his innocence. "I was just going to say sentimental show of solidarity."

"Riiight," Avery said, her eyes narrowing.

"Let's get some dinner," Carter said. "I'm suddenly famished." He slung his arm around Avery's shoulders and squeezed. "Thank you."

"Now you're talking," Harrison said, clapping him on the back.

Andie the waitress recognized them immediately. "Welcome back," she said. "You folks look like you got some sun on your faces. Have you been out exploring?"

Avery glanced at Carter and Harrison. "You could say that."

"And all this adventuring has made me hungry," Harrison said.

"And thirsty," Carter said.

"Well then, let's get you set right up," Andie said. "What's your poison?"

After she had returned with their drinks and taken their orders, the conversation returned to the hunt.

"I am glad to see that the three horsemen of the apocalypse haven't shown up," Harrison said.

"Weren't there four horsemen?" Carter said.

"Times are tough," Harrison said with a wink. "Even they had layoffs."

Carter snorted, beer dripping from his nose. Avery passed him a napkin without comment.

"I was half expecting to turn around and have them drive up in a boat while you guys were underwater," Harrison continued. "But no dice."

"Let's hope it stays that way," Carter said.

"That's the first time I've seen bones while diving," Avery said as she turned to Carter. "How old could they possibly be?"

"Believe it or not, they can last quite a while in shallow water."

"I would think deep water would be better for preserving remains," Harrison said.

"You'd think so," Carter said. "But it's just the opposite. The deeper water tends to be where the bacteria and tiny critters feed. Over time, those bones would be scavenged until they just dissolved into the ocean floor."

"Maybe the crevasse combined with the strong current helped keep critters away," Avery said.

"Could be," Carter said.

Avery's cell phone vibrated with an incoming call. "It's MaryAnn. FaceTime."

"Nobody's paying attention to us anyway," Harrison said. "Set it on the table and just turn the volume down."

"Hey, MaryAnn," Avery said. "The gang's all here."

"Hey, gang," MaryAnn said, twisting her mouth to one side when she saw Carter. "I'm so sorry about your friend."

"Thanks. How's Brady?"

"He's hanging in. I'm not sure he fully believes it. Told me to ask you if there's anything he can do."

"Tell him to check in on Jeff's mom when he's on the island. Let her make him dinner. I think she was lonely anyway, and I'd bet this has made it ten times worse."

"Done. I'll go along and see if she wants to come meet our senior volunteer group at the museum, too." MaryAnn smiled.

"Thank you."

"Were you able to get anything from Jeff's cell phone company?" Avery asked. "We have a new friend here I could pass the information to."

"I got stonewalled," MaryAnn said. "But if your friend is the kind who has a badge, maybe they'd have better luck. His account was with Vodafone, but so far I have no friends who know anyone there. I'll keep looking, though."

Avery made a note on a cocktail napkin. "Thanks."

"So I called because I've been digging into the ring you sent me photos of."

Avery put her wineglass down, leaning toward the phone.

"And?" Carter prompted.

"Well...I found it." MaryAnn's lips disappeared into a thin line. "Carter, do you have any idea what your friend did for a job there in England?"

"Not a one."

MaryAnn tapped one finger on the edge of her desk.

"What's up?" Carter asked, glancing between Avery and Harrison, who both looked as confused as he felt.

"Is it the Heart of the Night?" Avery asked.

"Nope," MaryAnn said. "Think higher profile. I just can't figure out where Carter's friend got it."

"We might have made some headway on that today, actually," Carter said. "There's an underwater cave here that has a topside where you could get air. I think pirates might've been able to hide treasure there four hundred years ago and not drown in the process."

"Not treasure like this," MaryAnn muttered, typing herself a note about the cave.

"What do you mean higher profile?" Avery wrinkled her forehead.

"That ring is part of the crown jewels." There wasn't a trace of sarcasm in her tone.

Avery would've dropped the glass had she still been holding it.

"I'm sorry, what?" She looked around when she said that and lowered her volume.

"The British crown jewels?" Harrison asked.

"No, the Australian ones." Avery poked him, turning back to MaryAnn. "How?"

"I can't figure that part out," MaryAnn said. "That's why I asked about Jeff's job. But I'd bet that guy from MI5 wants this ring because it could be a bona fide national treasure."

25

They stared wide-eyed into the phone screen as MaryAnn gave them a moment to process that. After stammering for a moment, Avery finally managed, "I'm sorry. Again: What?"

"That's pretty much what I said." MaryAnn nodded. "But I've consulted two different experts, without telling them why I was asking, and they both confirmed that the ring was a piece commissioned by King Charles I about a year before he was executed. Evidently, his son managed to hide the ring from Cromwell and the reformers, later adding it to the crown jewels when he recommissioned them after the restoration."

"How in the world would Jeff have just found a ring that belonged to the King of England?" Carter asked.

"That's the interesting part of all this," MaryAnn said. "According to the official records, maintained by the British government, this ring is locked safely away with the rest of the collection in the Jewel House at the Tower of London."

"So how does Jeff have photos of it—and why did someone kill him over it—if it's in a museum?" Harrison asked. "Could the one he found be a copy?"

Carter blinked at Harrison. "A collector paid Jeff almost a million pounds for a copy of a famous ring?"

Harrison shrugged. "A good copy?"

Avery remained quiet, her brain methodically working through the problem, turning the puzzle pieces this way and that while she listened to them hypothesize.

"The history of the ring is right on the Tower's website," MaryAnn continued. "The stone, a Burmese star ruby called the Eye of the Dragon, was gifted to King Charles. His wife, Henrietta Maria, had the stone set into an opulent gold band as a pinky ring for Charles's birthday."

"What about the mark we located on the band?" Avery said.

"That's where this gets really interesting. That is the hallmark of the king's jeweler," MaryAnn said. "He engraved it into every piece he made as a way of protecting and identifying his original work. If Jeff took those pictures, it is highly likely he possessed the genuine ring."

"But then there must be a report of the ring going missing, right?" Harrison said.

"You'd think so, but no," MaryAnn said. "In fact, I called a friend at the Royal Museums Greenwich who specializes in the Commonwealth period and the restoration, and he offered to put me in touch with the royal curator of the Tower museum."

"What did the curator say?" Avery said.

"I haven't contacted them yet. I wanted to talk to you all before making that call. Eventually my poking around is going to raise eyebrows."

"Good call," Avery said. "Let's hold off on that for now."

Carter glanced over at Avery. "Is it possible that someone could have created a fake good enough to fool the kind of private collector who would pay that much for a ring?"

Harrison scratched his head. "Well, if Jeff did try and pawn off a fake on a wealthy collector, I'd say that might explain everything that has happened. It would certainly speak to motive."

MaryAnn spoke up. "If there is one thing I've learned while working with you all this past year, it's never to assume something is impossible."

"So, it is possible the ring was a fake?" Avery said.

"Possible, but unlikely," MaryAnn said. "All of the pieces in that collection were handmade by a jeweler specially selected for the Crown. Back then, jewelry making was considered a true art form. People would apprentice for years at the shops of masters, learning the art. As such, each piece would have its own unique style and flaws even beyond the hallmark. Whatever the crafter had learned while working as an apprentice would likely carry over into their own pieces. Hence the hallmarks, more like an artist's signature."

"Then it's possible that an apprentice could have worked in secret duplicating a piece made by his master, right?" Carter said.

"For some quick extra cash, maybe," Harrison mused.

"Only one problem with that theory I can see," MaryAnn said.

"And that is?" Carter said.

"Rarity. Where would a young apprentice gain access to a five-carat ruby that would last centuries and still pass an appraisal today?"

"Okay, then how would you explain it?" Harrison said.

"I think I might know how it happened," Avery said as all eyes turned toward her. Before she could open her mouth to explain, their waitress returned balancing a tray with their meals.

"Who's hungry?"

26

London, 1664

Burgess returned to his quarters, exhausted and frustrated. He had planned to recover and return the stolen jewels to the king in short order, but it appeared his plan had been foiled by the thieves with help from inside the castle. But who?

On his bed lay a note. Handwritten ink on parchment, Burgess immediately recognized the familiar script. Alistair. He should've guessed.

You are beaten, my old mate. Be assured you will never find the missing jewels. Oh, what is my poor stupid lucky brother to do?

Captain Ace Mullins

Burgess paced his room, fuming. It wasn't lost on him that in dismissing the Christian name his mother had saddled him with as a lad, Alistair was surely making a clever reference to his claim that he was the eldest son of King Charles I, never mind the outright gall of referring to His Majesty as "stupid" or "brother."

He read the note again, fighting the urge to tear it to shreds. The arrogance his old friend displayed was infuriating. First to steal the jewels right from under his watchful eye and then to boast about it in the most condescending confession ever penned. Ripping up the letter would be foolish. If there was one thing he knew about Alistair, it was that his words often had more than one meaning. But Burgess's weary brain was no match for his friend's intellect.

He should have known. Who else would have been clever enough to pull off such a reckless heist? Had he known all along? Was he merely hoping that it was someone other than Alistair?

No matter, he thought. The stage had been set. There was no wiggle room here. He was bound by his oath to the crown to retrieve the jewels at any cost. Likewise, he knew Alistair would fight to the death to hold on to something he was convinced was his birthright. The fact that his old friend might well be right didn't factor into it. No one would care what Burgess thought. The captain of the royal guards held no sway in matters that had governed the royals and their business for centuries.

Kings took mistresses for many reasons, and children were often the result of those trysts. No one pretended to be heartbroken by it. The mothers and their children were always well provided for, the boys properly educated. It was at school where Burgess first met Alistair Mullins. Deemed exceptionally bright by his country teachers, Alistair was brought by the king to attend school in London. Burgess, the son of a guard captain and nurse, was paired with the boy. The king had envisioned his illegitimate son taking over the palace guard someday.

It did not work out that way, however. It took years, but once Alistair realized that no matter how hard he worked or how high his marks, he would never be accepted into the palace as family but only as staff—nothing more than a common servant to the crown—it wasn't long before he abandoned school, shunning his mother and society in general, proclaiming that the sea was in his Scottish blood. As years passed, Burgess received the occasional word of his old friend's exploits. Six months after joining his first pirate crew, at the youthful age of nineteen, Alistair led his first mutiny, successfully seizing control of the ship and proclaiming himself captain.

Alistair became Captain Ace Mullins, handpicking a loyal crew he led all over the North Atlantic and North Sea. They seized goods, sometimes entire ships, slipping in and out of ports with their contraband cargo. It had even been rumored that Mullins had taken over a village on the north-eastern coast of England.

Burgess studied the letter, hoping to unravel a cipher, but it was no use. This was the first and only time he and his old friend had ever been at direct odds. Burgess knew that they were now sworn enemies as sure as he knew that Mullins would prove to be a formidable opponent. Until and unless the stolen jewels were returned to the palace, he and Mullins would remain locked in battle until one of them was dead. Of this there was no question.

27

Everyone sat in silence until Andie dropped off their meals and departed, waiting for Avery to share whatever it was she had come up with.

"You actually have to speak for us to know what you're thinking," Carter said.

"Pirates." Avery smiled.

Carter and Harrison exchanged a glance.

"More words would be helpful," Harrison said.

"Carter, you told us that Jeff was obsessed by pirate lore, right?"

Carter nodded as he took a bite of his shepherd's pie.

"And Captain Chatty right here at the pub told us that Jeff had been asking about local legends during his visit here."

"Where are you going with this, Ave?" Harrison said.

"Yeah, not sure I'm following," MaryAnn said.

"I was thinking about the skeletal remains I found today. The coroner said they looked old, right?"

"I think the term she used was *ancient*," Harrison said, making air quotes. "Highly technical jargon, there."

"What if those bones belong to a pirate?" Avery said. "A pirate who stole that ring?"

"Bones?" MaryAnn's eyebrows shot up.

"It's a long story," Avery said. "But it might explain what's going on here."

MaryAnn cleared her throat and pointed to her computer screen. "Well sure, except...You mean the ring that's still locked inside the Tower of London? That ring?"

"Why couldn't the ring have been copied?" Avery asked. "I'm not suggesting that the ring Jeff found is the actual ring that belonged to the king, but pirate lore is full of treasure chests and jewels. If a pirate had another ruby, he could've had a jeweler or an apprentice make a copy of the king's ring. Who was the most active pirate around the time King Charles's wife commissioned his ring?"

"That would have been 1648." MaryAnn began to type. "I'd need to research a bit to be sure."

"I bet you'll find a guy named Ace Mullins," Avery said. "Just a hunch."

"I'd like to know if you think there could be more jewels where the ring came from." Carter put his fork down.

"I would bet the goons that killed Jeff think so," Avery said. "That's why they wanted to know where he found the ring."

"Or at least the person who sent them after Jeff does," Harrison added. "And after us, too. I thought this gig was supposed to be safer than my old one. Can't you two travel like normal people? You know, buy lame T-shirts, drink too much, ride around on one of those stupid electric scooters?"

"Hey, I love those scooters," Avery said.

"What fun would that be?" Carter grinned.

"You'd miss all the excitement, Harry," MaryAnn said. "You know you would."

"Which reminds me," Avery said. "Have you checked in with Inspector McGregor today?"

"I have not," Harrison said as he hoisted himself out of the chair. "But nature calls, so I'll take care of both right now."

"The internet is a beautiful thing," MaryAnn said, drawing their attention back to her.

"Did you find something?" Avery asked.

"I did indeed. It seems you're right again, Avery—there was one particularly infamous pirate around that time, Scottish by birth, named Captain

Ace Mullins. Apparently, Mullins was very active in the North Atlantic during the reign of Charles II. And get this: Mullins, whose given name was Alistair, famously claimed to be a bastard son of King Charles I."

"Oh my," Avery said.

"I imagine that was common back then," Carter said.

"It was," MaryAnn said. "Most kings had multiple mistresses back then, and like a dozen or so children between them."

"The nannies must have worked their butts off," Avery mused before she shook her head. "But that makes perfect sense—a pirate who thought the king was his father would have plenty of reason to copy a ring Charles favored. And like Carter said, a pirate treasure would be a heck of a secret to send us after."

"But then why didn't Rowan just say that?" Carter asked.

Avery shrugged. "Intel people are weird about information. Or maybe he really didn't know. Or he thought we'd think he was crazy."

"Any idea where this Ace Mullins is buried?" Carter asked MaryAnn.

"It doesn't say here," MaryAnn said. "But legend has it that many of the most infamous pirates were dumped in the catacombs in Paris."

"I read about that," Avery said. "The punishment was intended to act as a deterrent to piracy by not providing those charged with it with a proper burial."

"I wouldn't think that would be much of a deterrent," Carter said. "Not for anyone as immoral as a pirate. Anyway, I'm not sure that helps us much given where we think Jeff found the ring."

Harrison returned to the table.

"Well?" Avery said. "Any news?"

"McGregor said they are running down a couple of leads but not having much luck yet."

"Why am I not surprised?" Carter muttered.

"That's why we're helping Rowan." Avery patted Carter's hand, looking up at Harry. "Did McGregor say anything about MI5?"

Harrison shook his head. "Should he have?"

"I was just thinking that maybe having the feds come in, so to speak, would motivate him."

"Where did you all say you're staying?" MaryAnn asked.

"Blakeney," Avery said. "Why?"

"It looks like Captain Mullins and his merry band of miscreants spent a decade in Norfolk just up the coast from where you are—in the village of Heacham near King's Lynn. It's on the edge of a large tidal cove called The Wash. Perhaps you'll be able to scare up some answers and maybe a few ghosts there?"

"I don't believe in ghosts," Harrison grumbled. "Pirates or otherwise. But I do believe in modern-day pirates, like the ones who attacked us and killed Jeff. And if we're going to go after pirates made of flesh and blood, then I'd like to have my gun back."

"Can you send us a map of The Wash?" Avery asked.

"Done," MaryAnn said, pushing two keys on her keyboard with a flourish. "I agree with Harry about the gun—y'all be careful."

28

Avery was up before dawn scouring the internet for historical information pertaining to the map MaryAnn had sent the previous evening. She was on her third coffee before Carter and Harrison showed themselves in the hotel restaurant.

"Nice of you two to join me," Avery said.

"Morning," they replied in unison.

"Yikes." She leaned forward when they sat down, examining their faces in turn. "Looks like I may have to buy you guys some makeup of your own. Those are some angry-looking welts."

"I just need coffee, Ave," Harrison said.

As they fortified themselves with a traditional English breakfast, Avery filled them in on everything she had learned about the village of Heacham, King's Lynn, and The Wash.

"The area came under attack from Barbary pirates around 1633," Avery said.

"Barbary?" Harrison said. "As in Barbary Coast?"

"The very same. They sailed from Africa into northern waters to attack established trade routes around the British Isles and Western Europe. Their ships tended to be faster and lighter than the merchant ships, making them impossible to outrun."

"I wonder if Captain Ace Mullins learned anything from these Barbary pirates," Carter mused, cutting his sausage.

"That's what I was thinking." Avery nodded, finishing her orange juice.

Following breakfast, they packed up the rental and headed toward The Wash. It was only a forty-five-minute drive north from Blakeney, but the windswept landscape looked so different it could have been a world away.

"Look at this sandy beach," Carter said. "This isn't what I expected here."

"I'm wondering why there isn't anything on it," Avery said. "Who owns this much oceanfront property and leaves it empty?"

"It's probably privately owned," Carter said.

"By someone allergic to money?" Harrison asked. "A hotel here would bring in a fortune. Look at that view."

"Would you keep it like this if you owned it, Avery?" Carter said.

"I just might," Avery said. "But I'm not most people, either."

"The world could use a few more places like this," Harrison said, smiling at Avery. "And more people like you."

After parking in a dirt turnout nearby, they walked along the water's edge until they came upon what appeared to have once been a coastal fortress. All that remained were crumbling stone walls and buildings.

"You think this was the pirate outpost?" Carter said.

"If what MaryAnn told us was right, it must've been," Avery said.

"I can see why they picked this particular location," Harrison said. "It would have been difficult to approach without being seen, especially if pirates also ran the nearest town."

"Probably drove the British military wild, knowing it was here but being unable to do anything about it," Carter said.

"I don't suppose you have any idea what we should be looking for, do you?" Harrison said.

Avery scanned the area. "Underground bunkers or caves? If there was one thing pirates were good at, it was protecting their loot."

It took the better part of an hour for them to find the first cave entrance, just above the waterline in the side of a cliff that jutted out into the deeper water of the bay.

"Remind you of anything?" Carter wiggled his eyebrows.

"Sure does," Avery said excitedly.

"Given our history, I figure we've got about twenty minutes before this area is swarming with armed bad guys." Harrison raised one eyebrow.

"Good thing we've got you to protect us, Harry," Avery said.

"With what? A big rock?"

Avery patted his arm. "I trust you."

Harrison stood watch just outside the opening while Avery and Carter removed their shoes and waded into the cave.

It didn't take long for Avery's excitement to flag. The cave wasn't deep, and seemed devoid of both treasure and good hiding spots. Plus, it had been way too easy to get inside in the middle of the day, she realized.

"Are you thinking what I'm thinking?" Carter asked.

"I imagine so," Avery said. "Unlike the one we found in Maine, this one has probably been explored over and over."

"Yup. Way too accessible. If there ever was something here, it was likely removed long ago."

They returned to the entrance, where Harrison stood waiting. "Anything?" he said.

"Nothing," Avery said.

"Great. So, we're out of here, then?"

"Not so fast," Avery said. "I want a closer look at the ruins."

Avery and Carter slipped back into their shoes and socks, then headed for the ruins. The only interesting area of the rubble appeared to be the remnants of an ancient courtyard. Scattered about the yard were several dozen rudimentary stone grave markers. Some of the stones had symbols chiseled into them but due to wear from weather and time were nearly impossible to interpret.

"Check this out," Harrison said from the far side of the courtyard. Avery and Carter wandered over to examine Harrison's findings. There were rusted and crumbling hinges protruding from the stone attached to rotted pieces of a thick wooden door.

"It looks like it might have once been a cellar door," Avery said.

"Well, it goes nowhere now," Carter said as he bent down beside Harrison to peer inside the grassy depression.

"If it once warranted a door this thick, it's worth a closer look now," Avery said as she stepped past them and down into the hole.

She pulled out her cell and activated the flashlight app, methodically looking at each of the stones that comprised the mossy interior walls.

"Take a look at this," Avery said as she leaned in close to one of the stones.

"What is it?" Carter said, joining her in the basement.

"A drawing. An old faded drawing, but I can make out waves...and this looks like the opening to the cave we just searched."

"Great," Harrison said, standing above them. "Just what I wanted to go back and do again."

"We may have to, Harry," Carter said.

"It looks like someone may have hidden something in there after all," Avery said.

The tide was coming in quickly, so there was no way to repeat the leisurely search they had completed earlier.

"We're going to need diving gear," Carter said, looking at the rising water and pointing to the rental car.

After changing into their wet suits yards apart, Avery and Carter picked their way out to the bottom of the cliff and swam into the cave.

The water was above their waists and the push of the tidal current was strong. They had to fight against being flung into the back wall of the cave. The rock walls looked entirely different underwater, especially when illuminated by their diving lights.

Avery moved along the right side of the cave while Carter skirted the left. After searching for ten minutes, Carter shouted excitedly. Avery followed him, finding a rock about the size of a large cobblestone protruding just the slightest bit from the wall of the cave. In the brighter light of their diving lights, it was clearly a different color than the surrounding rock. The chisel marks at its edges made it look like someone had altered the shape of the stone so it would fit into the opening.

Sometimes, a change in perspective and lighting is all a person needs, Avery thought, swimming farther up than she would've thought, searching for the surface.

They both found it near the top of the cave.

"What do you think?" Avery asked.

"I think it looks like someone made a pretty well-hidden makeshift vault in that wall," Carter said.

"Can we pry that stone out of there?"

"I can try," Carter said. "Not real stoked about wrecking my dive knife."

"Let's give it a shot," Avery said. "Before the cave is completely submerged."

It took Carter several minutes of prying and working his blade around the rock before it began to loosen, but the stone finally slid free, revealing a small hollow they could now see had been carved into the rock. Lying inside was what appeared to be a bound leather journal. Avery snatched it up and they kicked off the floor hard, swimming against the tide and making it out just before the mouth of the cave was swallowed by a wave.

"That was close," Avery huffed as she climbed up onto a dry ledge.

"Are you two trying to give me a heart attack?" Harrison thundered. "I was getting ready to report a drowning."

"Just keeping you on your toes, big guy," Carter said. "No sign of our new friends?"

"Not so much as a headlight." Harrison pointed at the sopping journal in Avery's hand. "What is that?"

"It might just be what we came for," Avery said. "Let's get back to the hotel."

Avery luxuriated in a long hot shower, washing the ocean salt from her skin and warming herself in the process, her thoughts never straying from the journal lying on the bathroom counter. She didn't know what secrets it might contain but she wasn't about to let it out of her sight.

After dressing in a pair of faded jeans and a light sweater, she wrapped the journal in a towel and headed to Carter's room, where Harrison and Carter were waiting.

"Come on already," Carter said. "Let's get a look at that thing."

Avery placed the journal on the coffee table and carefully lifted the cover. The seawater had significantly damaged the outer edges of the pages, making the ancient ink run until it was virtually indecipherable.

"It wasn't wet until we broke into its hiding place," Avery said as she examined one page at a time. "And the middle of each page is still legible."

"We should photograph the pages now before anything else happens to them," Carter said.

"Good idea." Avery pulled out her phone and began to do just that.

"What do you think it is?" Harrison said.

"It looks like a mariner's logbook," Carter said. "Part star chart, part journal."

"Whoever kept this made a record of their travels," Avery said.

"There must be something important in there for them to go to all that trouble hiding it," Harrison said.

Before Avery could reply, something slid out of the back onto the rug. Avery retrieved it and laid it on the table beside the journal. "I'd say you might be right, Harry."

"Is that what I think it is?" Harrison asked.

"It sure looks like a map." Carter smacked his palms together and grinned.

"Half of one anyway," Avery said, leaning over the table.

"Can you read it?" Harrison asked, leaning over next to Avery. "What does it say?"

"Nothing we'd come across on one of those normal vacations you were wishing for earlier." Avery bumped his shoulder with hers and smiled. "Some of the writing is legible. But the drawing is incomplete. It looks like this is half of a map of something." She touched the edge of the paper carefully. "And here's a reference to a key."

"Where is the key?" Carter said.

Avery looked up. "With the other half."

"Of course it is," Harrison groaned. "Why couldn't these guys make anything easy?"

"Because they were pirates, Harry," Avery said with a wink.

"What else does it say?" Carter said.

Avery parsed the old English. "MaryAnn or one of her friends could probably read it better than I can, but I think it says the other half was hidden in a tunnel with the cursed bones of the pirate king."

"Pirate king?" Harrison asked as Carter took a step back.

"Cursed bones?" Carter's voice cracked and Harrison laughed.

"I don't think Jolly Roger is coming for you, kid." Harrison turned back to Avery. "Who the heck is the pirate king?"

"I don't know," Avery said. "But there's a sketch, look. It looks like the key is a sunburst-shaped amulet on a chain."

"Great," Harrison said. "An amulet, old bones, and a tunnel. Should be simple to find around here."

"Old bones and a tunnel makes me think about the catacombs," Avery said.

"MaryAnn said something about the catacombs." Carter snapped his fingers.

Avery looked up from the map. "Wait. If a pirate might have stolen something from the king, like the ring Jeff found, a logical place to hide out back then would've been France, right?"

"I guess," Harrison said. "But, assuming you're right, how would the location of wherever the rest of this map is have gotten back to the person who hid this in the cave?"

Carter, studying the image of the map he'd captured on his cell phone, spoke up. "Pirates were exceptionally good at moving news and information around because they traveled so much. Jeff told me that once. Someone could have easily passed half a map to someone on another ship for proper hiding."

"So now if we just had an idea who the pirate king might be," Harrison said. "Should we call MaryAnn back?"

"Why not Ace Mullins?" Carter asked.

"Of all the pirates there ever were, you think the guy we've been talking about since we got here was the pirate king?" Harry raised a skeptical eyebrow.

"I actually think I might, yeah," Avery said slowly. She pointed to Carter. "MaryAnn said Ace believed Charles I was his father, right? It tracks that his men would call him 'the pirate king.'"

"It sure seems like Mullins's story was tangled all up with the ring Jeff found," Carter said. "And that ring is probably at the center of whatever mess Jeff was in—that we're now in, too."

"Let me guess." Harrison pulled out his phone. "Call Marco. We're flying to Paris."

Avery shook her head. "Paris, sure, but I was thinking by train."

29

"Heard you folks had a scare diving the reef," Carleton the desk clerk said as they checked out.

"Not a scare exactly," Avery said. "But we certainly didn't expect to find a body."

Carleton blinked slowly. "A who?"

"It's a long story," Harrison said. "But the local constable has it under control."

Carleton shook his head. "Certainly glad you're all okay. I hope you'll come back and join us again."

"Thank you," Avery said. "But I think we've seen all there is to see here."

"You'd be surprised," Carleton said. "We have a good many repeat customers. Oh sure, some folks just come here to relax and eat tasty food. But others come again and again to explore the fields around the castle ruins."

"Castle?" Avery asked absently, signing the credit card slip.

"They were right popular for a time," Carleton said. "More even than today, after someone discovered a mirror out there that once belonged to the Queen of England."

Carter was halfway across the lobby when he stopped in his tracks and returned to the desk. "Come again?"

"The queen?" Avery looked up, the pen falling from her hand to the desk.

"That's what we were told by the experts," Carleton said. "The glass was gone but the silver frame and handle were still intact. For a while we had people poking around out there day and night with all manner of metal detectors and such. Not ever enough room at this or any other inn out here —they set up tents, they did. For years. It's manageable now, but we still see the diehards every summer."

"Where exactly are these ruins?" Avery said, thinking he might have been talking about the ruins they had visited yesterday.

"Town of Cromer," Carleton said as he handed Avery a flyer. "You'll pass right by them on your way if you're headed back to London."

They drove straight to the address on the brochure. None of them spoke a word the whole drive, but the excitement in the vehicle was palpable. Avery kept an eye peeled for followers but didn't see anyone. As Carter pulled into the lot, Avery noticed several people walking the area slowly, waving metal detectors over the grass.

"Not sure how this helps us," Harrison said. "If there was anything else to find, these vultures probably found it long ago."

"Not if they didn't know where to look," Avery said.

"Or who to ask." Carter grinned, pointing to a young female groundskeeper. "I got this."

Harrison rolled his eyes. "Make sure you tell her you're a famous diver, Romeo."

"Can I help it if women like to talk to me?"

The groundskeeper was an attractive thirty-something who greeted them with a smile. "May I help you?" she said.

"I sure hope so." Carter smiled, laying on the charm. "I'm Carter Mosley."

"Pleased to meet you. I'm Rebecca."

Harrison covered a snort with a cough when Carter's face fell slightly because the woman didn't recognize him. He and Avery each lifted a hand in greeting but stayed in the background, poking around the periphery of the grounds but staying in earshot while Carter chatted up Rebecca.

"My friends and I were wondering if you could tell us a little bit about these ruins. Seems like it's a popular attraction, and we're not sure when we might get back to this area."

"Americans, right?" she asked.

Carter nodded. "The guy at the hotel we've been staying at mentioned something about a mirror belonging to the queen being here. Could we see that?"

Avery glanced at him. Surely he didn't really think the mirror was still here based on what Carleton said.

"Well, see, that's complicated," Rebecca said. "Yes and no. That was quite a discovery, it was. But we don't have it. The mirror once belonged to Queen Catherine of Braganza herself. Part of the British crown jewels back in the seventeenth century."

Avery almost fell over, grabbing Harrison's arm to steady herself. Surely that was too coincidental to be an actual coincidence. Had the ring Jeff found made it's way to the water—or otherwise to Jeff—from here? There wasn't a good way for her to ask, so she fixed an expectant stare on Carter.

"You don't say," Carter said. "When exactly was it found?"

"About six years ago. A man named Aubrey found it buried about a half meter below ground."

"Any idea how it got here?" Carter asked.

"No, and nobody has found anything of value here since, despite an influx of treasure hunters." Rebecca gestured to the people roaming the grounds with their heads down.

"And the mirror really was part of the crown jewels? That's not just some local embellishment to bring in tourists?"

"I'm shocked that you would even think such a thing, Mr. Mosley." Rebecca feigned hurt before she winked. "No, it was authenticated by experts from London. In fact, Mr. Aubrey retired to the south of France three million pounds richer."

Carter whistled. "I guess I can see why people are still here searching. Tell me about the castle that once stood here."

"It was home to the Duke of Ravensmere."

"That sounds like a lofty title."

"It was. The duke was considered quite high up in the king's court. Some have speculated that the queen may have actually visited once. It's possible that either she or one of her maids might have dropped the mirror."

Carter nodded and glanced over at Avery and Harry. Avery was pointing at the ground.

"Would you know if there are any tunnels on the property?" Carter remembered the inscription on the map about the cursed bones of the pirate king.

"None that I know of."

"How about bones?"

"Bones?"

"Yeah, have any been discovered here?"

Rebecca twisted up her face at his comment. "Any bones would be over there in the cemetery. That burial site is the final resting place for the duke's line from the 1500s to the last Duke of Ravensmere, who finished drinking and gambling away the family fortune in 1847."

"That was quite a while ago," Carter said.

"To an American maybe. But to a country with any real history, like mine, that was practically yesterday." She grinned.

Carter feigned being wounded by her comment, making her laugh. "Thanks so much for your time, Rebecca. I won't take any more of it."

"My pleasure."

He started toward the cemetery, then stopped and turned back. "I don't suppose you can tell me where this property ends?"

"Sure," she said, pointing. "It's about half hour's walk into those woods."

"Thanks."

"No problem. Let me know if I can be of any further assistance."

"Will do."

Avery and Harrison followed Carter. As soon as they were out of Rebecca's earshot, Harrison mimicked her voice right down to the British accent.

"Oh, do let me know if I can be of any further assistance, Mr. Mosley."

Carter shrugged. "It's a gift."

"Or a curse?" Avery asked.

"Definitely a gift." Carter winked.

They roamed the cemetery, snapping pictures of various stones. Graves belonging to the upper echelon of the royal family, the blue bloods, appeared to have been grouped together at the center of the yard. The reoccurring last name Hollingsworth was engraved upon all but the stones memorializing the dukes. Each of those were numbered and merely identified otherwise as Duke of Ravensmere.

"It looks like there was a definite pecking order to this family," Avery said. "All those holding rank are clustered together here."

"Ah, the joys of royal life," Harrison said. "Think I'll wander this way and visit some of my own kind."

"Me too," Carter said with a chuckle.

"Notice anything about these markers?" Avery asked.

"Yeah," Harrison said. "Most don't have the dates listed."

"Except this one," Avery said. The grave marker she was looking at was badly worn. Some of the letters were completely obliterated by weather and time. She opened the camera on her phone and zoomed in on the stone.

"Can you make it out?" Carter said.

"Looks like it belongs to Anne Mullins," Avery said. "Devoted mother, died in 1657."

"What are the odds?" Harrison asked.

"Pretty good, I'd say," Carter said.

"Let's see what MaryAnn has to say before we jump to any conclusions," Avery said as she texted their friend the picture.

"Think there's anything else here that might help us?" Carter asked as he looked around the yard.

Avery shook her head. "No. But seeing this, I really think more answers are waiting in Paris."

30

They returned to London and boarded the train to Paris at the St. Pancras International station without incident. Carter was confident that they hadn't been followed during the drive from Blakeney, but he could tell Harrison was still wary.

"Did you get in touch with Rowan on the ride up?" Carter asked as the conductor left their first-class car, which was entirely empty except for the three of them. "Any updates?"

"I told him where we're going and that we have a lead on the ring, which might have once belonged to a king," she said. "He sounded doubtful, but said he trusts our instincts. And he asked if I'd been able to use any of my 'famous gadgets' to help before he thanked me six times in two minutes. He said Jeff's case is slow going, but he's interviewing two people this afternoon who might have a lead."

"He didn't say who?" Harrison asked.

"I didn't think we needed to know, so I didn't ask," Avery said. "We're going to Paris, remember?"

"In style," Harrison added, sweeping one arm at their surroundings.

"I'm surprised there aren't more people in this car," Carter agreed.

"Be thankful," Harrison said. "I plan to get some shut-eye, so that's just fine with me."

"We get a chef-prepared three-course meal as part of the upgrade, Harry," Avery said. "If you sleep, you'll miss it."

"Then make sure you wake me up when it gets here."

Harrison moved to the other side of the car and reclined, pulling his hat down over his eyes.

Carter moved to a table seat across the aisle from Avery. He kept turning over what Rebecca the groundskeeper had told him. He turned to speak with Avery, but she looked lost in thought as she stared out the window at the scenery racing by. Carter sighed, sliding his phone from his pocket, and pulled up the number for Jeff's fence. He knew this guy was their only hope for finding out who purchased the ring, and he had to at least try to find out. He stared at the number on the screen, his thumb hovering above it.

Damn you, Jeff, he thought. *Only you could get me in with the criminal underworld from beyond the grave.*

Carter pulled a set of earbuds from his pocket and plugged them into the cell, then pressed the number and waited for the call to connect. It rang several times before voicemail picked up and a twangy cockney accent said, "What is this, 1993? Bloody text me."

Funny, if Carter had been in the mood to laugh. Carter obliged, signing Jeff's name to the text. He waited, but there was no immediate response.

After a few moments, Carter locked the screen and pocketed the phone. The train had entered the tunnel, so the sunny countryside had become darkness with occasional glimpses of concrete. He looked over at Harrison, who seemed to have the right idea sprawled out in his reclining seat. Deciding to do the same, Carter leaned back and closed his eyes, attempting to quiet his noisy brain. The swaying movement of the train car as it rolled along the rails began to have the desired effect and soon Carter was somewhere between awake and asleep. He roused to the sound of the bathroom compartment door sliding open. Carter opened his eyes and glanced over at Avery. She was staring wide-eyed at the back of the cabin with her hands in the air. Carter jerked upright in his seat and turned to see someone standing near the door wearing a clown mask and holding a gun in one hand and a canvas bag in the other.

"Put all of your valuables in the bag," the clown growled.

Harrison, now also awake, sat up slowly. "You have got to be kidding me."

Keeping his eyes on the dark opening at the business end of the gun, Carter's thoughts returned to the image of Jeff bleeding out on the street. With no intention of meeting a similar fate, Carter stripped off his watch and held it out toward the clown.

"We don't want any trouble," Carter said.

"Give me your wallets and electronics too," the masked man said, gesturing toward Avery's open laptop.

"I don't think so," Avery said as she rose from her seat, hands still in the air.

"You must have a death wish," the clown said as he stepped toward her.

"Funny, I was about to say the same thing about you," Carter said as he moved toward the clown, hoping to distract him from the real threat. The clown swung the gun toward Carter, giving Avery all the time she needed. Carter watched the eyes behind the mask widen as Avery delivered a kick to the side of the man's face, knocking the mask askew. Her next kick targeted the wrist of his gun hand, nearly causing him to lose his grip on the weapon. The clown hollered for help, and before Carter knew what was happening, a second clown rushed through the doorway into their cabin coach.

"Oh, come on," Harrison said as he swung a right hook at their new arrival.

"You got him, Harry?" Carter said.

"Yeah, junior. Go help Avery."

Carter turned in time to see Avery send her assailant bouncing off the side of the coach, his gun skittering across the floor beneath the seats.

"Get the gun," Avery shouted.

Carter dropped down on one knee, trying to locate the weapon. He could see it had slid just past the next row of seats. As he scrambled down the center aisle in pursuit, he heard a fist connect with someone's face, followed by a cry of pain. As he reached for the gun, one of the clowns flailed backward into the wall, his foot kicking the handgun even farther from Carter's reach.

"Come on," Carter said, leaping to his feet in time to see Avery wind up for a roundhouse kick. Carter ducked just as her leg swept over him and into the first clown's jaw, eliciting another cry of pain and sending him sprawling into the next car, where a meal was being prepared.

"Gun," Harrison shouted from behind Carter.

Carter turned to find the second clown had drawn a weapon. Harrison punched the clown, knocking his mask off kilter, and the gun fired. The shot sailed wide, shattering the glass of one of the coach's windows.

"Will you hurry up?" Avery yelled.

"I'm trying," Carter said as he dove over a row of chairs toward where he had last seen the other gun. He lunged for it, grabbing the grip before it could be knocked away again. He rose up with the gun, searching for a target, just as another shot rang out. This one narrowly missed him, but struck one of the Eurostar kitchen staff who had run into the car to see what was happening.

When the cook fell to the floor, the clowns fled from the brawl.

"Check on him," Avery said to Carter, pointing at the wounded train employee.

Carter knelt. "Man, Avery, I'm not a doctor but I've been through loads of first aid training, and this looks bad." Carter looked up as the cook's face went pale and his eyes fluttered shut.

"Harry, can you see if there's a doctor anywhere on board?" Carter asked.

Harrison nodded and took off through the same door the clowns had used.

Avery knelt next to Carter. "How can we help?"

"We have to stop the bleeding," Carter said, lifting the cook's shoulder. The other man didn't move. "I think blood on both sides means the bullet went all the way through."

Avery stood and looked around, her eyes lighting on a nick in the sconce light casing in the wall behind them. "I think it hit the wall here," she confirmed.

"Hand me a couple of those blankets from the bin up there." Carter pointed and Avery moved to retrieve the blankets as Harrison returned with a short, balding man with wire-rimmed glasses and bright, intelligent eyes.

"This is Dr. Mike," Harry said.

The doctor knelt next to Carter, taking the blankets from Avery and asking Carter to help put pressure on the wound.

"You have a lot of experience with bullet wounds, Doc?" Harrison asked.

"I was an OB/GYN for thirty-one years," Dr. Mike said. "So no—but a bleed is a bleed, to some extent." He looked up at Harrison. "Can you come press on this and let me check his vitals?"

Harrison traded out with the doctor, who pulled a stethoscope and a blood pressure cuff from a black leather bag and leaned over the victim.

"How did someone get on board with a gun?" The conductor, who had followed Harrison and the doctor back into the car, fretted.

"It's pretty easy when there aren't any metal detectors at the station," Harry said.

Avery ripped off strips of sheets so they could tie them tightly around the wounds to keep the pressure steady. She helped the doctor secure the bandages and watched as Carter and Harrison let go, the blood flow not speeding up. The doctor pressed the stethoscope to the man's chest, and Avery held her breath.

Dr. Mike sat up and hooked the stethoscope around his neck. "That's helping, but he's still deep in the woods. We need to get him to a hospital." He looked at the conductor. "Can you call ahead to have an ambulance and medics with some universal donor blood waiting at the station in Paris?"

"And the police," Harry added, gesturing to the door. "The perps aren't exactly getting off before we get there."

"We need to find them. They've got my laptop," Avery said.

"But we've got their gun," Carter said, handing it to Harrison. "Let's go get Avery's computer back."

"We could use some thick tape or zip ties when we find these clowns," Harrison said to the conductor as they followed him into the next car.

"Right in this closet, sir." The conductor pointed, and Harry retrieved a handful of plastic cable ties.

They searched every car and restroom but were unable to locate the men who'd attacked them.

"I don't get it. Where the heck are those clowns?" Harrison threw up his hands at the back of the last car. "It's like they just vanished."

"Two men hurried out there," a passenger seated near the door said. "It's been a moment now, and they haven't returned."

"Well, they didn't just hop off," Harrison said. "This thing is going like 180 miles an hour."

"It only travels at 160 kilometers per hour in the tunnel, Harry," Carter said.

"Positively crawling," Harrison said.

"Where could they have gone from the platform on the rear car?" Avery asked the conductor, who had rejoined them with the news that the Paris police and a medical crew would be waiting at the station.

"If they didn't fall off? Only one place," he said as he looked up at the ceiling.

"Oh, hell no," Harrison said. "There is absolutely no way I'm going up on the roof of this thing."

"I'll go," Carter said a little too fast.

31

London, 1664

Burgess strode along the grand hall of Whitehall Palace on his way to the king's study, pausing to adjust his uniform. In truth, there was nothing out of place. His appearance was impeccable as always. His pause had more to do with his reluctance to deliver unwelcome news to His Majesty. Despite the days that had passed, Burgess had nothing new to report regarding the missing crown jewels.

He had been tireless in his pursuit of the thieves, overseeing massive searches of the woods, the tower, and a maze of subterranean tunnels, all to no avail. How the treasure could have been stolen without so much as a whisper or a dropped trinket was beyond comprehension. The note left in his room confirmed that Ace Mullins was responsible, even going so far as to gloat about besting his old friend. Burgess knew that Ace had to have entered the tower himself, but how? How did he do it?

Burgess continued his approach toward the king's den, nodding confidently as he passed one of his many guards, though he felt anything but confident. The thing eating him from the inside was that the time had finally come to inform the king that his own half brother was likely behind the theft.

The king had yet to arrive when Errol, his personal valet, allowed Burgess into the space. Burgess nodded to another of his guards before walking over to the fireplace, where he stood looking up at the life-sized oil painting of the king. The accusatory eyes of Charles II's portrait stared down at him. How was he supposed to tell the king something so vile? He had no idea what words to use that might soften the blow.

Charles entered the room like the monarch he was, confidence and intensity radiating off him like heat from an oven. He glanced at Burgess before turning and dismissing his valet and guard. The men closed the doors to the hallway as they departed, leaving Charles and Burgess alone.

"Well? Are you here to provide me with glad news?"

"I wish I were, my lord," Burgess said, watching the muscles in the king's jaw flex as he gritted his teeth.

"That is most disappointing, my friend. So, you have exhausted all leads?"

"Every lead pertaining to the location of the jewels, I confess."

Charles turned around and fixed Burgess with a raised brow. "What then? Have you identified the thieves?"

"One of them, Your Majesty." Burgess opened his mouth to say more, then closed it.

Charles approached, his eyes as dark and intense as Burgess had ever seen. "Tell me."

"I have reason to believe that the pirate Ace Mullins is responsible for this outrage."

"What reason?"

"A letter signed by Mullins has come into my possession."

"Where is this letter?"

Burgess gently removed the letter from the pocket of his coat and handed it to the king. He waited in silence as Charles read the letter.

"How?" the king said.

"He left it in my quarters, sire."

"Mullins was inside the castle?"

"Or he had another do his bidding."

"Why would a rogue pirate leave you a letter, Burgess?"

"Mullins is a boyhood friend of mine, sire."

Charles stared at the paper. "Who is his 'poor, stupid brother'?"

"He has always claimed it is you, Your Majesty." Burgess had to stop himself from taking a step backward when the king's face reddened. He watched as Charles stood before him, unblinking and unmoving. The rage was clearly forming inside of him.

"I will double our efforts to locate the jewels, sire."

"Bollocks!" Charles roared. "Damn the jewels. I want the head of that pirate."

"It will be done, Your Majesty," Burgess said as he nodded and bowed before backing away toward the door.

"Do not deliver him to the tower, Burgess," Charles said, stopping Burgess in mid-stride. "You will bring him to me."

"As you wish."

"And keep the Jewel House locked and guarded until this situation has been resolved."

"Very well, my lord," Burgess said with a bowed head, but as he opened the door to the hallway, he couldn't help but wonder what would become of his head if he failed to deliver Captain Ace Mullins. He knew if Mullins had a mind to hide, the finest detectives in all of London would be hard-pressed to find him. Let alone take him alive.

32

The conductor convinced the pilot to slow the train some, but not nearly enough to satisfy Avery. The Eurostar's normal cruising speed in the tunnel was about 160 kilometers per hour, or about a hundred miles per hour. In anticipation of Carter's stunt, they reduced the speed to an equivalent of about eighty miles per hour. Dr. Mike said any slower and the wounded cook might not live to see Paris.

"If they're up there," the conductor said, "they'll be hiding on their bellies. Probably waiting until we exit the tunnel before attempting their escape."

"How long until we're out of the tunnel?" Avery said.

The conductor checked his watch. "Another ten minutes or so. Once we clear the tunnel, though, the train will resume its normal speed."

"We really have to get this man to the hospital," Dr. Mike said when Avery opened her mouth to ask about maintaining the slower speed if needed. "His life is more important than capturing his attackers immediately. The police can always find them later."

"Hopefully, I'll have them by the time we leave the tunnel," Carter said as he started up the ladder to the roof hatch.

"Keep your head down," Avery said.

"Yeah, let's not lose your most marketable feature," Harrison said.

Avery shot him a glare and turned back to Carter. "Be careful. If it's too much, come right back down."

The wind smacked Carter in the face like a punch from Rocky Balboa as he poked his head out. He imagined it was much like sticking your entire torso through a moving car's window—if the car was zipping up the autobahn. The tunnel was nearly pitch black, the only exception being the occasional bank of side lights illuminating the lower half. Carter had ascended to the roof of the train from the rear car to make sure the clowns wouldn't be able to outflank him. Wherever they were hiding, he knew it had to be forward of his position. Fighting against the onslaught of howling wind, he pulled himself along the top of the car using whatever makeshift handholds he could find, inching forward into the darkness.

Carter had set the timer on his watch to go off about two minutes before the train would exit the tunnel on the French side of the channel and pick up more speed. The quicker he could close the distance between himself and his adversaries, the greater chance he would have of surprising them. He had made the choice to move without the aid of a light, a more dangerous maneuver from the standpoint of crawling atop a speeding train, but significantly lowering the chance that they might spot him. The clowns, not expecting to be followed, hadn't taken the same precaution. Carter could see two tiny pinpoint lights bobbing in the distance. He advanced toward them.

He had nearly reached one of the men when his watch began to vibrate, and the tunnel started to flood with daylight. They had almost reached the end of the channel. Carter elevated his body into a crouch, careful to stay as low as possible. Time was running out. The wounded cook needed medical attention, so the train had to speed up, and he was already having trouble keeping his balance—and his footing. Carter couldn't imagine what the high-speed train's normal 300 kph would feel like.

Daylight illuminated the men in front of him a split second before they stood up. Neither wore a mask now and Carter was slightly surprised that neither clown was one of the London thugs.

In the flash of sun, Carter also saw that his plan wasn't going to work: he'd thought the clowns would be lying flat and he'd be able to subdue them from a crouch, but they were crouching, too, which meant he needed to stand. Since he was fond of his head and wanted to keep it attached, that meant waiting until the train was out of the tunnel. So much for getting back inside before the train sped up.

Once in the sunshine, Carter sprang up and forward like a jungle cat, tackling the closest clown. He struck the man waist-high, wrapping him up like a defensive tackle and taking him down hard on the roof of the train. The man landed on his back but went down swinging, delivering a fist to the left side of Carter's head. Carter responded with a punch of his own to the man's jaw and an elbow strike to the solar plexus. A flash of movement caused Carter to bob to one side, narrowly avoiding a kick in the head from the second clown. Carter grabbed the leg and twisted to his left, pulling the man off balance and sending him crashing down on the roof near the edge of the car.

Feeling the speed increasing, Carter leaned hard into the brutal shove of the wind from the front of the train. The clown he was straddling had recovered and peppered several quick jabs to Carter's torso. Carter tried for an elbow strike to the man's head, but his assailant blocked it. Carter moved quickly, using the wind to his advantage—he jumped to his feet and back, letting the wind carry him a few extra feet and putting distance between himself and his assailants. The clowns regrouped. Standing beside each other, they moved toward Carter, their clothing and hair flapping in the wind like flags in a gale. The larger man on the left had a wide, slightly wild grin on his face. Carter knew that was a bad sign even before he saw the man pull a large combat knife from his belt.

Carter retreated as they closed the distance, matching him step for step. He glanced back over his shoulder to gauge how much room he had before the gap between cars would be a problem. Three more steps. Like it or not, it was fight or fall. Or maybe logic?

"I don't suppose either of you would consider handing over the bag you took," Carter shouted, holding up both hands. "We could even take a short break to look at the beautiful French countryside. What do you say?"

Knife Clown stepped forward and jabbed at Carter.

So a no on the logic, then.

Carter opted to attack the unarmed clown on the left, knowing he would make a nice shield against his friend's blade should it come to that. Dodging the knife, Carter charged his target and delivered a well-placed kick to the side of No-Knife's knee, buckling it and causing him to cry out in pain. As the clown reached down with both hands to grab his injured knee, Carter hit him with an uppercut that sent him pinwheeling off the top of the train. The man's scream was cut short as he collided with a passing electrical pole.

Not exactly what he'd intended. Carter leaned into the wind and recentered himself on the roof, eyes on the last clown standing. "That's gonna leave a mark."

"So is this." The clown slashed the blade at Carter's face.

Carter ducked again, then circled around to the man's left—away from the knife hand. Even one-on-one, the odds were still not in Carter's favor: the clown had fifty pounds and three inches on him. Maybe the size would make the clown slower?

What Carter really needed was a weapon of his own, but a quick glance around the roof of the train car didn't offer much hope.

Wait. Behind the clown, in the distance...Carter's eyes fixed on a large object racing toward them. It looked like a tree trunk had split down the middle, leaving one half hanging precariously several feet above the roof of the train.

Crouching low, Carter strained every muscle against the wind, which was intent on shoving both of them off the roof of the train.

"Last chance to give up," Carter said as the man swung again. "I really don't want to have to hurt you."

"That's where we differ," the man said, his smile widening as he parried with his blade.

Carter dodged. The knife flashed in the sun, slicing a hole in Carter's shirt.

Too close. Carter's gaze stayed fixed behind the clown.

Wait. Wait...

Now. Carter dropped onto his stomach. He looked up just in time to see the confused look on Knife Guy's face a split second before the broken tree trunk struck him squarely in the back, sweeping him from the train.

The wind roared in Carter's ears. It was all he could do to maintain his grip on the roof. He turned his head back to the hatch where he had climbed up. It was three cars back, too far for him to safely navigate a return. If he was going to make it back into the train, he needed a closer option.

"Over here," a voice filtered through the roar. "Come on."

He forced his head around to see Avery's sticking up from a hatch at the front of the car directly beneath him.

It was all Carter could do to crawl toward her. He kept himself as low as possible, head down as he inched forward. His hand slipped once, causing the wind to yank his arm backward, and for a second he didn't think it was still attached. Carter had done a lot of things people would consider risky, but never had a single element tried so hard to kill him—he could feel the pressure everywhere. The wind even rushed beneath his torso, threatening to lift him from the train like a kite. Bracing his feet, he found a new hand-hold, then resumed his forward momentum. He couldn't risk raising his head to gauge his progress, but he trusted Avery was there. At last, he felt her hands grab the collar of his jacket and tug him toward the hatch.

33

A dozen members of the Police Nationale and at least that many EMTs were waiting for them as the Eurostar rolled up to the gate at the Gare du Nord in Paris. News of the shooting had traveled faster than the high-speed train. Avery didn't need a translator to read the suspicion on each of the police officer's faces as they spent the next several hours recounting what happened aboard the train.

"And you say you are just vacationing with your friends," Inspector Aubert said to Avery, his accent bleeding thickly through every word.

"That's right," Avery said, flashing a smile. "We were on holiday in London and decided to take a trip to Paris at the last minute. I've always wanted to ride this train."

"And that's when these men wearing clown masks attacked you?" Aubert switched his attention to Harrison.

"That's the honest to God truth, Inspector," Harrison said. "We were just minding our own business when they burst in demanding our wallets, jewelry, and electronics."

"Uh-huh." The inspector's face said he didn't believe a word of it.

Carter leaned forward. "It's true, Inspector. We literally had to fight them off."

"And that's when one of the clowns shot a crew member?" Aubert asked.

"That's right," Avery said. "Then Carter chased after them."

"Onto the roof of the train?" Aubert raised an eyebrow.

"It seemed like a good idea at the time?" Carter said with a shrug.

"And both of these men met their demise while fighting with you on the roof, Mr. Mosley?"

"Well, I can't really take all the credit. One lost his balance and fell. The other got swept off by a tree limb."

"So here's what I'm struggling with," Aubert said. "We've spoken to all the other passengers and you three were the only ones targeted during this so-called clown robbery. How do you explain that?"

"Maybe they just decided to hit our car first," Harrison said. "We were in first class, and the car was empty except for us."

Aubert nodded. He stared at each of them for a tick before his attention returned to Avery. "How long did you say you and your friends are planning to stay in our city, Ms. Turner?"

"Most likely only a few days," Avery replied with a painted-on smile. "We were just hoping to catch some of Paris's highlights."

"Indeed." The inspector's eyes traveled down to the bag slung over Avery's shoulder. "I see you managed to recover your stolen bag."

She nodded. "It was the strangest thing. After Carter returned from the roof, we searched the entire train and found my bag hidden in a utility closet—along with their clown masks."

"What do you know about that?" Aubert tipped his hat and left the room, hollering in French about the masks and fingerprints.

———

Several hours after being released by the Police Nationale, they flagged down the first taxi they saw outside the train station. Avery told the driver to take them to the Montparnasse District. She watched his eyes light up in the rearview mirror, probably as he imagined a healthy tip for his services.

"There are a number of wonderful hotels in that area, mademoiselle," the driver said as he pulled away from the curb into traffic. "Would you like me to pick one?"

"Actually, I've already made reservations at La Reserve Hotel and Spa," Avery said. "It's on Avenue Gabriel. Do you know it?"

"I know it well. You made an excellent choice."

"Merci beaucoup," Avery said.

"De rien."

"I thought it was 'de nada,'" Harrison said, lowering his voice to keep the driver from overhearing.

"Wrong country, big guy," Carter said.

"C'est la vie," Harrison said, turning a serious face to Avery. "I don't think our new friend Aubert was buying the innocent tourist act, Ave."

"Would you?" Carter said. "We left two dead men and a nearly mortally wounded train employee on a two-hour trip."

"It could be worse," Harrison said. "One of you could have told him to call Inspector McGregor."

"I imagine he'll figure out who we are within the hour," Avery said. "After that he'll likely find out about Jeff and be on the phone to McGregor anyway."

"If I were him, I'd put plainclothes officers on us," Harrison said.

"Sure," Carter said. "That's what we need is the police tailing us everywhere."

"We'll keep a low profile while we're here," Avery said.

"Good luck with that," Harrison said. "You two are high profile even when you don't mean to be."

"How did those clowns find us anyway?" Carter said. "If they know who we are, why wouldn't they have thought we took your jet to Paris?"

"I'm still trying to work that out," Avery said. "I'll need to scan my computer and all of our devices again as soon as we check in."

"And why go to the trouble of stealing your laptop just to leave it in a closet?" Carter added.

"Maybe they had another accomplice on the train," Harrison mused.

"Oh, that's good," Avery said. "But it's just as likely they cloned the hard drive and had no use for the bag. Some type of high-capacity memory stick.

Probably planning to deliver it to someone after escaping from the roof of the train once it arrived here."

"Well, if they had it on them, whoever sent them isn't getting it," Carter said. "I'm positive of that."

"That only means whoever is behind this will send more clowns," Harrison said.

"Here we are, mademoiselle," the taxi driver interrupted, his face in the rearview more disturbed than excited as he rolled to a stop in front of the hotel.

Avery thanked him—and tripled his customary tip.

34

It turned out their taxi driver had been right. La Reserve Hotel and Spa was both charming and elegant. According to the hotel website, the grand dame's cream-colored stone façade and decorative balcony railings greeted thousands of visitors annually from around the globe.

Before they could step from the taxi, they were approached by a young man sporting a black suit, checked tie, and a black derby-style hat.

"Bienvenue, mademoiselle," the man greeted, taking Avery's hand as she exited.

"Bonjour," Avery said. "And good evening, for my fellow Americans here."

Carter and Harrison joined them on the sidewalk.

Without missing a beat, the concierge switched to English. "Welcome to La Reserve Hotel and Spa. Is this your first time here?"

"It is indeed," Carter said.

"Well, you are in for a treat."

"Jeez, Ave," Harrison said as he looked the man up and down. "I'm not exactly dressed for this place."

"Relax, Harry," Avery said. "I had Marco fly to Paris with the rest of our luggage. He's having everything delivered here within the hour."

"But I didn't pack any of my formal wear when we flew to California."

"I packed it for you," Avery said with a wink as she grabbed his arm and led him toward the hotel entrance.

They passed through a bright red door to the lavish lobby, where they were greeted by the maître d'hôtel, who was every bit as smartly dressed as the concierge, sans cap.

"You must be Ms. Avery Turner and company," the maître d' said.

"I am," Avery said. "I apologize for our delayed arrival. We were—held up."

"Literally," Carter said. Avery elbowed him.

"This place is great," Harrison said as his eyes surveyed their surroundings.

"Merci," the maître d'hôtel said. "We pride ourselves on attention to detail."

"Sounds like your old job," Carter said, giving Harrison a jab.

"How old is this place?" Harrison asked, ignoring the comment.

"The actual structure predates the hotel, monsieur. It was built in 1854 for the Duc of Morny."

"A duke, huh? Sounds important."

"Oh very, he was the half brother of Napoleon III."

"No kidding?" Carter nodded. "That's cool."

"I've always thought so, monsieur. If you're ready, I'll show you to your rooms."

"Please," Avery said.

The maître d' led them to the elevator, which they rode to the fifth floor. Painted red and trimmed in darkly stained hardwood, the hallways were every bit as elegant as the rest of the hotel. Nothing had been overlooked.

"These last three rooms on the left are yours," the man said as he held an electronic card up to a brass plaque mounted on the wall to the right of the door. "The rooms are identical. I'll give you a tour of this one."

They followed him into a spacious, brightly lit sitting area. The wall opposite the door they had come through featured glass patio doors that overlooked a small balcony with a table and two chairs. Avery's eyes peered through the glass to the horizon where the Eiffel Tower stood in the distance.

"Oh my God," Avery said. "The view is incredible."

"I'm glad you approve, mademoiselle."

"Approve?" Harrison shook his head. "I'm ready to move in."

"And all our rooms have this same view?" Carter said.

"Indeed, they do."

"Sweet."

He finished showing them around the space, which included a wall-mounted high-definition flatscreen, king-sized bed, large en suite with walk-in shower, and a deep cast-iron tub.

"I don't see a remote for the television," Harrison said.

"Really, Harry?" Avery said. "We're in Paris, and you want to watch TV?"

The maître d' grinned as he walked over to the table beneath the wall mounted TV. "This is the remote," he said as he waved a hand across the screen of what appeared to be a computer tablet.

"That looks like an iPad," Carter said.

"Actually, it is similar, only this one has been programmed to run everything in your room. You can select channels, movies, book a restaurant reservation, order room service, dim lights, turn on a bath...just about anything you might desire."

"Speaking of food," Avery said. "Could you tell me what time dinner is served in the Signature restaurant?"

"The restaurant opens for dinner at seven thirty," he said.

Avery couldn't help noticing that his eyes made a quick scan of their attire. Before he could say anything about the dress code, she spoke up.

"I assume that there is a dress code?"

The relief on his face was instantaneous. "Yes, there is. Smart to elegant is the preferred dress for dining."

"Perfect," she said. "I wonder if you might be able to help us with something before you go."

"Certainly."

"The remainder of our luggage and dress clothes are still aboard my jet, but they are due to arrive here at the hotel within the hour."

He held up his hand. "Say no more, mademoiselle. I will personally see to it that your bags are delivered to your rooms promptly."

35

They met in the lobby just outside the restaurant at six thirty sharp. Avery was dressed in a lemon-colored satin gown that left one shoulder bare. Harrison and Carter wore dark suits with bright-colored ties.

"Jeez, Harry, I forgot just how well you clean up," Avery teased.

"Why thank you, mademoiselle," Harrison said, doing his best to mimic the maître d' who had shown them to their rooms. "I keep this outfit for special occasions."

"Is this a special occasion?" Carter said.

"Hell yeah," Harrison said. "It's my first time in gay Par-ee. Hell, I've got a view of the Eiffel Tower from my hotel room. If that isn't special, then I don't know what is."

Avery turned her attention to Carter. "You don't look so bad, either, Mosley."

"Thank you, Ms. Turner," Carter said, giving her a slight bow. "However, my appearance pales in comparison to your beauty."

They followed a tall, attractive hostess to the table and ate their fill, each ordering another round of drinks before Harrison literally threw in the towel, dropping his white cloth napkin atop his plate.

"Man, I couldn't eat another bite," Harrison said. "That was fantastic."

"Don't you mean fantastique?" Carter asked with a corny falsetto accent.

"That too."

"Anybody want another drink?" Carter asked.

"Not me," Avery said. "I'm feeling slightly buzzed as it is."

"I'm good too," Harrison said.

"I guess I'm good as well." Carter sounded disappointed.

"Have another drink if you want one, Carter," Avery said. "You deserve it."

"Nah, it's okay. Did you hear back from MaryAnn yet?"

Avery nodded.

"And?" Carter said. "What did she say about the catacombs?"

"Aye yi yi," Harrison said as he signaled to the server. "Maybe I will have that drink after all."

"That there are some interesting legends, and this trip might prove worthwhile." Avery glanced around, thinking about all the times they'd been followed in the past few days. "And I'll tell you the rest in the morning."

Avery ordered a taxi to pick them up at the hotel after breakfast.

"Those guys on the train knew we were headed to Paris, Ave," Harrison said. "Not sure the cab is gonna help much."

"Yeah, but they don't know where in Paris," Avery said.

"Did MaryAnn hear back from her contact yet?" Carter said.

Avery nodded. "She's still exchanging emails and phone calls with a museum in South London. Apparently, they have an extensive collection of journals directly from the palace around the time of Charles I, Cromwell's rule, and the restoration of Charles II."

"What exactly is she hoping to find?" Carter said, holding the door for Avery when the cab pulled up outside.

"Any mention of the ring, its commission by the king, or the jeweler to the crown. The woman MaryAnn has been speaking with vaguely remembers reading something about a commissioned ring but can't remember exactly where she saw it. MaryAnn also told me she visited Paris when she was in college," Avery said, sliding into the car.

"Did she go to the catacombs?" Carter said.

"She was too afraid." Avery glanced up at the driver as he pulled out into traffic, then lowered her voice. "She researched them, though. She said we'll need to be careful, as there are a number of restricted areas that haven't been mapped and probably aren't safe."

"Shouldn't they be blocked off, then?"

"That's kind of the problem," Avery said. "They're the best chance we have of finding what we're looking for."

"Of course they are," Harrison said.

"She also said the police patrol around the inside of the catacombs, so we'll need to watch out for them too."

"This just gets better and better," Harrison said.

"Did she find anything more on Ace Mullins?" Carter said.

"She did. She was researching the history of French prisons and found a reference to Captain Alistair Mullins and his first mate being banished to the catacombs following his capture by the French navy. They were charged with firing on a royal ship. Apparently you can take the pirate out of England, but not the instincts out of the pirate."

"Did she have any idea where inside the catacombs we should be looking?" Carter asked.

"According to the history, Mullins wore his captain's coat and hat into the tunnels, pledging that they would never hold him."

"A cocky pirate, huh?" Carter said.

"Remind you of anyone, Ave?" Harrison chuckled as he nodded in Carter's direction.

"Here we are," the taxi driver said as he pulled to the curb and stopped.

They got out and waited as Avery settled up with the driver.

"Merci," he shouted out the window as he drove away waving.

"What was that about?" Carter said.

"I may have tipped him too much," Avery said with a shrug. "You ready?"

"Definitely," Carter said. "Let's go."

"Not me," Harrison said.

"Why not?" Avery said.

"For two reasons, if you must know. The first is I've seen enough dead people for one lifetime. I have no interest in doing the bone tour through an underground graveyard."

"What's the second?" Carter said.

"I've already had the displeasure of seeing you two grave robbers in action. You'll need someone who can bail you out if this hunt of yours goes sideways. I'll be in the café across the street drinking coffee, eating bread and cheese, and people watching."

"You hate people," Avery said.

"Why do you think I'll be watching them?" Harrison asked with a wink as he turned and headed toward the café.

"I guess it's just us," Avery told Carter. "You up for more bones?"

"I missed the skeleton you found on the dive," Carter said. "Figure I've got some catching up to do."

A line had already begun to form outside the ticket window. Avery and Carter paused outside the gate to read the posted sign.

Arrête! C'est ici l'empire de la Mort.

"I got the first part all right, but I have no idea what the rest of it means," Carter said. "But I'll translate it with Google."

"No need," Avery said. "It says: Stop! This is the Empire of Death!"

"Well, that's ominous. No wonder Harry didn't want to come."

"He's just being melodramatic."

"I don't know, Avery. There is something mildly disturbing about a mass grave as a tourist attraction."

"Come on," Avery said as she headed directly to the window and purchased two tickets. The attendant handed her the tickets along with an informational pamphlet.

She turned to hand Carter his ticket, but he was already engaged in a conversation with one of the docents.

"You're Carter Mosley, aren't you?" the attractive young woman said.

Carter grinned. "Guilty as charged."

"Oh my God, I knew it!" She actually squealed. "What are you doing in Paris?"

"Tourist stuff. Just like everyone else."

Avery leaned against the wall, watching the docent fawn over him. Her name tag read "Danielle."

"Would you mind terribly if I took a selfie with you?" Danielle asked excitedly.

"Not at all," Carter said. "Although, if I'm in the picture, is it still considered a selfie?"

Danielle laughed. "You're so cute."

Growing bored, Avery opened the map booklet and pretended to read.

"What should I know about the catacombs before I step foot inside?" Carter asked.

"You want the tourist version or the inside track?"

"Oooh, give me the good stuff," Carter said.

She giggled. "The catacombs were modeled after Rome's tunnel system. Many sections aren't mapped because none of this was ever intended to be open to the public."

Avery watched Carter pretending to be enthralled, like she hadn't told him most of this over breakfast and in the cab.

Danielle continued. "During the plague, they put the sick and the dying inside, hence the sign at the entrance. Entire sections of the city were banished to the catacombs, and as it began to fill up with bodies"—she leaned in and whispered—"they just left them."

"Gross," Carter said, exaggeratedly scrunching up his face in disgust while earning another giggle from his new best friend.

Avery rolled her eyes, wondering if his flirting would pay off with something they didn't already know.

"Supposedly, there are more than six million sets of remains. It's so incredibly sad."

"I don't suppose there are any famous historical figures inside," Carter said. "Like, I don't know...criminals...or pirates, maybe?"

Danielle looked both ways, then pulled Carter down so she could whisper in his ear. Carter pulled back, mouth agape, and said, "Really?" He seemed genuinely surprised, and Avery couldn't tell if he was serious or still flirting.

In response, Danielle nodded and said, "Oui, je jure."

Carter laughed, then asked her if he could take a selfie with her.

Having seen enough, Avery turned and walked toward the entrance to the attraction.

"You ready?" Carter said as he caught up to her, then turned and gave the giddy docent a parting wave.

"Are *you*? I didn't know how long you'd be with the president of the Paris chapter of the Carter Mosley Fan Club."

"Somebody jealous?" Carter asked.

"Hardly. Just ready to go. And very curious about what she whispered to you."

"She said that some criminals were taken deep into the most dangerous parts of the tunnels, chained, and left for dead. The thought was they would never be able to find their way out even if by some chance they managed to escape. And then she told me to say a prayer for my soul as we pass the third tunnel on the left."

Avery stopped in her tracks and stared at Carter. She couldn't help but remember a certain coal mine in Virginia. The memory made her shiver.

"They actually abandoned people in the dark?" Avery said. "With all the dead bodies?"

"Right?" Carter shook his head. "Talk about cruel and unusual punishment."

"What a horrible way to die."

"So, you still want to venture off the approved trail?"

"Of course," Avery said, recomposing herself and marching forward. "We've got something they didn't have."

"What's that?" Carter said.

"Lights. And each other."

36

When Avery and Carter got to the prayer-inducing tunnel Danielle the Docent had described, they found it guarded by a uniformed member of the local gendarme. Avery looked past the officer into the tunnel. She could see that there was a fork located a short way down that appeared to be the start of a steep descent.

"Jeez, that looks treacherous," Carter said, echoing her very thought. Avery nodded absently.

For the next twenty minutes, they wandered with the rest of the crowd, pretending to study a stack of human skulls built into one section of the catacomb wall.

"The crowd is starting to thin out, Avery. They're moving on."

"And?"

"And if we don't move on with them, Inspector Clouseau over there is liable to get suspicious, don't you think?"

"You're right." Avery glanced at the officer.

"Jeez, you'd think he'd have to pee eventually," Carter said.

Avery coughed, trying to cover her laughter. After composing herself she said, "Too bad he's not a pretty docent who follows you on Instagram, huh?"

"Bet I could have gotten a private tour from Danielle," Carter said, wiggling his eyebrows like Groucho Marx.

"Without question," Avery said. "Except I don't envision a middle-aged policeman being as susceptible to your charms, Mr. Mosley."

"Maybe not mine, but he might be to yours, Ms. Turner." Carter grinned.

"Excuse me?" Avery said.

"Come on, Avery. It goes without saying that you're extremely attractive. And when you're not giving orders or analyzing data, you sometimes even manage to be mildly charming."

"You think I'm attractive?" Avery said.

"I'm just saying, why don't you go flirt with the guy? I'll bet he's never been hit on by anyone like you in his whole life."

"There is no one like me," Avery said. "And I can be charming when I'm analyzing data."

"Some guys might enjoy you giving orders too," Carter murmured as he put a hand on her lower back and nudged her toward the cop. "Go on. Get him away from there and I'll slip into the tunnel as soon as it's clear."

"What about me?" Avery said.

"You follow me when you can."

"You mean *if* I can. What if he doesn't let me?"

"At least one of us will get a look."

Carter watched from the corner of his eye as Avery squared her shoulders and pasted on a smile, then pretended to wander away from Carter toward the policeman. "Bonjour," she said. "Je me demandais si vous pouviez m'aider."

"Je peux essayer," the officer replied before his eyes narrowed in suspicion. "Do you really speak French?"

"Only a little," Avery said, tossing her hair like a pro before stepping in a bit too close for propriety.

Girl's got game, Carter thought, watching for his chance to move.

"What do you need?" the officer asked.

Carter inched toward the tunnel as Avery got the officer to turn toward her.

"Well, I don't know if you remember me or not, but I was here yesterday and I lost a bracelet that once belonged to ma chere grand-mere. She was my favorite person in the entire world, and I am crushed."

"I don't suppose you know where you were when you noticed it was gone."

"It wasn't until I got back to my hotel. I've checked everywhere else; it must be here. I remember spending a great deal of time in this chamber."

Carter watched as Avery touched the cop's arm.

"It's funny, though, I don't remember seeing you yesterday," Avery said, lowering her voice.

"I was off yesterday," the cop blushed.

Get it, Avery, Carter thought. *Time to reel him in.*

Avery looked up at the cop through lowered lashes. "Can I tell you an embarrassing secret?"

"Of course. As a sworn officer of the law, I'm bound to keep it."

"Really?"

"Cross my heart," he said, pantomiming the act.

Avery giggled, a function Carter never even knew she possessed. That was going to get her thoroughly teased later. "I touched one of the skeletons yesterday. I know that probably sounds bizarre to you, but I've never touched a real bone before."

"Doesn't sound bizarre at all, miss. You'd be surprised what people get up to down here."

Avery turned and pointed farther down the main passage. "I may have reached a hand into that bone pile in the corner."

"May have?"

"Okay, I did. And my bracelet may have slipped off there. Will you help me look, officer?" She bit her lip and looked up at him, widening her eyes.

Hell, Carter would've waded through toxic waste to root through bones for her himself, and the cop was merely human.

Carter pretended to be engrossed in something on the tunnel floor, watching from the corner of his eye as the officer considered his options for a beat before taking the bait.

"Why not?" the cop said. "But let's make it quick, okay? I'm on duty here."

"You are a godsend," Avery chirped as she wrapped his arm in hers and led him away.

Shaking off Avery's complete personality transplant, Carter slipped stealthily under the rope and into the tunnel. He hurried past the fork, choosing the left because most people's instinct is to go to the right. Scurrying as fast as he could without making noise, he got down the incline and well out of sight, keeping as close to the wall as possible to maintain his balance in the darkness. He told himself the bones he brushed up against were rocks. He didn't believe himself, though.

As soon as he felt confident his light couldn't be seen, Carter pulled out his cell and turned on the flashlight. He scanned the nearby walls with the light. The horrors illuminated all around him made him wonder if perhaps the darkness had been better. He directed the beam straight down the tunnel, but the light didn't reach the end. Nothing ahead but thick, suffocating darkness—the kind of darkness that seemed to prevent a beam of light from penetrating more than a few feet at a time. Like the blackness was swallowing the light. He shivered with that unholy thought. And that wasn't even counting the dead people.

"Get it together, dude," he said aloud, spooked by the echoey sound of his own quiet voice.

Realizing that he needed to think of something else, he began to move forward again, this time humming a Jimmy Buffett tune about flip-flops and suntans. The farther along the tunnel he walked, the more the bones on either side of the passage encroached. He also noticed that the floor of the tunnel was no longer clear. Debris in the form of bones, rotted fabric, and fossilized sticks that may have once been torches. Stepping over and around the detritus, Carter continued.

The sound of his steps began to take on an odd, muted quality, as if someone had pressed some unseen noise-reduction button. The air was still and musty, and Carter suddenly found it difficult to breathe. A noise from behind caused him to spin on his heels, sweeping the light back in the direction he had come. But nothing was there. Had it only been his imagination or something else entirely? The all too vivid image of a dusty skeletal hand reaching out to grab him popped into his head, causing the hairs on the back of his neck to bristle.

"Not helpful," he said, closing his eyes, his breath quickening.

He opened one eye at a time, half expecting to see the ghost of Captain Mullins standing before him, sword in hand. But again, the passageway was empty and dark. Nothing but bones as far as he could see. And none of them were moving.

"Let's go back to thinking about saltshakers, okay, Carter baby?"

He turned and continued deeper into the catacombs. He'd heard of people descending into madness. He wondered if madness was a place you could walk to.

Still not helpful.

The debris field on the tunnel floor continued to increase until he was literally stepping on skeletal remains, the bones crunching underfoot. His light passed over the occasional radial or ulna bone still shackled in rusted iron for all eternity. His mind re-creating the sound of rattling steel as the captive's arm pulled against the bond in a futile attempt to be free.

Carter shook his head, trying to clear the cobwebs of fear weaving themselves around his psyche. He had come down here with a mission, and he would complete it. For Jeff. He paused to scan the remains, looking for the glint of silver or gold, any sign of precious metals. MaryAnn had told Avery that Mullins always wore the star necklace, but what if the French had taken it from him before he was led down here?

A new threat emerged in the form of a steadily shrinking ceiling. Adding to his feeling of claustrophobia, the tunnel of bones now closed in on Carter from every direction. As he shuffled forward, his mind retraced his steps. He had passed several other forks in the tunnel, with no way of knowing which to take. He'd guessed, staying with the left every time. What if Mullins wasn't even in this passage? What if he had guessed wrong and couldn't find his way back to daylight?

Carter staggered forward as his foot caught something. He looked down to see an entire skeleton laid out perpendicular to the tunnel floor. It was shackled at the wrists and ankles. A few scraps of rotted cloth hung limply from the torso. He paused a moment to collect his thoughts and slow his quickening pulse. This was so not cool. Everywhere he looked was a new and different horror fighting for his attention. As he stepped over the skeleton, he lost his balance and staggered into the left wall of the passage. He hit the wall hard with his shoulder on the way to the tunnel floor, landing sharply on one hip. Covering his head with his arms, he lay still as a multitude of stones and bones crumbled around and on top of him, obscuring the light in a cloud of dust and causing him to believe for a moment that the entire passage was caving in.

As the dust slowly settled, he lifted his head and looked around. The tunnel hadn't caved in, only a three-by-three-foot portion of the wall he had fallen against on his way to the floor. The hole revealed another passageway beyond the one he had been traveling on. He rolled onto his side and shined the light inside, partly wishing he could run screaming, and partly curious. If they just left all this out here for people to pay money to see, what had the people who used this place as a death chamber deemed worth hiding?

Carefully, Carter scooched and shuffled through the hole. Once inside, the space he found wasn't a passageway at all but a small chamber. He stood and dusted himself off, then moved the light beam along the walls on both sides of the cavern, starting at the floor and working his way up until the beam caught something near the ceiling on the right-hand wall. Nearly obscured by rock, the top of a human skull peeked out just enough to make him sure of what he was looking at. Inching closer, he saw the skull was in the mouth of a small, human-sized tunnel. As if someone had burrowed into the stone wall and then climbed up inside.

Carter stepped up onto a small ledge, putting himself eyeball to empty socket with the skeleton. Almost entirely intact, the thing was wedged into an impossibly narrow opening, as if the person had attempted to dig their way out of this space. *Digging with what?* Carter wondered as he repositioned his light inside the hole. The skull was turned toward Carter as if looking directly at him. Adding to the illusion, the eye socket shadows seemed to move, giving life to the skull and making Carter's skin crawl right up his arms. He'd had more than enough of this catacomb adventure by the time the beam of his light glinted off something shiny. Holding his breath, he trained the light directly on the spot. Metal...attached to a chain. A chain that was still wrapped around a skeletal hand. Carter's breath quickened again, but this time for an entirely different reason.

He'd done it.

"Hello, Captain Mullins," he murmured. "Or should I call you Ace?"

Carter reached into the opening, careful to avoid looking at the gaping eye sockets, and retrieved the amulet. As he withdrew it, the chain snared an arm bone, causing it to slide toward him. In a panic, Carter simultaneously yanked the necklace and stepped back, losing his balance. He pinwheeled in place for a moment before tumbling to the floor. This time he landed on his butt, striking the back of his head on the wall behind him and dropping his phone.

It took him several seconds to realize that he wasn't sitting in total darkness. As his eyes adjusted, he saw a faint sliver of light on the tunnel floor beside him. It reminded him of the cave near the reef. The flashlight on his cell was still on but pressed against the floor. He retrieved the phone, bathing the tunnel in light again. After checking to make sure Captain Mullins hadn't crawled out of his final resting place, Carter shined his light on the object in his other hand and saw for the first time what he had found: the golden sunburst they'd been searching for, its chain still wrapped around two metacarpals that had torn free from Mullins's skeleton.

37

Risking another look into the pirate king's tomb, Carter couldn't locate anything resembling a map. He wondered whether the map had ever been down here, or if the paper could've even survived through the centuries. Though the map in the journal had made it through just fine...until it got wet, anyhow.

After pocketing the medallion and returning the finger bones to their rightful owner, Carter crawled from the chamber into the tunnel, then headed back the way he came.

The return trip was uneventful aside from a few nervous glances back. He half expected to find Mullins's skeleton staggering after him in angry pursuit, accusing eyes sockets lit from within. His heart finally began to downshift into a more normal rhythm as he heard voices coming from the main tourist tunnel. He had made it out. With no sense of how long he had been down there, Carter could only hope that Avery was keeping the gendarme distracted.

No such luck, he thought as he caught a glimpse of the cop's back. He had returned to his post at the tunnel entrance.

Carter searched for Avery, hoping that she was doing the same for him. At last, her face popped into view. She was pacing in front of the officer still faux-fretting about a pretend lost bracelet. He heard the officer suggest that maybe she lost it elsewhere.

Carter, still well back in the gloom of the tunnel, needed to get Avery's attention, but he didn't dare risk activating the flashlight on his cell phone for fear the guard would see it. Instead, he held up the phone with only the screen illuminated in the hopes that Avery would notice.

It worked. He caught Avery's glance in his direction.

She promptly burst into tears and grabbed the cop's arm. Carter grinned as he saw the horrified look on the man's face. It was obvious that he had no idea how to console Avery as they began to draw the attention of passersby.

Avery's wails grew louder, and she collapsed into the officer's arms. Attempting to calm her, the cop walked with her, leading her several paces from his assigned post at the tunnel entrance. As soon as they were out of the way, Carter hurried from the mouth of the tunnel and ducked under the security rope. He blended into a crowd of onlookers, then stood watching the Avery show.

After several moments, he approached Avery, painting a look of concern on his face. "What happened, babe?" he said. "You okay?"

"She's fine," the officer said. "She's just a little bit upset about losing her bracelet."

"Is that all?" Carter said. "I thought you'd fallen. Babe, you shouldn't be bothering this nice officer about that old bauble."

The officer scowled. "It did belong to her grandmother, you know."

"Exactly," Avery snapped as she pulled free from the officer. "You don't have a sentimental or romantic bone in your body."

"Really?" Carter asked with a hearty laugh. "Would someone who didn't have any romance in them lose sleep searching so desperately for something you wanted so badly?"

"What do you mean?" Avery asked as she dried the crocodile tears with the back of her hand.

"Just what I said," Carter said as he slid a bit of the gold chain out of his pocket, careful to keep the medallion hidden from the officer.

"You found it!" Avery launched herself into his arms, planting a kiss on his dusty cheek.

"Looks like you just became the hero, pal," the cop said.

"I guess so," Carter said, blushing for real as the feeling of Avery pressing herself against him began to have an effect. He shook the sensation off and slid back into character. "We should probably get out of the officer's hair, babe. Thanks again, sir."

"Yes," Avery said as she released Carter and turned and hugged the officer. "Thank you so much."

"Au revoir," the officer said, touching a finger to the brim of his cap.

Carter kept one arm around Avery as he led her toward the entrance of the catacombs and away from the cop.

"Holy history, Batman," Avery said as soon as they were out of earshot. "I can't believe you actually found it."

"Did you really just call me Batman?"

"Why. You like it?"

"Yeah, kind of," he said, pushing his chest out proudly.

"Good. Don't ever call me 'babe' again."

"Deal."

"Come on, Caped Crusader. Let's go find Harry."

Avery, Carter, and Harrison sat surrounding an outside table at the café directly across the street from the entrance to the catacombs. They sipped coffee while doing their best to look like every other tourist as Avery passed the medallion to Harrison.

"I can't believe you actually found this thing," Harrison said as he turned the amulet over in his hand. "Do you have any idea how long the odds of that happening are?"

"You wouldn't believe what we had to go through to get our hands on that," Carter said.

Harrison looked directly at Avery. "If it was anything like your last graveyard adventure, I don't want to know."

"It wasn't like that at all," Avery said as she looked around the café to make sure nobody was watching them. "Besides, the catacombs are a tourist attraction, Harry."

"Riiight. And I'm sure neither of you violated any of the tourist attraction regulations while acquiring this?"

Avery crossed her arms in defiance. "No, Harry, we didn't."

"Maybe you didn't, but what about Indiana Jones over here? He didn't get covered in dirt and spiderwebs walking through the tourist area."

"I did have to explore an off-limits area to find it," Carter conceded.

"Uh-huh," Harrison said.

"We can talk about this later," Avery said as she took the amulet back from Harrison and returned it to her pocket. "Any sign of our friends?"

"No. No clowns or undercover members of the Police Nationale, at least not so far as I could tell. And I was watching closely."

"You think we really lost the goon squad?" Carter said.

"Not on your life," Harrison said. "More likely they're tired of losing operatives like the two they lost on the train. I imagine they *are* watching and waiting for us to do the heavy lifting." Harrison pointed toward the amulet. "Finding that was a big step toward whatever it is they're after."

"You can bet there is someone else out there who would love to get their greedy hands on it," Carter agreed.

"Then I suggest we get it back to the hotel and check in with MaryAnn."

They paid their café bill and returned to the hotel without incident. Avery couldn't help noticing that Harrison kept his head on a swivel, falling naturally into the role of protector once again. She wondered if he had reached out to his friends in the law enforcement or intelligence worlds yet.

They each returned to their respective rooms, Carter to shower and Avery to video chat with MaryAnn.

"Jesus, Mary, and Joseph," MaryAnn breathed. "I can't believe y'all found it, Avery."

"Actually, it was Carter who braved the depths of the catacombs while I played the damsel in distress."

"I bet you played it wonderfully. What did you think of the catacombs? Pretty disturbing, right?"

"I've never seen so many bones in my life," Avery said. "So many they even constructed retaining walls out of bones to hold them all. It's totally surreal."

"Right? Kind of gross and fascinating all at the same time."

"So, what do you think?" Avery said. "Is there a chance that this medallion will help us find the remaining treasure?"

"Assuming there's treasure to find...I'm not sure yet. It makes sense that Mullins might have copied King Charles's ring with a ruby he pilfered somewhere, and the medallion Carter found today may well contain a key. Or it might just be an ancient piece of tin. Any luck finding the other half of the map?"

Avery shook her head. "Nothing. According to Carter a sheet of paper might not have survived all those centuries in the catacombs. Even clothing worn by the dead was reduced to scraps."

"That's too bad. But I might have a lead on a duplicate."

"Do tell."

"I'm still waiting on a few return phone calls, but I did locate an avid collector near you who is particularly fascinated with Captain Ace Mullins."

"I know the feeling," Avery said.

"By the sounds of it he has amassed a sizeable collection of pirate artifacts and lore over the years."

"Well, that sounds promising."

"I'm trying to set up a meeting for you."

"Great! Where is he located?"

"In Senlis, but I don't have the particulars yet. I'm waiting on a call."

"What do we do in the meantime?" Avery said impatiently.

MaryAnn laughed. "You're in Paris. Enjoy yourselves. I'll be in touch as soon as I hear something."

Avery hung up and dialed Rowan.

"Ms. Turner," he said by way of hello. "My superiors tell me your train ride to Paris was an eventful one."

"They heard right." Avery didn't suppose there were many secrets that could be kept from British intelligence. "But we're here, and working a couple of leads on the ring and your top-secret secret. How is your investigation into Jeff's murder coming?"

"It's starting to get some traction," he said. "I'm MI5, I never talk cases over the phone, but I have four persons of interest, as your American police officers call them, and I'm confident we're on the right track. We just have to find them."

"Kind of like the ring." Avery laughed.

"Race to the finish?" Rowan asked.

"You're on."

38

They met in the hotel lobby thirty minutes later.

"Well, you look better than the last time we saw you," Harrison teased Carter. "Doesn't he, Ave?"

"He does clean up nice," Avery said.

"Enough about me," Carter said. "What did MaryAnn have to say? I bet she couldn't believe I found the medallion."

"She was amazed," Avery said. "I sent her photos of both sides of it."

"Does she think this amulet thingy is the key to finding some kind of pirate treasure?" Harrison said.

"In fact, it might be a key," Avery said. "But we still need to locate the rest of the map."

"I don't get it," Harrison said. "If it is the key, why do we need the rest of the map?"

"Not *the* key to finding it, Harry. A key. MaryAnn and I think the amulet might be a cipher. When we find the other half of the map, the amulet may help us decode what we're looking at."

"If we find it, you mean," Carter said.

"Right. MaryAnn is looking into a collector in Senlis. Apparently he has a thing for old Ace Mullins. She thinks the map could be there."

"Great," Carter said. "So do I. Let's go talk to him."

Avery put up one hand. "MaryAnn doesn't actually know this guy, so she's dealing with a third party to try and set up a meeting for us."

"What are we supposed to do in the meantime?" Carter said.

"I don't know about you, Junior Mint," Harrison said, "but I've always wanted to see Paris, and here I am. I say we take in some of the sights."

"I couldn't have said it better myself," Avery said. "Where should we start?"

"Where else?" Harrison grinned. "The Eiffel Tower, of course."

Thanks to the Tower's proximity to the hotel and the beautiful weather, they opted to walk. Avery stopped to take pictures of a bridge and two flowerbeds, commenting on the lack of traffic.

"I always assumed Paris was like New York in terms of crowds, but this is so peaceful." She waved one hand at the smattering of tourists milling about the Tower. "Can you imagine catching the Empire State Building on a day when there are this few people?"

"I figured it would be way more crowded than this," Harrison agreed. "Thought we might have to purchase something like that Fast Pass thingy we got at Disney to skip the lines."

"I suppose the Tower has been here a long time," Avery said. "Over a hundred and thirty years."

"You remember when they built it, Harry?" Carter asked.

"Just wait your turn for grays and aches, junior," Harrison said.

"Maybe the excitement wore off after all this time," Avery mused, ignoring them both.

"Not for me it hasn't." Harrison tugged her sleeve. "Let's go see."

Avery had purchased their tickets online, so after clearing the security screening, they moved into an elevator line for the first level.

"These elevators only hold a hundred people at a time," Avery said.

"Okay, so maybe there are a few more people here than I thought," Harrison grumbled. "We could take the stairs though, right?"

"We could." Avery raised a brow at the suggestion.

"It's six hundred steps up to the first level, Harry," Carter said.

Harrison pursed his lips as he considered it. "Waiting is good. My pop said it builds character."

It took another twenty minutes before their group was in the queue to ride the next elevator to the first deck.

"Sweet," Harrison said. "We're next."

"You excited, Harry?" Avery asked as she wrapped her arms around one of his.

"Yeah, I am. I've wanted to do this since I was a little kid, Ave."

"Well, I'm glad you're finally getting your chance," Avery said before turning her attention to Carter. "Any word from Jeff's fence?"

"No," Carter said as he pulled out his cell phone. "He hasn't gotten back in touch with me yet." Carter quickly thumbed in a message, then hit send. "Let's see if that lights a fire under him."

"What did you say?" Harrison asked as they shuffled into the lift.

"That we need to meet with the buyer to view the piece. And I pointed out that Jeff's murder was likely connected to that transaction, meaning whoever bought the ring might be next. The sooner we meet with the buyer, the closer we may be to finding the killer."

"Speaking of killers," Avery said. "Isn't that one of the guys from the hotel in London?"

"Where?" Carter said, spinning around to face the glass wall of the elevator.

"Right over there," Avery said. "Light-blue windbreaker."

"I don't see anyone, Ave," Harrison said.

"I got nothing," Carter added.

"I can't see him now either," Avery said. "But I swear it was one of the guys who attacked us in the hallway as we were leaving the hotel in London."

"You sure you're not seeing things?" Harrison said. "I've been on the lookout all day and haven't seen a trace of any of those guys."

"Maybe I'm just jumpy," Avery said with a sigh. "I guess I just keep expecting them to show up."

"Here we go," Carter said as the elevator began to rise.

After the Tower, the river, and a stroll through a nearby park, they were exhausted by the time they decided to return to the hotel. Avery hailed a taxi for the four-block trip.

"Man, this tourist thing is tiring," Harrison said.

"I still can't stop laughing when I think about you in the park trying to get that mime to talk," Avery said.

"I figured all those years of questioning bad guys with your mom would've given me an advantage. No such luck. Though, none of them wanted to speak with me either."

"Where do you want to have dinner?" Avery said.

"Doesn't really matter to me," Carter said.

"Can we keep it casual?" Harrison said. "I don't feel like getting dressed up again."

"Your one for this decade was last night, huh?" Avery teased.

"Our hotel has an outdoor restaurant," Carter offered. "The menu looked pretty good."

"Work for you, Harry?" Avery said.

"Sounds perfect."

"Alfresco it is," Avery said.

Avery sat back in her chair and dabbed at the corner of her mouth with her cloth napkin. "That was delish."

"I second that," Carter said.

"It was pretty good, but I think I'm gonna need dessert," Harrison said.

The waiter approached the table in time to hear Harrison's comment. "You wish to see the dessert menu, monsieur?"

"You bet your bippy," Harrison said, earning a confused expression from the waiter.

"He means yes," Avery said, coming to his rescue.

"Very good, mademoiselle."

After the waiter departed, Avery's phone vibrated with an incoming text from MaryAnn.

Are you available to chat?

We're finishing up dinner. What's up? Avery typed back.

The collector I told you about—he's dead.

39

They took their dessert to go, retreating to Avery's suite for a private chat with MaryAnn via FaceTime on the laptop.

"Don't tell me one of our mystery goons got to him first," Avery said.

"I don't think so, no," MaryAnn said. "My contact knew of him but hadn't had contact in a while. Apparently he died recently of natural causes."

"I hate to be the suspicious one in the room, but I'm almost tempted to ask for an autopsy report," Harrison said.

"Where did his collection end up after he passed?" Carter asked.

"This is the part that's good for y'all: his children donated his entire Mullins collection to a maritime museum in Marseille on the southern coast of France."

"Any chance we can get in for a private viewing?" Avery asked.

"Way ahead of you," MaryAnn said. "I've already spoken to the curator. His name is Simon Desrosiers. I told him we were considering filming some of the artifacts inside his museum for Carter's television special."

"You mean the one that probably isn't happening now?" Carter asked. "My agent isn't even speaking to me at the moment."

"But Desrosiers doesn't know that," Avery said.

"Exactly," MaryAnn said. "You'll have to bring along a camera and pretend that you're chronicling everything for social media and the show."

"We can grab my high-end video unit from the jet," Carter said.

"I told him you'd probably want to interview him for the show, too, and he practically tripped over himself making accommodations for your visit. If I had to guess, he's probably out shopping for something to wear as we speak."

"Everybody wants their fifteen minutes," Avery said.

"I hope you don't mind that I set up the meeting with Desrosiers under false pretenses."

"Not at all," Avery said. "False pretenses are often handy, in my recent experience."

"I'll sell it hard," Carter agreed.

"I don't want to be the one to rain on this parade," Harrison said as he finished his dessert and placed the container on the coffee table.

"Then why do I think I hear thunder?" Avery asked.

"Let's assume we do manage to find the other half of this Ace guy's supposed treasure map." Harry leaned forward, resting his elbows on his knees. "How are you planning to get it out of the museum?"

"We'll have the images of it after we photograph and film it," Carter said. "We can study the details of the images later."

"That's all good in theory," Avery said thoughtfully. "But it might not help. What if the clues are contained within the paper instead of printed on it?"

"You two did just recover a four-hundred-year-old necklace from a heavily guarded tunnel of bones," MaryAnn said. "Grabbing a map from some dinky museum should be a piece of cake. I can book you on a train tomorrow, if you'd like."

The three of them exchanged glances.

"No thanks," Carter said.

"After our last train ride, I think I'd rather jump out of a plane," Harrison said.

"Now that, I'd be up for," Carter said.

Avery looked back at MaryAnn on the screen. "Thanks anyway, but after our experience on the Orient Express, I think I'll just reserve a car and driver. Can you send me the deets on the museum?"

"Consider it done. Good luck."

40

The next morning, they met in the café and spent a leisurely hour fueling up on coffee, croissants, cheese, and fruit. At nine o'clock sharp the hired car and driver were waiting outside of the hotel for them.

"Bonjour, Mademoiselle Turner," greeted the driver, a petite man with a pencil mustache and a jaunty little black cap, as he opened the car door for Avery.

"Merci," she said as she settled into the back.

Harrison and Carter waved him off and climbed inside with their bags.

"You wish to go to Marseille?" the driver asked as he slid behind the wheel.

"Yes, please," Avery said. "Do you know the town well?"

"Very well. It is, how do you say, a tourist ambush."

"I hope not." Avery laughed. "I think you mean a tourist trap."

"Oui, a tourist trap."

"Let's hope he wasn't right the first time," Harrison said, lowering his voice to address Avery and Carter.

Avery grinned as her phone buzzed.

"Rowan says he has a location on his suspects in Jeff's murder." She smiled wider, keeping her voice low and turning to Carter. "They're going to bring them in for questioning today, as long as their information is accurate."

That's wonderful, she typed back. *We're heading to Marseille to look for the other half of a map that might lead us to the pirate's secret.*

By the time they had reached the Paris city limits, everyone had settled in for the long drive. Their driver had finally given up on his attempts at conversation and Avery put the privacy wall up. She felt a little bit bad about shutting him down, but experience had taught her that getting chummy with strangers while searching for treasure never led to anything good. In fact, more often it ended with bleeding head wounds or being shot at.

Avery noticed that Harrison's focus had shifted to the traffic behind them.

"Something wrong, Harry?" she said.

"I think we've got a tail."

"Seriously?" Carter yelped, lowering his phone for the first time.

"See that gray Mercedes about three cars back?" Harrison said.

"I got it," Carter said.

"What makes you think it's following us?" Avery said. "There is a gray Mercedes everywhere you look over here."

"Because that one was parked directly across the street when we left the hotel."

"Could be a coincidence, right?" Carter said.

Harrison broke out his patented don't-be-stupid look. "If they were wearing clown masks, would you ask me that?"

"You think it's the police or more thugs?" Avery said.

"Can't tell," Harrison said.

"That car is high end," Carter said.

"Back home," Harrison said. "Over here they're like Fords—everybody drives them. Even the police."

Avery couldn't even tell if she was more worried about another goon squad or that the police knew about the amulet—and how they'd gotten it. After the incident on the train, Aubert would be foolish not to keep a close eye on them.

"Do you think there may have been cameras we missed in the cata-combs?" Avery asked. "Maybe they saw you take the medallion, Carter."

"No way. It was crazy dark and on the backside of a sealed wall where I found it."

"I can't say for sure that's not a cop, but I can say that's not what they're after if it is," Harrison said.

"How can you be so sure?" Avery said.

"Because, in a city the size of Paris, the police have bigger things to worry about than some necklace they didn't even know about twenty-four hours ago."

"Maybe it's the guys from London you didn't believe were following us at the Eiffel Tower yesterday," Avery said.

"Gotta say I'm regretting that now, Ave," Harrison said.

"Well, there is one way to find out," Carter said as he lowered the privacy glass. "Hey, driver, step on it."

"Plus rapide?" the driver asked.

"Oui, le jeuneur," Avery said.

The Mercedes kept pace with them briefly before it slowed and turned off.

"Okay, maybe I was wrong," Harrison said with a shrug.

"No worries, Harry," Avery said. "We'll just get there a little sooner."

41

The museum was stunning. Avery hadn't been able to glean much about it from the internet, so she was really seeing it for the first time. Carter was in character as soon as they stepped inside, while Avery and Harrison played the dutiful film crew.

"I can't tell you how excited I was to hear that you'd be filming here and interviewing me, Mr. Mosley," Simon, the white-haired curator, gushed. "I'm such a fan."

"Please, call me Carter," he said, beaming a great smile.

"I see you have your crew with you. Will you need any other assistance?"

"No, I think we have all we need," Carter said.

"Where would you like to begin?"

"Seeing as how you're the expert, I guess I'll leave that up to you."

"Right this way, Mr. Mos—Carter."

They spent the next half hour convincingly shooting both still images and film footage interspersed with interview clips of the curator talking with Carter and pointing out the highlighted exhibits. Simon was so completely enamored with Carter; Avery couldn't help wondering if they even needed the ruse.

About forty-five minutes after they arrived, Simon was called away by an employee to take an important call.

"My sincere apologies for the interruption," he said, frowning at the young woman who'd come to get his attention.

"No worries," Carter said. "Take your time."

Avery watched him go and turned to her friends. "We need to get a look at the Mullins collection. Just in case those guys in the Mercedes were following us—or any of our other assorted new friends decide to crash our party here."

"Good point," Carter said.

"Heads up," Harrison said. "Here comes Simon now."

"I am so sorry about that," Simon said. "I instructed my staff that I was not to be disturbed, but you know how that goes."

"Indeed, I do." Carter cast a glance at Harrison. "Good help is hard to find."

"What would you like to see next?" Simon said.

"How about the Captain Mullins collection?" Carter said.

Simon led them to a cold and dimly lit room in the basement.

"I must ask that you refrain from using any type of flash photography," Simon said.

"Of course," Carter said.

"I understand the need for lower light when preserving documents and such," Avery said. "But why the cold temperature?"

"Same reason," the curator said. "Warmer temperatures tend to speed up degradation of paper. Excuse me a moment."

He slipped into a back room, returning several minutes later with a large tray of glass-covered documents. The yellowed paper highlighted the age of the texts.

"Each of these letters were written by the pirate himself. You can match Captain Mullins's scrawl throughout each one."

"I'm surprised the writing is so neat," Harrison said as he leaned in for a closer look with the video camera.

"Mullins might have been a pirate, but he was also classically educated," the curator said. "Quite different from your Hollywood depictions of drunken pirates."

"I'll say," Carter said.

As Avery studied each of the documents, she realized the one they were looking for wasn't there. "These are incredible," she said. "I wonder: Do any maps drawn by Captain Mullins still exist?"

"Great question," Carter said. "My followers do love their pirate treasure maps."

"I'm sure," the curator said with a twinkle in his eyes. "I think I may have just what you're looking for."

With that, Simon slipped into the back room again, this time returning with a smaller case. Protected under glass was the other half of the map they had been searching for.

"Any chance we could look at this more closely?" Avery said, barely containing her excitement.

"I couldn't possibly remove anything from under glass," the curator said. "It's against museum rules."

"I won't tell anyone if you don't," Avery said, figuring a little flirting might work as it had with the cop guarding the catacombs.

The curator raised his nose snobbishly at her. "Young lady, whether you tell anyone or not, the paper is still very old and likely to crumble."

"You know, Simon, my followers love a rule-breaker," Carter said as he put his arm around the curator's shoulders. "Especially when it's unexpected."

"Well, I suppose one little peek couldn't hurt, if you're really careful," Simon relented as he produced a key. "And, of course, you'll need to wear special gloves." He pulled a pair out of his pocket.

"We'll be extremely careful." Carter flashed his pearly whites and clapped Simon on the shoulder. "And you will be forever known as a rebel."

"Thank you so much," Avery said, earning another look of disdain from Simon as he opened the case.

After donning the gloves, Avery carefully picked up the map and studied it. Carter did his best to distract Simon by peppering him with questions about Mullins while Harrison filmed their conversation.

Avery ran one of her hands lightly across the page. Even through the thin cloth she felt the small ripples. It was impossible to know whether the imperfections were flaws in the parchment fibers or impressions made by some type of invisible ink.

Simon was right, the map was brittle. There would be no way to smuggle it out of the museum without folding it, and the thing looked like it might break if she looked at it funny. She returned the map to its case, then took several close-up photographs using the low-light setting and the image stabilizer.

Avery had barely lowered the camera before Simon appeared at her side and relocked the display case.

"We can't thank you enough for your time, Simon," Carter said. "It has truly been a pleasure meeting you and touring your museum."

"The pleasure has been mine, Mr. Mos—sorry, Carter." Simon smiled. "I can't tell you how much I've enjoyed your diving videos. I feel like I'm a youngster watching Jacques Cousteau for the first time."

"Now that is high praise indeed."

"Let me walk you out," Simon said as he turned toward the hallway from which they'd come.

Avery turned at the same time, bumping into him. She reached out and grabbed his jacket as if to keep from falling.

"I'm so sorry," Avery said as she righted herself. "I'm such a klutz. Are you okay?"

"Yes, Simon, are you all right?" Carter asked, straightening the curator's coat.

"I'm fine. No harm done."

Avery and Harrison led the way as Carter made small talk with Simon all the way to the museum lobby. After saying goodbye, they walked back to the waiting car and driver as fast as they could without drawing attention.

"Oh my God," Avery said. "The fangirl at the catacombs had nothing on that dude, Carter."

"I was about to suggest you get a room," Harrison quipped.

"Jealousy is so unattractive," Carter said as they reached the car and the driver jumped out to open the door for Avery. "The important thing is we got photos of the other half of the map."

"We got more than that," Avery said, holding up the key she'd lifted from Simon's pocket.

"You know, I think you and Jeff would have gotten along well," Carter said, his jaw slightly loose.

"We gotta talk, Ave," Harrison said as he climbed in next to her. "When did you learn to pick pockets?"

"Had to be done, Harry," Avery said. "And I grew up riding the subway alone, remember?"

42

London, 1664

Burgess stared in anger at his once trusted subordinate while two other guards held him firmly. The stink inside the tunnel was a distant sensation that faded along with everything else not having to do with the stolen jewels, the pirate who had eluded him for months, or the traitor standing before him.

"We found him hiding down here, Captain," one of the guards said. "He was carrying this letter."

Burgess stepped forward and retrieved the note. He recognized the script instantly. Alastair Mullins.

"What are you going to do with me?" The guard, who'd proven loyalty and valor enough to be trusted with the tower—and the Jewel House—in the dead of night, widened his eyes as he met Burgess's flat stare.

"Me?" Burgess said. "I am not going to do anything to you."

Burgess saw confusion ripple across the man's expression. "I do not understand. Surely, I will be held to account."

"You will, but not by me. His Majesty has plans for you."

Burgess used his torch to read the note from Mullins.

. . .

So now you have discovered this captain's secret. A traitor in the ranks, another shame that must be borne by the royal family. It will join deeper shame in whispers among the court: those of a rogue bandit with royal blood never to be spoken of. But I am a bandit who has outsmarted you and your most loyal men. I wonder, will anyone rise to the challenge of recovering the crown jewels? Their theft is humiliating enough, but the inability to recover them will be an embarrassment for the ages, forever staining your legacy as Ruler of England.

Captain Ace Mullins

Mullins was clearly unafraid, continuing to taunt not only Burgess but King Charles himself.

Burgess looked up from the letter at his prisoner. "Why have you betrayed me?"

"I have never sworn anything to you, Captain Burgess. My loyalty resides as it always has—with the true heir to the throne, Captain Mullins."

"Captain Mullins is a traitorous pirate who has betrayed his king and country," Burgess growled. "As are you."

"Betrayal is all a matter of perception."

"Tell me where the crown jewels are hidden and I will ask the king to spare your life," Burgess lied.

The prisoner's mouth stretched into an arrogant grin before he spoke. "Captain Mullins told me you might make such a promise. I have no secrets to share, just as you have no assurances of mercy to offer."

"You would risk the king's wrath by taking Mullins's secret to your grave?"

"I am already dead, my lord."

"What are we to do with him, Captain?" one of the guards asked.

Burgess considered the question while he studied the insolent prisoner's face.

"Where exactly did you find him hiding?" Burgess said.

"There," the guard said, pointing down the tunnel toward a side egress.

"He was hiding just inside that tunnel."

It was Burgess's turn to grin. "Then there he shall spend eternity."

The prisoner's eyes widened as he realized what Burgess intended to do with him.

"Mercy, sir. I would rather have it over with," the prisoner pleaded.

Burgess pocketed the letter, then leaned in close so that his face nearly touched the prisoner's. "And that is exactly why I will not kill you quickly. You will die a traitor's death. Locked in this unholy place for all eternity, to contemplate the nature of your crimes. You have committed an unforgivable sin against the crown, and as such, against God himself."

Slowly, Burgess drew back from the man and turned to address his subordinates. "Chain him inside the tunnel, then seal it up from both ends."

"You'll never find the pirate king, or his secret," the traitor howled.

Burgess turned away and moved back up the tunnel toward the dungeons, listening to the screams of protest as they dragged the disgraced guard toward his final horror. The discovery of the traitor within the castle brought them no closer to the stolen jewels, or to Mullins himself, but it was a start. It meant that Mullins no longer had an inside accomplice. And the sealing off of the tunnel was more than a simple method of torture for a traitor. It meant Mullins would never again access the fortress above.

Burgess moved swiftly up the tunnel toward the castle. He had a letter from a pirate to deliver to his king.

43

Avery directed the driver to a high-end print shop she found online, about a five minute drive from the museum. The driver dropped her off, then took Carter and Harrison to scout out a hotel. Avery smiled at the clerk and asked about printing some photos to send to her folks back home. The clerk showed her how to print out the pictures on photo paper.

"What about paper?" Avery asked. "Is there a way to print out a photo I took of a cool old drawing on regular paper? Maybe a shade other than white?"

"Certainly. Like something on which you might print out an invitation?"

"That's exactly what I want."

The clerk led her to a bin of different colored sheets before excusing herself to assist another customer.

Avery selected a shade very near to the sepia tone of the map's parchment. She knew the high-def photo would capture some of the surface texture of the map, assuming the printer here was good enough. It took several tweaks of the settings before she obtained a quality copy. After examining it closely, Avery printed five more, allowing herself some insurance in case she botched the needed alterations.

Harrison was sitting out front in an unfamiliar car when she finished in the print shop.

"Where's the car and driver we used to get here?" Avery said.

"I sent him packing," Harrison said. "Didn't think it made sense to use a hired driver to commit a burglary. The fewer witnesses, the better. So I rented this."

"Good thinking," Avery said. "Any trouble finding a hotel?"

"None. And I think you'll like it. It's right on the water."

"Perfect. I just need to run into that hardware store." She pointed across the street.

The hotel staff recommended a fabulous restaurant within walking distance of the hotel. Ten minutes after arriving, they were seated on a deck overlooking the ocean. None of them discussed the evening's planned activity during dinner, preferring instead to make small talk while gazing at the twinkling lights of cruise ships in the distance.

As soon as the busboy departed with their dinner plates, Avery removed the protective sleeve containing the fake map from her bag and slid it across the table. "What do you think?"

"Jeez," Carter said. "It looks just like the real thing."

"How did you do that, Ave?" Harrison asked in amazement.

"I studied my photos. A crumple here, a crease there, a couple of strategically placed wine stains, and voila."

Harrison shook his head. "From pickpocketing to counterfeiting in mere hours. I hardly recognize you."

"Don't forget burglary, Harry," Carter said as he sipped his cabernet.

"She hasn't done that yet," Harrison grouched.

"I'm going to need your help for that, Harry," Avery said.

"I can't believe you're seriously going to break into a museum, Ave."

"Relax," Avery said. "It isn't like we're stealing anything."

"Oh good, because for a minute it sounded like you were going to engage my services in a burglary and theft."

"First of all, a burglary requires an unlawful entry for the purpose of committing another crime," Avery said.

"Yeah," Carter said. "This would be more like—trespassing."

"In order to steal a priceless map," Harrison said.

"I don't know how priceless it is, Harry," Avery said. "Do you? When you get right down to it, it's only half a map that nobody can read. And we're not stealing it, just borrowing it for a while. We'll return it safe and sound, I promise."

Harrison reached for the wine bottle. "I don't know why I let you talk me into this stuff."

An hour later, under cover of darkness, Avery and Carter stood at opposite corners of the museum's rear wall while Harrison worked the stubborn lock on the delivery doors with a pick set.

"Still all clear over here," Avery whisper-shouted.

"You really think this joint has the money for security?" Carter replied.

"Off-duty cops often come cheap," Harrison said. "But they also move slow, so just keep your eyes peeled." He kept his on the lock. "You're sure you disabled the entire system, Ave? I'm not keen on spending the rest of my life in a French prison."

"I told you, Harry," Avery said. "I hacked in and deactivated everything. The door sensors, surveillance cameras, motion detectors, everything."

"Oh, man, someone's coming!" Carter forgot to whisper, waving frantically at Harrison and Avery.

"I hope it worked, Avery." Harrison stood up and turned the knob on the steel door, pushing it open. "Because there's no going back now. Inside, fast and quiet."

Harrison shut the door behind them and locked it. Avery and Carter held their breath as the guard's flashlight—and whistling—reached the other side of the door.

The lock jiggled once. Twice. The third time was halfhearted, and the whistling retreated.

Blowing out long sighs, Avery and Carter turned to Harrison.

"He'll be back in a few minutes," Harry said. "Let's get what you're looking for and get out of here."

Using the low-light settings on the flashlight apps on their phones, they retraced their steps to the Mullins collection room. It took several minutes for them to locate the trays in the back room where only Simon had been earlier.

"Here it is," Avery said, producing the glass case containing the map. She unlocked it and removed the original, then slipped the counterfeit copy from the protective sleeve and positioned it in the case.

"Man." Carter shook his head. "Inside the case it looks exactly like the real thing."

Avery nodded. "And unless someone opens the case and actually touches the paper, there is no way to tell."

"I think you're a little bit scary, you're so smart," Carter said.

Avery secured the lock, then slid the original map inside the plastic document protector and replaced the case on the shelf where she'd found it, flashing a grin at Carter. "But you're glad of it, right?"

He nodded.

"Okay," Avery said. "Let's get out of here."

"What about the key you swiped from Simon?" Carter said. "You made a copy, didn't you?"

"Oh yeah," Avery said. "I almost forgot." She looked around the room for a moment before deciding to simply slide the original halfway under a corner of the area rug near where she had intentionally collided with the curator.

"What exactly is that supposed to accomplish?" Harrison said.

"Simon will simply think he dropped it when he ran into me," Avery said. "Trust me, Harry. He was so enamored with Carter he won't think twice about it."

They hurried through the museum, retracing their steps to the delivery entrance. As they neared the doors, Avery stopped in her tracks, immediately ducking out of sight. There was a vehicle idling in the lot with its marker lights illuminated.

A police vehicle.

"Maybe he knows we're in here," she said.

"You have got to be kidding me," Harrison said as he scooched down on the opposite side of the door.

"I thought you disabled the alarm," Carter said.

"I did," Avery said. "I disabled everything."

"Then why is there a police car sitting in the lot?" Carter hissed.

"I don't know."

"Don't get your shorts in a bunch, Carter," Harrison said. "It's probably the watchman we saw earlier either on his lunch break or taking a nap."

Avery crawled over to a nearby window where she could get a better look at the car and its occupant.

"Harrison's right," Avery said. "The guard is just sitting there drinking coffee."

"Great," Carter said. "Let's hope he gets a call or something. I don't want to spend my night locked inside a museum."

"Are you worried the exhibits are gonna come to life, slick?" Harrison said. "No stuffed tigers or dinosaurs in here."

Avery snorted.

It took fifteen minutes for the police officer to leave, and they wasted no time exiting the building, securing the door, and hurrying back to the car once the coast was clear. In the back seat, Avery used her laptop to reconnect to the museum's security system. In six minutes, everything was back up and running.

"We all good?" Harrison asked.

"It'll be like we were never there," Avery said.

"What happens if someone notices the cameras weren't recording for a period of time?" Carter said.

"They'll assume there was a temporary outage," Avery said.

"Let's hope you're right," Harrison said.

"I am."

They drove directly to the hotel and retired to Avery's room for a celebratory nightcap. Harrison poured drinks, while Avery and Carter laid out both pieces of the Mullins map.

"The entire map, the star amulet, everything we need," Carter said. "You really think we'll be able to find what Jeff was searching for?"

Avery looked up from the map. "I'd say the fact that we're still being followed means someone thinks we're on the right track."

"You might be right," Carter said.

"What's the plan for tomorrow?" Harrison asked as he handed them their drinks.

"I'm not sure yet," Avery said. "I was really hoping that we would hear back from Jeff's fence by now."

As if in response to her comment, Carter's cell phone chimed with an incoming text message.

"Are you psychic, too?" Carter asked, waving the phone. "The collector has agreed to meet with us tomorrow at one o'clock if we can get there by then."

"Where?" Avery said.

"The address is in Santorini."

"Greece?" Harrison asked.

Carter nodded. "He said the buyer goes by the name Papa."

"You're not serious," Harrison said.

"I'm only telling you what he said, Harry."

Avery picked up the amulet. "Tell him to let Papa know we'll be there."

"I'll have Marco pick us up at sunrise," Harrison said.

44

It was just after noon when they touched down in Santorini. Avery was surprised to find that Papa, the collector, had sent a car for them, since they had never met—or even spoken.

The passenger compartment was both luxurious and perfectly air conditioned. Bottled water was chilling in a cooler alongside ice and spotless glasses.

The driver, who barely said hello, kept the privacy panel up during the half-hour trip to the village of Akrotiri, located on the far side of the island. All three passengers were mesmerized by the gorgeous vistas. Every glimpse of the stunning turquoise Mediterranean only served to stoke Avery's excitement—the chase really was thrilling all on its own. A quick look at Carter confirmed that he was feeling the same way. She couldn't read the expression on Harrison's face, though. Something about him looked off. She knew he was struggling with her method of retrieving the remaining half of Captain Mullins's map.

Avery turned around in her seat to look at the road behind them. No one followed. Among many upsides to jumping in a private jet for a last-minute trip to Greece was that the likelihood of anyone tailing them was near zero. Erring on the side of caution, Avery had scanned each of their devices, as well as everyone's shoes, on the way to the airport in Marseille. She'd learned the hard way that she could never really be too vigilant.

The car slowed as their driver pulled off the main road into the mouth of a gated driveway. Avery watched as the driver extended his arm out the window and pressed a button on a pole-mounted voice box.

"I'm back," he barked.

They watched as the gate rolled back on its track, thick trees and foliage lining the curved driveway. The driver rolled over the patterned stone drive and around a bend. As they crested the edge of the cliff, the compound came into view. Set into the hillside like a shiny, modern pueblo, the multi-level mansion was painted brilliant white with large, tinted glass windows overlooking the Mediterranean Sea.

The driver stopped just short of a portico and exited the vehicle. He immediately circled the car and opened Avery's door for her.

"You must be Ms. Turner," a voice said from behind her.

She turned to see a short man with bronze skin and a beaming smile. He wore white shorts, tennis shoes, a cerulean short-sleeve dress shirt, and a straw Panama hat. She wasn't exactly sure what she'd expected a wealthy aristocrat from a Grecian island to look like, but the real thing was close.

"I am Sebastian Papadakis, but my friends just call me Papa."

"Great to meet you, Papa," Avery said as she shook his hand, then turned to introduce Carter and Harrison. "This is—"

"Mr. Harrison and Mr. Mosley," Papadakis said before she could finish. "I can't tell you what a pleasure it is to meet all of you. You must be hungry after your trip. Come. I've arranged lunch on the veranda."

As they followed him inside, Carter leaned into Avery and whispered, "Were you expecting expensive suits and bodyguards, or was that just me?"

"Kind of, but we live on an island and we don't walk around dressed up all the time."

The view from the veranda was breathtaking. Perched out over the water next to an infinity pool, the spotless area featured a shower, a half dozen teak wood chaise lounge chairs, and a built-in grill and wet bar. In the corner sat a glass-topped dining table with matching teak wood chairs, already set for four.

"Please," Papadakis said as he gestured to the table. "Make yourselves comfortable."

"Thank you," Avery said, as she pulled out a chair and sat down.

"Lunch will be ready in a few minutes; may I interest you in something from the bar?"

"A glass of wine would be lovely," Avery said as a servant materialized from behind a gleaming white stone partition.

"Wine works for me too," Carter said.

"And you?" Papadakis turned to Harrison.

"I'll take a beer, if you have one."

"Ah, a man after my own heart. Beer it is."

They made small talk until the drinks were served.

"Salute," Papadakis said as he raised his glass.

"This is fabulous," Harrison said after tasting the straw-colored beer bubbling in his pilsner glass. "What is it?"

"It's called Mythos and it's brewed right here in Greece. It is immensely popular."

"I can see why," Harrison said before taking another swig.

"Mr. Papadakis—" Avery began before he cut her off.

"Papa, please."

"Papa, we are grateful that you were so willing to entertain us. And quite frankly a bit—"

"Surprised?" Papadakis said, interrupting her again. "Given that we haven't met or spoken before?"

"Well, yes," Avery said.

"Ms. Turner, I have a passion for fine old things. People call me a collector, but the truth is it is an addiction. I have a deep fascination with history, and everything connected to it."

"I certainly understand that," Carter said.

"As soon as I learned who it was who was enquiring about the ring, I knew we had to meet."

"Did you know my friend Jeff?" Carter said.

"I never had the pleasure, Mr. Mosley. Our contact was indirect through money transfers. And please allow me to offer my condolences."

Carter nodded.

"You heard what happened to him?" Harrison said.

"Our mutual acquaintance thought I might be in danger as well," Papa said. "Who's hungry?" Papadakis said as another servant arrived with a large metal tray.

They dined on seafood and pasta while enjoying the sunshine and ocean breeze.

"I understand you have questions about the ring," Papadakis said as he pushed his empty plate away.

Avery nodded. "I do. I want to know if you think it's genuine."

"One hundred percent," Papadakis said.

"I've read that it wasn't uncommon back then to have copies made of precious jewelry, in case a coach was attacked by highwaymen or a home was burglarized," Avery said. "How can you be so sure the ring you have is the original?"

Papadakis grinned and signaled to his servants to clear the table. "Would you like to see my ring?"

45

Papadakis led them inside and down two flights of stairs before turning down a long white hallway. After several minutes Avery realized they had walked much deeper into the structure than should have been possible unless some of it had been carved into the cliff like a bunker.

Papadakis stopped at a large steel door, placing his thumb on an electronic keypad. Avery heard a clank as the door's mechanical lock disengaged. Papadakis pushed it open and waved them inside.

The room reminded Avery of the document room inside the museum in Marseille. The lighting was strategically placed to highlight each of the treasures contained within without exposing the items to damaging levels of light.

"This is one of my many collection rooms," Papadakis said.

"Do you have many collections?" Avery asked.

"Countless," Papadakis said.

"Is that a real suit of armor?" Harrison asked.

"Indeed, it is." Papadakis beamed like a proud father. "This particular suit dates back to the fifteenth century."

"Wow," Carter said as he approached the display. "It's hard to believe people actually wore these."

"Not everyone did," Papadakis said. "Most soldiers wore regular clothing and carried swords and wooden shields. The armor was reserved for those of higher stature."

"How much does it weigh?" Harrison asked.

"This one weighs about twenty-one kilograms but some of the suits from around that time are said to have weighed as much as twenty-five."

"And what would that be in the US?" Harrison asked.

"Harry is metrically challenged," Avery explained.

Papadakis laughed. "About fifty-five pounds, Mr. Harrison."

"I can't imagine wearing that much gear into battle," Carter said.

Papadakis caught Avery's gaze as it drifted to a lighted table at the room's center. Mounted atop a small pedestal under glass was the ruby ring. The crimson gem shone brightly, bathing everything around it in a rosy glow.

"Would you like to see it up close, Ms. Turner?"

"Very much."

Papadakis unlocked the glass cube and lifted it off the pedestal. "You asked how I know the ring is genuine. King Charles was known to carry herbs that he thought would help him live longer. Because of that he commissioned the ring to be fashioned with a hidden locket beneath the ruby."

"I know," Avery said impatiently, waiting for him to hand it to her. "I found that in the description on the Tower of London's website. But even that could have been copied, correct?"

"That is true," Papadakis said. "Though a fake this old would have been made before that information was public."

"You might be surprised what a smart person can do there," Carter said, looking at Avery.

"I might at that, Mr. Mosley. However, I know my history, and the stone mounted in the king's true ring contained a flaw that would prevent anyone from making a believable fake."

Papadakis slid open a hidden drawer at the front of the table and produced a glass document protector much like the one that had housed the museum map. Avery stepped forward to read.

"What is that?" Carter asked as he and Harrison moved in on either side of them.

"This is the legal description of the stone from the king's jeweler dated 1647. As you can see, the flaw is described in great detail."

Avery nodded as she read. The age of the document was obvious, and the description of the ruby's flaw was incredibly detailed and specific. Papadakis handed Avery an antique jeweler's loupe.

"See for yourself," he said.

Avery bent down and studied the ruby carefully from several different angles. The flaw was there, exactly as described. If she accepted the document as genuine, then there was little doubt that the ring was the one that had belonged to King Charles.

"You see?" Papadakis said.

Avery nodded, her eyes wide. "You're right. This ring was stolen from the king."

"Nearly four hundred years ago," Papadakis added.

"So, that means the ring in the Tower today must be a copy?" Carter asked.

"That would stand to reason," Papadakis said.

"I wonder if they know," Harrison said.

Avery paused to consider what this really meant. The pirate's secret... It wasn't as if her idea of hunting for Mullins's map was terribly original. And what if it wasn't his map at all? What if he, too, had been simply searching for stolen jewels, not harboring them as Avery and Carter had thought? Had someone double crossed the infamous pirate? Beat him at his own game? There were just too many questions still unanswered. And they weren't likely to find the answers here. Not from a man who had to pay a fortune for a piece of treasure that Jeff had likely found on his own.

"I can't thank you enough for showing us the ring, Papa," Avery said. "And for your hospitality."

"You are most welcome. I must admit I was intrigued when I found out who was inquiring about the ring."

"I'm afraid we've been searching for something that might not exist," Avery said.

"Well, at least we now know," Carter said.

"Either way, there are still three large well-trained mercenaries and a sniper on the trail of this ring," Harrison said. "You should take extra care."

"And the British government," Avery added, her face falling. She had promised Rowan she'd find the ring, and here it was, but should she tell him?

Papa hadn't done anything but buy it. And Avery had a hunch that whoever told Rowan to enlist her and Carter wasn't the sort of person who'd buy it back from Papa.

"Oh really?" Papa asked.

"MI5 has an agent looking for it," Avery said. "It's pretty hush-hush, and the ring didn't seem to be all they wanted, but you should be careful."

"I appreciate your concern. Both of you," Papadakis said with a wink. "But I assure you that I am quite safe here. Home court advantage, you see."

Papadakis bid them goodbye and instructed his driver to return them to the airport where Marco was refueled and waiting. Avery hadn't spoken two words since they left the compound. As soon as they were on the plane, Carter pounced.

"Okay, Avery, spill it. I know something is going on in that head of yours. I can practically hear the gears turning."

"Yeah," Harrison said. "I've never seen you leave a place so quickly. I figured you'd want to see more of Papa's collection. What gives?"

"As soon as I realized we were looking at the genuine ring, something occurred to me that hadn't before. What if Mullins didn't do what I thought? What if it wasn't him who copied the king's ring at all?"

"I don't understand what you're getting at," Carter said.

"What if King Charles replaced the ring with a fake?"

"Why on earth would he do that, Ave?" Harrison said.

"To hide the fact that it had been stolen," Avery said.

Harrison rubbed his chin. "So he didn't want someone to know it was gone, I see that, but how do you know it was stolen? Maybe Mullins made a map to something entirely different and this whole thing is a coincidence."

Avery leaned forward and held up one hand. "Follow me here: We've been saying this whole time that we don't understand why Jeff was killed, why people keep chasing and shooting at and spying on us, over this one jewel, no matter what it is or where it came from or who might want it. That's the whole reason we thought Rowan was right and Jeff was onto something else Mullins had hidden, right?"

"Right," Carter said.

"I've been reading about Mullins all week," Avery said. "And it turns out he didn't just think he was *a* bastard son of King Charles I, he thought he was the king's *firstborn* son."

"So?" Carter asked.

"So what if, maybe, a smart guy who became a pirate, who was convinced Charles II had stolen his birthright, stole the crown jewels after the restoration? They were more than pretty baubles then, they were a symbol of the king's power and divine right to rule England. What if that's the pirate's real secret?"

"You think Mullins stole the crown jewels." Harry sat back in his seat. "Like, *the* crown jewels. All of them?"

Avery nodded. "It would sure be worthy of MI5 being put on the case when the ring turned up, wouldn't it?"

"Wouldn't that be the first hit on a Google Search about this Mullins dude?" Carter asked.

"Not if Charles had them remade and replaced before news of the theft could get out," Avery said. That was the last piece that had clicked in Papa's basement, convincing her she had figured out a four-hundred-year-old secret.

Marco stuck his head out of the cockpit. "I'm ready to take off, Ms. Avery. Any special instructions?"

"Take us back to London, Marco."

46

The first hour of the return flight from Greece to London was uneventful and smooth, Avery deeply entranced by her laptop. She appreciated Marco's uncanny ability to calculate the correct altitude to ensure a comfortable ride on almost every flight. Harrison and Carter left Avery to her own devices until finally their curiosity got the better of them and they sat down in the seats directly across from her.

"Well, this looks like an ambush," Avery said as she looked up. "What's up?"

"Harry and I were wondering what you think might be our next move," Carter said. "I imagine you've got some ideas."

"I have many ideas," Avery said.

"Any that I'll like?" Harrison asked.

"I doubt it."

Harrison shook his head. "How did I know you were going to say that?"

"Because she got that same look in her eyes right before we left Papa's place," Carter said.

"What look?" Avery said.

"That look that says you just doubled down, and nothing is going to get in your way," Harrison said. "Not even common sense."

"So?" Carter said. "What gives?"

"I've been messaging with MaryAnn, and she thinks I might be onto something," Avery said. "She's our history expert and she said my theory isn't that farfetched."

"But if you're right—if—I'm concerned about what you're going to want to do next," Harrison said.

Avery sat back in her cream leather recliner. "Have you noticed that the attacks have stopped since Carter threw those men off the train?"

"They fell," Carter corrected.

"Whatever you say, Rambo," Harrison said, patting Carter on the shoulder.

"You and MaryAnn think they stopped trying to take us out intentionally?" Carter said.

"I do," Avery said. "I certainly don't think we've outrun them. Not after all the trouble someone has gone to trying to stop us."

"You think they've changed tactics, shadowing instead of attacking, hoping we'll lead them to the real crown jewels," Harrison said.

"That's exactly what I think," Avery said. "I think whoever is behind killing Jeff has already figured out that Jeff unknowingly found himself on the trail of the crown jewels. And I think that means they must know about the fakes. Or at least that they suspect it."

"Do you know how crazy that sounds, Avery?" Carter said. "That's conspiracy theory 101."

"Maybe not, actually," Harrison said. "I know a fair bit about British history and I've been thinking about what Avery said. Charles II lived in some pretty uncertain times. His subjects' opinion of his worthiness to rule changed like the wind. A theft like the one we're discussing would make headlines today, sure, but in a couple of weeks the press would move on and so would everyone else. Back then, showing weakness would have been the king's undoing. Having the crown jewels stolen out from under him would've painted Charles as vulnerable and ineffective, not worthy of the respect of his subjects, and certainly not a monarch blessed by the Almighty."

"Exactly," Avery said. "If we believe that Ace Mullins really did abscond with the jewels, Charles would have had every reason to commission replicas. France was ready to go to war with the British. Other leaders felt the empire was weakening after the whole Cromwell rule thing following Charles I's execution. A king as desperate as Charles II would likely resort to almost anything to hold on to his throne and keep his nation at peace."

"Yeah, but even if you're right, do you have any idea how difficult—no strike that, impossible—it would be to keep a secret like that for centuries? Even in the strictest of confidence, there would have been those who knew. Guards, servants, not to mention the jeweler or jewelers commissioned to create the replicas."

"That was a brutal time in history," Harrison said. "There were ways to keep people from talking."

"And maybe it wouldn't have needed to come to that," Avery said. "This was the 1600s. Maybe the few people who knew did talk about it. It's not like someone could blast it out to the whole world on Insta or TikTok back then. The circle of people who could've known was pretty small. If they told other people, the whole story could have been discounted as rumor or some wild conspiracy that was simply forgotten over time."

"I don't know," Carter said. "They're still talking about the Warren Commission."

"Yeah, but that wasn't three hundred and fifty years ago," Avery said.

"Suppose you're right, Ave," Harrison said. "How did Jeff find out about it, then? Something must have put him on the trail."

"That is a really good question," Avery said.

"I wonder if Jeff even knew what he had stumbled onto." Carter shook his head. "It could've just been blind luck. That turned out to be pretty bad luck, really. The exact same way Jeff seemed to happen onto everything else in his life."

"I still don't understand why they killed him," Avery said. "That's the nick in my theory—if I'm right about them following us, why kill Jeff?"

She turned to Harrison, who shook his head. "No idea. Let's say you are right about all of this, Ave. How exactly do you propose we find the real jewels?"

"I've been thinking about that, and I think the key lies in studying these maps. I've already found something I overlooked before."

"What's that?" Carter said.

"There was more than one treasure map. Here, let me show you." Avery spun the laptop around for them to see, then pulled up a photoshop program displaying the two map halves they'd recovered side by side. "Here are the pieces we found. Watch what happens when I try to merge them together."

"They overlap by a third," Harrison said, wide-eyed.

"Then there must be at least two of these in existence," Carter said.

"By lining up two different pin dots, I can create one complete image of the map," Avery said as she manipulated them into place over one another, then merged the images.

"How do we know that both maps are identical?" Carter said. "And why should we assume there are only two?"

"We shouldn't," Avery said. "But we've got to work with what we have, and right now this is it."

"And we still need to figure out how Ace's necklace interacts with this," Harrison said.

"I think I might have some ideas on that too," Avery said.

47

Avery returned to her research while Carter and Harrison retreated to their own seats to grab some shut-eye. After several hours of researching map keys that got nowhere, she gave up and focused on loading the map images and known data obtained from the logbook into the DiveNav program on her laptop. After an hour or so, the program returned two possible locations, both in a crowded neighborhood in the West End of London.

Avery looked around. Harrison was sound asleep and snoring. She got up and quietly made her way past Harrison and over to Carter's seat. He appeared to be resting with his eyes closed until she noticed the Bluetooth earbuds and his foot tapping to the beat of some unheard tune.

"Hey," she said as she gently shook him until his eyes opened.

"What's up?"

"Jeff's fence friend has been helpful. I mean, without him we wouldn't know the ring Jeff found was real."

"I guess. What are you getting at?"

"Do you think you could text him again?"

"Why? What more can he do for us?"

"I'm wondering if he might know a good thief."

Carter sat upright in the seat. "A good thief. Kind of an oxymoron, isn't it?"

"You know what I mean. Do you think he could put us in touch with an experienced thief?"

"I'm sure he can. The question is, will he?"

"And here's another question," Harrison said, no longer sleeping as he leaned over the seat in front of them. "Why do we want to talk to a good thief?"

Avery looked back and forth between them. Both sets of brows raised, both mouths set in a disapproving line.

She swallowed hard. "We need to steal the ring that's in the Tower."

"Are you crazy?" Harrison bellowed.

"Avery, the Tower of London is one of the most secure buildings in the world," Carter said. "How in the world do you think we—who have never stolen anything bigger than a key or a stick of gum—are going to pull that off?"

"Why don't you just use one of those loupe thingies to look at it in its display case, instead of stealing it?" Harrison asked.

"It wouldn't work, Harry. No one could see any detail from it through a display case. Besides, we wouldn't really be stealing it. Just borrowing."

"Yeah, like the map you 'borrowed' from the museum. How's that return going?"

"I haven't finished with it yet."

"Ave, if I didn't know better I would think you've completely lost your mind. Money can't buy your way out of the trouble you'd be looking at if you got caught. I can't even bear to think what Val would say if—" Harrison threw his hands up before finishing his thought. Avery knew he was trying hard not to say something he would later regret.

"I just need someone who knows about this stuff to look at it, Harry. Knowing what we're looking for and where it came from might help us narrow down where the rest of the treasure might be. Plus, it will make it easier to authenticate the find if Papa is right about his ring."

Harrison simply stared at her without speaking.

"I have no intention of keeping it, Harry. My mother always trusted me. Now I need you to trust me too."

"You know I trust you, Ave. It isn't that. And Val would be so proud of how smart you are, like she always was. Like I am."

"But?" Avery asked, unblinking.

"I'm not going to be a part of this, Ave. I can't be. But I guess I won't interfere either." With that, Harrison returned to his seat.

Carter pulled out his phone and turned to Avery. "You really want me to text Jeff's fence again?"

"I do. But I'd understand if you didn't want any part of this either."

"Want? Not really. But to heck with that. We're partners, remember? Besides, I got you into this."

"I can't walk away, Carter. The historical significance of this one is too big."

Avery watched as Carter began to compose his text message. He paused and looked up at her.

"Yep, Jeff would have liked you, Avery," Carter said. "He would have liked you a lot."

48

It was after midnight by the time they touched down at Heathrow. Harrison had booked them a three-bedroom presidential suite at the Four Seasons Hotel London on Park Lane. The fifth-floor suite overlooked Hyde Park and was only four miles from the Tower Bridge.

MaryAnn had taken care of their transportation from the airport to the hotel, so a car and driver were waiting as they cleared customs with their bags. They rode in silence through the darkened streets of London, arriving at the hotel just before one o'clock in the morning. Avery checked in at the front desk while Carter and Harrison shlepped the bags into the lobby.

They were riding the lift to the fifth floor when Carter's phone chimed with an incoming text message.

"Is that Jeff's guy?" Avery asked.

"Yup," Carter said. "He wants to meet us tomorrow morning at nine."

"Where?" Avery asked as the elevator doors slid open.

"The Tower Bridge."

"What are the chances of being thrown into the Thames?" Avery asked.

"I've got your back," Carter said.

"Tell him we'll see him there," Avery said.

True to his word, Harrison said nothing.

Despite her exhaustion, Avery tossed and turned most of the night. She had finally fallen into a deep slumber when her phone rang, waking her at seven thirty. The caller ID showed a British country code and a number she didn't recognize.

"Hello, this is Avery Turner," she croaked.

"Ms. Turner, this is Constable Paine calling from Blakeney. I hope I'm not calling at an inconvenient time."

"Not at all," Avery said after clearing her throat. "What can I do for you, Constable?"

"You had asked me to let you know if we had any luck in determining an approximate age of the bones you found. Well, we've got a result that I think you'll find interesting. Accounting for submersion in salt water, we've dated the remains as being more than one hundred fifty years old."

"Wow," Avery said.

"My thought exactly. We are working with a professor of history at Oxford, who has long been interested in cold case files, to see if we might be able to figure out who it was. I just thought you might like to know what you folks stumbled onto could be historically significant."

"Thank you so much for keeping me in the loop. I really appreciate it."

"My pleasure, Ms. Turner."

After ending the call, Avery picked up the hotel phone and placed a room service order for coffee and fruit. As she stepped into the huge walk-in shower, she couldn't help wondering whose remains she had found. Was it a criminal on the run who'd met their grisly end in the depths of the North Sea? Or just a diver who had bad luck with the current? Or maybe something else altogether?

She worked her hair into a lather under the warm spray as Harrison's words about her mother echoed in her head. Harry was probably right. Val most likely would have disapproved of her plan to execute a high-tech heist of the ruby ring from the crown jewel collection in the Tower. But if Valerie had taught her anything, it was that the only person she could fully trust was herself. If she was going to finish what Jeff started and solve the mystery surrounding the crown jewels, she had to go all in. Regardless of what Harry or anyone else thought.

The fruit went untouched because everyone was too nervous about the meeting. Avery and Carter settled for coffee to-go and a short ride in a black cab to the bridge, while Harrison said he'd amuse himself until they got back.

"We don't even know this guy's name?" Avery asked as they looked around.

"He wouldn't give it," Carter said.

"What does he look like?"

Carter shrugged. "Search me. All I know is he said he'll know us when he sees us. If there aren't any cops around, he'll approach us."

They spent the next twenty minutes scanning the faces of passersby while sipping coffee.

"I think I've made him," Avery said quietly.

"Where?" Carter looked around, following her gaze.

"Don't be obvious about it," Avery said. "But I think he may be that short muscular guy standing down there." She nodded her head in the direction she wanted him to look.

"Are you talking about the tatted-up guy with the spiky blond hair?" Carter asked.

"He looks like James Marsters," Avery said.

"Who?" Carter asked.

"That guy on *Buffy the Vampire Slayer*," Avery said. "Spike."

"You watch Buffy?" Carter's jaw hung a little loose. "I wouldn't have thought it was cerebral enough for you."

"Some of the best dialogue in the history of TV, and monsters to boot. Who wouldn't?" Avery said. "Look alive. Here he comes."

The Spike lookalike in question strolled over near them and lit a cigarette. He leaned his forearms on the railing while pretending to admire the River Thames.

"Mosley?" he said after a moment.

"Are you Jeff's friend?" Carter said.

"Friend? Probably not. Business acquaintance? Most def. I understand he met an untimely end."

Avery nodded.

"Sorry to hear it. He had a gift, Jeff did."

"You don't know anything about what happened to him, do you?" Carter asked.

The blond guy shook his head. "Jeff and I did a lot of business over the last year and a half. Why would I want him dead?"

Carter considered that for a minute before he stepped forward and offered his hand. "I'm Carter Mosley. What do we call you?"

"Call me Shannon."

"Okay, Shannon," Avery said.

"And you are?" he asked through a plume of bluish smoke.

"Avery. Avery Turner. Now, are you going to help us or not?"

"Depends on what we're talking about, Avery. What are we talking about?"

"We're looking for a master thief. And we're willing to pay you very well for your time and assistance."

"What makes you think I'm a master thief?"

"I don't. But I'm hoping you know a few," Avery said calmly.

"Let's say I am the person you are looking for. How big a score are we talking?"

"We have no—" Carter began.

"Bigger than anything you could imagine," Avery interrupted.

"You might be surprised how much I can imagine." Shannon tossed away the butt of his cigarette and immediately lit another. "My question is, is it bigger than anything you've ever seen?"

Avery cocked her head to one side. "What do you mean?"

"I mean, I do my homework and I know who you are and what you do. Avery Turner and Carter Mosley, famous treasure hunters from the States."

"So, does that mean you'll help us?" Carter said.

"Depends," Shannon said.

"On?" Avery said.

"On whether you're serious about this thing being more valuable than anything you've ever seen. If you aren't just having me on, I'll help you."

"Great," Avery said.

"For fifteen percent," Shannon said.

"Three percent," Avery said.

"Ten," Shannon said.

"You don't even know what it is," Avery said. "Five."

"I'll do it for seven percent of the take, or I walk right now."

"Done." Avery stuck out her hand.

Shannon hesitated a moment before shaking Avery's hand. "We have a deal. Now, follow me."

"Where are we going?" Carter said.

"My office," Shannon said. "I don't like discussing business out in the open."

49

Shannon led them through a maze of streets away from the bridge to a small, dingy pub called The Slaughtered Lamb. The three of them slid into an empty snug at the back of the establishment.

"This is your office?" Carter asked.

"Don't knock it, mate." Shannon gestured to the bartender.

"What can I bring ya?" the bartender asked as he approached them.

"My usual," Shannon said.

"Whiskey it is. And the rest of you?"

"I'm starving," Carter said. "Do you serve breakfast?"

"Of course. A traditional English breakfast."

"One order for each of us?" Avery asked.

"To drink?"

"Coffee for me," Avery said.

"I'll take a pint of stout," Carter said.

"What did I just order?" Carter asked after the bartender departed.

"Bacon, eggs, tomatoes, mushrooms, sausages, toast, beans, and black pudding," Avery said.

"Black pudding?" Carter wrinkled his nose.

"Don't forget the bubble and squeak," Shannon said.

"I'm afraid to ask," Carter said.

"Potatoes and cabbage, mate," Shannon said.

"Why do they call it bubble and squeak?" Avery said.

"It's the sound it makes while being cooked," Shannon said.

The bartender wasted no time returning with their beverages.

"Cheers." Shannon raised his glass and downed it in one gulp.

"Let's discuss qualifications," Avery said.

"Qualifications?" Shannon asked with a wry grin. "Like what?"

"Like circumventing high-tech surveillance systems, tight security, opening a vacuum-sealed case with a time lock and pressure alarm, and getting in and out of a verifiable fortress undetected."

Shannon laughed and turned to Carter. "What are you lot trying to steal, mate, the *Mona Lisa*?"

Carter didn't smile. Neither did Avery. Shannon's grin faded and his gaze returned to Avery. "You're serious."

"I never joke about treasure," Avery said. "Do you have the skills I require?"

"Let's just say you've come to the right man. But I'll need to make some arrangements."

"How much time do you need?" Avery said.

"Give me the afternoon and we can meet up again later," Shannon said.

"Where?" Carter said.

"Give me a sec." Shannon slid from the booth, pulled out his cell phone, and walked toward the men's room.

"Who do you think he's calling?" Carter said.

"Hopefully not the cavalry," Avery said. "The way this week has gone, I wouldn't be shocked if he came back with cuffs and told us he's an undercover cop."

"What?" Carter's eyes popped wide.

"Relax, Carter," Avery said. "I'm kidding."

Shannon returned several minutes later. "It's all set. I'll meet you tonight at six."

"Where?" Avery said.

"Dinner by Heston in Hyde Park. Black tie. On me."

"On you?" Carter asked, clearly surprised.

"Sounds lovely," Avery said. "We'll see you then."

They finished breakfast, then headed outside to hail a cab.

"Back to the hotel?" Carter asked.

"Actually, I had another stop in mind," Avery said as she raised her hand and hailed an approaching taxi.

"I'm almost afraid to ask," Carter said.

"Thought we'd take a tour of the Tower," Avery said.

"Why?"

"Recon."

Per Avery's instructions, the taxi dropped them one block from the Tower of London. She had no idea what type of outside closed-circuit systems they might employ, if any, but it was far better to be overly cautious than not cautious enough.

She pulled two ball caps out of her bag and handed one to Carter. She tucked her hair up under hers while Carter simply pulled his hat down low over his eyes.

After paying for a walking tour of the museum, they fell in with a large group and began their reconnaissance of the Tower. Avery snapped hundreds of photos, as she wasn't entirely sure which things would be important and which wouldn't. They toured the prison and torture chambers first, saving the Jewel House for last. The guidebook Avery had paid twenty pounds for in the gift shop boasted that the Tower of London was the most secure fortress in the modern world, housing a collection of priceless jewels valued between three and five billion pounds. She pointed out the value to Carter.

"Wow," Carter said with a whistle. "That's a lot of pounds."

"And far more than the single ring we've seen," Avery said. "Though Harry would say it's also a lot of years in prison if something goes wrong."

"Surely they would have added to the collection since old Ace Mullins's day," Carter said.

Avery snapped twice as many pictures in the Jewel House as any other place in the Tower, including several surreptitiously from beneath display cases. She waited until the throng of people had pressed in around her—to follow along with the docent's descriptions of what they were seeing—before making her move each time.

"Dammit," Avery said as she dropped to her knees, barely drawing a glance from the other tourists.

"What are you doing, Ave?" Carter whispered as he knelt beside her.

"I'm trying to find my contact lens," she whispered back.

"But you don't—"

Avery glared at him until he fell quiet. She moved a cloth table skirt out of the way, then crawled forward far enough to get a look underneath one of the display cases. There was a black box mounted to the underside of the stand. An LED light glowed green at the center of the box. She had no idea what the box monitored specifically but there was no doubt it was tied into part of the anti-theft system. She snapped a quick picture of it.

"May I help you, miss?" a voice said from behind her.

Avery quickly backed out from where she had crawled to see a security guard standing above her.

"I found it," she said as she stood, pretending to hold an item in her hand.

The guard looked confused. "Found what?"

"My contact lens. I need to rinse this off. Where is the washroom?"

"The lavatories are this way," he said, pointing toward a sign on the wall. "I'll show you."

"There's really no need. I can find it."

"I insist," he said.

She followed him away from the crowd.

"There you go," he said.

"Thank you so much," she said as she hurried past him and into the women's bathroom.

Avery hung out in the bathroom long enough to sell her story. When she stepped back into the hall, the guard was gone. She backtracked until she located Carter.

"Where have you been?" he asked.

"Just a little snag," she said. "It's all good now. Come on. I've seen enough."

As they passed through the exit, a security guard called out.

"Miss? Did everything work out with your contacts?"

"Perfectly," she said, painting on a smile to hide her nerves. "Thanks again."

"My pleasure."

"Jeez, Avery," Carter said as they walked out of the museum. "Cutting it a little close, aren't you? You're going to have me sounding like Harrison with all his dire warnings about prisons. I look washed out in orange."

"Next stop." Avery brandished the DiveNav. "The X on this map makes almost no sense."

Hopping onto the first trolley they saw, they caught a ride to London's West End.

50

Tension thrummed in the air like a drumbeat, though nobody wanted to mention it first. Avery knew the DiveNav had led them right back to where Jeff had been murdered only days before, but she didn't know how to apologize to Carter for it.

"What are we doing here?" Carter said.

"This is where the DiveNav pointed us," Avery said. "I'm so sorry."

Carter cleared his throat, shaking his head. "If the DiveNav says something is here, then something is here, I bet," he said. "Jeff was probably staying around here for a reason."

"Other than hiding or being broke?" Avery asked.

"Let's knock on some doors," Carter said.

They poked around a few of the nearby apartment buildings but turned up nothing. In the fourth, they found the building super. Carter showed the man Jeff's picture.

"Jeff, huh? Yeah, I recognize him, but not the name. I can't remember the name he gave me, but I know it wasn't Jeff. Heard the poor bloke got himself killed messing about with some bad elements. Damn shame. He still owed me rent money." The super's eyes narrowed with suspicion. "Why are you asking about a shady character like him? Did he owe you money too?"

"Nah," Carter said. "We're actually looking for a guy Jeff might have met with recently. You didn't happen to see him with anyone strange over the last couple of weeks, did you?"

"Son, everyone is strange in this neighborhood. But now that you mention it, yeah, I did see a guy with him who kind of stood out."

"Stood out how?" Avery said.

"Well, the guy I'm thinking of visited Jeff a couple of times. He was squirrelly, looked out of place. Dressed like a college professor. Tweed jacket. Carried a briefcase like a shield. Not a lot of briefcase carriers in this neighborhood."

"Can you remember anything else about the man?" Carter asked. "Height, weight, anything?"

"About my height, I guess. I'm about 165 centimeters."

"Five foot five," Avery said.

"Anything else?" Carter asked.

"Gray hair and glasses. Matter of fact, I saw Jeff giving him money. That was the last time I saw either of them—I remember thinking your mate owed me and he was paying this other bloke, so I wasn't going to take no excuses from him." The super shook his head.

"That tracks," Carter said. "Jeff owed everyone money. Though I've never seen a loan shark wearing tweed."

"It wasn't like that," the super said. "I got the distinct impression that Jeff was paying this bloke for his services."

"What services?" Avery said.

The super shrugged. "Wish I could tell you."

They thanked the man for his time, then returned to the street. Avery couldn't help wondering why the DiveNav had brought them here.

"What's wrong?" Carter said. "You're doing that thing you do with your face when you're frustrated."

"What thing with my face?" Avery shook her head. "I guess I'm just a little perplexed about why the DiveNav picked this spot. I mean the map that was supposed to be Mullins's makes it look like woods, but these buildings are all old."

"Well, they aren't Middle Ages old," Carter said. "We're near the city limits. Maybe this was all woods back then."

Avery stopped and looked at him.

"What?" Carter asked. "I'm not just a pretty face. I read stuff."

Avery looked around. "If that's true, then the treasure we're after could be buried under tons of concrete and steel in one of these foundations.

"I have to believe that it's more than just coincidence that the DiveNav sent us to the same place Jeff was staying," Carter said. "Maybe he was onto something beyond the ring."

As they reached the next intersection, Avery stopped and leaned against a lamppost. She pulled out her phone and began tapping the screen.

"What are you doing?" Carter said.

"The super said he thought the guy Jeff met with was a professor, right?"

"Right," Harrison said.

"Well, I'm trying to find one within walking distance."

"A college?" Carter said.

"Yeah," Avery said. "But there aren't any."

"What about a private school?" Harrison asked.

"Bingo," Avery said after a minute. "There's a private high school less than a half mile from here. Let's go see if we can find Mr. Tweed Jacket."

51

As they drew nearer to the school, the surrounding neighborhood grew nicer and more gentrified by the block.

"How do you want to do this, Avery?" Carter said as they entered the school grounds.

"Not a clue. We only have a description of the man we're looking for and he might not even work here."

"Pretend we know what we're doing and that we belong here," Carter said. "Most of the con men I ever met made their living by looking like they belonged. It worked for a few of the cops I knew, too."

"People see what they want to see, right?" Avery said.

"Precisely."

They entered through the main doors and started down the center hallway. The space was jam-packed with students, some on their way to the next class, some loitering. Avery strutted past them as if she were a teacher who knew her way around until she found a student who looked both smart and friendly enough to ask.

"Excuse me," Avery said. "I'm wondering if you can help me. I'm looking for a teacher, but I don't know his name."

The teenage girl looked past Avery at Carter with a wary eye.

"Who is he?" the student said.

"That's my brother," Avery said, giving her best eye roll convincer.

"Gotcha," the student said with a laugh. "What's this teacher look like?"

"Gray hair, tweed jacket, glasses."

The girl smiled. "You're looking for Mr. O'Leary."

"Where would I find him?"

"The 'kick me' notes the boys tape to his back are probably easier to spot than he is."

"What does Mr. O'Leary teach?" Carter asked, stepping up beside Avery.

The girl froze, staring at Carter, her eyes getting wider and her breath coming faster until she began flapping both hands in front of her face. "OMG, you're him, aren't you?" She squealed. "You're Carter Mosley."

"Guilty as charged." Carter smiled.

"I absolutely love your videos. Can I get a selfie with you?"

"Sure." Before he could say more, the girl put an arm around him, snapping several pictures with her phone.

"Do you have any idea how pea-green jealous all my besties are going to be when I tell them I met you?" Her eyes went wide. "What do you lot want with Mr. O'Leary?"

Carter leaned in close to her and lowered his voice. "It's not for public knowledge yet, but it's really important that we speak with him." He gave her a provocative wink and Avery worried the girl might melt into a puddle right there in the hall.

"You never told us what he teaches," Avery said, attempting to pull the girl back to the here and now.

"Medieval history through the early modern period. The worst most boring class ever. Not surprised he don't tell people outside this place."

"Where can we find him?" Carter asked.

"Room 24," she said, pointing the way. "It's just around the corner."

"Thank you," Carter said, shaking her hand. "It was nice to meet you."

She blushed and hurried off down the corridor.

"I don't get it," Avery said, shaking her head as she stared after the girl. "But you just made Mr. O'Leary about a thousand times cooler. Let's hope he's half as enamored with you as that teenager was."

As they approached room 24, a man resembling O'Leary exited with a brown paper bag in one hand and an apple in the other.

"Mr. O'Leary," Avery said. "We were wondering if you could spare us a minute of your time."

"I'm on my way to lunch, young lady. If you would like to—" He stopped in mid-sentence and gawked at Carter. "You're Carter Mosley."

"I'm going to have to pry his head through the door to get out of here," Avery groaned, focusing on O'Leary. "Can we talk inside your classroom?"

"Of course we can," O'Leary said as he did an about-face and led them inside. "Come right in. Wow, Carter Mosley. To what do I owe this pleasure?"

"We're here about Jeff Shelton," Carter said.

"Jeff? Why?"

"He was a friend of mine."

"I'm very sorry for your loss."

"Thank you," Carter said.

"I must say I'm surprised to hear you knew him."

"We understand that you were doing some research for Jeff," Avery guessed.

"I was," O'Leary said. "He hired me to find out everything I could about a pirate from the Golden Age named Mullins. Captain Ace Mullins to be exact. He wanted to know what was true and what wasn't, of the legends he'd found online. I was surprised that he was so interested, to be honest."

"But you helped him anyway," Carter said.

"Money is money," O'Leary said, his face reddening. "And it wasn't like he was asking me to do anything illegal."

"Did you find out anything notable?" Carter asked.

"As a matter of fact, I did." O'Leary paused to look at Avery. "Are you interested in hearing this?"

"Please," Avery said.

"Okay, well, I researched the man extensively. I learned that Mullins ran a band of pirates out of Norfolk but trafficked throughout the North Atlantic in sugar and fine silks mostly. His ship, the *Rogue Raven*, was involved in several documented skirmishes, winning them all."

"Any idea where the *Rogue Raven* is now?" Avery said.

"It's rumored to be hidden and rotting in a cave somewhere on the UK's northern coast."

Avery immediately thought of the cave Carter found near the reef, where they believed Jeff may have found the ring.

"What about lost or buried treasure connected to Mullins?" Carter said.

"You sound like Jeff. No, I didn't uncover anything like that during my research. Mostly, it seems like Captain Mullins spent a great deal of time dealing in things that King Charles II would likely want. Currying favor that would garner him invitations to parties that Charles himself might attend. There were rumors that Mullins and Charles were half brothers."

"We heard that very same rumor," Avery said.

"I don't suppose you can remember Jeff's last question of you before he was killed," Carter said. "Maybe something he was particularly interested in."

"Of course I can. He was asking about topographical maps from this region."

"Where we are right now?" Avery asked.

"Well, yes. But he wanted maps from the 1600s."

"And did you manage to find anything?" Carter said.

"It took some doing, but I did find several. It's hard to believe now, but this entire area was wooded back then. The borders were different."

"How so?" Avery asked.

"Where we're standing right now would have been about three kilometers outside of the city."

"How did Jeff react to the news or the maps?" Carter said.

"Same as always. Matter of fact. Unruffled. He did ask me several times about some old hollowed-out tree or trees."

"Does that mean anything to you?" Avery said.

"No, and I told him so. This entire area was cleared to make way for the city's expansion. Any trees like he was describing would have been cut down centuries ago."

Avery noticed four boys standing in the doorway, mouths agape. "Well, thank you for your time, Mr. O'Leary."

"How about a pic before we go?" Carter said. "I'll post it on my social media sites."

"That would be wonderful," O'Leary said.

Carter put an arm around O'Leary like they were old friends while Avery snapped the picture with Carter's phone.

"Thanks again, Mr. O," Carter said as they headed for the door. "Hey, kids, study hard and listen to Mr. O. He's the man."

As they walked down the hall toward the exit, the excited voices of the students could be heard peppering O'Leary with questions about how he knew Carter Mosley.

"That was nice of you, Carter," Avery said. "He may just be the most popular teacher in the school from now on."

"Kids can be brutal sometimes," Carter said. "And if I can brighten someone's day with a selfie, where's the harm?"

"You just brightened that guy's whole life," Avery said, clapping Carter on the back as they stepped out through the school's front doors.

"What do you make of the hollow trees thing?" Carter asked.

"I don't know," Avery said. "But it's interesting."

"You know what else would be interesting?" Carter asked.

"What's that?"

"Lunch, followed by a nap. I'm wiped."

52

Shannon waited just outside the bar when they strolled into the lobby of Dinner by Heston at five minutes till six, and even Avery had to admit he'd cleaned up well. Dressed in a suit and tie, with his hair combed neatly, he hardly resembled the punk rocker wannabe they had met that morning on the bridge.

Accompanying Shannon was a tall, athletic-looking man with piercing ice-blue eyes and a killer grin that came complete with dimples. Shannon introduced the man as Duval.

Ten minutes after they were shown to a table, the only thing Avery had been able to figure out about Duval was that he had very expensive taste in wine. She recalled Shannon saying dinner was on him and wondered if he knew the price of the vintage Duval had ordered for the table.

As they dined, Duval regaled them with quiet stories from his sordid past. The conversation never lagged despite the one-thousand-pound elephant loitering in the room. Avery could tell that Carter was charmed, though, and the restaurant's waitstaff was so overly attentive she couldn't help wondering if Duval and Shannon might be regulars. Or even owners.

As soon as the dessert plates were cleared and the restaurant began to empty, they got down to the business at hand.

"Shannon tells me you're looking for a veteran acquisitions man," Duval said. "What exactly is it you hope to acquire?"

Avery studied him for a moment, then looked him dead in the eye and said, "The Eye of the Dragon ruby."

Duval sat back in his chair. He appeared to be considering what she'd said. He glanced around the table. Carter nodded. Shannon didn't so much as blink. Duval's gaze returned to Avery. "Are you mad, love? You're talking about the bloody crown jewels."

"I'm neither mad nor your love. I don't sleep with criminals."

Duval laughed and raised his wineglass toward her. "Fair enough, I know where I stand, then. Brilliant."

"I only want the ring temporarily. Long enough for the absolute best authenticity expert to lay eyes on it and tell me if it's real." Avery figured that if the ring in the Tower was truly fake, that lent her theory about the rest of the collection a lot of credibility—and she would be able to tell Rowan the real ring had been fairly sold and was private property, while also handing him the rest of the ancient crown jewels to return to his bosses, so maybe he wouldn't be too mad.

"Let me get this straight." Duval chuckled again, shaking his head and putting his glass on the table. "You want to risk life in prison to steal something that's damn near unstealable, just so you can have some git tell you it's legit? Of course the ring is real. It's part of the crown jewels. What makes you think it isn't?"

"I have my reasons," Avery said. "And it wouldn't just be some git. I have the best expert in London." Or she would by the time she had the ring, anyway.

"Let's assume for a moment the ring could be removed from the Tower. How exactly are you planning to return it, if you don't mind me asking?"

Avery said, "I figured we'd put it back the same way we stole it to begin with."

Duval looked at Shannon. "You left out the part about Ms. Turner being crazy."

"I'm not crazy," Avery said.

"And I'm not in the habit of stealing things just to turn 'round and give them back. Charity is not my bag, darlin'."

"It wouldn't be charity. I'm prepared to pay you one million pounds for your help." Avery held out her hand. "Half when I take possession, the remainder after the ring has been safely returned to the Tower."

"Wait a minute," Shannon said. "My cut was supposed to be a percentage. How does this work?"

"That's your problem, not mine," Avery said.

Shannon's face reddened. Avery knew better than to make an enemy out of him over something as silly as money.

"Assuming Mr. Duval signs on, I'll pay you one hundred thousand pounds for your time after the job is complete."

"You're serious, aren't you?" Duval said.

"As a heart attack," Avery said.

Duval looked at Carter. "And you lot? Are you in with this too?"

"I'm in," Carter said.

"Avery calls the shots here," Harrison said.

"So, are you in, Mr. Duval?" Avery said.

Duval appraised her in silence.

"Maybe you aren't as good as we heard," Avery said, causing a smile to spread across Duval's handsome face.

"You are something, darlin'. I'll give you that. But the thing is, I'm better than you heard. Count me in. I still think you're mad, but it's your money." Duval recharged their glasses, then raised his in a toast. "Here's to living on the edge."

"Cheers," Avery said.

Duval drained his glass and poured another. "Drink up, mates. We've got a lot of work to do."

53

Avery and Carter spent the next several days preparing for and studying every aspect of what Duval kept referring to as "the Heist," while Harrison took himself on a food tour of London—true to his word, he stayed clear of Avery's plan and refused to hear about it when they did see him.

Duval maintained a private warehouse in Whitechapel where he kept many of his rare acquisitions. But the warehouse served another purpose, too: it was where he kept his skills sharp. Picking locks, cracking safes, bypassing state-of-the-art motion systems, fooling surveillance systems with electronic loops, scaling buildings for upper window and rooftop break-ins. It was enough to give any cop or security company nightmares.

"Jeez," Carter said upon seeing it for the first time. "This is like Bruce Wayne's bat cave."

"Sans Alfred, I'm afraid," Duval said.

Many of the training aids were modular, meaning Duval could alter the layout to mimic nearly any scenario. After reconfiguring the training course, Avery and Carter practiced on models identical to the security systems that Avery had photographed at the Tower. If there was one thing she learned while working with Duval, it was that his middle name should have been Thorough. He left absolutely nothing to chance.

Duval wrote a checklist of things they would need to be proficient at disabling or bypassing if they hoped to pull off a heist of this magnitude. One by one, over the next twelve days, they slowly checked things off the list. But as they came up on two weeks of working together eighteen hours a day, the few areas that were giving them trouble started firing tempers.

"Stop calling it a heist, okay?" Avery snapped as the door's pressure alarm sounded for the fifth time in twenty minutes. "It isn't a heist. We're only borrowing the ring."

"You keep telling yourself that, darling. If we get caught trying to steal the Eye of the Dragon, there won't be a single judge or barrister in Great Britain who will believe a word of it. Best intentions be damned, make no mistake, this is a heist."

"Whatever," Avery said.

"What about the changing of the guards?" Carter said. "Can we use that to our advantage?"

"I think we can," Duval said. "It looks like the four a.m. change gives us the best chance of avoiding detection. It will still be dark, and the security detail will consist of the fewest yeoman. But we've still got a big problem."

"And that is?" Avery asked.

"The security doors at ground level." He pointed to the one she was using for practice. "Even if we manage to get over the walls undetected, there are simply too many sensors on and around the Tower doors."

"There must be a workaround of some kind," Avery said as she opened her laptop. "A code of some sort we can crack. Or a system I can hack."

Duval turned to Carter. "She always this driven, mate?"

Carter shook his head and chuckled. "You have no idea."

"What about this?" Avery pointed to her screen. "Will this help?"

Duval and Carter walked around behind her to see the computer screen.

"What exactly am I looking at here?" Duval asked.

"These are the maintenance log reports from the Tower," Avery said.

"Can I ask how you managed to get a hold of these?"

"You can ask," Avery said.

"Seems like you've already broken in, darling." He looked at her with unfettered admiration.

Avery scrolled through the spreadsheet pages as they read the most recent problems and/or fixes. One entry stood out as promising. "What about this?" Avery said, pointing.

"A high tower window in the Jewel House with a broken latch," Duval read the entry aloud. "And it hasn't been fixed yet."

"It's a low-priority repair because it's not leaking and it's fifteen feet up," Carter said.

"It's bleeding perfect, that's what it is." Duval grinned and leaned toward Avery. "If I didn't think you'd slap me I'd kiss ya, darlin'."

"Scaredy cat," Avery said.

"This is exactly how we're going in," Duval said. "By way of the roof."

54

Avery planted her climbing shoes against the wall as she dangled by a rope and harness more than thirty feet above the concrete floor of Duval's warehouse. She had never been rappelling in her life, but she had done quite a bit of rock climbing at the local gym, and now with Duval's personal instruction, she had grown more than proficient over the past two days. Not surprisingly, Carter admitted that he had taught rappelling at one point during his adrenaline-fueled jack-of-all-trades youth.

Duval had been patient with Avery as they practiced several basic moves. Muscles she hadn't even known existed were sore. Duval and Carter had fashioned a climbing wall to mimic the exterior of the Tower. Dimensionally, it was an exact replica right down to the window they would be using to enter. The black suits they wore were skintight one-piece affairs that made Avery a little self-conscious.

"I could watch you move in that getup all day, darlin'," Duval said as he dangled on the rope just below her on the training wall.

"That's exactly what I was afraid of," Avery muttered.

In truth, the suits weren't all that different from the wetsuits that she and Carter wore while diving. The major difference was that the material had thousands of microprocessors embedded all over it. The purpose of the chips, Duval had explained, was to make the suits virtually invisible to motion sensors.

"And these things really work?" Carter had asked the day before, after Duval explained what they did.

"Better than a stealth bomber, mate. Here, let me show you."

Duval led them into a small mockup of a room. The twelve-by-twelve-foot space consisted of four ten-foot-high walls with two doors at opposite ends and a closed ceiling.

"Give me a second to activate the sensors, then I want you and Avery to walk through the room and exit through the other door." He went out to a control panel. "Okay, walk on through. And spend as much time as you want exploring the inside of the room before you exit."

Avery and Carter did as he instructed, moving all over the room and contorting themselves in various positions as they tried to set off any unseen sensor. After several minutes they exited the room and circled back to Duval.

"Well, what do you think?" Duval said.

"It feels like you're lying," Avery said.

"I didn't see a single sensor," Carter said.

Duval grinned and handed each of them a pair of black-framed glasses. "Put these on and I'll activate the sensors again."

"Those look like you swiped them from Roy Orbison," Carter said.

"Ooooh-oooh, pretty woman," Duval sang as he leered at Avery.

Avery shook her head but couldn't suppress a grin.

"Okay, now look again," Duval said. "And feel free to walk through the room."

Avery and Carter wandered through the room again, stopping at its center. Everywhere they looked, infrared beams crisscrossed the space, thin as cat whiskers. There was literally nowhere to move without bisecting multiple beams simultaneously, and yet no alarms sounded. Like an electronic invisibility shield.

"Wow," Carter said. "There must be hundreds of beams in here."

"Thousands, mate," Duval said.

"Why don't these glasses trigger the sensors?" Avery said as she removed hers and held them up in front of her."

"Because they're equipped with the same microprocessors as the suits, even the lenses." Duval turned to Carter. "Roy the Boy may have been a cool cat, but he didn't own a pair of these."

Avery was startled out of her reverie as the rope she was hanging from suddenly went slack, causing her body to drop at least ten feet until she was below Duval and Carter. She quickly reached for the braking mechanism on her harness and squeezed. The brake engaged and she jerked to a stop.

"What just happened?" she demanded.

Duval grinned down at her. "Failure drills, love."

"You did that on purpose?" Avery asked, making no attempt to hide her anger.

Duval slowly lowered himself until he was adjacent to her. "It might seem like I'm just some giant British prick, but you hired me because I'm the best. What you're asking me to do is to drag two amateur burglars with me to steal one of the most well-guarded pieces of jewelry on the bloody planet. We're not nicking some piece of your grandmother's fine silver here, love. If something goes wrong while we're hanging upside down from the Tower, at night, with armed guards everywhere, I need to know that you and Mr. Instagram aren't going to lose your cool. Got it?"

Avery took a deep breath, then nodded. "Got it."

"One million pounds may sound like a lot, but it isn't," Duval continued. "You could have offered ten million, but it won't be any easier to spend if I'm in prison. I'm not doing this for my health or your money. I'm doing this because it's a challenge and I love a challenge. And because you asked nicely. So, we will practice every aspect of this job until I'm comfortable having you accompany me on the job. Both of you. Or we can call the whole thing off right now. Your call."

In the few days they'd been together Avery hadn't seen this side of Duval. It was obvious that there was more to him than the renegade playboy he pretended to be. There was a serious professional thief living just below his chameleon-like persona.

She stared into his blue eyes.

"So, are you committed to this?" Duval pressed.

Avery nodded. "I am."

Duval looked up at Carter. "And you, Mr. Instagram? Are you all in?"

"One hundred percent."

"Brilliant." Duval's attention returned to Avery and the smile returned to his face. "From the top then, love?"

She didn't snap at him for calling her that again.

———

They broke for lunch just after noon. Avery's phone rang with a call from Rowan she ignored—something about talking to the secret police while planning a heist on a national landmark seemed wrong. A couple of minutes later, the phone rang again. She put her sandwich down and groaned, then smiled when she saw Harrison's name.

"Are you all toured out?" she asked when she picked up.

"Hardly," he said. "This is a big city. I do have a question for you, though. That phone number that Jeff called last before he was killed— MaryAnn said she couldn't find anything on it, right?"

"Right. Though I forgot to ask her again amid all the other things I was asking her."

"Don't bother," he said. "I have it."

"You...what?"

"See, it's like this. If you're embarking on a life of crime, I'll balance the scales by solving one. None of these British cops are moving fast enough for a decent homicide investigation, so I jumped in. Good karma, and avoiding boredom."

"And?" Avery asked.

"Dustin Merriweather, twenty-seven. He's a guard at the Tower of London," Harrison said.

"No kidding?" Avery's eyes popped wide and she tried to subdue her reaction. She could tell Carter later but didn't think she should mention this to Duval.

"Seems from the cash in his wallet and the timing of that large deposit, maybe Jeff was thinking along the same lines you are."

"Bribery might have been an easier route," Avery acknowledged. She just wouldn't have known who to ask.

"I have the guy's number if you want it," Harrison said.

"I am maxed out on people I can trust this week who aren't me and you," she said. "And bribery and collusion are also crimes."

"True."

Avery caught Duval heading her way out of the corner of her eye and told Harrison she had to call him later.

"I'm on the case," he said.

She clicked off and pocketed her phone as Carter finished his sandwich and pointed to hers.

"You going to eat that?" he asked, looking around.

Avery pushed it toward him.

"Still admiring the bat cave?" Duval asked, joining them.

"More wondering how my life might have turned out if I'd met you six years ago," Carter said.

"It's not all peaches and cream, mate," Duval said. "I've been at this a long while. Some of what I do is legitimate, work for insurance companies and the occasional wealthy bloke or lass who wants to feel better about their security."

"And the rest?" Avery said.

"Let's just say a few of my more high-profile acquisitions have put a target squarely on my back, love."

"Whose target?" Carter asked.

"Take your pick. Rival thieves, people who were too tight to maintain their insurance policies, and one couple who still have a thorn up their arses because I embarrassed them."

"It must be exciting," Carter said. Avery was pretty sure he was thinking about Jeff.

"That is one of my life's most desirable perks." Duval hoisted his soda. "Cheers, mate."

They spent the rest of the afternoon focused on the ring itself after Duval's friend Patrick dropped off the last piece they needed to make all this work.

Avery had insisted on going with Duval when he visited Patrick in a different warehouse located in a seedier part of town the week before.

"Patrick's an interesting bloke," Duval had warned her. "Never looks anybody in the eye, but one of the smartest people I've ever met—including you, love. He's a tech geek with the soul of an artist. A bit odd, but today I'm glad I know him. Nobody else could do what we're looking for here."

"You still haven't told me exactly what we're getting," Avery said. "Only that it's going to cost me."

"Probably less than bail. Definitely less than prison." Duval had winked and held the door for her to walk into Patrick's shop, where the air had the sharp tinge of molten metal, but the cube-shaped workstation in the center held every kind of high-tech machine Avery could imagine, from the computers and high-definition monitors to the chip writer, the 3D printer, and the laser microscope.

Looking around, she knew why they were there.

"You're making a copy of your own," she said.

"Technically of your own, you're paying," Duval replied. "A special dummy that will hopefully keep us out of the clink."

Avery had smiled when Shannon strolled in and handed Patrick a piece of paper. "I checked the specs three times," he said. "Papa was very specific." He glanced at Duval and smiled at Avery. "I don't need to know what you lot are up to. Patrick here asked me for the lowdown on the ring I sold for Jeff, and now I'll be right on my way."

Looking at the copy of the Eye of the Dragon, the stone glass and the metal iron under a gold finish, Avery felt a flash of electricity from her hairline to her toes. They were really doing this. Duval turned on the sensors in the training room and tossed the ring inside, watching with a satisfied smile as it landed and rolled.

"You trying to break it before you can use it?" Patrick looked at the floor.

"Checking the function, mate," Duval said. "Nice work."

Patrick saw himself out and Duval turned his attention to the ring's storage case. He studied the pictures Avery had taken beneath the display case while pretending to search for her lost contact lens.

"I didn't know you wore contacts," Duval said absently as he flipped through images.

"I don't," Avery said. "But it was the only thing I could think of that wouldn't draw the suspicion of the docent or guards standing nearby."

"I'm impressed, love. You may have the aptitude for this life after all."

"So, how do we get the ring out of the case without alerting every yeoman warder in London?" Carter said.

"I think I've worked that out," Duval said as he produced his own set of detailed photographs of the Jewel House.

"Where did you get these?" Avery said.

"What?" Duval said. "You didn't honestly think you cornered the market on the pretend tourist trade, did you? I have dozens of full-blown disguises, outfits, body-weight prosthetics, phony casts, slings, and wigs. You name it, I've probably got it. I've taken reconnaissance to a whole other level. Or did you think I still used the old 'pull your hat down low' trick?"

Avery and Carter exchanged a glance.

"Yeah, who would try that?" Carter said.

They passed the photos around as Duval explained the plan.

"What you're looking at here is a two-part item security system. The ring itself is in a padded velvet setting. That pad contains a weight sensor likely set within a few grams of the ring's actual weight, so our mission is to fool the sensor into thinking the ring is still there."

"Kinda like that first Indiana Jones movie, right?" Carter asked.

"She's a bit more technical than a bag of sand, mate, but yeah, that's as good a metaphor as any."

"You mentioned a second part to the ring security," Avery said.

"That would be the motion sensor inside the case."

"How can you tell there's a motion sensor from these photographs?" Carter said.

"I couldn't," Duval said. He produced another photo taken with a filter. "But from this one I could."

The picture clearly showed two perpendicular beams of light crossing the inside of the case at a point directly above the ring.

"Patrick's little device here operates on the same principle as the body-suits we'll be wearing. You saw it—as long as we get the weight right, breaking the motion beams won't matter."

"That doesn't sound too bad." Carter sounded optimistic.

Duval grinned. "That's because I haven't mentioned the floor pressure mats and the window contacts."

"Don't forget the helicopter," said Avery, who had heard Duval on the phone earlier.

"Helicopter?" Carter's eyebrows shot up.

"How did you think we were getting on the roof?" Duval asked.

55

The helicopter pilot was a longtime friend of Duval's named Miles. His chopper was designed for stealth operations, painted flat black and equipped with special rotors that produced significantly less noise than the traditional style. But as Miles explained, less noise wasn't the same as no noise. They would need to rappel to the roof of the Tower one after the other using a single line as quickly as possible. The longer the chopper hovered above the grounds, the more attention he was likely to garner.

The plan was that they would zip down to the Tower roof, rappel to the damaged window, make entry, spend a maximum of four minutes inside the Jewel House, then rappel out the window and down to the lower roof, where they would signal Miles to return and pick them up. But as Duval had warned them repeatedly, things seldom went according to plan.

Already, the weather wasn't cooperating. Originally, forecasters had called for a calm, overcast night, but the wind had picked up and now there was also the threat of scattered showers. While the wind and rain might help provide cover for their arrival, it came with its own set of difficulties, not the least of which was trying to reach the roof of the Tower safely on the first try.

Avery was so excited and nervous, every inch of her skin tingled as they lifted off from the airfield and headed toward the Tower. They had covered every angle. Practiced every maneuver. Knew each other's jobs so well that no verbal communication would be necessary. Duval told them whatever happened now was completely up to fate. Succeed or fail, everything would be over within the hour.

Avery sat in the darkened cargo hold of the chopper, across from Carter. Duval was up ahead standing near the side door they would drop from. She busied herself by running down a mental checklist of her assignments. Everything that was expected of her and what to do if something went wrong. Duval had planned for multiple contingencies, but Avery couldn't help wondering what might lie ahead that they weren't expecting.

A low-wattage red light illuminated at the forward end of the cargo hold. Avery and Carter stood as Duval waved them forward.

"Here we go," Duval said as he double-checked their harnesses and connectors. "You ready, love?"

Avery nodded, her stomach in knots.

"I was talking to Carter," Duval said with a wink. He was so charming, it was too bad he was a criminal.

Avery smiled.

"You sure?" he asked gently.

Avery nodded more vigorously.

"Okay. Get geared up, then."

The light changed to green as the chopper ceased its forward progress and hovered above the target.

"Go, go, go," Duval said.

Carter moved first, clipping his harness to the drop line, then stepping out of the helicopter into the dark of night. Avery stepped out right behind him.

Remembering what they'd practiced, she feathered the braking mechanism to control her rate of descent. She couldn't see Carter below her, but the darkened roof of the Tower loomed closer. And then she was down, her feet contacting the gritty surface of the roof. Carter, having already unclipped himself from the line, helped Avery with hers. Quickly they moved to opposite sides of the roof so Duval wouldn't crash down on top of them. Duval landed without incident smack in between them. In one smooth motion, he unhooked his harness and let go of the line. The chopper departed immediately, taking the muffled thump of the rotors with it. The three of them spent the next several minutes crouched on the darkened roof waiting for any sign they had been detected. Five minutes passed but nothing changed. No alert from the bailey, no bright search lights, nothing. The only exception was of an atmospheric nature as a cold drizzle began to fall.

They had discussed the possibility of inclement weather and what it might mean for their operation. "Moisture tends to make things wet and slippery," Duval had joked when Carter had asked if the rain would alter their plan. While they all knew they would need to take greater care in the execution, the plan moved forward. Avery was hoping the inclement weather might even be a blessing, as security would be less likely to spot them outside the Tower because human nature would make the guards reluctant to be outdoors.

Duval signaled again as he moved toward the edge of the wall with the damaged window. He uncoiled the rappelling line from the waistbelt of his harness, quickly securing it around one of the blocks protruding from the top of the Tower wall before he tossed the other end over the side. Avery and Carter repeated the maneuver with their own ropes and stood at the ready while Duval went over the side first. They peered over the edge, waiting as he lowered himself to the aumbry with the damaged window. Avery kept her eyes peeled for any of the roving yeomen who might be patrolling below, but the courtyard appeared empty.

Duval signaled up to them that he was in. Carter tapped Avery's arm and pointed downward. She nodded and stepped up onto the roof's edge. She clipped her harness to the rope and started down the side of the Tower just as she had countless times during their practice sessions. As her feet bounced along the wet stone, she tried to imagine that she was still inside the safe, dry confines of Duval's warehouse, and not where she was. Before she knew it, she had reached the entry point and Duval tugged her inside the Tower, where she switched lines and made her way down the wall while Duval waited for Carter.

Avery unclipped her harness and stepped back. As soon as Carter was inside and on the ground, Duval raced down the wall like a panther and raised four fingers, signaling exactly how much time they had to complete the mission and get out. Avery and Carter nodded and moved in the direction of the case with the ring.

Avery's heart raced as she realized that the clock was ticking.

Nothing looked the same as it had during the visit she and Carter had made only days before. Part of it was the reduced lighting, and part of it was the eerie emptiness. They didn't belong there. Avery paused to get her bearings, and Duval turned and signaled for her to follow him. It was clear that he had done a more thorough job of reconnoitering the Tower than she and Carter had.

With their bodies and faces completely covered by the dark fabric, they moved like shadows as Duval led them through a maze of riches in the jewel room. Avery fought off a nervous giggle as she imagined them as the Blue Man Group dodging their way silently through hundreds of infrared beams. Without the high-tech suits and headgear, they would've been discovered in seconds. Avery and Carter followed Duval to the case where the ring was on display.

The lighted cases containing the many jewels Avery had seen previously were all dark, making their mission seem even more like the burglary it was. A momentary feeling of uncertainty washed over Avery. Was Harry right? Was she crazy to have suggested this in the first place? She took a deep breath and willed the feeling away. It was too late to back out now. She was here for the right reasons and was determined to see this through.

Duval worked quickly while Avery kept an eye on the timer on her watch. They had already spent almost a minute and a half locating the ring. It took Duval an additional forty seconds to pick the lock and open the case. Like synchronized swimmers, they moved as one. Duval lifted the cover to the case as Carter reached inside and grabbed the ring, moving it slowly while Avery slid the counterweight disk into place.

The dummy ring had been fashioned to accurately match the exact weight and size of Papa's ring by using the information that Shannon recorded when he had fenced the real ring for Jeff. But this was the first test of the copy's accuracy—they were counting on the fact that the real Eye of the Dragon and the one in this case, both made by hand centuries ago, were the same in order to trick the sensors. What if they weren't? Avery held her breath, waiting to see whether an alarm would sound as Duval closed the lid and relocked the case, but once again, nothing happened.

Holy crow, they'd done it. She tucked the ring into a velvet pouch and slid that into her pocket.

They retraced their steps quickly and confidently. As they rounded the corner, Duval held up a hand, signaling Avery and Carter to stop. He pointed to the window, which was standing open.

"What is it?" Avery whispered.

"The rain," Duval said, pointing to the water running down the wall. Avery knew, as they all did, if rainwater reached the floor it could set off the sensors. "We need to hurry."

"Are they that sensitive?" Carter said.

As if in answer to his question, an alarm sounded, security lights flashing. Avery heard the hiss and clank of automatic door locks engaging.

"We gotta go now," Duval shouted as he clipped onto the special line outfitted with the same sensors as their suits and began to climb. "Come on, move!"

They raced up the wall to the window. Duval leapt up onto the ledge. Avery watched him clip onto one of the outside ropes, then disappear into the storm. Carter signaled Avery to go next. She shook her head and shoved him toward the opening.

"I'm right behind you, Carter," she shouted. "Go."

As soon as Carter stepped out into the darkness, Avery grabbed onto her rope just as the first of two armed guards appeared at one of the glass doors that led into the room. She fumbled with her clip as she watched one of the guards press an ID card to the electronic lock. While climbing around the rainwater-soaked ledge, Avery slipped and fell, gripping the windowsill with her fingers and kicking her feet, trying desperately to hoist herself back up. By the time she did, the guards had managed to open the door.

"Stop!" one of them bellowed as he pointed his weapon at her.

Without looking back, Avery climbed onto the outside ledge and leapt out into darkness as a shot rang out.

56

Rowan paced back and forth across his bedroom floor, fingernails digging into his palm as he listened to the words tripping out of his cell phone.

"The Tower has been breached. The Eye of the Dragon ruby is missing. The thieves are nowhere to be found. The building was surrounded in minutes. It's like they vanished into thin air."

The director general was a whiner. Rowan had almost zero respect for the man, but as he was his immediate boss, Rowan had to at least pretend to play nice.

The director's breathless tirade continued. "This situation is unprecedented. That ring belonged to King Charles II, for God's sake. Do you hear what I'm saying?"

"I do," Rowan said.

"The ring must be returned quickly and quietly before the damned media catch wind of this. The only good thing is the early hour. The on-site staff is minimal. They have been quarantined and ordered not to speak of it."

As Rowan listened to the man prattle on, he grew more incensed at the thought that someone would have the audacity to attempt such a bold and blatant act against the Tower of London. But more than that, in addition to the intel having been spot on, it meant they could now proceed with the next step.

"Do you understand why I'm calling you?" the director demanded, raising his voice to a shrill whine.

Because I get things done, he thought. *Things you don't want to know about.* "Yes, sir, I do," was all he said.

"We have billions in that tower, Rowan. And the museum brings in millions from tourists annually. Do you have any idea what would happen if people found out that our security is beatable?"

Rowan didn't bother responding to such an obvious rhetorical question. He was confident he did know.

"I want you to assemble your own team. There will be no paperwork filed regarding this incident. Zero reports. I don't want to know what you're up to. Just see that it gets done by any means necessary. We will cover all your expenses fully and quietly as always."

"Understood. I'll get started now."

"See that you do." With that, the director disconnected the call.

Rowan stared at the phone for a moment, fantasizing that it was the director's scrawny neck as he squeezed. The act brought a smile to his face.

Rowan immediately dialed another number.

"Talk to me," the voice on the other end of the line said.

"We have a situation with the crown jewels," Rowan said.

"We've been expecting this, sir."

"Load up. I'll meet you in thirty minutes."

Avery's left calf felt like it was on fire. She did her best to ignore the pain as she hurried after Duval and Carter across the roof of the lower building, but she felt the blood trickling down her leg through the skintight suit. The wind was gusting now, driving the rain sideways. Avery didn't need Duval to tell her that the chopper wasn't coming back. It was plan B time.

Plan B involved hooking onto a steam pipe at the exterior of the building, then rappelling down to the ground. The only problem was plan B hadn't factored in their discovery. They could hear shouting down below.

The building was surrounded. As far as Avery knew, they didn't have a plan C.

Duval pointed to a maintenance door on the side of a large air-conditioning unit, and they ran toward it. It took him several moments to pick the lock on account of the rain and darkness, but he got the door open, and they slipped inside, resecuring the door behind them.

They each activated their penlights and scanned the area.

"What's the plan?" Carter asked.

"I'd say we're moving to plan C," Duval said.

"We have a plan C?" Avery asked.

"I'm working on it," Duval said as he looked around the darkened space. He pointed to an aluminum grate covering the ductwork that entered the building. "Here, give me a hand prying this off."

They removed the grate, then carefully leaned it up against the wall.

Avery tried to hide her injury, but Carter caught her limping.

"You're hurt," Carter said.

"It's nothing," Avery said.

"You're bleeding, love," Duval said as he trained his light on the back of her leg. "What happened?"

"I got shot as I was leaving through the window."

"Jesus, Avery," Carter said. "That looks bad."

"It's fine," Avery said. "We just need to get out of here."

"She's right," Duval said as he stripped off his backpack and handed it to Carter. "First things first. I'll scout out this duct. If it's clear, I'll signal back with my light. You send all the packs down, then crawl down yourselves. Got it?"

"Got it," Avery said.

They waited several minutes for Duval's signal, then slid the packs down to him one at a time. Carter forced Avery to go first. She could tell he was upset about her injury. Not the fact that she had gotten injured, only that she'd tried to hide it.

The air vent they'd chosen led to a public restroom. Once they were all safely inside, they stripped off the bodysuits and changed into the street clothes they'd packed with them. Duval, who appeared to have thought of almost everything, brought out a small first aid kit and did his best to clean the wound on Avery's leg.

"Looks like it passed right through the skin," Duval said. "Nothing major injured besides some skin and fatty tissue."

"Who are you calling fat?" Avery snapped.

"I only meant—"

"Just bandage it and save the commentary, okay?" Avery said.

"I've got to clean it out first. Prepare yourself. This is gonna hurt like hell."

Avery grimaced as he applied peroxide to the wound, but didn't let out a peep. Not that it wasn't extremely painful, but she wanted neither to alert the guards nor to have Duval think she was weak.

After he'd cleaned and bandaged the wound, they finished changing into their street clothes.

"Now we look like tourists," Carter said.

"What do we do with these bodysuits?" Avery said.

"They come with us," Duval said.

"Wouldn't it be better if we just tossed them in the trash?" Carter said. "What if they search us?"

"No way. Our DNA is all over these," Duval said. "And Avery's blood. We'll have to just take our chances that we don't get stopped."

"What time does this place open?" Carter said, running his arms through the straps of his pack and hoisting it onto his back.

"Not until eight," Avery said. "We'll have to stay hidden for a couple of hours until we can blend in with the paying customers."

"I may have a better idea," Duval said.

They exited the bathroom and moved along a windowed hallway that provided an excellent view of the Tower. It was surrounded by uniformed guards.

"I guess walking out the front door isn't an option," Carter said.

"No, but the good news is that they are all focused on the wrong direction," Avery said.

"It won't take them long to figure out what happened," Duval said. "Follow me."

Duval led them further inside the empty building. As they neared an intersection with another corridor, the sound of rapidly approaching foot-falls echoed around them.

Avery didn't need any signals to know that this was it. Quickly she ducked into the alcove of a doorway, pressing herself as flat as possible against the locked door. Carter and Duval followed suit on the opposite side of the hall.

Three more yeomen came into view, then turned sharply to the right and continued up the corridor and out of sight.

It took Avery a moment to realize that she'd been holding her breath. Duval signaled for Avery and Carter to remain where they were while he checked to be sure the coast was clear. Avery didn't know what was both-ering her worse, Carter staring daggers at her, or her leg, throbbing like it was being beaten with a drumstick. Several minutes later Duval returned and waved for them to follow.

They resumed their silent refuge into the maze of ancient stone passages.

"Where are we going?" Carter whispered. "The longer we're running around in here, the more likely it is we'll be found out. We should have stayed in the bathroom."

Duval turned abruptly, causing Carter and Avery to nearly trip over each other. "Look, I get that you're stressed. But you hired me to help you grab the ring and I've done that. If you don't think they would have gotten around to searching that bathroom, you're not as bright as I'd hoped. I know more about this fortress than most of the people who work in it every day. You can either start trusting me, or you can go turn yourselves in to the guards. I'll try and remember to visit you once a year in whatever English prison they truck you off to die in."

Avery took both of them gently by the arms. "Let's just stick to the plan, okay?"

Carter whipped his head around to face Avery. He opened his mouth to respond, then apparently thought better of what he might say, and closed it.

"Please, Carter," Avery said.

"Fine," Carter snapped as his attention returned to Duval. "Lead on, McDuff."

It took them another five minutes and two more close calls with guards before they made it down to one of the castle's sub-basements.

"Where are we?" Avery asked.

"The white dungeon," Duval said.

"Hoping to give us a taste of what lies ahead if we get caught?" Carter asked.

Duval stepped forward and got right in Carter's face. "Actually, I was hoping you might have enough self-preservation skills left to give me a hand with this grate."

"What grate?"

"That one," Avery said, pointing to the floor beneath their feet.

Carter looked down and saw for the first time where he was standing. He stepped back and bent down on the side opposite Duval. "Where does this lead?" he asked as they struggled with the weight of the rusty iron grate.

"Well, it's been a while since I researched this room," Duval said. "But if my memory is correct, it will eventually lead us to drainage tunnels."

"Where do the tunnels lead?" Avery said.

"To the Thames," Duval said as he helped Avery down through the opening to the tunnel below.

Carter dropped down into the tunnel next, followed by Duval. After they were all safely standing in the darkened passageway, Carter helped Duval slide the grate back into place. It dropped into its frame with a *clank*.

Three penlights roamed the heavy darkness that is particular to subterranean spaces, trying to get a feel for their surroundings.

"Which way is out?" Carter whispered.

Duval pointed the beam of his light down toward the trickle of water running beneath their feet. "Follow the water, mate."

Duval took point, with Avery following, while Carter brought up the rear.

"You said these were drainage tunnels," Avery said. "Drainage for what?"

Duval kept walking. "Trust me, love, you don't want to know."

57

They trudged along through the dark, dank passage in silence, each of them lost in their own thoughts. What they were trudging through, though, God only knew. Duval stopped and held up a hand as they approached a bend in the tunnel.

"What are we stopping for?" Carter said. "Don't tell me you're lost."

Duval turned around to face them. The reddish light reflecting off his eyes gave him a devilish appearance that unnerved Avery. He stared at Carter without speaking for what felt like an eternity. At last Duval looked at Avery. "Your boyfriend is a bit of a wanker, love. Has anyone ever told you that?"

"I've often thought the same," Avery said. She didn't say Carter wasn't her boyfriend because it was probably better to let Duval believe that.

Watching Duval look around, Avery began to giggle silently at the ridiculousness of their situation and at Duval's use of British slang to describe Carter. Soon her giggle morphed into a full-blown case of laughter, which she was doing her best to suppress. It was catching, and Duval and Carter joined in. When everyone had caught their breath and the tunnels were silent again, Duval cleared his throat.

"I stopped here because the city maps show there's supposed to be another tunnel near the first bend in this one," Duval said. "A slightly newer one, cut in to connect to the city sewers about a hundred years ago. Here is the first bend. But I see no tunnel."

"Well then," Avery said as she trained her light on one wall, "let's find it."

Most of the surface area of the damp stone walls was covered by a thick, mossy growth, some of it hanging like ivy, concealing whatever lay beneath. It took several minutes before Avery discovered tendrils of moss moving outward as if something was pushing against them. She reached out and brushed the hanging flora to one side, exposing a smaller passageway, narrower and shorter by half a foot.

"Is this what we're looking for?" Avery called.

Both men hurried over.

"Well done, love," Duval said. "I feel air flow, which can only mean one thing."

Duval moved to duck inside, when Carter stopped him.

"I'll take lead for a while, if you don't mind," Carter said.

Duval stepped back and gestured for Carter to enter. "By all means."

One by one they moved into the cramped passage, continuing their downhill trek toward whatever awaited them on the other end. In addition to the tighter confines of this tunnel, Avery also noticed that the dank, musty odor from the previous tunnel had morphed into something far more foul smelling.

"What is that?" Carter asked before Avery could utter the words herself.

"What's what?" Duval said from the rear of the line.

"That putrid smell," Carter said.

"Other than the reason I allowed you to go first?" Duval offered an impish grin.

"What do you mean?" Avery said.

"I mean, this runs into the city's modern sewer system, which was cut in out here years after the tunnels under the fortress were hollowed out."

"So, we could literally be walking in—" Carter said.

"Crap." Duval nodded.

"That's just great," Carter said as he attempted to straddle the water flowing beneath their feet.

"Hey, you offered to take lead, mate," Duval said. "I was just trying to be a team player."

"How thoughtful," Carter said.

"Remind me to throw out these shoes," Avery said.

A few hundred steps later, they noticed a change in both the tunnel's dimensions and angle of trajectory as they began a long and gradual ascent upward. Avery wondered how long it would be before they reached street level. As if in answer to her thought, she caught the sound of a large vehicle rumbling past them overhead.

Carter paused and turned to face Avery and Duval. "Is that what I think it is?"

"Sounds like traffic to me," Duval said. "We must have crossed into a storm sewer. Keep an eye peeled overhead for manhole covers or any other egress to the surface."

"Try and pick a manhole on a side street," Avery said. "We'll be less likely to get run over."

They stopped at a rusted ladder consisting of rungs of rebar set into the concrete wall of the sewer. The ladder led up to a short circular tunnel capped by a steel lid. Avery couldn't tell if it was a manhole, only that she could see a pinprick of daylight shining through it.

"Why don't I climb up and take a look?" Duval said as he grabbed hold of one of the rungs.

"Why you?" Carter challenged.

"It doesn't have to be me. I just figured you wouldn't want to lose your head to a passing truck."

"Good point," Carter said. "All yours, *mate.*"

Avery and Carter stood at the bottom watching as Duval climbed up.

"Yup, it is a manhole," Duval hollered down.

"Can you lift it?" Avery said.

"Hang on a minute," Duval said as he pressed his shoulder up against the lid.

Avery watched the circular cover shift, flooding the entire tunnel with daylight.

They scrambled up behind Duval and found themselves on a side street where two children astride their bicycles on the sidewalk had stopped to watch them. Avery walked over to them.

"Whatcha doing down there?" the smaller boy asked.

"Fixing a sewer blockage," Avery said, clapping her hands together as if knocking off debris. It was the only thing she could think of that might placate their curiosity.

"Where are your uniforms?"

"We are undercover agents for the sewer department. We don't wear uniforms."

"Seriously?" the other boy asked.

"Yup," Avery said. "Don't worry. It's as good as new now."

"What was blocking it?" the first one asked.

Avery leaned in close as if sharing a secret. "You do not want to know." With that, she waved her hand in front of her face while turning up her nose in disgust.

"Gross," both boys said in unison before pedaling away furiously, laughing.

Carter and Duval replaced the cover and joined Avery on the sidewalk.

"What did you tell them?" Carter said.

"They think we're undercover sewer operatives," Avery said.

"Brilliant," Duval said.

They paused for a moment to take in their surroundings. The Tower of London was visible a half mile in the distance.

"Jeez," Carter said. "I thought we walked a lot farther than that."

"It's easy to get disoriented underground," Duval said.

Avery pulled out her phone and contemplated calling Harrison.

"You calling a cab?" Carter said.

"That's exactly what I'm doing," Avery said as she opened the taxi app on her phone.

"Good idea," Duval said. "We've got to get you back to the hotel and get that leg wound treated properly."

"Yeah," Carter said. "Harrison will skin me alive if that gets infected."

Harrison might skin all of us alive anyway, Avery thought as she punched in their destination.

58

As Avery had predicted, Harrison was beside himself with worry by the time they arrived at the hotel. They had made one quick stop on the way at a pharmacy for first aid supplies, peroxide, tape, gauze, and Neosporin.

"I told you this was a horrible idea," Harrison said, glaring daggers at both Duval and Carter. "And why didn't anyone call me with an update?"

"We were busy trying to avoid capture—and bullets." Duval gestured to Avery's leg.

"It's okay, Harry," Avery said. "I'm fine. Really."

"It's not okay," Harrison snapped. "And you're not fine. Breaking into the Tower of London was a ludicrous idea in the first place, but you got yourself hurt, too. The entire Met police force is probably out searching for you guys right now."

"I don't think so," Duval said.

"What are you talking about? Of course they are."

"I think he might be right," Avery said. "We didn't see any extra police activity on the way back here. And our taxi driver was a news junkie. His radio was tuned into a news station the entire time. We would have heard something."

"I suspect they're playing this close to the vest," Duval said. "Keeping it in-house."

"Why on earth would they do that?" Harrison said.

"Think about it, mate. If word got out that you could steal jewels from the Tower of London and get away clean, it would reflect very poorly on their entire security staff. Hell, everyone with a mind to pick a pocket would think it was open season at the Tower."

"You can't honestly think they aren't going to do anything about it?" Harrison gaped.

"I never said that," Duval said. "They've likely got some heavy hitters on retainer for just this type of thing. And those lads will stop at nothing to recover this ring."

"That's just great," Harrison said.

Carter opened his mouth to add something, but one look from Harrison stopped him cold.

"Not one word, Carter," Harrison said. "I swear to God if anything happens to Avery because of this little stunt, you won't need to worry about all the king's men. I'll kill you myself."

"The whole thing was my idea, Harry," Avery sounded weary.

"Before we move on to killing each other, we ought to get your wound cleaned and treated, love," Duval said.

"He's right," Avery said. "I need a long hot shower and a change of clothes before we do anything else. And remind me to burn these."

Avery's luxurious marble walk-in shower was equipped with wall jets that relaxed every muscle in her tired body. The high-pressure streams stung the open wound, but she knew it would help to clean out any debris the bullet had left behind.

She changed into a clean shirt and shorts, allowing Carter to treat and dress the wound properly. Harrison oversaw the entire operation, continuing to fuss over her.

"It's just a flesh wound, Harry," Avery said. "The bullet grazed right over the skin. No real damage. I'll be fine."

She knew her words wouldn't have any lasting effect, as Harrison was worried about more than just her injury.

"Harry, did you happen to catch anything about the burglary on the telly?" Duval said.

"No. And I kept switching channels, but no one was talking about it. You're probably right about them keeping a lid on this. That's exactly what I would do."

"What about these people you think might be coming after us?" Carter said. "Any thoughts about who they might send?"

Duval nodded. "I've got a few ideas."

Avery stared at the ring sitting on the coffee table as she waited for MaryAnn to respond to her text. She didn't have a loupe or a professional eye, but it looked exactly like the one Papa had shown them. One of the rings had to be a fake. The only question was, which one? The Greek collector had seemed certain that his was the genuine article, but there had been no way for Avery to determine the provenance of the certification papers he'd shown them.

Harrison took a seat next to her. "You scared me."

She leaned her head on his shoulder. "I'm sorry. You get anything else on Jeff's killer? I know Rowan had people he was interviewing last week, but I stopped taking his calls and I don't know what came of it."

"What did you quit talking to him for?"

"Felt weird, planning this heist while I was helping MI5. Just trying to keep everything in its lane," she said. "I can call him later, though."

"I spoke with the Tower guard Jeff was trying to pay off, Merriweather— he denied ever having heard of Jeff until I showed him the phone records, and then he told me a sob story about his mother needing surgery. I don't think he's our man, for the record, seeing as how he never got paid."

"Does his mother need surgery?" Avery asked.

"Vital records says his mother died eight years ago," Harrison said. "So I think he's just greedy. Or desperate. Or both."

Avery nodded. "No other leads?" She was beginning to think Jeff's killer was just going to walk away.

Harrison touched his chin. "The guard said something about Jeff not trusting the people he'd been dealing with. That was on my docket for today until you went and got your international theft patch and then got yourself shot."

"People he'd been dealing with...like Shannon?" Avery's eyes went to Duval, who was on the balcony that faced the Tower, talking on his phone and studying the city below.

"Maybe," Harrison said. "I don't know yet. I need to dig a little more. This day is making me wonder if Jeff wasn't unnecessarily trying to avoid drawing attention to himself. Seems like that might have been the smarter play given what we're seeing now, doesn't it?"

Avery nodded absently, the events of the past several weeks shifting in her mind, making room for that idea. She gripped Harrison's arm, the rest of her going still.

"You okay?" He put his other hand on top of her suddenly viselike one.

"Harry, what if these people didn't kill Jeff because they wanted to steal the ring, or even because they were worried about him telling Carter?" Avery asked softly.

"What other reason you got, then?" Harrison asked.

"The same reason they backed off of us after a few days, watching instead of intervening, the same reason there's nothing on the news about this missing ring. Secrets." Avery sat up straighter and released Harrison's arm. "They aren't after the ring itself at all. What if the real goal was to try and keep the fake crown jewels from being discovered?"

59

Avery jumped to her feet and began pacing, mumbling mostly to herself.

"To keep a secret that has stayed quiet for hundreds of years, I bet people would go pretty far," she said. "I mean, how much money must they rake in every year on tickets to tour the Jewel House? If the internet got hold of a story about fakes, it would cost the government a fortune."

"That makes more sense than anything we've come up with so far," Harrison said. "Though by that logic, we're in serious danger."

Avery shook her head. "Not as long as they think we might lead them to the rest of the stolen treasure, we're not."

"How do you figure?"

"They could've killed us ten times in the past few weeks. Probably more that I don't even know about. At some point, their objective shifted."

"To what?"

"Getting the original jewels back—quietly. They might kill us once we've found them, but until then, I'd bet we're the safest people in this city."

"So..." Harrison stopped.

"What?" Avery asked.

"Nothing." He stood. "I need to make a couple of calls. I don't disagree with your theory, but use caution if you go anywhere, especially if you take that ring with you."

"I promise," Avery said, standing and waving for Duval to come inside when he got off the phone.

Duval had offered to contact his authentication expert while Avery reached out to MaryAnn for hers. Keeping the number of people in the know as small as possible was a necessity, but a second opinion regarding the authenticity of both rings couldn't hurt.

Her phone buzzed a call and Avery checked the screen. MaryAnn. Avery answered on the first ring.

"Tell me you're all okay," MaryAnn said breathlessly before Avery could utter a single word.

"We're all fine," Avery lied as she looked down at her bandaged leg.

"Thank God. I've been worried about you ever since—well, you know."

Avery knew she had chosen well when she had hired MaryAnn. Not everyone would have been as smart as she about avoiding details over a wireless connection.

"We need help from one of your resources," Avery said. "It concerns authenticity."

"I understand. How soon do you need to see them?"

"Ten minutes ago."

It turned out that MaryAnn's expert was not only close by, but available to see them immediately.

Avery had the hotel order a car and driver for them while she ordered one of her own.

"Why do we need two cars?" Carter said as she hung up the phone.

"Because she's worried about being followed, right, Ave?" said Harrison, who'd finished his phone call just in time to invite himself along.

Avery grinned at Harrison's insightfulness.

"You don't miss a trick, do you, Harry?" Duval said. "How many years did you say you were a copper?"

"Too many." Harrison sounded gruff, but Avery could tell he was taken with Duval's rakish charm.

"I figure two of us can travel in one of the cars, while the other two wait a few minutes for any tail to take the bait," Avery said. "If no one follows, no harm done. But if the first car, the decoy, is tailed, the second one will know about it, and we can respond accordingly."

"What are appropriate measures?" Duval said.

"May I?" Harrison asked.

"By all means," Avery said.

"Well, Avery will be in the second car regardless of what happens. If the first car picks up a tail, they will call the occupants in the second car, alerting them to the problem. The first car will then lead the tail on a wild goose chase, never going anywhere near the original destination where our appraiser is located. Avery and her partner can continue unmolested to the intended destination."

"And what if there is a second tail?" Carter said.

"If there are two tails, we will have to improvise some other way of getting Avery to the appraiser without leading either of the followers there," Harrison said.

"May I?" Avery said.

"By all means, milady," Harrison said.

"We'll have our drivers execute U-turns or sudden lane changes followed by quick turns onto side streets to make it difficult for the tails to stay with us. Once my car is out of sight from the tail, I can easily jump out and continue to my location on foot. As long as they continue to believe that I'm in one of the cars, they will follow them until the cows come home."

"What cows?" Duval said, his forehead creased in confusion.

Avery laughed. "It's an American colloquialism."

"Ah," Duval said. "I'll try and remember that one. And which of us is to be in the second car with you?"

"Since we will require two different authentication experts to examine the ring, I figured it should probably be the two of us," Avery said, drawing a disapproving look from Carter.

"Grand." Duval's grin showed off his dimples.

60

Fifteen minutes later Harrison and Carter climbed inside the car ordered by the hotel, giving the driver a fake address six miles from the appraiser's location. Avery and Duval stood off to one side of the portico, waiting for them to depart.

"How long do we wait?" Duval said.

"Let's give it a few minutes," Avery said. The traffic moving in the direction that Harrison and Carter's car had gone was heavy, making it impossible to know if they had picked up a tail yet, but Avery was confident that Harrison would know before long.

Several minutes later, the car Avery had ordered with her app drove up to the front of the hotel and parked. Avery and Duval provided their driver with another phony address close to where she really wanted to go. If they didn't end up being followed, Avery planned to change their destination at the last minute, making sure that even the driver wouldn't know where they were headed.

They'd been on the road for less than three minutes when Avery's cell phone rang with a call from Harrison.

"Well?" Avery said without fanfare.

"We picked up two different tails within sixty seconds of leaving the hotel," Harrison said.

"I spotted one of them," Carter hollered in the background.

"Yeah," Harrison said. "I think we may have an inspector in training here, Ave. How about you guys? Anything on your end?"

Avery double-checked with Duval before responding. He shook his head.

"I think we're in the clear," Avery said.

"Okay," Harrison said. "Keep us posted. Carter and I were thinking a nice long tour of the British countryside might be in order. We'll keep these guys occupied as long as we can."

"Thanks, Harry."

Avery disconnected the call and sat back in her seat. She toyed with the idea of giving the driver the correct address to save them some time and legwork, but—on the off chance that their driver might become part of the problem—she opted to have him drop them off at the address she had already provided.

While Duval kept an eye out for trouble, Avery squared up with the driver. They crossed the street and waited for the taxi to drive out of sight before doubling back and proceeding to the real destination.

It took them another ten minutes to make the trek. MaryAnn's connection was waiting for them inside.

"Avery?" the woman asked as she greeted them at the door to her flat. "I'm Maura Toomey."

"Avery Turner," she said, shaking the woman's hand. "And this is Duval. Thank you so much for agreeing to help us."

"My pleasure. Come on inside."

The building's drab exterior provided excellent camouflage to what lay inside. The gallery-style lighting offered an air of superiority to expensive oil paintings lining each wall. The Afghan floor coverings and sculptures and vases atop Queen Anne–style furniture pieces appeared no less valuable.

"Your home is gorgeous," Avery said. "MaryAnn never mentioned you were a collector."

Maura grinned. "MaryAnn and I go way back. She is the reason I've managed to acquire some of these pieces."

"They are beautiful," Duval murmured, his eyes roving over everything.

"Thank you. Can I offer you anything before we get started?"

"That's most kind of you," Avery said. "But we're actually tight on time and we'd like to get started."

"I completely understand. Do you have the ring?"

Avery carefully removed it from a hidden compartment at the bottom of her purse.

"You don't take any chances, do you?" Maura said, making no attempt to hide her admiration.

"Believe it or not, we've taken quite a few recently," Duval said.

Avery handed Maura the ring and watched her eyes widen.

"MaryAnn never specifically commented on what you were bringing me," she said. "Only that it was of a very sensitive nature."

"MaryAnn's good that way," Avery said.

"She's also evidently the queen of the understatement," Maura said, looking up from the ring to study Avery's and Duval's faces. "Can I ask where you got this?"

"You can ask," Avery said.

The woman hesitated a moment. "Okay, I understand. Follow me."

She led them to a wall at the back of the flat, where a single oil painting hung. They watched as she reached up and slid the painting to one side and leaned forward until her face was mere inches from the wallpaper. After a moment the wall began to swivel in, revealing a hidden room behind it. The room was a walk-in vault of sorts. The large, windowless, well-lit space was equipped with a half dozen wall-mounted security monitors, a table, several chairs, and a cluttered desk. Atop the desk sat three large computer monitors. One normal-looking door stood at the center of a side wall. Avery assumed it must have led to a bathroom.

"Welcome to my research lab," Maura said.

"How very double oh seven of you," Duval said. "Or should I have said Moneypenny?"

Maura laughed in appreciation. "My business requires me to cross paths with all types of collectors. Not all of them are of the savory variety."

"I can only imagine," Avery said, casting a quick glance at Duval.

"Come. Make yourselves comfortable."

As they stepped inside the space, the wall swung back to its original position, sealing the room off from the world. Avery and Duval turned to watch as several large steel tubes slid into matching holes at the seams of the false wall, clunking home as they did.

"This place is like Fort Knox," Duval said.

"I tend to research better when I'm not disturbed," Maura said with a wink. "This is a fully operational safe room. Self-contained, bombproof, bulletproof, air conditioned, and all my online connectivity is protected by the most advanced firewalls you can imagine."

"Oh, I can imagine quite a bit," Avery said.

"Ms. Turner's kind of a tech genius," Duval said.

"Then you can fully appreciate what I must do to keep this place secure. I saw you checking out that door. Beyond that door is my own private collection, not for display, and a vast library of ancient tomes. All climate controlled of course."

"Of course," Avery said as she pulled out her cell to send a quick update to Harrison and Carter.

"I'm afraid that won't do you any good in here," Maura said. "I should have mentioned it."

Avery looked at the phone's screen. There was no service.

"Lead is the only sure way to keep prying eyes out."

Maura spent the better part of the next hour researching the ring and studying every aspect of it through her specialized equipment. She made several trips to the back room, muttering to herself, then returning with the occasional ancient book. At last, she removed her glasses and sat back in her chair, rubbing her tired eyes. She returned her glasses to her face, then handed the ring back to Avery.

"Well?" Duval said.

"What did you find?" Avery said. "Is it real?"

"What you have here is an excellent copy of the original ring, which was gifted by the queen to King Charles I in the 1640s. The real ring was the only piece from the crown jewels that survived Cromwell. It was King Charles II's prized possession because it belonged to his father. He said it was a symbol of his right to the throne."

Did he, now? Avery didn't say it out loud but smiled to herself.

"A copy?" Duval exclaimed, shocked.

"An excellent copy," the woman continued. "One that would likely fool anyone, maybe even the king himself, but the historical notes I located pertaining to the original stone gave it away."

"And the actual ring?" Avery said.

"Is still safe inside the Tower of London, along with the rest of the crown jewels."

Avery and Duval exchanged an uneasy glance.

"I hope you weren't fleeced too much for this ring, assuming you were told differently."

"The cost could have been substantially higher," Avery said as she considered how close she had come to being killed at the hands of a yeoman warder.

"It isn't like it's worthless," Maura continued. "That is a real natural ruby mounted in a real solid gold setting. Priceless even. Just not with a royal history."

"What makes you say it's priceless?" Duval said.

"The hallmark I found under the band. May I?" Maura said, holding her hand out to Avery.

Avery returned the ring to her.

"You see this mark? It's worn but still legible. All fine British gold and silversmiths used hallmarks on their work centuries ago. It's the equivalent of a painter signing their work."

"Is there a way to identify the jeweler?" Avery said.

"I already have. This hallmark belonged to a smith named Rory Taylor."

"And who's he?" Duval said.

"Taylor was once the most gifted artist in Cheapside. He was a jeweler to the Crown and much of the king's court during the mid-1600s."

Maura handed the ring back to Avery, who returned it to the false bottom of her purse.

"This has been fascinating," Avery said as she rose from her chair. "I can't thank you enough for taking the time to meet with us."

"Not at all," Maura said. "I always love being part of any historically relevant find. While that may not be the ring you had hoped, it is still quite old and valuable."

61

As soon as they were back on the street, Avery pulled out her cell to phone Harrison. She turned to Duval. "What do you think?"

"I think that might be total bollocks."

"She came highly recommended," Avery said, sounding more defensive than she'd meant to. "And I trust MaryAnn implicitly."

"And I trust my expert implicitly, love. I want my guy to look at this before we rush to any judgment about this ring's provenance. Okay?"

Avery nodded. That was fair, and second opinions were a good policy to keep.

"Jeez, Ave," Harrison said. "I was beginning to worry—"

"We were beginning to worry," Carter said from the background.

"Whatever, junior," Harrison said. "Are you okay? Did you meet with the woman? What happened?"

"Duval and I are fine. We just left and we're headed to our next appointment. I'll tell you all about it when we see you. Where are you guys?"

"Hell if I even know," Harrison said.

"We're near Northampton," Carter shouted.

"You heard that?" Harrison said.

"Yeah," Avery said, surprised. "That's a long way from here."

"We got sick of driving in circles. I don't know who wants to kill us more, our driver or the guys tailing us."

"Would you mind playing decoy just a little bit longer?"

"It's your dime."

Avery and Duval caught another taxi to Hackney, on the other side of London. They both watched the entire way, but again there was no sign of a tail. As they neared the address Duval had given the driver, Avery couldn't help but feel uncomfortable with their new surroundings. This neighborhood felt much different than the last.

"Are you sure about this guy?" Avery said as they stepped out of the cab and onto the sidewalk.

"Don't let the neighborhood spook you, love," Duval said as he paid the driver in cash. "I've had a professional relationship with this bloke for as long as I can remember. Come on."

Duval's expert looked so much like a history professor from Avery's days at Princeton that she almost called him "Dr. Banks" at least five times during their visit. Unlike MaryAnn's contact, Mason's apartment had no safe room and no eye scanners. It looked to Avery like everything this man might need for research was locked up tight inside his head.

"It's not the original ring," Mason declared as he returned it to Avery after a once-over.

"What?" Duval said. "Are you sure, mate? Check it again."

"I don't need to check it again. This is a copy. An exceptionally good copy. Extremely valuable to the right collector, but it's not the ring that belonged to King Charles."

"Do you know much about the real ring?" Avery said, trying to smooth over the feathers that Duval was beginning to ruffle.

"I know all about the Eye of the Dragon, Ms. Turner. The real ring was one of Charles II's most cherished possessions. It was originally a gift from

Charles's mother to his father. The king kept the ring with him almost constantly."

"You said almost," Avery said.

"Well, on occasion the ring would need to be on display at major public celebrations."

"And you're sure this isn't that ring?" Duval said, his annoyance clearly on display.

"I'm sorry to disappoint you, my friend. But this ring is not part of the crown jewels."

As they bid Mason adieu, Avery thanked him for all his help while Duval sulked.

As soon as they were outside the building, Duval began to pace the alley. "Why would a fake ruby ring be housed in the Tower of London? It doesn't make any sense."

Avery considered sharing her theory with him but quickly thought better of the idea. If she was right about the ring, she might well be right about everything.

Although Duval had been instrumental in helping them acquire the fake ring from The tower, she didn't want him involved in what might come next.

"I know you're disappointed," Avery said. "But at least we know the truth. That's two independent experts who agree that it's a copy. I'll see to it that the remainder of your payment is deposited in your account."

"My payment? I couldn't care less about the money. I want to know where the real Eye of the Dragon is, love. This is personal now. I nearly got myself killed stealing a fake."

"*You* nearly got yourself killed?" Avery said, raising her brows. "I'm the one who got shot, remember?"

Duval stopped suddenly and grabbed Avery's arm. "You don't get where I've gotten in life without knowing people, love, and I have gotten to know you rather well. You wouldn't be cutting me loose unless there was something bigger happening here. Whatever you've got planned, I want in."

"That was never part of our deal." She removed his hand from her arm with a warning glare.

He took a step backward. "Maybe we can have a new deal."

"You agreed to help me steal the ring for one million pounds, remember? That's all you get, *love*."

Duval grinned and opened his mouth to respond before his eyes widened as his gaze shifted past Avery. Avery turned in time to see Carter and Harrison approaching on foot. Closing in on them from behind were two of the goons from their previous London visit, guns drawn.

62

"Well, well, well," the larger of the two men said. "If it isn't the treasure hunters." He poked Harrison in the back with the barrel of his gun. "Move it, grandpa."

They stopped walking within arm's reach of Avery and Duval. She made eye contact with Carter and Harrison.

"I'm not sure you want to start out by age-shaming him," Avery said.

"Gotta agree with her on this one, mate," Duval said.

"I'm not your mate," the goon said. "And what is the old-timer going to do about it?"

"This," Harrison said as he spun to his right, driving an elbow into the side of the gunman's head. Dazed, the man staggered to one side, giving Carter the time he needed to drop down and sweep the legs from under his assailant.

Avery made effective use of the distraction as she located a discarded wine bottle on the ground next to a dumpster. "Carter," she yelled as she tossed the bottle in his direction.

Carter snatched the bottle by the neck and swung at the second goon, who was wrestling with Duval. The bottle shattered over the left side of the goon's head. Avery watched the man's eyes roll back before he collapsed onto the pavement, his gun skittering away.

As Carter scrambled after the gun, Avery and Duval moved toward Harrison, whose goon had gained the upper hand after whacking Harrison with the butt of his gun.

"That's enough of that," Harrison's goon said as he stepped back and trained the gun on Avery. "Try anything stupid and the chick gets a bullet. We understand each other?"

"Yeah," Harrison said as he climbed to his feet, rubbing the back of his head.

"How about you, glory boy?" the goon said to Carter. "You gonna drop that gun or do I put a hole in your girlfriend?"

"Nope," Carter said, as he dropped the gun on the ground and held his hands out to the sides. "I got it."

"Now, chicky," the first goon said as he refocused his attention on Avery. "Hand over the ring."

"Chicky?" Avery blinked.

"This guy just doesn't learn," Duval said, shaking his head.

"I might have let the first one go," Avery said. "But now you're starting to get under my skin."

"Good," the goon said with a laugh. "The ring. Now."

"I haven't the faintest idea what ring you're talking about," Avery said, looking down at her hands.

"The one inside your pack."

"Carter, watch out," Duval shouted as a third goon raced up behind him.

Carter ducked and moved to the side, attempting to avoid the incoming tackle, but he was tripped by the second goon, who had regained consciousness.

Avery's goon used the distraction to put Avery in a headlock from behind, the gun still in his hand.

A few feet away, Carter's attacker deflected two attempted punches and used Carter's momentum on the second one to his advantage, letting Carter stumble before he closed his hands around Carter's throat. "How's this gonna look on Instagram?" He laughed as Carter's eyes bugged wide, his fingers clawing at the meaty hands locked around his throat.

"Not as good as this," Duval said, pummeling Carter's attacker in the ribs and forcing him to let go and stumble backward when one of them cracked. The man's yelp drew the attention of Harrison's attacker for just long enough—as soon as his goon was distracted, Harrison pounced, delivering a crippling punch to the gunman's solar plexus. The man staggered backward, and Harrison twisted the gun from his grasp.

Duval delivered a knee strike to the back of the man who'd been choking Carter, sending him flying.

Still struggling with her own assailant, Avery set her feet, then used all her strength to flip her goon over her back and onto the ground. The hard landing on his back knocked the wind out of him. Before he could do more than blink, Harrison stepped on his chest and pointed the gun at him.

Unafraid, the criminal came up shooting, blood blooming across Harrison's shirt as he staggered backward.

"Harry," Avery screamed as Harrison dropped his gun and hit his knees.

The sound of approaching sirens filled the air. Without hesitation, the first goon fled with his gun. Still struggling with Carter, the second goon snatched a board from the ground near the dumpster and swung it wildly, catching Carter's chin. He used the distraction to take off right behind the first, both leaving their downed partner without a second look.

Carter covered Avery's assailant while she checked on Harrison.

"Harry, are you okay?"

"I think so, but it burns like a son of a b—"

Avery gave him a warning glare.

"Son of a gun, Ave. That's what I was going to say."

"Sure you were," Carter said.

"Any thoughts on how we're going to explain this?" Harrison asked through gritted teeth.

"I don't know but we'd better come up with something quick," Carter said, pointing at the goon lying on the ground. "I think this guy is dead."

Avery looked around. "Where's Duval?" she asked.

Police vehicles slid to a stop, blocking both ends of the alley, sirens screaming and lights ablaze.

Several uniformed officers swarmed them as Avery and Carter laid the guns on the ground. The officers wasted no time handcuffing everyone. Including the motionless man Avery had left on the ground.

As Avery lay face down on the ground, she saw a set of familiar dress shoes walking toward her. The owner of the shoes stopped and knelt beside her.

"What is it with you Americans?" Inspector McGregor asked.

"Good afternoon, Inspector," Avery said. "I bet this looks kind of funny."

"Funny isn't a word that readily comes to mind, Ms. Turner."

63

London, 1665

In the growing gloom of twilight, Burgess exchanged a wordless nod with the guard standing post outside the king's chambers. The man was one of many guards under Burgess's charge and though neither spoke, both men knew why Burgess had come. It was the moment Burgess had dreaded for many months. This was the moment that he would admit his failure to the king. Burgess had been unsuccessful in his efforts to locate the elusive pirate known as Captain Ace Mullins. He had failed to recover the missing crown jewels. Burgess had let down not only himself but his country and his king. Though he was a loyal and trusted servant to His Highness, Burgess had no idea how the king would react to the news. There was no greater shame for a leader of the palace guard.

He had followed every lead, checked every rock, run down every hint and whisper. He knew what happened: his traitorous employee had given Mullins a guard uniform and entry into the Jewel House that night, and Mullins made off with the jewels. But no amount paid to snitches, no number of witnesses sought had brought Burgess anywhere close to the jewels. He had heard Mullins escaped the country and was hiding in Paris, but the French certainly weren't inclined to be of any use.

He was a good leader and an honorable guard, but as a detective he had failed.

He reached out to knock on the heavy wooden chamber door, when it abruptly swung inward. Standing before him was the king himself, his eyes piercing directly through Burgess like a sharpened blade. Burgess cast his own eyes downward toward the stone floor of the castle corridor.

"My lord," Burgess said, shame radiating off him like waves of heat.

"You have news, Captain?" Charles demanded.

"I do, Your Highness. But I am afraid it will not please you."

After what seemed an impossibly long silence, the king spoke at last. "Come," Charles said as he moved away from the door, allowing Burgess to enter.

Burgess moved to follow, exchanging another glance with the sentry as he passed. Burgess couldn't help but wonder if he would ever set eyes upon the man again. At least in this life.

Charles led him into the bedchamber where Burgess had first broken the news of the theft many months before. Unsure of exactly what the king had planned, Burgess waited for him to make the first move. The king moved to an oversized chair and sat down in front of the cold fireplace. Burgess remained standing near the entrance to the room.

"Come, Leon," the king commanded in a softer than expected tone.

Shocked, Burgess stood planted in the doorway. In all the time he'd known Charles, the king had never referred to him by his given name.

"What's the matter?" the king said.

"Nothing, sire," Burgess replied. "It's just—"

"You didn't know I even knew your Christian name, did you?"

"I was unaware, my lord."

"Come in, Leon, and take a seat. Let us talk as equals."

Burgess did as instructed. After he was seated across from the king, Charles asked him to speak his mind.

"As I said before, I come with distressing news, Your Majesty. I am afraid I have failed you."

"How have you failed me?" Charles said.

"You have tasked me with finding and bringing to justice Captain Mullins and I have not accomplished this task."

"And the crown jewels?"

Burgess hung his head in shame. "I have not succeeded in locating the jewels either, my lord."

The king seemed to ponder Burgess's admission before speaking again. Burgess couldn't help but wonder how much longer His Lordship's benevolence would last.

Charles sighed. "Mullins is a wily and unpredictable creature. I'm not even sure he understands what drives his need for revenge."

Burgess stared. The king sounded thoughtful. Contemplative. Not at all angry.

The king regarded him a moment before rising and crossing the room toward the fireplace. Burgess watched as Charles turned to face him, placing one arm upon the mantel. It was impossible not to notice the striking similarity between the oil portrait hanging above the mantelpiece and the actual king himself.

"The loss of the jewels is quite distressing, Leon," Charles said. "I'll not deny it."

Burgess nodded in agreement but remained silent. He watched as the king moved to the other side of the room where a massive writing table stood in one corner. He had visions of the king retrieving a dagger and returning only to plunge it into his heart. But that wasn't what happened. Instead, Charles reached into a hidden compartment in the wall behind the desk and retrieved a large ruby ring. Burgess felt his own eyes widening in astonishment at the sight, for he recognized it instantly. It was the Eye of the Dragon, part of the crown jewels and one of the most prized items the king possessed. Burgess studied the ring as the king drew nearer and held it out to him.

"My lord," Burgess said, refusing to accept the offering.

"It's all right, Leon. The ring is not going to bite you. I promise."

Slowly Burgess raised his hand and watched Charles place it into his palm.

Burgess held the ring close to his eyes, studying its beauty and detail, the heft of its weight. "It is exquisite, sire."

"I'll not disagree," Charles said.

"But how?" Burgess said as he handed the ring back to the king. "I know this ring was taken from the Tower by Mullins."

The king returned to his seat, ring in hand, and sat down. "The truth, my friend, is that this is not the actual Eye of the Dragon."

"I don't understand."

"It is a copy. A reproduction of the original ring commissioned by me to be created by a master craftsman."

"He must be a sorcerer, my lord."

The king grinned as his eyes returned to the ring. "Hardly. But it is true that the man's work is unequalled."

"And the remaining jewels?" Burgess said. "What of the others?"

"They, too, are being remade from the finest precious metals and jewels available. Soon the crown jewels will be complete and back in their rightful place in the Tower."

Burgess eyed the ring again. "Then what of Mullins? What if he tries to sell what he has stolen from you? Or tells others of the deception?" Burgess tried to pull back the last words even as they left his lips, but he was unsuccessful. For just an instant he saw Charles's eyes grow dark and disappointment crease his brow. But it was gone as quickly as it had come.

"Forgive me, my lord. I should not have made such a callous comment."

"No, my friend, you are right. It is a deception I suppose, but a necessary one to maintain the power of the monarchy in the eyes of our enemies. And to hold intact the public's perception of the Crown. Whether they realize it or not, real power is bestowed upon leaders by the people. But only as long as they believe their leaders are strong. Any display of weakness, and that power is repossessed."

"And what of Mullins?"

"Mullins is many things, but foolish is not one of them. He knows he would be put to death if caught, so it is unlikely he would try and sell the jewels if he hasn't already. His prattling missives seem to indicate this was never about wealth, but about power and humiliation. And so I have decided to call his bluff, and beat him at his own game. As for any claims he might make regarding his pieces being the genuine crown jewels, my word as king would certainly supersede the word of a pirate. Wouldn't you say?"

"Indeed, I would, my lord. Indeed, I would," Burgess said.

"The one thing you must do for me, Leon, is make sure the pirate's secret dies with us. No one must ever tell the tale. No one must ever know the truth." He plucked the ring from Burgess's palm and slid it onto his finger. "It is done. He is beaten. And you are free to carry on with life as it was before this began."

"Of course, sire." Burgess bowed. "I don't deserve your kindness, but remain ever thankful for it."

"Go home, good and faithful servant," Charles said. "And simply tell no one."

64

McGregor, assisted by one of the uniformed officers, helped Avery to her feet, then removed her restraints.

"I want some answers," McGregor said.

"Harry's been shot," Avery said, rubbing her wrists.

"It's not that bad," Harrison said. "Really, I'm fine."

"I'll explain everything as soon as you get him some medical help," Avery said.

"I'll hold you to that," McGregor said, nodding to one of the uniformed officers.

They spent the next twenty minutes recounting what had happened from the moment the goons appeared in the alley.

Harrison leaned against the rear of one of the police vehicles as the EMT attendants checked and cleaned the wound on his arm. The gun used by the goon who shot Harrison turned out to be a small-caliber weapon, a blessing, as the bullet barely managed to penetrate his clothing let alone his skin. The goon Avery had fought with hadn't been as lucky.

"This man really should get this wound checked by a doctor," one of the medical technicians said as he looked to Avery and McGregor for help.

Avery opened her mouth to reinforce the diagnosis, but Harrison beat her to it.

"Forget it, Avery," Harrison said. "It's not going to happen. I'm completely fine." He turned his attention to the EMTs. "Just patch me up and move along, youngsters."

Avery turned to McGregor. "Can't you make him go to the hospital?"

"Me? I can't even make you three keep out of trouble. Tell me again how you happened to be in the neighborhood?"

"Sightseeing?" Avery said.

"Here?" He looked around with his brows under his hairline. "Why don't I believe that? Perhaps one of you could explain to me why our witness up there says it was four on three?"

Harrison shrugged. "Search me. In a donnybrook like the one we just had, it's difficult for a bystander to tell whether there were six or seven participants."

"You're saying they're lying?" McGregor said.

"Just mistaken," Avery said.

McGregor's frown betrayed his disbelief.

"I've lost track of how many times we've been attacked now," Carter said as another EMT cleaned his head wounds. "You must have some idea who these guys are, Inspector."

"At the very least, the dead guy must have some ID," Harrison said. "You know, the one you just whisked away. I'm not sure how you folks do things over here, but where I come from, we lock down a scene and keep the body where it is until the medical examiner and the crime scene techs have had a chance to examine everything."

Avery caught McGregor's eyes as they glanced downward. He was hiding something, but she had no idea what it might be.

"Well, I'm proud to say that we do things differently than you Americans," McGregor said. "And the man you claimed was killed by one of your missing assailants had no identification on him. We're trying to match his prints."

"You must have some idea who he is," Harrison pressed. "Christ, I've seen him three times just in the short time I've been here."

McGregor ignored Harrison's comments and addressed Avery. "Anything else you'd like to share with me, young lady?"

Avery shook her head and tightened her grip on her bag. She wanted to talk to Rowan, but she wasn't telling this guy a thing. "No, I think we've told you all we know."

"Well then, thank you all very much for your help. We'll be in touch. Would you three like an escort back to your hotel?"

"No thanks," Avery said as she exchanged a glance with Harrison. "We'll find our own way back."

"I'm afraid I must insist," McGregor said.

"What the heck was that?" Carter said as they stood in front of the hotel, watching their police escort drive away.

"It's called the bum's rush," Harrison said. "McGregor knows more than he's telling us. He's hiding something."

"But what?" Avery said.

"I don't know enough to be sure, but I'm getting some ideas." Harry looked around. "Anyone know where the hell Duval ran off to?"

"I suspect the police make him uncomfortable," Avery said. "Might have been better for us not to be seen with him, honestly."

"Still," Carter said. "Not cool to just ditch us like that. So, what's our next move?"

"I'm thinking," Avery said.

Harrison checked his phone and muttered about needing to sit down, disappearing into the lounge without a backward glance.

Avery threw her hands up at Carter. "You have somewhere to be, too?"

"I figure we should get that thing into a safe, and ourselves into clean clothes," Carter said. "Don't worry about Harrison—he'll share with the rest of the class when he knows he has the right answer."

They retired to their respective rooms to clean up and change, with a plan to regroup in the hotel restaurant in an hour.

Avery locked her door, put the ring in the safe, and picked up her phone, tapping one side of it as she considered what to say to Rowan.

He was the government. And she was more sure after that last go-round with McGregor that the government wanted this whole thing kept dead quiet. But he hadn't stricken her as insincere, and she wanted to know what he had found out about Jeff's murder.

The experts had both said the ring she had was a good copy—and Rowan wanted the ring.

We found it, she typed. Send.

Her phone rang immediately.

"That was fast," she said when she picked up.

"Where?" His voice was sharp.

"How did your suspect interviews go?" Avery asked. "I've been working too hard on this project to ask."

"Where did you find the ring?" Rowan asked.

"Why do I have to answer you before you answer me?"

He took a deep breath. "Apologies, Ms. Turner. It's been a...very stressful day. You're sure the ring you found is the one Mr. Shelton had?"

"Positive."

"And you have it with you?"

"With all the people who've chased and shot at us? Not a chance," Avery lied. "It's in a safe place."

"That's wise," he said slowly. "How can I arrange to have it picked up?"

"You can tell me who killed Carter's friend," Avery said calmly.

"Miss Turner, I'm afraid murder investigations are terribly complicated endeavors—" he began.

"Surely your file must include a note that my mother was one of the most decorated homicide detectives in NYPD history," Avery interrupted. "I understand the difficulty. I also know we had a deal. I'll tell you where to find the ring when you deliver the shooter."

She hung up, knocked back a shot of scotch from the bar cart, and went to shower.

Had she just poked a hornet's nest? Maybe. But her mother had always said urgency from the detective was the key to a collar. And with Harrison working the case from this side, she felt better about their odds of catching the killer—mostly, she wanted to see what Rowan would do next.

As she showered off the fight, she decided her bathroom back home needed one of the huge, multi-jet showers she was enjoying in the hotel before she noticed her leg was bleeding again. She cleaned and dried the wound carefully. She had no intention of seeking medical attention at the local hospital or walk-in clinic where they would undoubtedly ask uncomfortable questions that might lead someone to call the authorities. She figured McGregor would like nothing more than to learn she'd been shot and hadn't reported it.

Avery rooted through her purse until she found what she was looking for, a small nearly empty tube of superglue. She knew there was a reason she hadn't discarded the adhesive, but she couldn't have imagined that reason would be to patch up a gunshot wound. Satisfied with the results, she wrapped herself in a towel and walked into the bedroom. Her phone was vibrating on the nightstand with a voicemail from MaryAnn. She snatched it up and returned the call.

"Sorry I missed you," Avery said.

"I'm glad to hear your voice," MaryAnn said. "Everything okay over there? I mean you'd tell me if something was wrong, right?"

"Of course I would," Avery said as she double-checked the freshly mended wound. "You have something for me?"

"Actually, I do. I spoke with a curator friend of mine in Greenwich who remembered seeing something in an old journal collection written by someone within the Royal Court around the time of the restoration. The author was a man named Leon Burgess and he was a guard captain at the Tower of London."

"A three-hundred-year-old journal?" Avery said.

"Nearly three hundred and fifty," MaryAnn continued. "And I doubt Captain Burgess could have ever imagined his journals being sold to a museum one day."

Careful what you write down, Avery thought.

"Anyway, there is a passage from near the end of Burgess's life where he mentions secrets, regrets, and lessons he wished he had taught his own children. He also references some sort of cover-up."

"About the crown jewels?"

"He doesn't go into any detail, even on his deathbed, but given where it's mentioned, I'd say whatever happened weighed on him heavily."

"Would you email all of the relevant pages to me?"

"I already did. Check your inbox."

Avery scanned through the attachments before she slammed her laptop shut, yanked clean clothes on, and went to find Carter and Harrison.

Harrison was in the bar, nursing a scotch and soda, and Carter was asleep on a chaise on the suite's balcony. Given her conversation with Rowan and what had happened to Jeff, Avery rounded them up in the suite's plush living area, passed out cocktails, and shut the heavy drapes for good measure.

"You think McGregor is watching us?" Carter asked, watching her fuss with the drapes. He sipped his drink, wincing as the alcohol stung his split lip.

"Of course he is," Harrison said. "That's exactly what I'd be doing. He doesn't trust us any more than we trust him."

"I definitely think he knows more about our attackers than he's letting on," Avery said.

"The people who killed Jeff," Carter said, a dark cloud passing over his face.

"I know he does," Harrison said.

"What do you mean, Harry?" Avery asked.

"Just what I said. I snapped a picture of the dead goon's face before they carted him off in case McGregor was stonewalling us."

"And?" Carter asked.

"And I was right. I sent the picture to my contact at Interpol, and he ran the image through their facial recognition software and came up with a name."

"Who is he?" Avery asked around a mouthful of bread.

"He wouldn't give me the name, but he confirmed that the guy was a contract killer believed to have been operating throughout Western Europe for the past decade. Apparently he has wracked up quite a few kills."

"Why didn't he kill us, then?" Carter said.

"I'm guessing because his orders were to recover the jewels," Harrison said. "And they figure you two are the way to do that."

"Guess we better avoid finding them for a while longer, then," Avery said. "But you think McGregor knows all this?"

"He knows something. But I can't tell what for sure."

Avery tapped one finger on the edge of the table. "Rowan said he didn't get anywhere with the interviews he did last week," she said. "But I told him we'd found the ring, and he got tunnel vision. He wants it. Badly. Maybe because of his orders, but it's hard to tell."

The police are one thing, but getting on the wrong side of MI5 is probably a lousy idea, Ave." Harrison scratched his head.

"I told him he could have the location of the ring Jeff stole when he tells me who the killer is."

"You don't think he'll just come take it?" Carter's eyes widened.

"I guess then we'd know if he's a good guy or not," Avery said. "But I also told him I don't have it."

Harrison looked pensive for a moment and then shook his head, saying nothing.

Avery noticed, but didn't comment, leaning toward the guys. "I learned a couple of things today. First, MaryAnn's authenticity expert said the real Eye of the Dragon, the one Papa has, was King Charles II's prized possession because he believed it was a sign that he was chosen by God to lead England."

"Oh, but Mullins..." Carter bounced in his seat, pointing at Avery.

"Exactly. So here's what I think: Mullins stole the jewels, not to sell them, not even to have them. He wanted to humiliate Charles. But he did want the ring."

"Because of what it meant." Harrison nodded along. "Sounds about right."

"So then where is the rest of the treasure?"

Avery opened her laptop. "MaryAnn also found something. She sent us photos of some journal pages written by an old Tower of London guard. A captain named Burgess, written just before he died."

"Deathbed confessions. Interesting," Harrison said. "What did Burgess say?"

Avery skimmed the journal entries again, looking for the passage that had jumped out at her. "My hope is that we sealed the secret in with the traitor, and that hell awaits all who were part of the conspiracy. My regret remains failing my king, but all trace of this memory dies here with me." She started there, then went back and read all the pages aloud.

"So, what do you think?" Avery asked when she had finished.

"I want to know what branch off the main tunnel Burgess was talking about," Carter said. "The only offshoot we saw was the one we took that passed under the sewer, and according to Duval that wasn't added until about a hundred years ago."

"The notes say it was sealed off before Burgess died in 1678," Avery said.

"With a traitor inside," Harrison said. "But not Mullins." He looked at Carter. "Right?"

"Seems very possible."

"It does indeed," Avery said as she rose and crossed to her bedroom. "And I'm pretty sure the cover-up has to do with the jewel heist. Which reminds me." Setting the computer on the table, she jumped up to run to her room and returned a moment later with the water damaged book they'd found in the cave outside Blakeney. "I remember seeing something about a tunnel in here."

"Yeah, but didn't we think that was a reference to the catacombs in Paris?" Harrison said.

"What if we were wrong?" Carter said. "What if it was the tunnel we used to escape from the Tower?"

"Not the one I read you before. There was something else...Here it is," Avery said, reading. "*He sealed my tunnel just as I knew he would, creating a loss of his own making.*'"

"What does that mean?" Harrison said.

"I really wonder if this is Mullins talking about Burgess," Avery said.

"It does fit with Burgess's notes about a sealed tunnel," Carter said.

Avery raised the journal to eye level and peered at it, poking at the page edges. "Harry, hand me that file on the end table," she said, pointing to his end of the sofa.

"You're gonna do your nails?" Harrison said and he passed it over. "Now?"

Avery gave him her best scowl before using the file to gently separate two pages that were stuck together.

"I've got another entry here," Avery said, squinting at the cramped writing. "Guys, listen! According to this, sometime later, Mullins and his crew were set upon by a lower, more ruthless band of pirates. They staged a sneak attack while Mullins and a few of his men were separated from the crew. Because they wanted the ring that belonged to Mullins's father."

"The king," Harrison said.

"Oh, man," Carter said.

"Mullins gave it up to save the rest of his crewmen. It had a profound effect on him judging by his notes. He considered it to be the one bit of his heritage that he possessed while everything else would be passed on to his more fortunate brother. Which means—assuming the ring we saw in Greece was the real Eye of the Dragon—Mullins didn't drop it or hide it in the reef where Jeff found it."

"Then who did?" Harrison said.

And exactly how well did Captain Burgess and Ace Mullins know each other? Avery wondered. Both of their writings alluded to having been acquainted, but how? Avery shook off the question for now. The bigger question was how to return the ring in her bag to the Tower of London before someone came for it—as someone surely would. By now security would have tightened substantially, and the guards should have been able to figure out how they gained access to the Tower in the first place. Which meant that rappelling back inside wasn't an option. No, this time they would need to go in the same way Mullins had nearly four centuries ago.

"Who wants to join me on a tour of the sewer tunnels leading into the Tower of London?" Avery asked.

"I'm in," Carter said.

"Are you two completely unhinged?" Harrison thundered. "You were nearly killed the last time. Why on earth would you want to go back?"

"I told you, Harry," Avery said. "I was only borrowing the ring. I needed the experts to look at it. Now it's time to return it."

"And how exactly are you planning to do that?" Harrison said. "You don't think you'll just be able to waltz in and hand it to someone, do you?"

"Of course not, Harry," Avery said.

"The rappelling option we trained so hard for is out, as we seem to have lost our ride," Carter said. "So, what are you thinking, Avery?"

"Well, first, we should be able to use their own tour schedule to our advantage."

"What makes you think they're still giving public tours?" Harrison said.

"You said it yourself, Harry," Avery said. "There hasn't been a single mention of the break-in on any of the British news channels."

"She's right," Carter said. "Someone is more afraid of public embarrassment than stopping us."

"I wouldn't count on that second part," Harrison said. "I agree that they'd want to keep the break-in and theft quiet, but if it were me, I'd be coming after you with everything I had at my disposal."

"You're probably right," Avery said. "But we have one big advantage."

"And that is?" Harrison said.

"Nobody would ever guess that we'd be stupid enough to break in again to return the ring," Carter said.

"Only because they don't know you," Harrison said.

65

It was still dark when Avery and Carter slipped down through the same manhole cover they'd used to make their escape several days before. Harrison joined them this time, but only to drive them to the entrance point in a car Avery had rented and to make sure they got underground okay. He did his best to try to talk them out of it, but Avery remained steadfast.

Knowing what they would be up against allowed Avery and Carter to bring the correct gear with them. They wore typical tourist garb, which they would need for the second part of their plan, underneath a lightweight outer shell that would be easy to peel off while still protecting them from the foulness awaiting them in the tunnel.

"You still sure about this, Avery?" Carter said as they retraced their steps along the dark tunnel toward the Tower of London. "You know, it's not too late to reconsider."

"We're not just down here to return the ring, Carter. What do you think the chisels and hammers are for?"

"I get that, but what if we don't find this walled-up tunnel? And what if you're wrong about what Mullins did with the rest of the treasure?"

"I'm not wrong," Avery said. "Harry's right, they are keeping a lid on the theft just like I knew they would. Just like they did all those years ago.

Anything to avoid embarrassment and to keep from showing the castle's vulnerability."

"And if you're wrong? What if we can't find our way back to the tower tunnel? What if we can't find the tunnel Burgess wrote about?"

Avery stopped walking and turned to face him. "Then we simply return the ring like we planned, then get out of there. No one will ever be the wiser. You'll just have to trust me on this, Carter."

Carter sighed. "Let's do this."

A half hour later they crawled into the main tunnel that led to the Tower dungeon.

"I told you we'd find it," Avery said as she turned around to gloat.

"Um." Carter pointed as his eyes widened.

"What?"

"Don't freak out, but you found more than the tunnel."

Avery felt her skin prickle with fear. "Oh, please don't tell me that there's a rat on my pack."

"All right, I won't tell you. Just. Don't. Move."

Avery did her best to remain still while Carter shrugged off his own backpack and pulled out the hammer.

"What do you want me to do?" Avery whispered.

"Nothing. Don't do anything. Just stay put and close your eyes, okay?"

Avery listened to the sound of Carter walking around behind her. A moment later she felt something large shift on her pack followed by a sickening crunch and a thump.

"Okay, I got it. You can turn around now."

Avery opened her eyes and turned. Lying motionless on the floor of the tunnel was a rat the size of a small dog.

"Oh my God."

"Always expect the unexpected," Carter said. "Isn't that what Duval told us?"

"Yeah, although I don't think that's what he had in mind," Avery said as she gave the dead rodent a wide berth. "Speaking of rats, where is Mr. Risk Taker now?"

"You mean now that he got his million bucks?" Carter said with a shrug. "I guess maybe it was all about the money with him after all."

Avery wasn't so sure.

———

They waited in the tunnel until they knew tours were well underway, then slipped back through the grate into the dungeon. The floor grate was in an alcove slightly out of view of the main room portion of the tour, providing them with some cover as they shed their outer layer of clothing and backpacks, then stowed them in a recess. They knelt in the shadows, waiting for their chance to slip into a group unseen. It wasn't long before they heard a tour guide talking and several members of the group laughing at a joke the guide had made.

"Okay," the tour guide said. "Unless any of you feel the need to spend some time in the iron maiden, we should move on."

"You ready?" Avery whispered, amid the sound of the crowd chuckling and moving away.

"After you," Carter said.

Avery was surprised by how easy it was to blend into the group. Apart from an elderly couple who gave them a cursory glance, no one else, not even the tour guide, seemed to notice the recent arrivals.

They followed along with the group, laughing with the others at the canned humor as if they hadn't heard the presentation before, until they finally came to the public restrooms.

"For any of you needing to use the facilities, this would be a good time," the tour guide said.

"Back in a sec," Avery said as she scooted off toward the women's room.

Avery secured the latch on the stall door, then flushed the toilet to mask the sound of her removing the tank cover. She pulled the ring from her pocket and studied it one last time before dropping it into the water tank.

A knock on the stall door froze Avery where she stood.

"Will you be much longer?" a desperate voice called out from the other side of the door.

"Be right out," Avery said, her voice cracking.

With another flush she carefully returned the tank top to its original position.

She unlocked the stall door and strode past the impatient young woman.

"All yours," Avery said with a smile.

Avery and Carter hung back from the tour group until they were forgotten, then quickly made their way back to the dungeon. They changed footwear and donned the coveralls again before dropping down into the tunnel. Carter struggled with the grate for one tense moment after it failed to seat properly in its frame. He waited until the next tour group had moved on before attempting to make it sit flush. Finally, it dropped into place with a *clunk*.

"Let's get a move on," Avery said.

They moved along the tunnel slowly, occasionally knocking their hammers against the stone while training their lights on the walls looking for anything that might indicate a walled-up entrance to a side tunnel. Any sign that the stone might be of a different vintage.

"You never told me how you were planning to let them know about the ring," Carter said. "I mean, you're not just going to hope some custodian discovers it in the toilet, are you?"

"Email," Avery said. "We'll send a note by way of a private untraceable server to the address listed on the museum's public website."

"I like it," Carter said.

"I'm glad you approve."

Twenty minutes later Carter stopped walking. "I hate to say it, but this might be a fool's journey."

"It's here, Carter," Avery said. "I know it is."

"I know it's hard to give up, Avery, but sometimes it's the right thing to do. I dragged you and Harry all this way to try and save Jeff from whatever he was into, and we failed. But we have managed to take his search further than he could have imagined. I might even go so far as to say we uncovered some seriously cool history. But I'm not sure how much further we should take this."

Avery shook her head. They'd come too far, risked too much to quit now.

"Come on, Avery," Carter said. "For all we know, someone may have discovered the tunnel we're looking for back around the time they put in the sewers."

"It's here, dammit," Avery shouted as she swung her hammer at the wall. "It has to be here."

One of the stones Avery had struck shifted, then tumbled back inside the wall, leaving a dark hole in its wake. They heard it land with a thud on the far side.

Staring at each other with wide eyes, they moved toward the hole for a better look. Their lights revealed another long dark passage on the other side.

"Forget everything I just said, okay?" Carter said as they stepped back and began knocking more stones from the wall.

It took them several minutes to knock out enough stones to make the hole big enough to pass through. Avery could feel the sweat building up under her coveralls.

"You ready?" she asked, winded and grinning like a fool.

"After you, Your Highness," Carter said, bending at the waist like a loyal subject.

66

Stepping through the wall into the dark, still passage was like stepping back in time. The change in the air was hard to describe. It was just as dank and moldy-smelling as the other tunnels they had passed through, but there was an odd stillness associated with this one Avery would have been hard pressed to describe. She shivered as she moved along the tunnel. She wasn't sure if it was from her sweat-soaked clothing or the realization that they were the first two living souls to enter this space in nearly four hundred years.

"It's a little creepy," Avery said.

"Oh." Carter held his light over her head and pointed with his free hand. "A lot creepy. There's the traitor Burgess mentioned."

Avery froze, her eyes locked on the crumpled skeleton chained to the wall by one old iron shackle. "I've seen about all the dead people I can handle for a while," she squeaked.

"Same," Carter said, leading her past the bones by flattening himself up against the opposite wall. Avery looked at the ceiling and moved her feet, focused on the only question that mattered now: Were the stolen crown jewels also buried down here?

"Come on," Avery said as she led the way.

Not wanting to chance missing something, they moved their lights over every square inch of the tunnel as they walked. These tunnel walls weren't nearly as smooth as the other passages had been, almost like it had been hurriedly dug out with small tools.

"I wonder if Mullins dug this hims—" Avery started to say before stopping short.

"What is it?" Carter hurried to her side.

Avery stood, staring into a shorter, narrow alcove about ten feet deep, just where the tunnel started to turn uphill. Stacked at the back were two large wooden trunks.

"You don't think," Carter said.

"Only one way to find out," Avery said as she brushed past the cobwebs and stepped inside.

The trunks were banded with rusted steel and chained with padlocks.

"Don't suppose you brought your super-duper treasure chest skeleton key with you?" Carter said.

"Not this time, I'm afraid."

Carter shed his pack and removed several items. "Then I guess it's hammer time."

Using the hammer and chisel, Carter and Avery made quick work of ancient, rusted padlocks on both chests. They hoisted the top one and set it on the floor next to the other.

"Man, this is heavy," Carter said.

"You'd think we'd be used to it by now."

"I think you should do the honors," Carter said as he stepped out of the way.

"You sure?"

"Absolutely," Carter said. "Just know, if we went through all of this to find two chests full of scrap metal or candlesticks, I'm gonna go postal."

"Don't worry," Avery said. "If that's all that's in these, I'll join you."

As Avery raised the first lid, the tunnel glowed from the light reflecting off the trunk's contents.

"Oh, man," Carter said.

Speechless, Avery dropped to her knees. The trunk was filled to the brim with all manner of jewels, precious metals, and heirloom pieces, each rivaling any museum collection she'd ever seen. She recognized several from the doubles she'd seen up in the Jewel House.

"Oh my God, Carter. We did it. We found the stolen crown jewels."

"You did it, Avery."

Avery spied a small leather-bound journal lying half-buried among the treasure. The spine cracked and split as she opened the cover, but the pages were still largely intact. She recognized the handwriting instantly.

"What is it?" Carter said.

"A note from Ace Mullins to the king."

"You really were right," Carter said. "But why would Mullins go to all the trouble to break into the Tower just to leave the jewels in the basement?"

Avery looked up at him. "You can ask that after what we just did?"

"Touché."

Avery held up one finger as she read. "He hid the treasure nearby in a stand of hollow trees until he knew Burgess and the guards had moved on, continuing their hunt elsewhere. Then he returned the treasure to the tunnel. He knew they would wall up the tunnel once they figured out how Ace had broken in. The only pieces he kept were the ring belonging to his father and the mirror that his mother had used from the queen's dressing table on her visits to the palace, because it was her favorite."

"But all his scheming was for naught," Carter said. "Charles outsmarted him and kept the theft a secret by having fakes made of every piece."

Avery nodded. "They've been protecting and giving tours of replicas for centuries while the real crown jewels were walled up down here."

"Only one problem left," Carter said. "How do you propose we get these out of here?"

Avery grinned and reached into her own pack. "With these," she said, holding up several bundles of nylon straps. "And this," she said, holding the DiveNav in her other hand.

Avery attempted to triangulate a shorter way out of the tunnels that didn't involve a ladder, while Carter prepared the trunks for travel using the nylon straps.

"These are still going to be bulky to move," Carter said. "But I think the straps will allow us to drag them without too much trouble. You make any headway with that thing?"

"I'm pretty sure if we followed this tunnel to its conclusion, we would end up right in the same neighborhood where Jeff was staying."

"You think Jeff figured something out that led him to that neighborhood?"

"Absolutely." She nodded.

"We have no way of knowing what's at the other end now, though. It very well may be blocked."

"You're right," Avery said. "And I don't want to drag these any farther than we have to."

"My point exactly," Carter said. "Let's stick with the route we know. Getting these out of here is going to be hard enough without dragging them into a dead end."

"Agreed. I sure would like another look at that map we found, though. I still think there is something else involving sunshine, the map, and the amulet you found in the catacombs."

"You might be right. But maybe we can just count our blessings for one day, huh? I mean, we found the treasure, and nobody is trying to kill us at present. I call that a good day."

"You're right. Let's get these out of here."

It was slow going, but despite the weight, the trunks glided smoothly across the tunnel floor on the nylon straps. Avery and Carter stopped numerous times to rest, but their adrenaline kept them moving toward the connecting sewer tunnel.

Nearing the mouth of the tunnel, they froze as the beams of several flashlights illuminated their faces, blinding them where they stood.

"That's far enough," a baritone male voice commanded.

Avery struggled to see past the brightness. Four silhouettes stood, each with a light and gun trained on her and Carter. She recognized two of the men as the goons who fled immediately after Harrison was shot. The third was new to the party and stood in front of the last one until the taller man stepped around.

"Weapons down, gentlemen," Rowan said, smiling at Avery and Carter.

They exchanged an uneasy glance.

"Splendidly done, you two," Rowan said, waving at his companions to stow their weapons as he put his hand out to shake Avery's hand and then Carter's. "I wasn't sure you'd find these—I wasn't even sure until today that they really existed—but you've done it. The Crown thanks you, Ms. Turner, Mr. Mosley. We can take it from here."

"How do we know you're not thieves?" Carter asked. "If it's all the same to you, we'll take the trunks up to the proper authorities."

"Don't be ridiculous, Mr. Mosley," Rowan said. "I am the epitome of the proper authority, here today to serve truth and justice, I assure you. I'm so pleased we happened across you two."

"Happened across?" Avery's eyebrow went up. "Since when does MI5 skulk around in sewer tunnels looking to happen onto anything?"

"We spotted you on the security cams in the Tower," Rowan said. "Given what you'd told me about your day earlier, I wanted to make sure you weren't followed by anyone with ill intent, so I brought my team down." He raised both hands, his facial expression hurt. "You've done so much for Britain. I was just trying to get you back home safely, Miss Turner."

Avery glanced at the other men. "They attacked us today and shot my assistant."

"A misunderstanding," the tallest goon said, following Rowan's lead and raising his hands. "You were in the company of a known thief."

"You didn't identify yourselves as law enforcement," Avery said.

"We are called the secret service for a reason, miss," Rowan said, putting his hand out. "Please, let us help you carry that. We know a faster way out, and it won't be safe here for much longer."

67

Avery had less than a split second in which to consider their situation as she exchanged a glance with Carter. They had worked so hard and come too far to have their discovery snatched right out from under their noses. Rowan was the police, and his team was armed. Her brain scrambled to come up with a workable solution, but she couldn't see one. Outnumbered and unarmed, there really was no other option than to comply.

"Those trunks are quite literally full of priceless history," Avery said. "How can we be sure your intentions are honorable?"

"You can't, not for sure," Rowan said. "But from where I stand it doesn't look like you're in any position to challenge my word."

Avery released her grip on the straps and stepped away from her trunk. After a moment, Carter followed suit.

"Where is the ring?" Rowan asked.

"In Greece with a private collector," Carter said because he knew Avery wouldn't and he didn't like the way the tall guy was looking at her.

Rowan kept his eyes on Avery. "And the one you stole from the Tower last night?"

"In a toilet tank. Middle stall, third floor ladies' room," she said. "I don't think—"

"Miss Turner," Rowan said. "Respectfully, your service to the Crown is complete. You have the thanks of the king himself, but this is over. Indeed, it never happened at all. You are still currently free to go."

Avery trudged past Rowan, Carter directly behind her. Neither of them looked back or spoke until they reached the manhole and began to strip off their coveralls.

"How angry are you?" Carter said.

She threw her hands up. "I don't even know what to think," she said. "It fits, on one hand, with the government trying to keep this quiet."

"And they didn't kill us," Carter added. "That's a point for cop over thug."

They climbed out of the manhole onto the street above. This time there were no neighborhood kids eyeballing them.

"I can't believe we just lost everything," Carter said as he slid the cover back into place.

"We didn't," Avery said, remembering that she had slid Captain Mullins's journal into her pack. "Not everything."

Duval was waiting for them outside the hotel.

"You've got a lot of nerve showing up here," Carter said.

"Calm yourself, mate. I just wanted to make sure Avery hadn't forgotten about the rest of my commission."

"Commission?" Avery said. "You're lucky I couldn't find a way to withdraw the initial deposit. The deal was you help us recover the ring, determine whether it was genuine, and return it. You were curiously absent during that last part." She turned to Carter. "You didn't see him down there in the tunnels, did you?"

"Nope," Carter said. "The only rat I saw was the one I whacked with the hammer."

Harrison drove up to where they were standing in the rental. "What happened to keeping me up to date? I was worried sick. And what is he doing here?"

"It might be best if we didn't have this conversation out here," Avery said, looking around to see who might be watching them.

Carter opened the rear door of the rental and looked at Duval. "Get in."

Harrison drove them around, watching for tails, while they talked.

"Well, did you return the ring or not?" Duval said.

"We returned it," Avery said. "No thanks to you."

"Yeah, sorry about that. But I didn't think you'd want the police connecting you to me."

"Oh, is that why you took off?" Harrison asked. "I thought maybe it was because we were getting shot at."

"They connected us to you anyway. That's why they were shooting," Avery said.

"What?" Duval and Harrison asked in unison.

"We found the jewels," Avery said. "Pretty much where I thought they were. And those guys from the fight this morning? They showed up with Rowan, who thanked us for our service to the Crown and took the trunks right after he dismissed us."

"You're kidding." Harrison stopped the car.

"Not a bit here that's funny," Avery said.

Harrison turned on Duval. "Do you know an MI5 intelligence officer named Rowan?"

Duval shook his head. "No. What makes you think I would know anyone at MI5?"

"Oh, come on," Harry said. "Unlimited funds, security consultant, high-end burglaries, access to night-mission helicopters...Should I continue?"

Duval remained silent as he appeared to be formulating a response.

"What are we missing?" Carter asked.

"What do you know about a black ops sector of the British government?" Harrison asked Duval. "Because I'm nearly certain that's who killed Jeff Shelton. I'm waiting for some confirmation and a list of names."

Avery gasped before she looked between Harrison and Duval. "Harry, the calls you made earlier?"

"To a friend at Interpol who's running a check for me," he said.

"Look, love," Duval said. "I'm not naïve enough to think the government isn't involved in some shady doings, but outright murder? Seems a bit far-fetched. This isn't some Ian Fleming novel."

"I verified Rowan's story last week," Harrison said. "He has a long history with the military and the police."

"So we did the right thing, then, I guess," Avery said.

Harrison tapped the steering wheel. "Here's the thing that's bugging me. I can't imagine a sworn intel officer of the British government taking an order or even getting involved in a secret that doesn't somehow threaten national security. MaryAnn said Mullins's jewel theft was a big deal back when it happened. If it had come out then it would have made the king look weak to England's adversaries. But that break-in is hundreds of years removed. Who would care now? At worst they might have to put up with some late-night groaners from Jimmy Fallon."

"Harry's right," Duval said. "This isn't some bomb code, it's just a bunch of moldy old baubles. A gold-plated embarrassment, but certainly not something worth killing over. Something is off."

"Rowan came to us and asked for our help finding the ring," Avery said.

"Fine time for you to share that." Duval shook his head. "The only way this makes sense is if these guys plan on keeping this quiet so they can sell the jewels." Duval turned his attention to Carter and Avery. "I'd say you just got had, mates."

Harry's phone buzzed and he pulled it out, his free hand going to his head before he flipped the screen around.

"Rowan was reassigned last year," he said. "To a top-secret sector of the agency that doesn't even keep files. He's a fixer."

"So, they do want to keep it a secret," Avery said.

"The ballistics on the rifle rounds from the bank roof match a government-issue rifle used by MI5 snipers. Didn't you say he had no leads on Jeff's death?"

"He said it's complicated."

Harrison flicked to the next photo. "Because the sniper who has that weapon is in his command."

"So you solved Jeff's murder, Harry?" Carter patted his friend's shoulder. "Thank you."

Avery shook her head and raised both hands. "So now what do we do? We can't just let the guys who killed Jeff get what they came for and walk away billionaires."

Duval rubbed his unshaven chin between his thumb and forefinger for a moment. "I might have an idea."

"I'm all ears," Avery said.

"There's only one way I know of to get even with someone who steals something from you."

"And that is?" Carter asked.

"Steal it back."

"And how do you reckon we do that?" Harrison asked.

"As it happens, I know a few blokes who could have given old Captain Ace Mullins a run for his money. What you want now is purely low-tech, and the guys I'm talking about are the best."

"Why should we trust you after you bailed on us?" Carter said. "What's to say you won't do it again after we reacquire the crown jewels?"

"I already explained my rapid departure. I have an allergy to law enforcement types. No offense, Harry."

"Okay," Avery said. "You've got our attention. Tell us more."

68

Despite Carter's protests, Avery gave Duval the green light to contact his friends.

"They are better for muscle than brains," Duval said.

"Maybe that's just what we need at this point," Harrison said. "I for one am tired of getting banged up and shot every time these jerks turn up."

Avery smacked her own forehead. "If they work for Rowan, they've been turning up not because they were tracking us with a gizmo but because I've been telling him where we're going. Every step of the way except the one place they didn't show up: Duval's warehouse. I thought MI5 watching out for us was helpful."

"You had no way to know, love." Duval patted her shoulder as he left the room with his phone in his hand.

While Duval rounded up his friends, Avery called the Tower of London's main office and told them to send someone to the restroom to get the ring in case it wasn't too late, then called MaryAnn and asked what she could find on Rowan. "Harry's Interpol contacts confirmed his background: former British military, special ops, military intelligence, and finally recruited into MI5."

"This guy sounds like a real 007," MaryAnn said, typing. "What do you need from me, exactly?"

Harrison ambled over and Avery put the phone on speaker. "Harry's here, MaryAnn."

"Hey, Harry," MaryAnn said. "Yes, I am still feeding your fish. They're all happy, I promise."

"Thank you. Anything on this Rowan character?"

"We're trying to figure out which side he's on and where he would've gone." Avery pulled up the dark web and began searching for references that might correspond to Rowan in any way, pausing after a few minutes of searching. "I can't locate any mention of this guy on the dark web. How about properties he may own, MaryAnn?"

"Give me a sec."

Avery could hear MaryAnn typing frantically.

"Okay, I might have something here," MaryAnn said. "There are two addresses associated with him. The first is right in London. It looks like a posh upper-floor condo in the pricy end of town. Apparently, they pay MI5 special ops very well."

"Or he inherited some money," Avery offered.

"Or he's dirty as he—" Harrison began.

Avery shot Harrison a warning glance, cutting him off midsentence.

"Heck. I was going to say dirty as heck, Ave."

"Sure you were, Harry," MaryAnn said with a chuckle.

"What about the other property connected to him?" Avery asked, attempting to keep them on track.

"It looks like he owns some acreage out in the countryside near Sufton Court," MaryAnn said. "According to the description on the deed, the land is mostly undeveloped, apart from an old shack. Let me jump on Google Earth real quick."

"Maybe the guy likes to hunt in his off time," Harrison said.

"Or maybe he needs a place to hide the crown jewels he just stole from us," Carter said.

"I can't see anything new on the land. There is one tiny structure at the southeast corner that seems to match the deed description, but I don't know how recent this satellite image is."

"If he's MI5, it's unlikely that his property would be available for public viewing," Harrison said. "That view might be just for show."

"Well, there's only one way to find out," Avery said. "Let's pay Mr. Rowan a visit. Just to see what's what with our own eyes."

"Be careful," MaryAnn said. "I don't want to lose you guys."

"You just don't want to be saddled with Harry's fish forever," Avery teased.

"Well, that too," MaryAnn said.

Duval's friends turned out to be anything but what Avery had conjured up in her mind. Instead of a gang of burly head-breakers, they looked more like yoga instructors or former gymnasts. Trim, fit, and polite, their names were Javier, Reggie, and Oscar. Despite their unlikely outward appearance, Duval vouched for all three men when they met back at his warehouse.

"They are more than capable of handling anything we might encounter," Duval said.

Avery could see that Carter and Harrison still weren't convinced.

"Perhaps a demonstration," Javier, the smallest of the three, offered.

"That's a good idea," Harrison said.

"Here you go," Oscar said as he tossed a padded training vest at Harrison.

"Oh no, not me," Harrison said. "As it is I get my butt handed to me by Avery on a regular basis. Besides, I just got shot."

"That flesh wound?" Carter asked. "You call that getting shot?"

"I don't remember you being wounded by anything more than a discarded bit of kindling, junior," Harrison said as he tossed the vest to Carter. "Seems like you're overdue for a butt kicking."

"All right." Carter slid the vest around his torso and began to tighten the Velcro straps.

Avery watched as Javier suited up in the same padded outfit as Carter. Each suit included a boxer's training helmet and gloves, similar to the ones that Avery and Harrison trained with at home.

"What do you say we go at this at like half speed and power?" Javier said.

"Don't hold back on my account," Harrison said. "I'm kinda looking forward to watching Carter get his."

Carter grinned. "You heard the man."

"I really think we should go easy to start," Javier said.

"I won't be," Carter said before slipping the mouthguard in place and moving toward Javier.

Javier countered Carter's approach as both men danced around one another, each calculating his opponent's movements and tells.

Avery could feel the excitement building, wishing she was in the pads instead, but the last thing she needed was to have her leg wound tear open again.

Carter danced around until he had Javier backed into a corner. As he moved to deliver a punch, Javier ducked and swept Carter's legs out from under him, sending him crashing to the canvas.

"Very impressive, Carter," Harrison said.

Carter recovered quickly but Javier had already moved away. Avery could tell Carter was upset about being taken down so easily as he charged at Javier.

Again, Carter wound up and delivered a combination of punches, two to the body and one uppercut to Javier's head, none of them connecting. Javier simply dodged each blow as if they'd been delivered in slow motion.

Harrison turned to Avery. "I wish we'd had these guys with us when we met Rowan's goons."

Avery was thinking the very same thing.

"Come on," Carter said, his frustration showing. "Are you going to dance around all day, or can you actually fight?"

Javier looked to Avery for a sign. She gave a wary nod. Immediately, Javier pounced, releasing a flurry of punches to Carter's body and head. Each one rocked the larger man until it was clear that Carter was no match for his quicker and smaller opponent.

Carter backed away from Javier and regrouped. This time he came at Javier like a bull. Before Carter could throw a single punch, Javier spun on the ball of his right foot, his left leg coming around high until his foot connected with Carter's head, snapping it backward and dropping him to the floor like a stone.

This time Carter lay there clearly stunned by the kick. Javier moved in and offered his hand to help Carter up.

Avery could see Carter was weighing his options.

"Just take his hand, Carter," Avery said.

"Or don't," Harrison said. "Javier hasn't even broken a sweat and I'm rather enjoying this. I could use some popcorn."

At last Carter grabbed Javier's hand and struggled to his feet.

"Well?" Duval asked. "Are you convinced?"

"How are the other two?" Avery said.

Reggie spoke up for the first time. "Javi is the weakest fighter of the three of us."

Avery looked back at Carter, who was clearly dazed, with his helmet in one hand. "If he's the weakest, I'm glad I didn't get in here with either of his buddies," he said.

"What about weapon proficiency?" Harrison said.

Oscar answered, "Javier is the best."

"Welcome to the team," Avery said.

69

The undeveloped property MaryAnn located for Rowan was situated in a sleepy, wooded hamlet called Woolhope in Hereford about three and a half hours west of London. They loaded up two nondescript vehicles with all the necessary gear they'd need for a proper reconnaissance, then hopped on the M4.

"Any idea what to expect?" Reggie asked Avery.

"None, but given his military experience and the fact that he is employed by British intelligence, I'd say we should prepare for almost anything."

Duval nodded his agreement.

"Let's not forget, if we want to assume Rowan has been behind everything that has been thrown at us, he has been a step ahead of us the entire way," Carter said.

"If you're right about that, he'll expect this," Javier said.

"Good," Oscar said. "I like a challenge."

"This must be it," Duval said as they rolled past an unmarked dirt road leading into a thickly wooded area. Standing back from the road, almost out of view, was a small, weathered structure that might have served as a gatehouse or guard shack.

"What do you want to do?" Duval asked.

"Don't stop," Avery said. "Keep going and we'll try and find someplace nearby to park."

They pulled into a parking area about a half mile beyond the dirt drive. The lot appeared to be a parking place designed to accommodate hikers and bird watchers.

"Good luck trying to fit in here," Harrison said. "We look as much like birders as we do like birds."

"Don't sell yourself short, Harry," Carter said. "With that hat and a pair of binoculars, you'll fit right in."

Oscar laughed.

"Don't encourage him," Avery said, shaking her head.

"So how do you want to do this?" Carter asked.

"We operate under the assumption that Rowan must have a country getaway back there somewhere," Duval said.

"Or a bunker," Harrison said.

"Anything is possible given what we know about him," Avery said.

"Let's grab a couple of bicycles, and Avery and I can pretend to be riding, then enter the woods near the driveway and check out that guard shack," Javier said.

"Why don't I take Carter and Duval with me, and we'll do a bit of pole work," Reggie said.

"Pole work?" Carter asked.

"I don't care what your plan is," Harrison said. "I'm not wearing pasties."

"I could have gone the rest of my life without that image in my head, Harry," Avery said.

"Not that kind of pole work," Reggie said, chuckling as he stepped out and slapped a brightly colored, magnetized Crown Communications sign on the side of the van. "No better way to find out what he's up to than checking out his communication links, right?"

"Sounds good," Oscar said. "Harry and I will monitor everything from here."

"I see you guys have done this before," Harrison said.

"Once or twice," Javier said as he exchanged a knowing glance with Duval.

Avery and Javier coasted to a stop close to where Reggie's van was parked on the side of Broadmore Common. They drank from their water bottles while pretending to rest. Carter and Reggie were already in position near the base of the telephone pole while Duval, who had donned an orange vest, was directing traffic around the operation.

"If I didn't know better I'd think they really were checking telephone lines," Avery said.

"Reggie probably knows more about communications than most of the real techs," Javier said. "As soon as the road is clear of approaching cars, we'll scoot into the woods, okay?"

"Right behind you," Avery said.

They stashed their bikes just out of sight behind a thick stand of evergreens and approached the shack from the rear.

"Empty," Javier said. "Like I figured. This building is more for show than anything."

"Good," Avery said. "That will make things easier."

"Not necessarily. I noticed trip wires surrounding the perimeter just beyond the shack. It's going to be tough to get a look at whatever is down that road without giving ourselves away."

"Not if we do it electronically," Avery said as she removed her laptop from her pack and began typing.

"What are you doing with that?" Javier asked.

"Hacking into Rowan's system. If he really has a secure hideaway here, he'll need internet access to run his security systems, right? Bingo."

"Bingo?"

"I've located his Wi-Fi signal. Now I'll access his system."

"What are you, some kind of tech genius?"

"Something like that." Avery smiled.

Harrison sat in the passenger seat of the SUV, nervously drumming his fingers on the armrest while he and Oscar monitored the radio for updates from the others.

"Don't mind telling you, I'm a nervous wreck," Harrison said.

"I thought you used to be a cop, Harry?" Oscar said. "You must have done this kind of thing all the time."

"Not really. I mean, yeah, we did a lot of surveillance, but never on an MI5 officer. And never with Avery in the crosshairs."

"You two are very close, I've noticed."

"She's like my niece or the daughter I never had. Her mother, Valerie, and I used to be partners. NYPD."

"Detectives?"

Harrison nodded. "Val and I worked homicide side by side for almost two decades."

"Where is her mother now?"

"With the angels. Killed in the line seven years back."

"Sorry, mate."

Harrison nodded. "I guess I'll always worry about Avery."

"Well, don't worry too much, Harry. She's in there with the best."

"Okay, I'm in," Avery said.

"Into the Wi-Fi?" Javier asked, eyes wide. "Dang. That was fast."

"No, silly. I'm into his entire system."

Avery pulled up several camera feeds on the screen of her computer. "Here we go. Looks like he has a couple dozen cameras inside and out."

"That's quite an impressive surveillance system for a country getaway," Javier said as they got their first look at the property hidden from the road. "He does pretty well for a guy on a government salary. Check out the vehicles. Oh. And the muscle."

A half dozen luxury four-wheel-drive vehicles sat parked in the dooryard. Several men roamed the grounds on foot. On the far side of the yard sat two tanker trucks with no discernible markings.

"Must be his extracurricular activities that pay for this," Avery said.

"What's with the trucks?" Javier asked.

"No idea."

They saw several large outbuildings, but one structure caught their attention.

"What is that?" Javier asked, pointing at the small odd, wedge-shaped steel structure depicted on the screen.

"I don't know," Avery said. "It's too small to be a hiding place."

"And yet, two sentries are standing guard beside it."

"It could be a bulkhead," Avery opined. "Like the entrance to a storm cellar."

"Storm cellar?"

"Yeah. Pretty common in the southern parts of the US or anywhere tornadoes are apt to spring up."

"We don't see much of that here."

"Whatever it is, it's getting quite a lot of attention."

"What do you suppose Agent Rowan has stashed inside?" Javier asked.

"A pile of royal silver and gold, I'd imagine."

"Where is this Rowan chap?"

"Right there," Avery said as she pointed him out.

"The guy talking on the landline?" Javier asked.

"Yup, that's the guy who snatched the crown jewels right out from under my nose. Wish I could hear what he's saying."

"With any luck, Reggie's already listening in."

"Anything yet?" Duval hollered up to Reggie.

"Hang on," Reggie said, holding up an index finger as he listened over his earbuds. He only caught the tail end of the conversation before the caller disconnected.

Reggie worked quickly to uninstall his equipment from the line, then started back down the pole.

"Well?" Duval said.

"This is definitely the place. Rowan was talking to someone about a jewel expert and an exchange."

"That's it? Where and when?"

"He ended the call before I could get anything else. Something's up. Seemed like he was in a hurry to get off the line. They may be onto us."

"Not good," Avery said.

"What's not good?" Javier asked, concern making his voice too high.

"Someone just ran up to Rowan and said something. Then Rowan looked up directly into the camera."

"Damn," Javier said as he keyed the mic on his portable. "They made us. Repeat, they made us. Abort."

"Roger," Duval's voice said over the radio. "Watcher, copy?"

"Copy," Oscar said.

"I don't understand it," Avery said as she quickly disconnected from the system. "Rowan must have someone monitoring his systems from the inside."

"It doesn't matter now," Javier said. "We've got to get out of here. Come on, Avery. Move, move."

Avery stuffed the laptop inside the backpack, then grabbed her bike as she scrambled through the woods after Javier.

They reached Broadmore Common just in time to see Carter and Duval hurrying toward the van. As Avery straddled her bike and began to pedal, she heard what sounded like several vehicles rapidly approaching on the dirt drive.

"What about Carter and the others?" Avery hollered over her shoulder.

"Don't worry about them," Javier said. "They can handle this, Avery. But we're exposed out here. So, beat feet."

Avery did her best to keep her eyes forward while pumping her legs as hard as she could. She heard Reggie's van doors closing just as the first gunshot blasted.

70

"What the hell happened back there?" Harrison barked as Avery and Javier peeled off their gear and got settled inside the SUV.

"Rowan's men made us," Avery said, toweling the sweat off her face. "I don't know for sure, but I think he may have had someone monitoring his systems from the inside. They must have picked up my hack."

"We heard gunfire," Oscar said.

"Yeah," Javier said. "They fired at the van, but I don't think they even realized Avery and I were part of it. Just two bicyclists enjoying the countryside."

"Where are they now?" Harrison said. "How come they didn't chase you back here?"

Javier grinned at Avery. "They met with an accident. I scattered a few spikes at the end of the drive, flattening their tires. The first vehicle they sent got rear-ended by the second. Both out of commission."

"So, they may have made the van?" Harrison said.

"I doubt it, Harry," Avery said as she watched Duval and Carter remove the magnetic decals. "Anyway, they'll be searching for a communications van."

Oscar looked back at Avery in the rearview mirror. "Where to?"

"Back to London," Avery said. "We know where he's keeping the jewels. Now we need to know what he's up to."

"What he's up to?" Harrison asked. "Isn't it obvious? He's probably planning to sell the jewels."

"Rowan appears to be loaded, Harry," Javier said. "Something in my gut tells me this wasn't ever about money."

"Then what?"

"That's what we're going to find out," Avery said.

Back in London, Avery immediately began scouring the dark web for tracks that Rowan may have left behind. She knew he'd be smart enough to cover his tracks with aliases and coded language. And he likely had an insider on the payroll. Probably the same person who sniffed out her hack of his systems. She had underestimated the MI5 officer twice; it would not happen a third time.

"What are you doing?" Carter asked.

"Going undercover," Avery said without looking up from her laptop.

"Didn't we just do that?"

"Not that kind of UC work. This is purely electronic snooping. I'm using the dark web to see if I can't figure out what Rowan and his band of merry men are really up to. I don't like feeling like he played us to get the jewels, and I want to know what we helped set off here."

"You don't think it's just for the money, either?"

"No, I don't. If money's all he wanted, he could have buyers lined up, or he could hide the jewels and take years selling them piecemeal. No, I think Javi was right, and he's up to something else. Something that requires a great deal of capital to pull off."

"Like what?"

"I don't know yet, but whatever it is, I think Jeff's discovery and sale of the real Eye of the Dragon ring set this whole thing in motion."

"What whole thing, Ave?" Harrison asked absently as he plopped onto the couch.

It was well past midnight and Avery was fighting to keep awake when she practically tripped over what she had been searching for. It was a private chatroom thread between many users, one of whom went by War On. Her heart began to beat faster as she realized one of the users was online.

Using state of the art software she had modified herself, Avery had managed to hack into the chat while keeping her online presence cloaked from the other users. But she was still concerned about how quickly she'd been detected when she'd hacked Rowan's security system. Whoever Rowan hired to police his systems had talent. Avery couldn't help but wonder if the tech guru was someone Rowan had worked with over the course of his many years of service to the Crown or just another hired mercenary.

Trying to keep up with the conversation was like watching a tennis match as the words scrolled at lightning speed. Compounding the problem was that everything appeared to be written in code. None of it made any sense to her. It might as well have been a foreign language. Certain words leapt off the screen, though. Words like *exacting revenge, exposure, cover-up,* and *treason.* Avery couldn't decipher the overall meaning with an exhausted brain and abundance of data, but it was clear that many of the posters were upset about something.

During a lull in the online conversation, Avery opened another screen and began checking out the history of War On's posts. Most of them were much less coded but far more disturbing. It looked as though the user had a serious axe to grind with the British government dating as far back as the execution of King Charles I. And their hatred extended all the way to the UK's current prime minister and the entire British parliament. She wondered how many of the posters were individual accounts and how many were duplicates. Some of the language used made her suspicious that a percentage of the accounts belonged to the same person.

War On's posts went back several years. Some of them alluded to unnecessary chronic illness and the death of British soldiers due to low-level exposure to VX gas while conducting chemical warfare drills. He described the Chemical Weapons Convention as a farce, claiming that no government will ever trust any other enough to cease developing and stock-piling chemical weapons. Soldiers, he argued, were merely expendable numbers on a spreadsheet. War On accused the entire British government of conspiring to cover up the program and its victims.

Avery alternated between reading from the list of older posts and checking for updates on the active thread. The next post she opened was the one she had been searching for. War On claimed to have access to clas-sified files belonging to MI5. Her stomach muscles tightened. Was this disgruntled user Rowan? And if so, was he planning some type of revolt against his own government? Was that the real reason for stealing the crown jewels? To fund a mission? She couldn't believe what she was seeing. She opened the next dated post.

War On went on to talk about an upcoming event. Something dramatic enough to force a policy change and make the government admit their past crimes. Avery could feel the anger in the words.

She scrolled on and on, finding more of the same.

Her eyes were drawn to the live thread as a line of symbols popped up on the screen. Although she didn't entirely understand what was being discussed, the overall tone of the back and forth was disturbing. It looked like some type of attack might be imminent. But who were these people, and what were they talking about attacking? Before Avery could postulate further, the entire thread disappeared from her computer screen.

"What the...?"

She tried refreshing the link but got an error message. Someone had deleted the thread and kicked her off the page. She sat back and stared at the screen. Had they figured out that she had hacked in? Was their software higher tech than her own? Who would have better software than she did? MI5? Could this be an inside job?

Avery disconnected from the dark web, then disconnected from her internet connection entirely. She opened her spyware program and ran a scan of her entire hard drive. If she really was up against the British govern-ment's premier spy agency, it was best not to take any chances. If they had detected her online presence, then there was no limit to how advanced their software was.

It took close to thirty minutes before she was sure that no malicious software had invaded her hard drive. She opened a new search bar and typed in the symbols she had seen on the thread. They turned out to be the chemical code for something called soman gas. The word sounded familiar, but she couldn't remember where she'd seen it. She searched again for the word *soman*. This time the search returned hundreds of pages of information about a gas far more deadly than its chemical cousin sarin. Soman was described as a clear, colorless, tasteless gas that produced an odor similar to mothballs. Avery scanned through additional pages. Sufficient exposure would cause death. Symptoms included blurred vision, constricted pupils, vomiting, elevated heart rate.

Her eyes widened as she recalled the two tanker trucks she and Javier had seen on Rowan's property. Was War On planning a terror attack on British soil? If Rowan was War On, Avery had just handed him all the money he could possibly need to finance an attack.

71

"I'm fairly confident that War On is Rowan," Avery said. "In one of the posts, he even mentioned access to classified MI5 files."

"It's an anagram," Duval said. "Rowan is War On, same letters in a different order."

"I'll be damned," Harrison said.

"How did I miss that?" Avery asked, clearly embarrassed.

"Because you were distracted by the possibility of a soman gas attack?" Harrison asked.

"Maybe he's planning a ransom demand," Carter said.

"No way," Javier said. "He could have just as easily sold the crown jewels and kept the money. Based on what Avery saw online, this one is for keeps."

"Where are you going, Harry?" Avery asked as Harrison got up and headed for the door.

"I gotta make a call."

"Harry," Roger Antonin croaked. "Do you have any idea what time it is?"

"Sorry, man. I wouldn't be bothering you if it wasn't important."

"It's always important with you."

Not only was Antonin one of NYPD's homicide commanders, but he was also wired into the upper echelon of the FBI. And he owed Harrison several big favors.

"I'm listening, Harry. What do you need?"

Harrison laid out the information that Avery had given him. Antonin remained silent on the other end of the call. If it wasn't for the sound of his breathing, Harrison would have assumed the man had fallen back to sleep.

"Now you know why I think it's urgent," Harrison said.

"Do you know how many people rant and rave online about their governments, Harry? Christ, we used to dump all over our bosses ourselves, remember? Most of those sites are just disgruntled geezers spouting off to feel important again. You sure you're not just overreacting here?"

"I'm not overreacting, Rog. I think this guy is a loose cannon. And I think he's planning to take out the whole of the British government. Parliament, the prime mister, maybe even the Crown."

"This gas you're talking about. Soman. That stuff is some kind of expensive, Harry. Even if this War Games guy—"

"War On," Harrison corrected.

"Whatever. Even if he wanted to attempt something like you're describing, do you have any idea how much of that stuff he'd need? It's not like he can just go down to the gas station and fill up his tanks. He would need a supplier. Probably a hostile foreign power who would only do something like this if it served their purposes. And do you know how much something like that would cost?"

"How much?"

"Half a billion, maybe. A billion. I don't know. A lot."

"What if I told you this guy has access to that kind of money?" Harrison said.

"And how would you know that?"

"Because he got it from us."

"Say again?" Roger sounded more awake now.

"It's a long story. Let's just say it involves the crown jewels."

"The crown jewels? One of the most heavily guarded treasures in the world? Those crown jewels?"

"That would be the ones."

"You're saying he stole the crown jewels?"

"In a manner of speaking, yes," Harrison said.

"Forgive me if I seem doubtful, Harry. A story like that would be all over the news."

"Not if they didn't know the jewels were missing."

"Why do I get the feeling I don't want to know how you know that?"

"Trust me. You don't." Harrison heard Antonin sigh. "So, will you help me?"

"I'll make some calls, okay? But don't do anything stupid until you hear back from me."

"You called Commander Antonin, didn't you?" Avery asked as Harrison walked back into the room.

Harrison nodded.

"What did he say?" Avery asked.

"He's going to make a few calls."

"While you were gone, I called Inspector McGregor," Avery said.

"Did he believe you?"

"No. He put me on hold while he checked to see if the crown jewels were still in the Tower."

"And?"

"Then he thanked me for the laugh and asked when we were going home."

Harrison shook his head as he looked around the room. "Now what? Are we supposed to save the world? A computer genius, a social media star, a retired cop, and a den of thieves?"

Duval raised a finger in the air. "Exceptional thieves, mate."

"Whatever, Hans Gruber. The point is, how did our little breakfast club get into this in the first place?"

"And it wouldn't be the entire world, Harry," Carter said. "Just the UK government."

"Don't be so sure of that, Junior Mint. What do you think some third world arms dealer is going to do with a couple billion dollars' worth of jewels?"

"Harry's right," Oscar said. "Arms dealers love wars."

"And a couple billion dollars could help start a big one," Reggie said.

"So, how do we stop this?" Carter said.

"We steal the treasure back and stop the transfer," Avery said absently.

"Here we go," Harrison said as he collapsed onto the couch.

"How's that, love?" Duval asked.

"We steal the treasure back from Rowan," Avery repeated. "We know where he has it, right, Javier?"

"Well, it's probably in that storm cellar thingy we saw those men guarding."

"Which means he hasn't taken delivery of the soman yet," Avery said.

"We need to consider that Rowan has either already cleared out of the compound or is preparing to vamoose as we speak," Duval said.

"All the better," Avery said. "Our best opportunity to steal back the treasure would be while it's in transit, right?"

Oscar and Reggie nodded in agreement.

"She's got a point," Javier said. "But how do we know where the transfer is supposed to take place? Didn't they kick you off the dark web page?"

Avery powered up her laptop and began typing furiously. "But they didn't kick me out of his server."

Reggie looked at Carter and Harrison. "She can just hack into any account she wants?"

"As long as I've got the IP address," Avery muttered without looking up.

"Remind me to start sending letters again," Duval said. "The post is underrated."

A grin spread across Avery's face.

"What?" Carter walked over to her. "You got something?"

Avery nodded.

"Where?" Harrison asked.

"When?" Reggie asked.

"Ten o'clock tomorrow morning. Farnborough Airport. He has contacts in the old Iraqi army."

Duval circled his finger in the air. "Mount up, boys. We've got ourselves a date."

72

They availed themselves of Duval's warehouse for the preparation. Javier, Reggie, and Oscar arrived with an oversized van and more weapons than Avery had ever seen in one place. Carter captured the moment with short video clips taken using his cell phone, with the understanding that neither their faces nor real names would ever be used on screen.

"Josh will forget all about LA," Avery said as she watched him document the moment. "And so will the production people."

"Assuming we survive this," Carter said.

"Don't you think this might be a bit of overkill here, Ave?" Harrison grumbled.

"Not when you consider what we're up against," Avery said.

"Exactly my point," Harrison said. "We shouldn't be involved in this anyway. I mean, this Rowan guy is MI5, for Pete's sake."

"Maybe not for long, mate," Duval said.

"What do you mean?" Carter said.

"I got some inside scoop on ol' Rowan from a bloke I know. Seems he's colored outside the lines one too many times and now he's on shaky ground with the agency."

"How do you know that?" Avery asked. "I thought you said you weren't a part of any of this stuff."

"I'm not. At least not directly. But I've got friends everywhere. These intelligence groups don't operate in a vacuum, love."

"That's even more reason that we shouldn't be a part of this," Harrison said. "Rowan is a loose cannon."

"Don't forget seriously unhinged," Javier said.

"Who else is going to stop him?" Avery asked. "We called the London police and the FBI. No one believes us. Besides, Rowan wouldn't have the money for this if we hadn't practically handed him the treasure."

"We didn't exactly have a choice," Carter said.

"If I hadn't found it, he'd still be looking," Avery said. "Besides, remember how I told you I needed some adventure in my life? What's more adventurous than trying to save the world?"

Harrison shook his head. "I've regretted that conversation every day since. Pretty foolish of me to hope that scuba diving with Boy Wonder here and finding two treasures would have been enough."

"If things go well for us, Carter will have a wildly popular new story for social media. Maybe even a documentary."

"I'll be sure to worry about Carter's TV career when my lungs are burning up from contraband poison gas." Harrison made a sour face.

They were packed up and on the road to Farnborough Airport well before dawn. Breakfast consisted of power bars and large thermoses of coffee en route.

"Cheers," Oscar said as he raised his insulated mug of coffee in Avery's direction.

"I can't thank you guys enough for helping us," Avery said. "It's very gallant of you."

"Don't mistake greed for gallantry, Miss Turner," Reggie said. "I have no love for the government, here, there, or anywhere, but I don't fancy the idea of a poisonous gas floating all over London either. Mostly, though, I do fancy money."

"Well, whatever gets you on board, I'm glad you're here."

"What exactly are we looking for?" Harrison asked.

"A plane carrying the Iraqis," Javier said. "It will likely be a small cargo plane. They'll be carrying the soman with them."

"Our window will be small," Oscar said. "Their transport will probably only be here long enough to transfer the soman to Rowan and his men and take delivery of the crown jewels."

"Won't they need to refuel too?" Carter said.

"Not necessarily, mate," Duval said. "It all depends on where they flew in from. It's highly unlikely they came directly from Iraq. I imagine they staged nearby before flying in here. If I'm right, they won't need to spend any time refueling. This will be a quick transaction. We'll need to act fast if we hope to disrupt this thing."

"Let's not use words like disrupt when discussing soman, okay?" Harrison barked, his eyes widening at the thought.

"Relax, Harry," Avery said. "It will be in liquid form, which is much more stable."

"Oh, good. And here I thought we were in real trouble."

They arrived at the airfield just before eight o'clock, giving them what they hoped was a two-hour window to set up on their targets. Javier pulled the van off the road into a small dirt turnout about half a mile from the terminal, just outside the airport perimeter fence. A small rise kept them semi-hidden.

"Parking here will keep us from standing out like a neon sign," Oscar said. "But if Rowan is paying attention at all, he'll spot us."

"It won't matter," Avery said. "Once the plane lands, we'll move into position."

"You're the boss," Javier said.

The plane touched down on the runway early, at exactly 9:37.

"Good thing we got here at eight," Duval said. "That's mighty likely their plane landing now."

"They're early," Harrison said.

"Probably excited about taking delivery of the royal jewelry," Carter said.

"Or maybe they don't want to be around that soman stuff longer than they need to," Reggie said.

"I second that," Harrison said.

Duval and Oscar bailed out of the far side of the van, then moved toward the airport's perimeter fence, keeping low as they crossed the roadway.

Reggie climbed up on top of the van with his high-resolution binoculars. Lying flat to conceal himself, he gave them a play-by-play through the roof hatch.

"It's definitely the Iraqis," Reggie said.

"Can you see anything happening?" Avery asked.

"Yeah, looks like Rowan's guys have a box truck for transport. Three guys wearing fatigues are moving a large wooden crate toward the back of the truck."

"That's got to be the soman," Javier said. "The canisters are probably inside the crate."

"Great," Harrison groaned.

"We're in position?" Duval asked over the radio.

"Roger that," Javier said.

"Can you see Rowan?" Carter asked.

"No, I don't see him anywhere," Reggie said. "Okay, wait. There's a pickup pulling up next to the plane. It's Rowan and some other guy driving."

"Good," Avery said. "I don't want him wriggling his way out of this."

"What are they doing?" Duval radioed.

"Just talking," Reggie said. "A couple of the Iraqis look really antsy. If we don't want to be spotted like sitting ducks, we better make our move."

"Okay," Avery said to Javier. "Give Duval and Oscar the signal and let's head for the gate."

Avery watched through the window as Duval and Oscar slid through the holes they'd cut in the wire fencing and headed toward the runway. Javier pulled the van back onto the pavement and drove at a normal speed toward the gate. Reggie maintained his position low upon the roof.

"They spotted us," Reggie said. "Whatever you're planning, now would be a good time."

"Pull up to the gate and stop," Avery said. "We'll make like we've got a flat tire."

Javier stopped directly in front of the chain-link gate, blocking it, then climbed out of the van. Harrison joined him. Carter and Avery remained inside the van, since they couldn't take the chance that Rowan would recognize them.

"They're headed this way, Ave," Harrison said, his voice cracking as he spoke.

"Pretend you're checking one of the tires."

Avery watched through the glass as Rowan and two other men sped over in the truck, stopping about twenty feet from their van.

"Piss off," Rowan yelled at them. "You're blocking the damn gate. Get that thing out of here."

"Sorry, mate," Javier said. "But there's something wrong with the steering. I think maybe we've got ourselves a broken tie rod."

"You've got to be kidding me," Rowan said as he and the driver and one of the Iraqis stepped out of the Jeep and approached on foot.

Avery grinned at the ruse as she and Carter used the distraction to slip out of the van's rear doors and circle around to the back of Rowan's truck.

"You must be able to back it out," Rowan said.

"Not without steering I can't."

Avery and Carter kept low to avoid being spotted by the men standing near the plane as they made their way around to the back of the truck and looked inside the bed.

"It's the chests," Avery whispered.

"I know," Carter said. "We dragged these halfway through the London sewers."

"Come on, give me a hand."

"What are you doing, Avery? You're gonna get us killed."

"We take back the jewels, the transaction never happens. The Iraqis will leave with the soman canisters."

"You hope," Carter said as they struggled with the weight of the first trunk.

They made it about halfway back to the van before someone began shouting from the direction of the plane.

"Hurry," Carter said.

Avery's hands were covered in sweat, causing her to lose her grip. Her end of the trunk crashed onto the pavement with a loud bang.

Rowan spun toward them and fired his weapon.

Avery and Carter took cover behind the van as Rowan shouted to his men, commanding them to grab the cylinders. Reggie and Javier traded shots with Rowan and one of his men. Avery heard distant shouting and the sound of gunfire from across the runway as Oscar and Duval engaged the men from the plane. Rowan's driver cried out as he was hit. Still shooting, Rowan and the Iraqi retreated to the truck and backed away at high speed, turning at the last second and racing toward the plane with one crate of jewels still in the payload.

"You guys okay?" Javier asked as Reggie jumped down from the roof.

"We're fine," Avery said. "Where's Harry?"

"Under the van." Reggie laughed.

"Yeah, it's all fun and games until someone loses an eye," Harrison said as he crawled out from under the vehicle. "Great plan, Ave."

"Hey, we managed to recover half of the jewels," Carter said.

"We got bigger problems," Javier said. "Rowan and his guys are getting away with the gas."

"But the Iraqis didn't get the jewels," Avery said.

"Looks like they're settling for half," Reggie said as he pointed out the men loading the trunk onto the plane.

"Help me load this chest into the van," Harrison said to Carter.

They struggled with the weight but managed to secure it inside.

"Let's go," Avery said as she hopped through the van's side door. "Rowan's getting away with the soman canisters."

"We aren't going after him in this," Javier said.

"Why not?" Harrison said.

"Because they shot out one of our front tires," Reggie said.

"We need to find another vehicle and fast," Avery said as she watched the box truck plow through a gate about a quarter mile behind them.

"How about this?" Carter said as he ran over to a vintage motorcycle with a sidecar parked unattended in the small lot beside the gate.

"You've got to be kidding me," Harrison said.

"You need a key to start that, mate," Reggie said.

"Not if you know how to hotwire it," Carter said as he stripped the covering from one of the ignition wires.

"What about you guys?" Avery said.

"Don't worry about us," Javier said as he lugged the spare tire around to the front of the van. "We'll get this changed and catch up as soon as we can. Just go."

Carter revved the motorcycle engine. "Come on," he shouted.

"But...Duval and Oscar," Avery said. "We can't just leave them."

"Here they come now," Reggie said, pointing to the two men running across the tarmac toward them. "Go on, Avery."

"Come on, Harry," Avery said as she straddled the bike and wrapped her arms around Carter's torso.

"If we somehow manage to survive, I'm never going to forgive either of you for this," Harrison said as he squeezed himself into the sidecar.

"Hang on," Carter said as they shot past the van and out onto the road in pursuit of Rowan's truck.

73

They raced along the A3 through Guildford and Wandsworth and headed back toward London. Any conversation was limited to shouting back and forth due to the wind whipping past them in the open-air vehicle.

"Shouldn't we be wearing helmets or something?" Harrison yelled from the sidecar.

"Probably," Carter yelled back.

Rowan had a good head start on them, but Carter kept the throttle wide open, giving them the occasional glimpse at the back of the truck.

"Has anyone been keeping track of how many laws we've broken?" Harrison said. "I'm trying to come up with an approximate figure for my attorney."

"I haven't," Carter said. "But I think stealing this motorcycle must have added to our tally."

"Your tally, you mean," Harrison said. "I didn't hotwire anything."

"Look on the bright side, Harry," Avery said. "Maybe we'll get adjoining cells."

"You think Rowan's heading back to London?" Carter asked.

"I know he is," Avery said. "And I think I know why he picked today."

"Why?" Harrison said.

"Because he's planning to attack parliament."

"The building?"

Avery nodded.

"How could you know that?" Carter asked.

"Because I read online that King Charles is planning a ceremonial visit today."

"Great," Harrison said. "Forget prison. If we crash that party, they'll just shoot us where we stand."

"Not if we can stop Rowan before he gets there," Avery said.

They were nearing the city limits before they caught up to the truck. Traffic both helped and hindered their progress, but the smaller vehicle allowed Carter to swerve through traffic and draw nearer to Rowan's truck until at last they pulled alongside.

"I don't suppose either of you thought this out, did you?" Harrison said.

"Not really," Carter said.

"I thought we might wing it once we got to this point," Avery said as she tapped Carter on the shoulder. "Aren't you a surfer too?"

"Yup. Why, what were you— Hey, great idea!" Carter shifted in the seat. "You take the controls, okay?"

"Got 'em," Avery said as she grabbed onto the handlebars, keeping the throttle open.

"Are you trying to get us killed?" Harrison yelled.

"Come on, Harry," Avery said. "I know you and Mom used to get into high-speed chases."

"Yeah, but we were on four wheels and wrapped in Detroit steel at the time. Not this rolling deathtrap."

Carter stood upright on the foot pedals as Avery steered them closer to the side of Rowan's box truck.

"Watch out!" Harrison shouted as the truck swerved toward them.

Avery matched the maneuver, gliding away from a sure collision. Carter kept his balance as he stepped up onto the seat.

"This is what you call a great idea?" Harrison shouted.

"Like riding a bike, Harry," Carter said. "Okay, Avery, get me closer."

"You've got it," Avery said as she inched closer to the side of the cargo hold.

Carter reached out and stepped at the same time, grabbing onto the rack mounted to the roof of the truck before he scrambled up onto the roof.

Avery saw the surprised look on Rowan's face in the truck's side mirror when he saw Carter's acrobatic move. Rowan swerved harder toward the motorcycle and Avery steered to the left.

"Watch out, Ave," Harrison shouted just as a horn blared from the vehicle on the opposite side of the motorcycle.

"Sorry," Avery yelled to the other driver with a wave. She braked and fell in behind Rowan's truck.

"What can I do to help?" Harrison said.

"A prayer wouldn't hurt, Harry. And maybe try calling Inspector McGregor again."

Carter crawled along the roof of the truck toward the rear, where he knew the soman canisters were. Carefully he climbed down until he was standing on the rear bumper, then opened one of the rear doors and jumped inside.

Rowan continued to swerve, causing the door to bang open and shut. Carter grabbed onto the rails running along the inside walls of the payload. The canisters were still intact inside their wooden crates, but the heavy crates were sliding around on the floor, threatening to squash Carter like a gnat. He looked around helplessly for something he could do but there was nothing—knocking the crates off the back of the truck only risked puncturing the tanks and releasing the deadly contents. He looked toward the front of the payload for any access to the cab but the wall between them was solid. His only option was to head back outside and try to get into the cab and incapacitate Rowan.

"Any luck with McGregor?" Avery said.

"I couldn't hear him that well, but I think he finally believes us. I think he said something about sending the cavalry, but it was hard to tell with all the bloody this and bloody that."

"Better late than never," Avery said.

"Now what's he doing?" Harrison said as they watched Carter secure the rear door, then climb up onto the roof.

"He's going after Rowan."

"Who does he think he is, Rambo?"

Avery glanced up ahead at the looming spires of the Palace of Westminster. "You'd better hope he is because we're almost out of time. Look."

"Don't tell me, that's where parliament meets," Harrison said.

"Okay, I won't tell you, but those limos probably mean the royals have already arrived."

"I'm gonna have a heart attack before this thing is over, Ave. A full-blown heart attack."

Carter felt like he was trapped on a giant slide as he struggled to hang on to the roof of the swerving truck. He didn't know if it was because Rowan was intentionally attempting to dislodge him or if it was due to the increasing traffic. Either way he knew he had to breach the cab if he wanted any chance of stopping Rowan before they reached parliament.

He grabbed onto the metal rail affixed to the left side of the box's roof and dragged himself forward until he was looking directly down onto the roof of the cab. Backing up a bit, he grabbed the rail with both hands, then lowered himself to the side of the cargo box, bracing the toes of his boots against the base molding. The truck swerved again, nearly sending him flying into the side of a double-decker bus. He hung on for dear life, his torso and legs banging against the side until the truck straightened again. He glanced up and saw the approaching spires of the Palace of Westminster for the first time.

It was now or never. He leapt forward onto the cab's running board, grabbing onto the mirror bracket to stabilize himself as he made eye contact with Rowan through the window. He watched as Rowan lifted the handgun toward him and fired. Carter ducked beneath the window just as several bullets shattered the glass, raining shards down on him. Rowan's attention shifted as the truck swerved again, narrowly missing a line of stopped cars. Carter saw Rowan's gun tumble to the floor. It was all the distraction Carter needed as he hoisted himself through the window and wrestled with Rowan for control of the steering.

Carter was surprised by Rowan's strength as they traded punches. Rowan caught Carter with a devastating elbow to the chin that rocked him backward. Now half lying across the bench seat, Carter swung his legs up and drove his boots into the side of Rowan's face, knocking his head into the A-pillar. Rowan's body slumped forward, unconscious. The truck sped up as the weight of Rowan's body pressed down on the accelerator. Carter grabbed the wheel and looked up just in time to see the traffic directly ahead stopped in every lane. With no time to dislodge Rowan's foot from the gas pedal, Carter fastened his safety belt, then turned the wheel sharply toward the biggest tree he could find. The truck sideswiped a parked vehicle, then jumped the curb and slammed into the thick trunk. The last thing Carter saw was the hood crumpling toward the windshield.

74

Avery ignored the shouts from nearby police officers as she leapt off the motorcycle and ran to the front of the truck. Steam was rising from the massively damaged front end, and she found the left door jammed shut. Climbing up on the running board, she leaned in through the window opening and saw Carter hanging motionless from his seatbelt. Rowan's mangled body was slumped over the steering wheel.

"Get down from there, miss," a voice commanded from the ground behind her.

"Not until you get him some help," Avery shouted back.

"She's with me, officer," Harrison said.

"Fine, but—"

"You need to clear this area and get a hazmat team in here," Harrison said, cutting him off.

"And why is that?"

"Because there are several canisters of a deadly gas in the back of this truck, and they might be leaking."

Good old Harry, Avery thought as she gently ran a hand over Carter's forehead.

Carter slowly came to, coughing and grabbing his chest. "Oh, man does that hurt."

"I knew you were too tough to die in a fender bender," Avery said with a soft smile. "You okay?"

"I feel like I got kicked by a mule."

"More like a big tree."

Harrison climbed up beside Avery. "You okay, Carter?"

"Yeah, I'll survive. Not sure I can say the same for Rowan, though. Did we stop the attack?"

"Yeah, *we* did," Avery said as she reached in and kissed him on the cheek. "We did."

An ambulance took Carter to the hospital while Avery and Harrison spent the next several hours answering some tough questions from the local authorities. Avery was beginning to wonder if they might not be able to talk their way out of this one when Inspector McGregor showed up and dismissed the other detectives.

"You know, I've never seen tourists cause as much trouble as you three have," McGregor said. "How do you do it?"

"Trouble just seems to find us, Inspector," Avery said.

"Looks like I might owe you an apology."

"For what?" Harrison said.

"For not believing you. You got yourself mixed up with some pretty bad characters when you came to Jeff Shelton's aid. We've known about MI5's internal investigation into Intelligence Officer Rowan for some time but couldn't get a handle on what exactly he was up to."

"So, what we heard was true?" Avery said. "The MI5 brass knew he was unstable?"

"Aye, for a while now. Unofficially, I think the agency has exploited his tendency to be a loose cannon when it suits them, and that's the only reason he's still employed there. But I doubt they knew he was capable of an attack like the one you prevented today."

"What about the soman tanks?"

"Our hazmat people have removed them. You were lucky. None of the tanks were compromised. Harry tells me that you guys probably saved every member of parliament and even the king himself."

"Like you said, we were lucky." Avery shivered.

"Well, lucky or not the British government owes you a debt of gratitude that I'm afraid we'll never be able to repay."

Avery clapped one hand over her mouth. "The jewels! I almost forgot. Is there a way to track them and get them back now?"

Harrison and McGregor exchanged glances that Avery couldn't quite decipher.

"What?" she asked.

"Your friends did the right thing, Ms. Turner," McGregor said.

"I don't understand." She looked at Harry, because Carter was getting medical care after nearly getting himself killed stopping the truck. What friends?

"Duval, Oscar, Reggie, and Javier fought off the Iraqis and recovered the stolen jewels, Ave," Harrison said. "The others wanted to make off with them, but Duval actually talked some sense into them, and they handed everything over to the authorities."

"You're kidding." Avery's jaw loosened. "I guess you really can teach an old dog new tricks."

"Not hardly," Harrison said. "I offered up the same payment for services that we promised to Duval. I didn't think you'd mind."

Avery shook her head. "Of course not. Money well spent. They will probably want a big press conference or ceremony for the recovery of the crown jewels, right, Inspector?"

Harrison and McGregor exchanged another look.

"I'm afraid there won't be any official acknowledgment of the recovery," McGregor said. "The king asked me to personally convey his thanks to the three of you for what you did, but the original theft of the jewels from the Tower of London would be extremely embarrassing if it ever came out. I'm sure you can understand."

Avery sighed. "C'est la vie."

"There is another matter we need to discuss, though," McGregor said.

"What's that?" Avery asked.

"It seems that the Tower of London was burglarized again recently.

Several unknown individuals rappelled down from the roof in the middle of the night and broke in through a window."

"How horrible," Avery said, doing her best to project innocence. "Was anything taken?"

"Well, yes and no. The thieves made off with a valuable ruby ring known as the Eye of the Dragon. Belonged to the last King Charles, in fact. But then, oddly enough, they returned the ring several days later by placing it into the tank of a museum water closet."

"What a strange coincidence," Avery said.

"Very." McGregor shook his head before turning to Harrison. "You sure you don't know anything about that, Detective Harrison?"

"Don't look at me," Harrison said. "I'm afraid of heights."

75

Avery helped Carter from the limo across the tarmac to her Gulfstream, where Marco stood waiting. Carter hobbled on crutches, a knee sprain as his only souvenir of the treasure hunt. All things considered, he said it wasn't the worst thing.

"Welcome back, Ms. Avery," Marco said.

"It's good to be back, Marco," Avery said.

"What happened to you, Mr. Mosley?"

"It's a long story, Marco," Carter said.

"Yeah, but he'll have plenty of time to tell it while he milks this injury for all it's worth," Harrison said as he wrestled with the bags.

"Come on, Harry," Carter said. "After all, I did risk my life for king and country."

"It's not even your country, junior," Harrison said.

"Ms. Avery, who is that man waving to you?" Marco said as he pointed toward the limo.

"That is Inspector McGregor of Scotland Yard," Avery said as she returned the wave.

"That was nice of him to escort you to the airport," Marco said.

"Nice had nothing to do with it," Harrison said as he passed Marco a piece of luggage. "He just wanted to make sure we really left this time. Oh, and to return my gun."

Confusion creased Marco's forehead.

"Like I said, Marco, it's a long story," Carter said.

Marco studied Harrison and Carter. "What happened to your faces? It looks like you lost a fight."

"You didn't see the other guys," Carter said.

Avery laughed as she helped Carter up the steps onto the plane. "Europe is a dangerous place, Marco."

"Not for normal tourists," Harrison grumbled.

"Home, Miss Turner?" Marco asked.

"With a quick stop in Marseilles to return something to a friend of Carter's," Avery said.

Three hours later, the map was back where it belonged, Simon was even more in awe of Carter's bravery than he'd been a week before, and the Gulfstream was at cruising altitude, headed for home in the Florida Keys. Harrison sat in the cockpit, regaling Marco with a colorful recounting of their adventure while Avery and Carter lounged in the leather cabin recliners with laptops open, trying to catch up on everything they'd missed.

"You hear back from your agent yet?" Avery asked.

"Yeah. He's still pretty pissed about me taking off in the middle of filming, but I think I managed to pique his interest in a new project."

"Not about the crown jewels, I hope."

"I don't want to end up in a London prison. No, this would be a reality type drama involving the lives of four professional thieves."

"Anyone we know?" Avery asked with a wink.

"Maybe."

Avery closed her laptop and gazed through the window at the clouds drifting past and the deep blue Atlantic far below.

"Whatcha thinking about?" Carter said.

"I was just wondering how the ring Jeff found ended up at the bottom of that reef."

"Who knows? It might have come from that 150-year-old skeleton you found. Maybe that person was a descendant of the pirate who stole it from Ace Mullins. Or maybe some rich guy bought it before meeting his maker in a watery grave. Either way, as the finger rotted off the bone beneath it, the ring could have simply washed up onto the reef."

"I guess. I still wonder, though. Do you think Jeff was interested in Ace Mullins before he found the ring or after?" Avery said.

"It's a mystery," Carter said. "And not one we need to solve. Overall, I'd say we did what we set out to do when we came here."

"You think Jeff would approve?"

"I know he would," Carter said with a grin. "Especially the less than legal stuff. He *really* would've liked Duval."

"And we did save England," Avery said. "Still wish we could have met King Charles."

"That would have made a cool video for my followers," Carter said.

"You might have been knighted, Sir Mosley."

"I like the sound of that, Lady Turner. Anyway, now the royal family has a set of spare crown jewels."

Avery laughed. "Yeah, I guess they do."

"So, what's next?" Carter asked as he closed his laptop and tossed it onto the seat beside his.

"I just want to go home and relax by the ocean. Enjoy a nice boring day on my nice boring beach and a few nice cold boring drinks."

"Something with an umbrella?"

"That sounds pretty good right now," Avery said.

"How about some scuba diving?" Carter asked.

"I think I've had enough adventure for one week."

"Okay," Carter said. "But what about after my knee heals up? Maybe a month from now we can find some more trouble to get into. You know how much you love a good adventure, Avery."

Avery's face stretched into a grin. "What exactly did you have in mind?"

The Pharaoh's Tomb
The Turner and Mosley Files Book 4

An ancient mystery ignites a modern day treasure hunt.

When an artifact with the potential to destabilize the Middle East disappears, experts Avery Turner and Carter Mosley are summoned to retrieve it. Their destination: Egypt. Their target: a centuries-old relic—a small pin of solid gold, shaped like an ancient goddess.

Needle, meet giant haystack.

Landing in Cairo, the pair are immediately blindsided by a hailstorm of bullets—clear proof that their reputations have put a target on their backs. Navigating through layers of corruption and in a race full of cutthroat treasure hunters, they must outsmart others who are just as desperate to find the pin.

With the situation escalating and a colleague going missing under suspicious circumstances, the odds seem stacked against them. But when a connection between the pin and a forgotten Egyptian queen emerges, the duo begin to think they are onto something.

As danger knocks and adventure calls, Avery and Carter learn that some legends are more real—and more valuable—than gold.

Get your copy today at
severnriverbooks.com

ACKNOWLEDGMENTS

So many people had a hand in getting this book into yours, and we are ever thankful to all of them. Our fantastic team at Severn River Publishing: Cate, Amber, Lisa, and Randall, who helped make the story, the cover, and the pages shine, and pushed us to reimagine parts of the story in more clever, dangerous ways, thank you for all your hard work. Our agents, John Talbot and Paula Munier: thank you for your unending support. And last but never least, we'd both like to thank our families for keeping us on track and making sure the story got told: Karen Coffin, Justin Walker, and all three littles, you are the talent behind the scenes that we'd be lost without. As always, any mistakes you find are ours.

ABOUT BRUCE ROBERT COFFIN

Bruce Robert Coffin is the award-winning author of the Detective Byron Mysteries. Former detective sergeant with more than twenty-seven years in law enforcement, he is the winner of Killer Nashville's Silver Falchion Awards for Best Procedural, and Best Investigator, and the Maine Literary Award for Best Crime Fiction Novel. Bruce was also a finalist for the Agatha Award for Best Contemporary Novel. His short fiction appears in a number of anthologies, including Best American Mystery Stories 2016.

Sign up for The Turner and Mosley Files newsletter at
severnriverbooks.com

brucerobertcoffin@severnriverbooks.com

ABOUT LYNDEE WALKER

LynDee Walker is the national bestselling author of two crime fiction series featuring strong heroines and "twisty, absorbing" mysteries. Her first Nichelle Clarke crime thriller, FRONT PAGE FATALITY, was nominated for the Agatha Award for best first novel and is an Amazon Charts Bestseller. In 2018, she introduced readers to Texas Ranger Faith McClellan in FEAR NO TRUTH. Reviews have praised her work as "well-crafted, compelling, and fast-paced," and "an edge-of-your-seat ride" with "a spider web of twists and turns that will keep you reading until the end."

Before she started writing fiction, LynDee was an award-winning journalist who covered everything from ribbon cuttings to high level police corruption, and worked closely with the various law enforcement agencies that she reported on. Her work has appeared in newspapers and magazines across the U.S.

Aside from books, LynDee loves her family, her readers, travel, and coffee. She lives in Richmond, Virginia, where she is working on her next novel when she's not juggling laundry and children's sports schedules.

Sign up for The Turner and Mosley Files newsletter at
severnriverbooks.com
lyndee@severnriverbooks.com